Also by Douglas Clegg

WELCOME TO

The Abyss line of cutting-edge psychological horror is committed to publishing the best, most innovative works of dark fiction available. ABYSS is horror unlike anything you've ever read before. It's not about haunted houses or evil children or ancient Indian burial grounds. We've all read those books, and we all know their plots by heart.

ABYSS is for the seeker of truth, no matter how disturbing or twisted it may be. It's about people, and the darkness we all carry within us. ABYSS is the new horror from the dark frontier. And in that place, where we come face-to-face with terror, what we find is ourselves.

"Thank you for introducing me to the remarkable line of novels currently being issued under Dell's Abyss imprint. I have given a great many blurbs over the last twelve years or so, but this one marks two firsts: first *unsolicited* blurb (*I* called *you*) and the first time I have blurbed a whole *line* of books. In terms of quality, production, and plain old story-telling reliability (that's the bottom line, isn't it?), Dell's new line is amazingly satisfying . . . a rare and wonderful bargain for readers. I hope to be looking into the Abyss for a long time to come."

—Stephen King

The Children's Hour

DOUGLAS CLEGG

A DELL BOOK

Published by
Dell Publishing
a division of
Bantam Doubleday Dell Publishing Group, Inc.
1540 Broadway
New York, New York 10036

ISBN: 0-440-21867-5

Printed in the United States of America

Published simultaneously in Canada

November 1995

10 9 8 7 6 5 4 3 2 1

RAD

For Sky Nonhoff

Thanks to R.S., Goldmann Verlag, and to Jeanne Cavelos and Jacob Hoye at Dell, who have made this writer feel welcome; and to Kay McCauley for all the good stuff. Thanks as always to the Cleggs and the Silvas. Special thanks to Tyler Montague Fulcher, Barbara Michaels, Kim & Elaina, Lyndi Coté, Laurent Bouzereau, Edward Lee, Laurie Drake, Wayne Edwards, Robert Weinberg, Ellen Datlow, John Scoleri, Peter Enfantino, Sheryl & Mark & Sarah Parrott, Linda Marrow, William Relling, Jr., Marty Greenberg, Richard Gilliam, Gabe & Sandy, Kurt & Amy Wimberger, Bentley Little, the Laymon clan, Kathe Koja, Rick Lieder, and to Carly Simon.

I must acknowledge, without naming them, the wonderful families who took me into their homes (and hearts) in West Virginia for a good part of 1994 while I researched this novel. Thank you.

1.

He awoke suddenly, brought to consciousness by a smell.

Another sense, too, something he'd acquired recently, nothing specific, more instinct than sense, something within him that told him his quarry was near. It was as if he had a radar for some of them— *maybe if you know them, you sense them, or maybe (heh-heh, my insane friend) they sense you and send out unseen feelers to find you.*

He reached for the mallet. It was still there, beneath

the rags he'd used as a pillow. His whole body was soaked with sweat from whatever fever dream had been buzzing inside his head. He wiped the back of his neck with his left hand. His neck and legs were sore.

How long had he been asleep? Sleep was a problem. After all he'd been through, his body was wearing him down, forcing him to sleep too much. And he was supposed to be on watch. He had appointed himself the one who would not sleep and the last thing he remembered was he had been sitting up, listening for them, waiting for them. Somehow, he'd been tricked into falling asleep.

The man trusted no one now. He was careful not to wake the others as he rose up from the straw. Only three of them left. Only three. His side still ached from a recent wound. He managed to force the pain down deep into his flesh, to forever pretend that the pain was only a vestige of some past incarnation. Had to bite his lip, too, because when he finally stood, it felt as if his legs would buckle and he'd fall again. He held onto the edge of a wooden post that was draped with chains and hooks.

Blood had dried on one of the larger hooks, blood and some hair. Maybe some skin, too, matted with the hair and blood, or maybe he was so used to the grue by now that he imagined it everywhere.

He glanced at the others. He didn't want to alarm them with what he was about to do. He was still not positive that any of them were who they claimed to be. The sleeping forms, wrapped in blankets and straw. They didn't have the smell to them, but he mistrusted his own senses more than anyone or anything.

He moved silently through the workroom, grabbing the tool belt from its peg on the cork wall. He could've taken a gun. There were plenty to go around, a veritable arsenal, but a gun never seemed to do the job right. What he had learned in the past twenty-four hours was that it was not enough just to do it and walk away—it took some time, it took patience, this kind of job. You had to watch them suffer before you knew they were truly dead.

He hefted a mallet in his right hand, swung it back and forth as if it were an old friend, and walked out the barn door. His palm was sweating around the mallet— he wondered when the mallet would become a part of him, melded into his flesh, until he was, himself, no longer a man, but a function of something higher—a tool of flesh and blood and wood and steel. He had never had much religious sense, but sometimes the voices told him what to do, sometimes he believed what they said. Sometimes he thought he was meant to be here, this time, this place, this hour.

The light was hazy, not dark yet, and he knew that if he was going to kill them it was going to have to be dark, because he wanted to look into their eyes and see the thing that he was killing—not them, but what was behind them, what gave them their inspiration. He tried not to think of them as Them, with a big T, be- cause it was making him nervous as hell to even think about what they were without adding the larger fear to it. *What if I'm crazy? What if I'm one of those psycho killers who imagines that everyone else is a them?*—a fleeting thought, through his brain; he ignored it.

It would've been almost impossible to find them in daylight, anyway, but at night, hell, they'd come to him. They'd approach as if they were supplicants com- ing to the altar and he'd just take them out.

Well, it wouldn't be that simple.

He'd probably get some fight out of at least one of them, maybe all. Who wanted to get his head bashed in, anyway? He knew he was crazy, thinking these things, but what was a man to do? He couldn't just let it all go, all the hurt, and give in. *When you give in, they get you. When you give in, they take you over and do things to you you don't want done, they get you over to their side, and then everything looks different.*

The trees leaned, cowed by the strong wind, as if his arrival had made them bow down. *But you're not God, remember that,* a voice told him, *you're just you, and you're going to look them in the eyes, one at a time, and you're going to have to bash them and spear them and they're going to know you, what you're thinking, they're going to have already half crawled into your brain, punching buttons as if you're a computer until they find out what's on your mind, and then they're going to do whatever they can to stop you.*

He could smell one of them in the air—they stank, had that stink of humanity—the wind was icy, and the stink made him want to retch. He clutched the mallet more tightly. The worst of it was, they smelled like people, just like people who maybe haven't bathed in a while, the strong stink of human flesh.

In the grove, at the edge of the property, he thought he saw someone standing there.

He felt for the tool belt, for the screwdriver.

He'd gone hunting once, when he'd been young, and learned of a phenomenon where a hunter, looking for deer, sometimes took a shot at another human being because the hunter wanted to see a deer so badly that he actually mistook a man for a deer. Not just any man, either—it was often a friend.

It was the problem with them, they looked so much like anybody else. You couldn't really know for sure until you plunged the screwdriver into them. It wasn't simple, Life. It wasn't gray, either—things were definitely black and white, at least for him. *Good and Evil, and you're either for us, or against us. The only way to live, now. Well, the only way to survive.*

But what if he was wrong? He could look in their eyes, but if he didn't see what he was looking for, would he kill them anyway?

Maybe I'm just a madman, maybe I had a breakdown and the stress of the shit-hole world has dropped down on my shoulders. Maybe I'm just another Ted Bundy or John Wayne Gacy out to hammer everyone I'm para- noid about into the ground, bash their faces so I don't have to see their eyes staring at me, twist the old Phil- lips head number two into that sweet little place be- tween their ribs where a nice plump heart's just waiting to get skewered.

Have to keep my mind on right here, right now, no veering off. They'd want that—you go careening off the edge of a cliff in your mind, and they got you. Once they get you, they put you where they want, and who knows what happens to you, how they hollow you out like a canoe and turn you inside out and then you're not who you think you are, oh, no, boys and girls, you're something altogether different and you look in the mir- ror but you don't see yourself, no no no, you see some- thing else and then you want to break the mirror be- cause of what they did to you, no thank you, ma'am, I ain't buying none of that.

He watched the bent over trees. The sky was dark- ening—not much after four, but getting dark fast. *Never find them in their hiding place—have to wait, sometimes, 'til they come to you.*

"Hey!" he shouted. Friendly like, neighborly, put- ting the mallet behind his back a little so whoever was standing there wouldn't completely suspect him. They weren't too smart, these people, and when they were fresh, before they ripened, they had a little bit too much of what they used to have, so they weren't always the smartest things.

You are insane, the voice inside him said, *this is just a dream, it has all been a dream, you've been drunk and abusing your wife and family and you drank a couple of six-packs of Rolling Rock and you went over the Edge.*

(The voice in his head knew about the Edge.)

Someone came out from among the shadows of the grove. It wasn't an It or a Thing or a Them.

It was a boy. Dark hair, pale skin, wearing a hooded sweatshirt with the hood pulled down. On the front of the sweatshirt, which was blue, were the words: *If Virginia Is for Lovers, Then West Virginia's for Us Decent Folks.* He couldn't actually read the sweatshirt from that distance; he just knew what the words said because he'd bought the sweatshirt for the boy, himself, not two days before, thinking it was kind of funny.

He knew the boy.

He's one of them, though.

The boy smiled.

The man with the mallet stood motionless. His fingers felt numb.

The boy started running towards the man, shouting.

The man pulled the mallet from behind his back.

When the boy reached him, the man took him in his free arm and brought the mallet to the side of the boy's head, ready to bash it.

You are insane, the voice inside said.

Am I? Well, go to hell, he told it.

He held the boy's head tight in his arm and stared down into those eyes as darkness blossomed all around them. He was looking for the light there, to see if he could see the boy's inspiration, if he could see the thing that fueled the boy. If it still existed there.

Tears shone in the boy's eyes.

"Dad? Daddy?"

The man would only have a few seconds to perform the operation.

But he had to be sure.

He had come too far, from such a far-off land—the territory of sanity and reality—to lose it all in a moment's hesitation.

But he had to be absolutely sure that the boy was one of them before he carved into the boy's heart.

They were tricky that way, because you might slip up and stab one of your own kind—it wasn't like in the movies or books, where all it took was a good jab in the right place—it was bloody and you had to stab them over and over, until there was nothing left pumping—it was just like killing your own kind, only they weren't, they were another species, practically, and if you didn't hunt them down, they'd hunt you.

You'd be the deer in the forest to them.

The voice inside him said, *you are tired of this, aren't you? You just want them to take you so you'll be one of them, so you won't have to fight anymore. You don't need to fight anymore. Everyone you love is gone, everything you've ever lived for, vanished. If you kill him, you kill yourself. Look at him, look at his face, his skin, his eyes, you were once like that, remember? When you were his age, in this very place, you set this in motion, you and your friends. What has brought you to this place? You have brought yourself. Who is this boy? He is you so many years ago, running through the groves, setting this in motion so that you will one day return only to pierce your son through the heart as a just sacrifice for what you and your kind have done.*

And the man knew then that he was insane, because, although he was holding the boy and raising the mallet to strike, he saw what he thought was the light of day come up all around him, a color of light that he had never seen before, and the boy was not what he had seemed a second ago, but a creature of mutilation and putrefaction. The world became liquid all around them, until all light was like a river, and the man fumbled with the mallet and dropped it. He tried to reach for the screwdriver to press it into the boy's flesh before it was too late, but something grabbed his hand and pulled him through some kind of opening, as if the world were only a removable layer of skin.

And on the other side, she stood there as beautiful as he had ever remembered her.

She opened her mouth to speak, dark water spilling from between her lips.

"I know you're not her," he said. "I know I'm standing outside a barn, holding my son in my arms. There's a town just down the road. And apple trees. It's cold. It's getting on night. I know you can't be her. I don't know what you are, but I know you're not her." Was he shouting? He couldn't tell—his breathing was difficult. He felt a pain in his chest as his heart beat wildly. Unbidden tears streamed down from his eyes as he tried to see her as she was, rather than the way she presented herself.

Her face froze in its expression. Then, for a moment, he knew clearly that the voices within him were the beacon of his insanity: she was, indeed, who she looked like, and she was trying to talk to him, but the voices in his head were getting louder, more raucous, shrieking across his nerve pathways. He knew the world was not the insane place that he had been living in, that it could not be, that the creatures he had been slaughtering could not be anything more than simple human beings. His own obsessions had brought him to this.

He felt the screwdriver in his hand and turned its blade towards himself.

You failed once before, the clearest voice in his head said, *so do it, do it right. Do it now.*

He pressed the blade against his chest and was about to give it a good shove, when he felt a searing numbness in his leg, and he fell to the ground—the sound of a gunshot—a burning around his right calf. He closed his eyes. Rock salt? When he opened them, it was night, and the boy stood over him, looking at him. He could see the barn and the darkening sky. From nearby a man shouted, "What the hell are you trying to do to that boy?"

Shot, I've been shot, damn it, you don't shoot your own kind.

But of course you do, you always kill your own, it's the law of man.

And what you don't kill, the wild things get.

He looked up and recognized the other man, the one holding the gun, and tried to cry out to him. Although he trusted no one at this point, he knew that this man with the gun thought that he was rescuing the boy from the clutches of a madman. The man would try to help the boy.

The man with the screwdriver knew it was too late, knew that they'd tricked him, almost made him kill himself, and now they would descend upon the man with the gun, too, and all would be lost.

The game was over.

Now he knew the boy was one of them.

The boy, who looked just like a boy, a perfect imitation, resembling so closely, in so many insignificant details his own son, looked at him.

Then the boy turned his head in the direction of the man with the gun and sniffed at the air just like a wild animal detecting its prey.

The man lay there and for one second, like another scent, came the smell of memory and all that had happened in just a few days, all that had turned him from a sane man into someone who believed that darkness had fallen across the universe.

He remembered where he had been just a week before, how different things had been, how normal life had seemed, how balanced.

How unspeakable it had become.

2.

From the Journals of Joe Gardner/when he was eighteen:

I will not go back to that place as long as I live. It's bad, and everything it touches rots. I don't care if my mother's on her deathbed, I don't care if my dad's being tortured by Nazis, and I don't care if it goes to hell. I know what it can do, that place. I know where it can take you.

And I'm not ever going back there as long as I live.

I know what it is.

It's a hunting ground.

THE BEGINNING:
WE ALWAYS RETURN
TO OUR FIRST LOVE

PATTY GLASS AND HER VANISHING ACT

1.

From the *Colony* (West Virginia) *Press Leader,* April 8, 1972:

Patricia Frances Glass, 12, is still missing. After thirty-four days, the search has finally been called off by sheriff's deputies . . .

2.

The signposts of life are, more often than not, grounded in some simple act; for Patty Glass, in 1972, it was an act that she didn't even know she had participated in.

It was spring, and the ground was mushy from the rains. There was that swampy smell that always came with the rains, too, like the sewers had begun flowing into the river, and the river had flooded the low ground. Somewhere nearby lay a dead animal, maybe a possum or a raccoon.

The boys—there were two of them, and two girls, too—wouldn't've minded finding the dead animal and seeing if its guts had been pushed out, because as kids went, they were healthy in their interests, which included some truly repulsive things.

They'd gone frogging before the sun was up, and Hopfrog already had a big burlap sack full of croakers. Being of insensitive nature, Hopfrog Petersen was going to use the frogs for scare tactics—his mother had an inordinate fear of slimy things, and it was his only way of getting back at her for the damage she was doing to his mind with her religious zeal. Patty was not exactly Hopfrog's girlfriend, but she was one of many seventh graders who had a crush on him. His real name was Homer, which he despised more than wedgies, but in spite of his name and nickname, he was indisputably the handsomest boy in the county, perhaps in the world, at that moment. At least as far as Patty was concerned, he was.

Hopfrog didn't think much of his own looks, except insofar as he could manipulate people—which, he discovered when he was about five or six, could go a long way in a town like Colony, West Virginia. Florrie Everett, who ran the Five N Dime, would kiss him on the forehead and give him extra candy; the girls all did his homework when it was too difficult for him; even his father, who worked at the furniture factory as a customer service rep, seemed to go easy on him and say, in his defense, "the boy just shines, Boston, you can't get mad at a boy for just shining." (Boston was his mother, and it was her real name.)

But Hopfrog and Patty were not the only kids on this expedition. Lo and beholden, as Hopfrog's own mother would say in her misuse of language, there, trailing Patty, were Joey Gardner and Missy Welles. Joey loomed over them, a boy doomed to play basketball with all the coordination of a drunk; he was terminally gawky, as far as Hopfrog was concerned. Didn't even like having him along. Joey was okay, on the scale of bullies versus wieners—although he leaned to the wiener side—but he seemed to have terminally bad breath and the beginnings of a problem with b.o. Hopfrog Petersen and Joey Gardner were not the best of pals, on top of all this. Hopfrog considered himself a loner, even with the girls flocking after him, and wasn't sure if having someone like Joey along was good for his image. And the only reason Joey was there at all was because (as everyone from fifth grade on had known) Joey had a humongous crush on Missy (whom he called "Melissa") and wouldn't leave her alone. Missy was there because Patty had dragged her along, and they were just about inseparable and often insufferable —well, Hopfrog was quickly becoming a misanthropist in his brief span of years, and was right then wishing that he'd gone frogging all alone.

They were crossing the old Feely property out on Lone Duck Road and had to take a detour. (Hopfrog being the natural-born leader, *he*, in fact, led the troop across the back of the old barn, away from the farm-house windows so Old Man Feely wouldn't take any shots with rock salt at their vulnerable asses.) There was a slender clutch of woods near the gray-boarded barn, all piney and dark, even in broad daylight—which it was not, being still six A.M. and hardly more than purple light all round. Hopfrog, with Patty Glass clutching his free hand (the other held the croaker sack), followed by Joey and Missy, tramped across the muddy grass that was like Old Man Feely's hair, all thin and droopy, to the woods. Old Man Feely wouldn't even see them in time to go for his shotgun; Hopfrog knew that if they could stay to the northeast of the farm, they would go unseen.

And as he stepped into the pines, he heard a twig crack in front of him.

He looked up into the red coal eyes of Old Man Feely, and then noticed the rest of him: five feet four inches from the ground, fat like a pig at the fair, his overalls half buttoned—Old Man Feely must've been pissing in the woods, 'cause the denim around his crotch was soaked. His plump head was beaded with water, too. In one hand was a bucket full of dark water, in another, his shotgun.

Hopfrog stood perfectly still, as if it would make him invisible. Joey and Missy and Patty weren't so smart; when Hopfrog looked over his shoulder, finally, every-thing seemed like it was in slow motion as Joey went running back across the field. Missy and Patty practi-cally clung to each other in terror and shock; it was up to Hopfrog and Hopfrog alone to avert this disaster-in-the-making.

He turned back to face Old Man Feely.

He took his croaker sack—all those beautiful bull-frogs, at least a dozen—and tossed it to the old man.

Old Man Feely dropped his bucket and his gun to catch the croaker sack. Hopfrog turned and pushed Patty and Missy forward and screamed, *"Run!"* Joey was already ahead of them by about twenty feet. Hopfrog, feeling like he was running through molasses air, pushed at Patty. Missy slipped in the mud, so he grabbed the back of her collar and lifted her up as he ran.

For just a second he glanced back to Old Man Feely, and it was like looking at a pagan god:

There was the little man, surrounded by frogs, standing there as if he were summoning all the powers of the universe.

And then, Old Man Feely went for his shotgun.

Rain began coming down, and sunlight was coming up, and Hopfrog was sliding across the grass just like he was on his skateboard—

When he felt something in the seat of his pants—

Then, he heard the shot—

Then, and only then, did Hopfrog know he was up shit's creek without a paddle, as the burning salt found the most tender flesh of his posterior.

He fell.

3.

Back then, in the early 1970s, Colony was still called, by some of the old-timers, New Colony. A man who claimed he was the incarnation of the prophet Moses had a vision of an angel settling down over the crest of House Mountain in 1723. He and his band of ragged followers started a short-lived colony when the land was still part of the Virginia Colony; then, after the American Revolution, the religious group had disappeared, probably gone farther up into the Malabar Hills; then, New Colony was left to itself to grow wild again, until the next century. The area was reborn as an ill-conceived tobacco plantation that ran from the Paramount River to the north and west sides, all the way southeast to House Mountain, well over a hundred acres, actually. The deed to the plantation, circa 1836, was limited to only a hundred, so that Stephen Friar and his sons lost much of the nine hundred acres they were using free and clear. Then, in the War Between the States, the plantation was destroyed, and the land went bad, which often happens after years of tobacco farming and days of war. The Friar boys were all dead by 1865. The Feelys, the Glasses, and the Reynolds worked what there was of farmland. An unincorporated area had already sprung up, a corners of sorts owing to a crossroads. Then, a town grew. Some of the land was useful, some useless, as Mennonites came into the valley, and then departed within thirty years, leaving behind farmhouses and furniture. There were the mines, too, across the Paramount River into the Malabars, a few of which had been reduced to high plateaus by strip-mining. The mines, too, had their days, but most of them were abandoned in Colony before Hopfrog and his friends were born, although there were plenty of old-timers still around with cases of black lung and stories of cave-ins and coal-mine canaries that never died. The last mine in town, and the last quarry, failed and closed by the mid-1950s. The furniture market out of West Virginia burst wide open because people in the other states wanted country simplicity, and Colony, the incorporated township, was officially born—a mayor and a police department and a Decency League and everything—after the Colony Furniture Company was formed in 1948 and built the Colony rockers, imitating a simple Mennonite design. These were the rockers that America's grandmothers sank into. This is how towns are born, not from land or water, but from an idea of what to sell to a million people that they don't need but must have anyway.

After World War Two, Colony seemed to settle into its own routine. The Colony Furniture Company still employed most of the employable residents who had not developed a trade of their own. The miners who wanted to ply their trade headed over to the other side of the Malabars (or "Mallomars," as Joey Gardner called them) and worked rock and cave. The town became a getaway commuter place for people from Charleston who wanted a quieter, gentler life. They even had a train stop, just up from the Miner's Lodge, although the train waited for no man beyond the requisite ten minutes. Main Street was long and fat, and half the shops were boutiques because of the nearby Civil War battlefield stopover, officially named Flushing Farms, after a previous Mennonite owner, called, more popularly, Fleshling Farms, because of the buried dead. A plaque by the highway read: *Two hundred Confederate soldiers died at the battle of Colony, a victory for the Union Army, May 1864.* Although West Virginia had separated from the South, the residents of Colony looked more kindly on Lee's Virginia than on Lincoln's Union. There were banks and restaurants, and, clearly, by 1972, when Hopfrog, Joey, Missy, and Patty were twelve, it bore no physical resemblance to the original plantation. Still, its traditions and rituals remained firmly rooted in the memory of tobacco-growing, and there existed a code of honor and the kind of chivalry which is most often spoken of by men and women who dreamed of a world that was long vanished, and possibly never existed.

As Hopfrog's grandfather often said about Patty Glass, who claimed to be related to Thomas Jefferson by way of uncertain ancestry, "there's lots of mules in this town who spend half their lives braying about how their ancestors were fine Arabians."

It was Patty that Hopfrog felt sorriest for, of all the girls in school, not just because she was a snob and could trace her ancestry back not only to Jefferson, but the Friar Plantation, as well, but because he knew that she was adopted from an agency in Winston-Salem. This was something they had in common.

A bond.

So when he fell in the mud at the Feely place, with rock salt biting his butt, he told her to go on and leave him there, to get the hell out before she got rock salt in her butt, too.

And, later, he wished he hadn't told her to go.

Maybe, he thought, *just maybe she'd still be alive if I'd held onto her real tight.*

4.

"Patty, Jesus!" Hopfrog pushed at her, but she kept trying to help him up. Rain was coming in sheets now; Joey and Missy had already run off someplace. *Damn Patty for staying behind.*

Patty was crying—she always fell apart whenever anything happened that she hadn't anticipated. She was tugging at Hopfrog's sleeve in a feeble attempt to lift him.

"Get the hell out of here, for Christ's sake!" Hopfrog spat at her. "He's gonna shoot you, too!"

Patty Glass leaned forward and planted a big kiss right on Hopfrog's mouth; he recoiled, but it felt good. For a second, in the illusion of her kiss, the threat of impending Old Man Feely was gone. The rain dried and the sky became a beautiful blue. But then Patty let go of him, and he slid back into the mud.

He looked up at her face.

Between the tears and the rain, she looked as if she were shining with water.

He heard the frogs croaking behind him.

"Hopfrog," Patty said, looking down at him, and then up to, presumably, stare into the squash face of Old Man Feely.

"Just run." Hopfrog gritted his teeth.

Patty caught her breath, and then ran off. Hopfrog watched her go behind the barn.

Then he felt the shotgun poking his shoulders.

"Git up, pig boy," Old Man Feely said.

Hopfrog pushed himself up from the mud with his hands, and turned to face the man. "I was you, I wouldn't call nobody else a pig," he said.

Old Man Feely had the gun pointing at Hopfrog's face.

Hopfrog tried to imagine what rock salt in the nose or on the cheeks might feel like, and he thought of how his face would be scarred, thus taking care of his reputation as the handsomest boy in Colony.

But there, on Old Man Feely's shoulder, sat a big old bullfrog.

Hopfrog looked from Feely's face to the frog, and back again.

They could've been distant cousins, mother's side.

It was possibly the shittiest day of his life so far, but Hopfrog just couldn't help himself, what with the rain, the rock salt in his rear end, and the frog on Old Man Feely's shoulder: he just got the giggles.

"What you laughin' at?"

The giggles had him so hard he couldn't even answer. He fell down in the mud and rolled to the side. "Okay!" he shouted, "just shoot me, you want, just shoot me!"

But Old Man Feely would have none of it. "You goddamn kids trespassin' all over my property, I see you back here, I'm gonna put somethin' stronger'n salt in my gun, you hear?" Old Man Feely had the funniest voice; he never spoke without shouting, and there was always something in his shout that was like firecrackers.

Old Man Feely stomped off towards his farmhouse, and the last Hopfrog saw him, the bullfrog was still sitting up on his shoulder, too.

Hopfrog watched Feely set his gun down on his porch, and then open the door of the house and go inside.

He glanced around to try and see if he could salvage any of his croaker sack, but the frogs had generally dispersed in the morning rain.

As he was looking for the escaped frogs, he heard the scream.

5.

Missy Welles and Joey Gardner heard it, too.

They stood huddled together (to give Joey some credit in the social department, he'd managed to slip his arm around Missy's shoulder without resorting to the false yawn routine), behind the stone wall that defined one edge of the Feely property.

It was definitely coming from the direction of the old barn.

And they'd both seen Patty run into it after Hopfrog had fallen.

Joey didn't think it was Patty's scream—she'd screamed often enough in her life for him to distinguish hers from anyone else's.

It was a single scream, and was cut off quickly as if someone had clapped a hand over the mouth of the person screaming.

Joey looked at Missy; Missy watched the lightening sky—a flock of starlings, startled by the sound, took off in a dark cloak towards the river. The morning was deep blue, as if the chilly wind had blown some of the color off House Mountain's flat blue top.

6.

Hopfrog went towards the sound.

It had come from the Feely barn, and he was wondering if it had been Patty, or maybe some animal hurt in there.

He glanced at Feely's front door to make sure that the Old Man wasn't going to check the noises out. A light switched on in the second story—Old Man Feely was probably upstairs counting his money. They said in town that he was a miser who had found a Civil War treasure buried under his house and was hoarding it for judgment day.

Pretty sure that Old Man Feely was occupied, Hopfrog walked around the side of the barn, to the back end of it—all the kids knew there were some loose boards back there you could swing to the side and squeeze through.

Hopfrog noticed footprints in the mud—Patty's shoes.

He waved to Missy and Joey, and whisper-shouted, "Come on, guys. It's Patty."

He waited for his two friends to come over and then they went between the boards, into the old barn, not knowing that they were beginning the greatest and most terrifying adventure of their lives.

For they heard Patty Glass's last cry; a shriek, really.

And in that sound all of their fates were bound together and sealed and tied forever to their hometown of Colony, West Virginia.

7.

"And that's the story about how Patty Glass disappeared, over twenty years ago," the man said to the boy.

"But you're not done yet," the boy said, "a story can't end until it's all told."

"Any good storyteller will warn you that a story's over when the teller tells all he knows. It doesn't really matter whether it's all told or not."

"I don't get it, Dad," the boy said, "how'd she disappear?"

The man shook his head. "Nobody knows. She just vanished. Those kids found one of her shoes—just like Cinderella. Only there wasn't any Patty in it. She was just gone."

"Didn't they see anything in the barn?" the boy asked.

The man looked out the window.

The leaves were brilliant red and orange, but even so he only saw a gray world out there, out where people lived and breathed. He didn't go out there much—at least not much more than he had to. It scared him—he hated admitting it even to himself—just the ordinary world, how people were with each other, the mysteries of everyday existence which he could not fathom. His son was his main connection to it, an emissary of life beyond this house, bringing in the smells and stories and triumphs of a child's world.

Children were beginning to walk the streets in costumes of ghosts and goblins and witches and ghouls and pirates and heroes and princesses.

He looked at his son—the boy, dressed as Batman, waiting for his mother to arrive to take him trick-or-treating.

The man said, "They saw things in the barn, of course. But sometimes the mind plays tricks, don't you think? Like on Halloween? Tonight? Ghosts are out, demons, even."

The boy shivered. "You're just trying to scare me."

"I know, I know, and your mother will be furious with me, won't she?"

The boy smiled. "I like getting scared. So, did Hopfrog and Joey and Missy see ghosts?"

"Not exactly. What they saw was something less scary. It was a well."

"Like a wishing well?"

"Yup. In the center of the barn. Only strange thing was, there was this cross on top of it, like it was part of a church or something. Like someone had pulled it off a church and had stuck it on the well."

"That's weird."

"Sure is. And when Hopfrog was in the barn, he thought he heard someone talking down the well. He thought he heard Patty. But when he told people, and

they went to the barn, there was nothing down there, nothing in the water at all. Just water. Lots of water."

"No Patty?"

"No Patty. That's why you kids shouldn't ever go out to the Feely place. It's not a good place to play at all."

"Okay. Dad? Mom told me you used to be called Hopfrog when you were a kid, only once you lost your legs, you didn't like being called it anymore."

His father grinned, remembering the insensitivity of youth. He drew his wheelchair back from the window and pushed himself over to be closer to his son. He reached out and gave him a hug, practically crinkling up the Batman cape permanently. "I want you to tell your mom I still love her, okay? She's still angry at me, but you can tell her that, right?"

His son looked uncomfortable. "I guess so. And Dad? Can I ask you something else, please?"

"Shoot."

"If the Feely place is so bad, why don't they just burn it?"

But his father, who was known as Homer Petersen, and lived in his late mother's house two blocks from Main Street in Colony, West Virginia, and was in his mid-thirties, had no answer to that.

His mind was wandering now, not morbidly, as it had been in the past few weeks, but wondering what his other friend was doing now, the friend who had been smart enough to get the hell out of this place in time, before it had started crippling him, too.

This place.

These hundred acres of nightmares.

The wind picked up outside. The man who had once upon a time been called Hopfrog, shut his eyes and thought he heard a voice from the past whispering through the eaves of the old house.

BORN TO RUN

1.

The same night that Homer Petersen was telling his son about Patty Glass's disappearance, Joe Gardner was in Baltimore. He was not at home with his wife and kids sorting through the Halloween loot of Snickers, Necco wafers, and candy corn in their renovated townhouse on Pratt Street. He was down at Fell's Point getting good and plowed on a fine local ale called Oxford Class. It had a golden texture to it, that's what Joe thought, and could be sipped or guzzled, whatever the mood.

The bar was called Franklin's and had a big fat portrait of Ben Franklin holding a foaming mug, as if he'd been in just the other day to hoist a few. The place had an old tin ceiling with all kinds of fancy markings on it and the walls were red brick, built sometime in the last century, crumbling now, cracks between the bricks, cracks on the mahogany bar. *Just like me*, he thought, *a few cracks showing through.* Joe had promised his wife a year before that he wouldn't do this kind of thing anymore—go to a dive and get shit-faced, but Ben Franklin's was no ordinary dive, and *when you get news like I got today, hell, it seems like the right thing to do. Besides*, he rationalized, as he often did, *I'm joining that fine tradition of writers who can't get through a crisis without a cold one.*

But I won't look at women, no sir, not me, that I have forsworn.

He kept his eyes on Ben Franklin, or the chilly mug in his hands, or the bartender, who looked a bit like the Tenniel illustration of the Jabberwocky from *Through the Looking-glass*—all gangly and long, with a lampreylike face and a Fu Manchu mustache.

"More?" The Jabberwock bartender asked.

"I think four has done me in. Hey," Joe added.

"Yeah?"

"You got a mother?"

"Everybody's got a mother."

"Not like my mother."

"How old are you, buddy?"

Joe had to think a minute. "Almost thirty-five."

The bartender shook his head. "Get a life, my friend, get a life."

Joe wanted to protest and say that he had a life, he wrote essays and stories and novels, but when he thought about it again, he realized it wasn't much of a life at all. "My mother's dying," he said. "She's dying. Leave it to her."

The bartender moved away, not interested.

"Damn her for dying," Joe said, and lifted his mug in a toast to old Ben. "She's dying and now I've got to go back there, Ben, for more than a day, Jesus, for maybe a week. A whole week in hell, Ben."

A woman, a blond—he saw her hair peripherally— sat on the stool next to him.

I am not going to look at you. And not just for the obvious reasons that I'm married and I shouldn't even be in here, but because you're going to look like her, I just know it. I will look at you with your blond hair, and instead see a woman with brown hair and deep almond eyes, because, lady, I am haunted, but only in the normal fucked-up way that guys are always haunted by their first loves. Men are all assholes, lady, don't you know that yet?

He could tell that she wanted to speak with him, maybe just for a friendly chat, but he was scared of those friendly chats, because they could turn into something else, and he would just end up punishing himself if he spoke with her. He kept his eyes on Ben Franklin.

When he was finished with his ale, he set the mug down, and swiveled out of the bar stool in the opposite direction from the woman. It was time to go home and sober up, get the kids ready, make sure he was ready, too, ready to face that memory that never seemed to die, no matter how many beers he drank, no matter how many nights he lay awake, listening to the sound of his own heartbeat and remembering the sound of her voice like he was a radio tuned only to her frequency.

Tomorrow we leave, he thought, *tomorrow we head*

for the armpit of the universe and look the devil in the face.

Joe Gardner walked home to sober up, in the icy wind that came up from the harbor, not minding the cold, not minding the early dark of autumn, knowing that his doom was somehow sealed.

He bought a pack of cigarettes at Fitzpatrick's corner store and though he wasn't even a smoker, smoked half of it while he walked up seven more blocks to his home. The first thing his wife said when he walked through the door, observing the cigarette hanging from his mouth, was "Don't you start up another bad habit on me."

He stubbed the cigarette out in a saucer and shrugged. "Lung cancer, emphysema, stroke; nothing compared to dear old Mom."

2.

After Aaron finally wound down from sorting through his candy, after both he and Hillary were quiet in their beds, Joe sat in front of the television and just stared at the screen. The show, *Cops*, was on, and a policeman was chasing down a man who had been growing marijuana in his backyard. Joe wanted to change the channel, because he usually watched the news, but he didn't even have the energy to pick up the remote. He felt a freeze in his muscles and bones. The thought of going to visit his mother paralyzed him. His wife sat beside him, resting her head on his shoulder.

"Remember the hamster Aaron used to have?" she said.

"Huh? Yeah. King Tut. Not just any hamster, but a long-haired blue hamster."

"Right. Well, remember how Aaron neglected him for a couple of months? Fed him and everything, but didn't get him outside his cage to run around?"

Joe nodded, and laughed. "Hamster paralysis."

"That's right. That's what the vet called it. It didn't move so its body just gave up. Is that what you're going to be like when we go to see your mother?"

Joe nestled his chin above her scalp. She smelled so good. He closed his eyes and inhaled: sweet and fresh. "Yes," he sighed. "I'll get hamster paralysis." He laughed, but he sounded like he'd been hollowed out.

"No, you won't. Because you're not going for Joe."

"I'm not? Well, I'm not going for her, either."

"No, you're not. Guess who you're going for?"

"I have no idea."

"You're going for Aaron and Hillary so they can finally meet their grandmother before it's too late."

Joe sighed; wishing he had another drink, but knowing it was better he didn't. "I guess I think too much about myself. All those bad years."

"And it was a long time ago now."

"Not to me. Feels like yesterday."

After a few minutes of breathing her sweet aroma and the feeling of her body against his, he said, "It sure would go a long way to making me forget the past if we made love right about now. What do you think?"

"Oh, I don't know. How about if we sat like this for a while longer? Then, maybe, we can see where it leads," she said.

"Sounds good," he said, slipping both hands around her, feeling the comforting warmth; and until he went to sleep that night, it helped him forget the nagging feeling that if he ever set one foot in the town of Col-

ony, West Virginia, again that it would be his doom.
They did not make love that night, but it was all right.
They went to bed, and, ignoring each other's snoring,
fell asleep.

He awoke in the middle of the night, sleepwalking,
standing in the hallway of the townhouse, the last image of a dream in his head—

*a girl with berry-stained lips, holding a child in her
hands, holding it up for him, as if offering him some of
what she had tasted.*

3.

From the Journals of Joe Gardner/1995:

This morning, we go.

*Jesus, I do not want to, and not just because of my
mother, but because of that other thing, that thing I
did, that thing that every last person in the town knows
about and probably still remembers. I'd say fuck 'em
if they can't take a joke, but you and I know that nobody ever takes a joke in this life. Nobody laughs when
you throw something in their face. Last time I went, I
hid the whole time. But this time's going to be different. Damn it, I hate being an adult. All right, I'm a
coward, I know it, I just don't want to go there, you
can't make me. Please let some miracle happen and let
us get down there and find that town has been wiped
off the face of the earth—as it deserves to be. God—I
will believe in you if you will do this for me—please,
please.*

Don't make me go.

*(How can I expect some God to help me if I don't
even believe in anything?)*

We'll be there by early evening. So close and so far away.

Too damn close.

It's funny how just the idea of going back home sometimes does things to you.

4.

It was November, and he hadn't been back to his hometown in at least seven years, not since Hillary was born—and then, only for a day, without his wife and family, just to pay his respects after his father died.

That was the story, anyway.

Truth was, he had skipped his father's funeral, had made it about as far south as Alexandria, Virginia, and had spent the night at a motel off 395 drinking himself into a stupor rather than continue down to that hell-hole. He hadn't even felt guilty about missing the funeral; he knew he was a bad son, the worst, but he could not bring himself to go home, as if there were an invisible barrier, a glass wall, keeping him out. He lied to his family, told them what a somber occasion it had been, how he had barely said two words to his mother, how the place was as ugly as he had remembered it.

Joe reasoned that he hadn't been back because time went so fast after thirty; his wife knew it was because he didn't like to remember what had happened back then. Not the Patty Glass thing when he was a kid (he had never even spoken about that with anyone since), but when he was a little older.

And now, he was almost there.

Colony.

In Fredericksburg, he'd stopped at a gas station for

coffee and a fillup. While his family waited in the car, he went to use the restroom. It was a garden-variety pit of a restroom, which wasn't so awful, so he did his business, and then caught a glimpse of something in the mirror, something which shook him up in a way he would not be able to explain.

He had seen her, briefly, in his own face.

Mother.

In his eyes, as he was getting older, he saw the flecks of dark brown on cinnamon, the kind of stern, tense glance she had.

It was as if the closer he got to her, the more she emerged from beneath his own flesh.

I'm a grown man. What the hell is wrong with me?

He washed his face off with the ice-cold water, and looked at his reflection in the mirror until she went away. Until it was just Joe, dark hair, pale skin, a few imminent wrinkles around the eyes and maybe the forehead, his hair thinning in places he didn't like thinking about—but still Joe, and no one else.

He didn't talk much the rest of the way down, and it seemed to take forever (of course, as Aaron pointed out, Joe had taken the longest route possible in his effort to avoid going home). Then, the signs started: Colony, West Virginia, 50 miles; Colony, 22 miles; Colony, 14 miles. It felt like he was counting down to a rocket launch.

Joe took the long cut that went along the quarries, not far off the river. Trees were still bursting with the golds and oranges of fall, shining and damp from a recent rain; the grass was dull, but dewy; the air, so clean it was almost unbreathable.

"I forgot it's so pretty," his wife said. "The whole area. We haven't gotten out into the country in forever."

Joe did his usual head-nod-and-rotate as if to say, *pretty only goes so far.*

Aaron was sitting up in the backseat poking his fingers at his Game Boy, behaving fairly decently since he'd been warned that if he went into any kind of tantrum or mood, the Game Boy got the deep six. Hillary slept, her head propped up against the car window with a pillow. It had taken far too long to come down through the mountain roads after the urban and suburban sprawls of Baltimore, and then Northern Virginia. He was impressed that neither of his kids had put up any fuss.

If anyone's done that, it's me.

"How much farther?" Aaron asked, setting his Game Boy down for the first time since breakfast.

Joe's wife smoothed the map out on her lap. "Seven miles? Maybe?"

Joe looked at the rounded hills, and the blue-gray valley. "You can always smell it before you step in it. That's what old Hop used to say."

"Oh," his wife said, faking a laugh.

"I know, I know," Joe grinned, "I should be more . . . forgiving or something."

"Mr. Cynical, right, Mom?" Aaron said, leaning forward, resting his chin upon the back of the front seat, between his father and mother.

Joe glanced at his son in the rearview mirror. The kid looked like his mother; neither Hillary nor Aaron got Joe's dark hair, or eyes, or the little ridge to his nose. Thank God for that. He was always afraid that a daughter of his would inherit that nose and feel forever cursed because she didn't get her mother's slightly turned up nose that was so WASP-perfect-to-form that sometimes it was hard to tell she had an ethnic heritage at all.

He looked back at the road; it narrowed and curved, and he had to slow down some, until finally the two lanes melted to one lane, with a sign on its edge.

"What's that mean?" Aaron asked, pointing to the sign. He sometimes got things backward—Joe didn't like to think it might be dyslexia. He preferred to think it was some kind of originality or creativity; but it worried him, his son's inability to read well. He was bright in other respects, everything but reading. "Y-eye-old?"

"It means to let someone else go first. Like being polite," Joe's wife said. "It's pronounced 'yield,' like 'field.' Y-I-E-L-D."

"Keep going teacher-lady," Joe said, quoting from an old movie. He raised his right arm and rested it along her shoulders. She leaned into him.

After what they'd been through, it amazed him, sometimes, how a simple touch was like healing.

And then, Joe stopped the car.

He didn't realize that he'd already begun shivering.

His wife said, "Honey? We can go—there's no one else on the bridge. Joe?"

But the world's sounds drowned for a moment or more and Joe felt as if he were not at the edge of a bridge, but beneath frozen waters.

Someone whispered in his ear, "Joe? Is that you? Joe?"

It was a girl's voice.

It was as if someone had switched on some juice and sucked Joe back into the vacuum of memory.

To a special time in 1978, when he was eighteen.

5.

What is it you want the most? Money, love, fame, happiness? Make your choice, you only get one. Make it, and blow out the candles, spin the wheel, say the prayer. You only get one of them, so make it last.

What is it you want the most?

My name's Fate, Mister Fate to you, children, and whatever it is you want the most, make sure . . .

Very sure . . .

Because I'm gonna make sure it's the one thing you never get.

6.

He was just eighteen and he had a Ford Explorer, bought cheap from a man in Stone Valley for six hundred bucks, the truck was what was called Ford Yellow, and was dented in three places, but Joe was going to hammer the dents out and maybe clean up the transmission some, and replace the left headlight, which was chronically dark.

Seventy-eight was shaping up into a good year for him in most ways, at least in the ways that counted. Back then, he was a smart boy even though he had dropped out of high school in the middle of his junior year to work in his father's garage full-time. Grades were never a problem: he aced the classes he enjoyed and flunked what bored him (including chemistry, geometry, and Phys. Ed.) His father had never finished high school and had never, in his own words, "given a rat's ass goddamn" about education, higher or lower. Joe's mother was furious at both her husband and Joe, but Joe had plans that involved money, and his father was paying him top dollar for Colony, West Virginia, in 1978, a good seven dollars an hour, more than he'd make in the furniture factory, more than he'd make if he went all the way to Charleston with his limited talents and his ambition of being a writer.

Joe figured that he'd get his diploma by hook or by crook somewhere down the road. Writers didn't need educations, anyway. What did Shakespeare need with an education? Or Jack Kerouac? Or John McDonald? Or anyone who wrote a half-decent sentence?—such were his arguments when he turned seventeen. It was hard enough listening to Bruce Springsteen records all the time and feeling like that, like he just wanted to get Melissa and have her wrap herself around his engine and take off—well, sometimes living in Colony was like living in hell, and did Bruce Springsteen have to go get a bachelor's degree to write "Born To Run"? Somehow, Joe doubted it. These arguments had soured in his mouth by the time he was eighteen, and watching his buddies graduate from Colony High, while he went back to being a grease monkey, and Hopfrog Peterson, that son of a gun, was even going all the way to Morgantown for college, while Joe—who knew in his heart he was smarter—was going to be stuck in Bumfuck, Egypt, for the rest of his life, saying, "regular or unleaded?" and "check under the hood, miss?"

But he had done it all for Melissa.

Sweet Melissa.

He had been in love with her since sixth grade, and he would love her until the day he died.

And she loved him, too.

Neither could wait until they got married.

Couldn't wait.

Had to get married as soon as they were both on their own.

Melissa's family wanted her to go to college, too, but she wanted to marry Joe, and he loved her more than life itself.

That's really the start of trouble in life: when you can't wait for something, particularly love.

In a town like Colony, patience was not only a virtue, it was a requirement.

It had taken nearly a hundred years for the town to call itself a town.

What would four more years be? That's what Melissa's dad wanted to know.

But to Joe Gardner who had carved JG LOVES MW TO DEATH on an oak tree near the old quarry, and to Melissa Welles, time was the enemy. Everything was NOW NOW NOW.

7.

"What do you know about love? Either one of you?" Gary Welles said. Melissa was upstairs, hiding, embarrassed probably that her father was taking this new tactic in dealing with Joe. Gary ("Mister Welles to you, boy,") stood in the doorway of his house, his hands akimbo on either hip, his legs braced as if waiting to get socked in the jaw.

And sometimes Joe wanted to sock him, too, because he was the kind of bully that Joe had hated all his life. Joe wanted to tell him that he knew why Melissa's mother sometimes had bruises, or why her little brother Gordon was practically autistic at thirteen; but he only wanted one thing, to see Melissa, and he knew that getting in a fight with her father wasn't going to help anything.

Besides which, Joe wasn't much for a fight—not that he'd ever been in one to know, but no matter how often his own dad pulled him aside to teach him how to box, he just never got the hang of it.

But Joe had size on his side. At eighteen, he was six foot three, his shoulders were broad if often slumped, and he projected strength.

Melissa's father, on the other hand, was small and wizened, which made it all the more maddening when Joe thought of the guy beating up on Melissa's mother.

"Love," Gary Welles said, continuing the lecture, "love isn't this kissy-flower-steam-the-car-window-at-the-drive-in thing like you kids think. It's commitment and security and care and service. It's raising children with the right morals and values."

"Okay, Mr. Welles, I get your drift," Joe said, "but how old were you when you got married?"

Gary Welles narrowed his eyes as if trying to avoid some verbal trick. "Nineteen."

"And Mrs. Welles?"

"Well, sour owl dung, boy, you can't compare Mrs. Welles and me marrying in 1949 with you two. Things were different then. The war helped us grow up fast. I had a steady job, I was able to support a wife."

"I can, too. I make enough, and I'll take another one on weekends, if I have to."

"What about college, boy? Melissa's going to go to college. I ain't gonna have some pregnant girl running back here because she can't do nothing herself. My wife and me, we want something more for her than wife to a grease monkey. We want her to get up in the world."

"You mean you want her to marry up, don't you?"

"I didn't say nothing of the sort."

"You want her to go to college, not so she can learn something, but so she can marry a premed student or someone who's gonna be a lawyer, or something. You think just because of my mother that I'm white trash or something."

"No, boy, you got me all wrong."

"My mother is a good woman, Mr. Welles." Joe felt he was lying.

Gary Welles seemed like he was about to say something, then hesitated. Slowly, he said, "I won't argue with you there."

Joe shut his mouth. He wanted to open it and start up again, because this guy really set him on edge, but he knew it would end in a spitting contest, and all that would happen would be that Gary Welles would be further convinced that Joe Gardner was not suitable for his daughter's hand.

Gary went and stood on the edge of the wraparound porch. The few street lamps haloed the antebellum houses on Stonewall Avenue; the lights were yellow, and buzzed slightly, to the point that Joe often thought they were going to explode sometimes. You could hear the crickets and locusts, all maracas in the trees, and beyond them, the ocean-wave-crashing sound of the big trucks on the mountain pass, their horns, too, like the cries of whales in mating fever, calling out to each other in darkness.

Gary Welles drew a cigar from his breast pocket. He always wore three-piece suits, even on the sultriest of nights, as this one was; there were clearly blotched islands of sweat beneath each armpit. Mr. Welles was a salesman for Colony Furniture and although the sales force was known as stupid and deceitful, it was Mr. Welles who headed the northeast region, the biggest sales territory of all, and so, to his face, in town, he was kowtowed to; you couldn't risk offending the man who was so good at getting rich idiots in New York, Boston, and Washington, D.C., to fork over hundreds of dollars for what amounted to an eight-dollar rocker, mass-produced, and hit several times with a lug wrench to antique it.

"So, Gardner, Joe, boy, wouldn't you be happier if Melissa got out of this hole and lived a better life?" Gary Welles smoked his cigar. For a moment, Joe felt that he'd let his guard down.

"Yeah. Yes. But I think I can be part of it."

The man turned to face him, smiled kindly, reached over and patted Joe on the shoulder, drawing Joe towards him with a slight pressure. Joe stood beside Melissa's father.

He said, "Joe. Let me tell you about myself. Let me tell you about a man who was once a boy like you, fresh from the Good War, come back home to marry his sweetheart. How I bled my knuckles carrying Colony rockers door-to-door, was up by four A.M. to catch the train up to the cities. How I sacrificed everything for my family. And the big question, Joe, always is, my boy, was it worth it? Was all that doing without and sleeplessness and fingers to the bone bullshit, was it really worth it? And you know the answer." Long puff on the cigar, stinking smoke coming at Joe, making his eyes water. "You know the answer?"

"I guess."

"I don't think you do, Joe. I think kids today are too young. The answer, boy, isn't yes. Just the opposite. If I had it to do over again, I'd've waited. I'd've courted Melissa's mama another three, four years, when I had some savings, when I could devote time to a family. She would've waited. When a woman loves you, Joe, she waits. When you love someone enough to let her pursue her dreams, trust me on this one Joe, you'll wait. What's a few years if love is eternal?" Gary Welles looked Joe in the eyes and blew smoke at him.

Joe's eyes teared up as much from the smoke as from the sentiment.

From behind both of them, Melissa's voice:

"Damn it, Joe, don't you listen to him." And before Joe could turn, there she was, in her button-down shirt and jeans and penny loafers—she grabbed his arm and tugged him almost halfway down the porch stairs. "Let's get the hell out of here," she whispered, and turned and shouted to her father. "Will you quit it with your poison for once in your life?"

8.

They made love in the bed of his truck, something that was still a mystery to him, an article of faith, a marriage vow, unbreakable, unstoppable (and insatiable, most of the time). Her body was sacred and he took their communion more seriously than most teenagers. He took care that she had as much pleasure as possible, that she felt at least as much as he did, which was all shivers and gasps. There was a lot of fumbling, but it was sacred fumbling. He had never made love to another girl and never wanted to. He would spend the rest of his life with her and he would make sure she was the most fulfilled, happiest woman on the face of the earth. He was a Man now, and she a Woman, and the world was their Eden. People like her father were too old to understand about real love, about how sex bound two souls, how the very act of making love was the one seeking and finding its other half. Older people had lost that, people like his mother and father, they had betrayed their pure spirits long ago, they had perverted their love. But it was different with Melissa, it was like touching an angel. He savored the feeling when he was inside her, albeit with the Lambskin Trojan on, even then the feeling was of connectedness and pleasure and fire—God, he couldn't take it for long, but he had to, he had to for her.

When it was over, he kissed her sweetly, brushing the hair from across her forehead.

She grinned, whispered something, and put her jeans back on. It was nearly midnight. They had to flip coins as to whose music got to play on the tape deck. Melissa usually won. She wasn't a Springsteen fan and so the damned soundtrack from *Saturday Night Fever* kept playing in the background. He heard those high-pitched BeeGees every time he felt himself about to really let go and enjoy the moment, so it was just as well they were in the back of his truck and not somewhere more comfortable—disco never was really great make-out music, as far as he was concerned (but most of the time, he just covered his ears and pretended he was listening to the Boss singing about getting out of some pissant burg.)

Afterward, he almost laughed. "He'll kill me," Joe said, smiling, "Your dad's gonna kill me."

"He will if he sees us like this," she said, brazenly jiggling her breasts.

"Melissa Welles, you stop that," he said, but couldn't help laughing.

"After sex, you're shy. You weren't so shy an hour ago."

"And you're a quick learner. I always thought boys were hornier than girls."

She shrugged. Snapped her bra back in place and

slipped into her shirt. "The famous Myth of Manhood. Or maybe I'll make that page one hundred two in the book, *The Myth of Joe Gardner.*"

"So," he looked at her sidelong, leaning back on his elbow, "which chapter of my novel do you want to be?" He was in no hurry to dress; he thought he might look desirable to her, there, naked, in the moonlight, in the truck, even with the mosquito bites on his ass.

She leaned forward and kissed him on the forehead. "Every chapter, Joey. But no more myths, okay? I want us to get married soon. I love you and I don't care what Dad thinks about it."

"Are you sure he wasn't right about getting out of Colony?"

"Well, we can both get out. We'll manage. I've got my savings, and you've got some money. I think we'll do okay."

"And college?"

"I'll go at night or something. All I know is I love you and I want us to be together." She kissed him harder. He felt the blood start to rush to his lower organs, followed by that awful and wonderful hormonal tide rising up, unbidden.

As they resumed their lovemaking, in which Melissa kept her bra and shirt on but removed her jeans again, Joe wondered if she really loved him or was just a sex fiend.

She whispered, "Day after tomorrow, we can go over the mountain and get married in Stone Valley. Daddy won't have to know til it's too late."

Joe said, like a train picking up speed as it comes out of a station, "Yes Yes YES YES I LOVE YOU OH GOD MELISSA I LOVE YOU **YES.**"

The night was endless, the love was strong and

beautiful, but something buzzed around his brain in
the early morning,

What is it you want most, kids?

Love? Happiness?

What is it you believe in?

Love? Is that it, Joe? Love?

*I'll take it from you. I'll blow out that candle for you,
Joe, my boy, and every time you light another one, I'll
snuff it, too.*

9.

Hopfrog Petersen became best man by default. Melissa and Joe didn't want anyone to know who might
tell on them and Hopfrog, for all his winning looks and
natural charm, had alienated himself from most of the
town well before eighteen.

"Actually, Hop," Melissa said, giving him a hug,
"you're a very good man, but I hope I'm marrying the
best man."

Hopfrog shrugged. "Remains to be seen, man."
Hopfrog had started calling everyone "man" since he'd
tried marijuana off in one of the cornfields with the
Heads from school. He was going through something
of a cool phase and Joe was a little unnerved by his
bouts with drugs and booze. Hopfrog had even, it was
rumored, tried LSD once, which was way out of the
league of even the druggiest high schoolers of Colony,
but some kids thought he was lying about the "tab"
which sent him "flying" to a place where the world
was a "magic carpet ride." Hopfrog's hair was a little
too long, his clothes a little too tie-dyed, and his reading matter a little too　William Burroughs. Hopfrog

had gone to weird, in Joe's opinion, since about eighth grade or so.

It was the morning of graduation and while Melissa's folks were going to the ceremony, expecting her to be there, as she was practically the "fucking valedictorian," as she said in her crude language, she was instead running off with Hop and Joe to Stone Valley to see the justice of the peace.

Hopfrog had a VW bug left over from 1969 with flower power decals and upside-down flags and peace signs painted sloppily on the hood. He'd bought it in Blacksburg, Virginia, for two hundred bucks and a bag of weed. It ran as if it were, itself, stoned, if it ran at all. Joe was ready—he'd dressed up in a navy sport coat and khakis, his shoes were shined, and his hair was cut. He stood with Hopfrog, waiting for Melissa, tapping his foot, shifting his weight from one foot to the other, wondering if he should smoke a cigarette just to calm his nerves.

Hopfrog leaned against the hood of his bug and yawned. "Missy's always been late, man."

Something about the way Hopfrog said that, *Missy's always been late, man*, seemed too familiar. Sure, Hop had known her since birth practically, just like Joe, but he'd also known that Hopfrog looked at Melissa differently these days, not like a buddy, but like a woman. Joe didn't really like that. Then, he thought: *Shit, am I gonna be one of those hothead rednecks who's always getting jealous 'cause some guy is after his woman? No way.* "Yeah, I know, man," Joe said, ever the chameleon. "Hope your wheels don't break down like they did at Christmas."

"Look, dude, this bug is in primo condition."

"I'd've worked on it free down at the shop," Joe said. Sometimes he couldn't believe that Hopfrog had changed so radically since the vanishing of Patty Glass when they were still kids. After that, Hopfrog was never quite the same old Hop. He'd gotten into the drugs and partying too much and did strange things like running cross-country wearing purple granny glasses, or making his own special brand of brownies, to be distributed at lunch to the teachers' table—as it turned out, they weren't hash brownies at all, but had Ex-Lax laced through the dark frosting.

"I got some champagne in the back," Hopfrog said, pointing to the small bag in the back corner of the bug. Beside it was a pizza box from Luigi's. Hopfrog had thought of everything. He had been pretty much a leader before adolescence hit, and now, he was the outsider; but he still had the damned Boy Scout thing down. He was always prepared.

"Hey," Hopfrog said, holding a finger up into the air, "feel that?"

Joe stood still, as if he were about to miss something.

"No wind," Hopfrog said, "that means a storm. Always a wind from the hills, unless we got a front moving in. You know, the first of one of those summer storms. Lightning, thunder, the nature thing. We'll get rained out over in the Malabars. Probably have to spend the night in Stone Valley. So, do I get to sleep between you, or at the foot of the bed?"

Joe was taken aback. He was not the kind of young man to understand the difference between this kind of joke and a real request. It wasn't because he was dense. It was because he had spent the majority of his formative years reading and writing stories that never seemed to go anywhere, working in his dad's gas station and hoping against hope to get out of Colony before he went crazy. He didn't like the idea of anyone, even a friend, joking about Melissa like that.

Hopfrog must've read his face, "Aw, come on, Joey, sit on it and rotate, it's only a little wedding humor. God, you either hang out with your loony old man sniffing high octane or you're down weeping over Russian lit. as if some dead guy like Tolstoy were sitting right next to you."

"Gee, Hop, you sure know how to sum a guy's life up, don't you?"

"Just seems you've made a lot of stupid mistakes in your life, you know? Like, for instance, dropping out of school when you were practically a fucking honors student and putting up with your old man making you do the dipstick thing and even in third grade accepting that dare to jump the bridge—Jesus, I can't think of a time since your birth when you didn't see the wrong thing to do and head in exactly that direction, Joey."

"Hop," Joe said.

"Yeah?"

"Shut up."

"Oh. Okay."

"If you're trying to tell me what I think you're trying to tell me, butt out. I've known Melissa and I would get married since we were kids. You're not just the best man, you're the only man. All I want from you is a ride over the hills. If there's a storm, I'll pay for your motel room. If there isn't, I'll buy you lunch. Try and remember that you're a friend and not my second conscience, okay?"

Hopfrog nodded and from the look on his face, probably wished he was drinking that champagne in the sack right that very instant.

Joe was tense.

Hopfrog was getting tense, too. So tense, he drew a

Camel from his rolled up sleeve, lit it, inhaled deeply and exhaled a gray cloud of smoke.

It was going to be a tense day.

And it didn't get any better when Melissa Welles finally showed up.

10.

"I'm not sure this is the right thing," she said.

Eight little words.

The eight most terrifying words in the language when you're sure that you're doing the right thing and have been depending on her to feel the same.

She looked great. In Hopfrog's words she was her "kickassiest," a compliment as far as he was concerned, an obscenity to the more conservative element that pervaded the town.

To Joe, she looked more beautiful than he had ever thought at the very moment she said those disheartening words.

He felt his face go red. It had been too good to be true, all of it, from the time they'd met in fourth grade and he'd had a crush on her but had kept his distance, to the time in sixth grade when he gave her flowers and she kissed him; and when Patty Glass had run away or been kidnapped or had fallen down a well or whatever, she had cried, and he had held her, the first time he'd ever comforted someone else; or when she told him she loved him, in tenth grade; said she'd marry him, in eleventh.

And now, "I'm not sure this is the right thing."

She wore her graduation gown. She'd just come running from the ceremony. Her hands were tucked into the slits of the dark gown; she only put her hands in her pockets when she had something to confess. She didn't even have her overnight bag with her.

She wasn't going to marry him.

He could see that.

She started speaking but he didn't hear anything. He was beneath some current in the river. He was beyond all sound. All he could think of was that there was nothing left to live for. There was nothing worth having, or wanting.

Then she giggled. "Joe. Joey, come on. It's a joke. I love you, I'm all ready." From beneath her gown she withdrew her small red overnight case.

"Oh, my God," he sighed, and leaned forward, color coming back into his face, feeling the warmth of blood and sunlight and love again. He took her in his arms and kissed her lips and cheek and forehead. "I love you, too, oh, babe, I don't love your jokes, but I love you."

"Never could take a joke," Hopfrog said, slapping him on the back, spitting the butt of his cigarette on the street, "let's make like shit and hit the trail before the posse comes after us."

11.

They drove to the town limit and beyond, Hopfrog driving, Melissa and Joe together in the backseat. A storm was clearly coming down now from the Malabar Hills and they were almost at the Paramount Bridge, leaving the area, when Hopfrog, who was driving, said, "Looky there, boys and girls, a genuine wreckage of a car." He pointed off to the side of the road.

A Mercury Cougar lay on its side in the gully.

"There's Gump." Hopfrog nodded towards Joe's

cousin Dale Chambers. "Wanna say howdy?" The officer barely noticed them as they drove slowly by. The wreck was still smoking. Dale, known by most as Gump because of a cartoon deputy on TV who looked just like him, was scratching his head. Voices came over the policeman's radio in his black-and-white Ford Torino.

"I wonder what happened," Melissa said and leaned against Joe. Her breath was sweet. She was chewing Juicy Fruit gum. She smelled like Charlie!, a vial of which she always kept in her purse. Didn't mix well with his British Sterling, but what the hell. He liked her smell. "You think anyone's hurt?"

Joe leaned forward, sticking his face out Hopfrog's window. "Hey, Dale!"

Dale Chambers turned away from the wreck. He recognized Joe, waved, and then waved them on. But he still had a puzzled look on his Gump face. Joe noticed that there was no body in the car—as if someone had just wandered off, dazed and disoriented, from the wreck.

"Must be okay," Joe said, relaxing again into the backseat. He entwined his legs with Melissa's and thought it was going to be the happiest day of his life.

Hopfrog put his foot down on the gas and shifted gears. The VW hummed and growled to life again.

They drove onto the Paramount Bridge but when they got to the middle of the bridge, the bug stalled.

Joe whispered in Melissa's ear, "Now, what else could go wrong?"

Rain was beginning to fall.

It was to be the first storm of summer.

Lightning played blue and white across the far hills.

There was a nice smell of honeysuckle in the air, though. Folks in the hills always said that honeysuckle was like a protection, that it meant good luck. Joe liked smelling it now, mixed with that fresh smell of new rain.

Up ahead, a truck was barreling down the road, directly towards them.

"Damn car!" Hopfrog said, bearing down on the stick shift. The VW kept stalling out.

Something was funny about Hopfrog's face, something Joe couldn't pinpoint.

Joe stayed calm. Nothing bad was going to happen. The truck would stop at the other end of the bridge. He and Melissa would be married by three in Stone Valley. Hopfrog would get drunk on his own champagne and have to sleep in a cot in their room at a motel. He and Melissa would be married and happiness would be starting its slow roll towards them.

Right now, only the truck seemed to be rolling towards them and it was harder to stay calm by the second.

They only had seconds, after all.

Melissa whispered, "Why isn't that truck slowing down?"

Hopfrog seemed to be looking, not at the truck or the clutch, but at something in the sky and his mouth formed a small o as if he had never seen the sky before.

Something else whispered,

What do you want the most?

Think real hard, Joe.

But keep it a secret. Keep it to yourself.

'Cause it's the one thing I'm gonna make sure you never get.

12.

"Joe?"

He opened his eyes.

He was no longer a teenager.

He was in the Buick Skylark with his wife and kids.

His daughter, Hillary, was beginning to sing the "I love you" song from *Barney*. It reminded him for a second of Old Man Feely, because the tune was "This Old Man He Plays One."

It was no longer 1978.

Damn it. Or Thank the Powers That Be, one of the two.

"Joe? You okay?" his wife asked.

He glanced at her and worked up a smile. He was sweating. "We shouldn't've come back," he told her, "I shouldn't've anyway."

She reached up and felt his forehead. "A little fever."

"Jenny," he said, "this is where it happened."

She drew her hand back. "We could've taken the new highway down. Why this way?"

"I wanted to see it again. To see if it's changed any. It hasn't. All these years and they haven't put a better road or bridge through this side."

"You want me to drive?" she asked.

"No, I'll be fine." He started the car up again.

This time, he crossed the bridge safely.

3

THE LIFE OF A BOY

The worst things always happen in broad daylight.

Billy Hoskins actually thought this as he leapt off the
front porch of his house over on Third Street. The
worst things to a boy of nine tend to be considered
normal life to the grown-ups around him: arguments,
scowls, mocking laughter, scoldings, simple obscenities
under the breath. His mother started the fights—at
least, that's how Billy saw it. His father would come
home at lunchtime for a peaceful meal and Billy's
mother would start in. The fights were always about
nothing, at least as far as Billy could tell. The dish-
washer was broken, or the kitchen needed rewall-

papering, or Billy's dad had smiled at the waitress out at Hojo's the night before, or something silly. Billy didn't think he was going to get married when he grew up because wives seemed like such a bother. So, even though he'd been just about finished with his tuna sandwich and he had wanted to have one of the Chips Ahoy cookies that invited him from their package, open on the table where his mom had been clawing at them in her desperation to fill her mouth in order to keep out all the bad things she was about to spew, Billy shoved back from the table—almost knocking his chair over—as soon as his mom started in on how bad the heat had been the past summer and how dare his father keep her in the dark ages without an air conditioner. "There's sales down at Crawford's. We can get a kitchen unit and a bedroom unit, three hundred dollars. That's all."

"It's fucking November," his father said, "we're gonna have snow any day and you're gonna whine about that? Christ Almighty Goddamn it, woman. And why the hell's Billy home today? He should be in school, shouldn't he?"

"He had a fever this morning," his mother said, almost weakly. This wasn't entirely true, Billy knew. He had missed a lot of school this fall. His mother had slept in again, with that wine smell all around her, and he had just stayed in bed hoping the world would go away and both his parents would forget he even existed.

But then, around ten-thirty, she'd gotten up and he'd given his line about not feeling well. She'd put her frosty hand on his forehead and cried out, "Oh, my god, baby, you're burning up!" This seemed to happen whenever she'd been into the wine that she called her "Beau-jolly."

Billy stepped back from the table. They wouldn't even notice him as he took off, would they? They'd just sit there and bicker about things. At night they were too tired to argue, but in the middle of the day, it was always a fine time.

It was the worst thing, as far as he was concerned, and he was sick of it. He grabbed his hooded sweatshirt and hurriedly tugged it over his head. He felt as if he were dodging bullets whenever his parents fought. It was what his cousin Alec called a DMZ, which meant something about a zone, like the part of town where there was a sign that read: Not zoned for horses. Something like that. He thought DMZ might stand for Demon Mother Zone, which pretty much summed it up for him.

The shouting continued.

"Well, I know you, I know you won't buy me an air conditioner come June and they'll cost more then, too."

"Jesus, we might have to send Billy to a orthodontist in another year and spend a couple thousand on his teeth—he inherited them from your side of the family —and you want to buy a air conditioner in fucking November!"

"He don't need braces, not as bad as I need things around this house." His mother began weeping.

But, by that time, Billy was leaping off the porch and was off and running up the street, not really thinking about where he was going, but just wanting to run as far away as he could from them, from that house too. It was a bad house. They had moved into it two years before, from their little apartment above the grocery store on Main Street. Ever since they'd gotten into that house, it had all gone as sour as milk in the sun.

Billy hated the house. He wished somebody would torch it or something.

He stopped running when he reached the end of Third. It hit a dead end and Lone Duck Road. If he went to the left, he'd end up in town and would get in trouble for going so far. If he went right for about a mile, he'd end up in farmland, if he made it that far (and he never had, on any of his runs).

Straight ahead were Old Man Feely's apple orchards, all sweet and rotting with unpicked apples since the Old Man had gotten sick. All the kids went through there as a shortcut to school. Billy never had because he wasn't old enough.

But today, he was going to.

He would pick some apples that would be good enough to eat and run away. Some nice person might give him a ride—if you cut through Feely's property, and got across the creek, you could make it to the highway. He had heard about a boy who was about fourteen who had made it out there and had gotten a ride with a trucker. The boy made it all the way to Charleston before he was brought back home. Billy's uncle was a trucker and was really nice. Maybe a trucker like that would pick him up and take him on his route with him. Then Billy would get away for a while and maybe his folks would feel sad that he was gone (he imagined his mother crying all over herself, and his father shedding a little pearl of a tear wondering what they'd done to drive their precious child away. It made Billy smile to think of it.) Then, after he'd had his adventure, Billy would show up again and tell them that everything was going to be all right. "You learned your lesson," he'd tell them, just like his teacher Miss Gordon had told him so many times when he'd had his temper tantrums in school and she'd shut him in the little closet near the janitor's room. "You learned your lesson. Now you can come back and be a good boy again."

Being a good boy was important to Billy, but it was hard to do with all that yelling at home.

He ran up the thin dirt path that went between the scraggly apple trees. Exhausted, he slowed down and went in search of apples. He picked one up that was all shiny on one side, but when he turned it over, it was wormy and brown-rotted on the side that had rested in the grass. He found three or four more like this. He knew he had to have some apples or food of some kind for his journey—he should've grabbed the Chips Ahoy bag off the glass table in the kitchen before he'd run off. Then, he saw a few good apples, still on the tree, at the far end of the orchard. He walked that way and found more. He stuffed them into the kangaroo pouch of his sweatshirt. He got so many good ones that he had to put some into the back of his hood. You could never have too many apples for a journey like this.

He was getting tired and it seemed colder. If only he'd brought his Halloween candy. He'd be better off with candy since it came in wrappers and he could always sell it for money. He had counted twelve mini-Snickers bars in his sack from the night before and at least fifteen Baby Ruth bars (far too much candy corn, and since it was unwrapped and loose, it would be difficult to sell, he was sure). *Maybe*, he thought, *I should run back to my room and get it*. But it was a DMZ now. There was no turning back.

What was the use of dreaming about candy?

He'd never see it again, anyway. He'd never see his cat, Louisianne, either. He was positive now that he would never go home again. Thinking of how sad they'd all be without him, he wanted to cry but his eyes wouldn't water up.

He looked ahead: to the right of the orchard was the old barn. Beyond the barn was Feely's house. No lights were on in the windows. That was good. Other kids were scared of Old Man Feely. He was legendary in town. But Billy wasn't scared of anything that he couldn't see—and nobody ever saw Old Man Feely anymore.

The apple trees made ragged columns, like an army on a slope heading towards battle; then there were the woods, and the creek. But it would be a couple of miles to the highway. Billy wasn't sure if he'd ever gone that far.

Instead, he remembered the place his friend Mack had shown him, part of the slope from the orchard. It was a special place. He had caught Mack there, once, smoking cigarettes. Mack was thirteen, and could smoke if he wanted to (that's what he'd said at the time, anyway). And then, Mack had shown him the place, all covered over with rocks.

"What is it?" Billy had asked, peering down into the darkness.

"Part of the old mine," Mack told him, shining a flashlight down the path of the tunnel a ways. "They had to close off parts of it. I heard it goes all the way to Watch Hill. I heard that sometimes you can hear the dead people stumbling around in the mines trying to find their way out."

Billy had known about the mines because, right behind his house, there were a couple of pipes sticking up on a ridge in the lawn. His father had told him that it had been part of the underground mine, too.

Billy had asked Mack, "Ain't it kinda scary, down there?"

Mack had grinned. "Lots of bad things down there, Billy, but if you're with me, I can protect you from them."

Strangely enough, for Billy, that time sitting in the hole in the ground for a couple of hours on a Saturday, watching Mack smoke cigarettes, and telling scary stories to each other, was the best time he could remember ever having in his entire life.

So Billy decided to go find that hiding place in the dirt again. It didn't take long—the rockpile was still there. He figured that maybe he'd hide for a while and come out later to see how sad his parents were and how much they missed him. Then, maybe they'd be nicer and not yell so much. He wouldn't have to run away at all.

He rolled some of the rocks back, dropping a few apples in the process. Then, he took off his sweatshirt because moving the rocks made him hot. The hole seemed smaller than he'd remembered it—but then, he had grown a lot in the past year. He brushed spiders and gunk off the entrance and sat down in it. He squeezed himself back into the tunnel just a bit more. He could see all the way to Old Man Feely's house from his spot. Maybe it would be better to cover himself up again.

But it would be dark.

He didn't love the dark.

But what if Old Man Feely came out when he was asleep? What if that happened? Then he'd be in bigger trouble. And what if the other kids' stories about the Feely place were true? What if something haunted it?

I don't believe in all those scary things.

I don't.

No such thing as ghosts. If there were, wouldn't they have been out on Halloween last night? All he'd seen were other kids dressed up as ghouls and things, not actual ghouls.

Billy wasn't scared of things he couldn't see.

He pulled some of the rocks back in front of the opening, just enough so he could see out, but so that no one could see in.

He put his knees up until they were under his chin, closing his eyes for a second.

He didn't think he'd sleep. It was too early in the day.

Just for a minute. Try an apple. An apple a day keeps the doctor away. Don't keep the worms away, or the flies. Do worms fly? Flying around like an angel across the treetops . . . his thoughts spun into drifting sleep.

Billy Hoskins fell asleep at three o'clock in the afternoon, about the time that Joe Gardner and his family crossed the Paramount Bridge, and about the same time Homer "Hopfrog" Petersen parked in the handicapped space in front of Logan's Market downtown and spotted his ex-wife Becky walking her dog while Homer couldn't get out of the car even to say hi because he was overcome with fear that she hated him more than anything. It was about the same time that Colony, West Virginia, would experience a change of seasons, when winter would be coming on strong.

When Billy would awaken, it would be dark and cold.

Something would touch the back of his neck and he would be so afraid that his breathing would become rapid. He would turn around and follow the warm feeling down, down, down, scraping his knees along the way, but unable to resist.

And then, one final breath from his lips, and the feeling of having wandered into the real Demon Mother Zone, and with it, the certain knowledge that there was nothing, *nothing* he could do about it.

4

THE TRUCK DRIVER

The truck which had rammed into Hopfrog Petersen's small VW back in the seventies, did not go over the edge of the Paramount bridge. Instead, the driver managed to get it to the other side. He swerved a bit, and managed to blow gusts of dirt up before finally bringing his eight-wheeler to a stop. The driver jumped down out of the cab and ran back to the bridge where the other car had gone over.

A policeman was there (by his badge, the driver saw that the policeman's name was Dale Chambers), and the truck driver noticed another accident at the roadside, a Mercury Cougar, lying on its side, without a driver.

"You see it?" he asked breathlessly. "You see it?"

"See what?" The policeman seemed calm. "The accident?"

"No," the driver said, "that thing, that flash of light!" He would realize later that he was excited, in spite of the tragedy for whomever had been driving the VW. "It was a UFO," the driver said, "I know it was! I saw it come down, all silverlike. It wasn't like anything I ever seen before, it was like somebody parted the sky, like a big lightning crack came down in between the sky and earth, and came between my truck and the VW!"

"Mister, you got beer on your breath. I advise you to get a lawyer real soon." The policeman went to call on his radio for an ambulance, but the driver wandered to the edge of the bridge and looked up to the sky.

Although he would later be charged with vehicular manslaughter (and this charge would inevitably be dropped because a good lawyer can do a lot with the loopholes in the law), he would return often to this spot, considering it sacred, the place where he saw the flashing and exploding lights from the sky.

This was so many years back, and the man didn't tell anyone his story for fear of being thought insane.

Time passed. Some wounds healed.

The business of the living took over the town and then, one day, Joe Gardner returned to the place of his birth.

5

THERE ARE NO STRANGERS IN A TOWN LIKE COLONY

1.

On the other side of the Paramount River, inside the county, a sign:

Colony, West Virginia.
"The Friendly Place on the River
Home of the World Famous Colony Rockers"
Population, 1700.

Someone had spray painted across the lower edge of the sign:

Welcome To Colony. Now, go home. And yer little dog, too.

You take the train down from Harpers Ferry to get there, or you can fly in to the airport in Charleston, rent a car, and drive southeast almost to the Virginia border, to Stone Valley, say, and then wind your way through the Malabar Hills, another forty minutes to Colony from the top. If you know the back roads, you get there with greater difficulty, but with an appreciation for the beauty of the area, the clear sky, the trees still resplendent with red and orange and yellow leaves, the wind brisk but invigorating. A river winding on its outer edges made it look like a vast and fertile quarry surrounded by monoliths. Was it beautiful? No one who lived there thought so, but it was: it was beautiful as were all American towns that had seen their heydays at the time when the railroads ruled, when coal was king, when honor was a commodity that was valued above life, and when a certain degree of patrilineal inbreeding was considered genteel. It had the look of a tired county seat and yet Stone Valley, modern and stupid, held that honor. Colony was town on the inside, country on the out: a deer or possum might cross the old roads, like Lone Duck Road, or Paramount Road or the one called simply, the Old Road. There might be the smell of smoke in the air, from a cabin set back in the woods—the fireplace lit when the chill of early evening sets in. The taste in your mouth is like leaf mold and river ice, an acquired taste if you're not used to the country, a taste of memory wine if you've been here before, in your youth, in the days of green and summer and light that never faded.

Joe Gardner stood beside his Buick. Aaron needed

to pee and had been too embarrassed to get out at the paved road, so here they were, pulled over to the side of yet another dirt road. Aaron shivered a little as he peed. Joe noticed that Hillary was sound asleep in the back. Jenny took a hike over to the river's edge to stretch her legs. She was looking a little ragged; they all were. They'd been driving five hours, and after stalling on the bridge like that (Joe now assumed the car had stalled, he told himself over and over again, it had stalled—it wasn't that he himself had stalled, that his body had stalled, that his mind had stalled, but that the car was having its usual round of mechanical problems). Joe wanted to let the Skylark cool down a little.

Aaron finished peeing, and turned around without zipping his fly up. Sometimes Joe thought his son was quite possibly the smartest, most handsome little boy on the face of the earth.

And then there were those times when Aaron left his fly unzipped.

"X-Y-Z," Joe told his son.

Aaron glanced down and saw his own shirttail sticking out from his fly. He pressed it in, zipped up. "Dad?"

"Yeah?"

"Why is it that the pee keeps coming even after I think I'm done?" He had a deceptively sweet Vienna Boys' Choir sort of voice, vaguely cherubic, which he tried to disguise by lowering it an octave to sound more mannish. This was a very serious question, Joe could tell by the tone of voice.

"It's like plumbing. Must be you need a new washer."

"I don't think so. I think maybe I need a new dryer." Aaron laughed. Then, looking up at his father's face, "I can't wait til I get to shave."

Joe reached up and felt the day's growth around his chin. "You think it's a treat, do you?"

"No," Aaron said, "only we saw this movie in school where it says that when you get to shave, girls start liking you."

"It's not exactly like that. You want girls to like you?" This was a new twist; Joe hadn't expected to worry about Aaron and girls for another few years.

Aaron shrugged, "I guess . . . I guess I want everyone to like me."

"It's more important that you like yourself, Bean," Joe used the affectionate nickname that Aaron was quickly outgrowing.

"Oh," his son said thoughtfully, "well, in that case, I only like parts of me."

"Which parts?"

Aaron scrunched his face up a bit. "The parts that work. Like my hands and my brain and my feet when I run. The basics." Aaron was one of the most wonderful and strange kids that Joe knew: sometimes he made Joe believe in reincarnation, because the kid seemed preternaturally intelligent, as if he'd been around from another time. Joe had read books where people talked about old souls and young souls, and if there were such a thing, Joe thought he was probably a young soul, while his son was the old kind. Aaron whispered, almost under his breath, "And Mom says she wishes not all your parts worked quite so well."

It stung, that comment. Joe didn't need to ask Aaron to repeat it. He didn't even want Aaron to know that it was an important comment, something Aaron shouldn't be repeating. *Nobody's perfect.* It was his litany at this point, his rosary, his private prayer. *Nobody's perfect. We all make mistakes. What's past is past.*

Aaron might've figured it out, but recalling his own childhood, Joe knew you didn't figure it out until you were older, maybe in your late teens, when you saw something die between your parents, when you wanted to prove that your own kind of love was stronger than theirs, that it would last into eternity, not just break apart at the first pretty face. He didn't blame Jenny for having made those kinds of comments: *I wish your father's parts didn't work so well.* Jenny shouldn't have said it in front of Aaron, but when you got to the state that she'd been in, you probably didn't notice what you were letting slip.

All right, so I cheated.

Once.

I will write that I won't cheat ever again in my entire life if it makes you happy. I will be your slave and never ever look again at another woman if it will mean that every now and then you look at me tenderly again without getting that hurt look on your face. Okay?

He'd said all that in therapy, which they'd sped through from January to August. He remembered what his father had said, when Joe was fifteen, and had found out about his mother. *"Well, women have difficulties with us. She called me an asshole, Joe, and you can't argue with that. When you come down to it, all of us, all men on this planet, are assholes."*

Another thought, unbidden, the one that lurked there in his brain at all times, always, even before he had cheated:

You're evil.

You're evil just like your mother was evil.

You are possibly the worst human being on the face of the earth, you are lower than low, not just because you cheated on your wife and family, but because the moment when you were cheating, your son was dying.

Joe glanced down at Aaron and scruffed his hair up. Aaron grinned, but was watching the trees as if expecting to see a bear.

Joe wished it had never happened. It was a year ago now, at a bar in Baltimore, down at Fell's Point. A bar where you could barely see the person sitting next to you, where men and women did things in shadows.

She was there.

She was not nice, not sweet, not even very pretty, certainly not the beauty that Jenny was.

But she had one thing. That one thing.

She looked like her.

(He shivered whenever he thought of the name.)

Like Melissa.

Just in the eyes, really.

And the way she touched him.

Aaron said, "Dad, look!" He pointed across the road.

A flock of birds, dark against the fading sky, burst from nearby laurel bushes and flew up, chattering, coming together as one dark cloud, and then dispersing again.

Your son was dying. Paul. Aaron's baby brother. Hillary's baby brother. Something got him in the dark while you were sleeping with someone other than your wife. Something came out of the dark, something called sudden infant death syndrome—maybe—but maybe it was just God saying that if you screw around on your wife, you don't get everything you want, if you cheat your family out of their father, you don't deserve another beautiful little baby.

Maybe it was God. Or maybe it was something more idiotic, more brain dead and arbitrary:

Maybe it was fucking life.

Joe lived with these thoughts side by side with more mundane ones, and managed to function most of the time. Sometimes he just stared into space. He had lived a life where he had let two people he had loved die, and yet, here he was, with his wife and kiddies watching a flock of birds take off. They were on their way to Gramma's house. *Over the river and through the woods, indeed.* Aaron watched the birds with wonder. He looked so much like his mother, it was amazing, although Joe saw a little of himself, just a pinch or two, in the eyebrows that were like caterpillars mating, or the way his ears poked out from his wheat-sheaf straight hair, or in his incipient height—Aaron had shot up four inches in under six months.

Joe looked from his son to the billowing flock of birds. "They're late. We're going to have an early winter, and those guys are never going to make it to Florida," Joe said.

"Birds are neat." Aaron stuffed his hands in his pants pockets and hitched his shoulders up. "I wish I was a bird sometimes."

"And where would you fly to?"

"I dunno. Maybe China. Where would *you* fly to?" Aaron asked.

Joe watched the birds go up and over the sloping hill beyond the river, and then, out of sight. "Anywhere but here," he said.

He followed Aaron over to Jenny who was stepping over the low bushes and moving into the dusky stand of trees along the hillside. She seemed to be looking for something. Jenny had never really been out of the larger cities of the Northeast; in fact, Baltimore was the smallest city she'd ever lived in—she'd only ever been to the country when she needed to get to the beach, or as a rest stop off a major highway.

When Joe approached her, she turned at the sound of his footsteps on twigs. "I saw a deer," she said, "I

know I did." She kept her voice whispery and held a
hand up for Joe to stop making so much noise with his
damn shoes (he could translate this just by the flick of
her wrist). She motioned for Aaron to step up beside
her, and when he did, she put her arm around his
shoulder and leaned into him.

She pointed into the woods.

Joe moved forward as silently as he could.

He looked to where she was pointing.

A small doe stood beside a tree, chewing at its lower
branches. It was thin and more shades darker than Joe
had remembered deers being. Its eyes didn't seem to
register the intruders. It seemed close enough to
touch. Even though he'd seen deer before, it had
never been with his family. This seemed different, almost sacred. Maybe it was a good sign, after all. Maybe
coming here was the right thing to do, and the right
timing.

Aaron turned around and said, "Look, Dad, it's
Bambi."

Joe smiled. He liked his son, he liked his family, he
liked his life.

*His father had advised him, before the wedding,
"Don't fuck this up, Joe, because once you do, you
spend the rest of your life working on the engine without ever driving the fucking car."*

My mother's dying, but life is still worth it.

Then a piercing wail came up from somewhere behind him, the doe took off into the woods—it was a
child wailing—*not just a child you asshole, it's your
child, it's Hillary*—like a reflex, he spun around and
ran towards the Buick—he had left the door open,
damn it, she'd been asleep, but she was only three,
what was he thinking? Anything can happen to a three-
year-old, his heart raced faster than his feet.

He got to the side of the car. The door was still open.

And Hillary was sitting up screaming bloody murder because she'd awakened from her nap and everyone had left her behind.

Joe imagined the therapist's bill for her, when she was about seventeen, several thousand dollars—all because when she'd been three, they'd left her in the Buick for ten minutes by herself in the middle of nowhere.

He unstrapped her from her harness, and took her up in his arms. "Hilly Hilly," he said, rubbing his nose softly against hers.

Her face was wet with tears. She stopped crying and inhaled deeply. She said nothing. She knew enough words, but she'd gotten really good lately at withholding her thoughts from him as a form of punishment.

She's a fast learner.

He kissed her cheek and hugged her tight; turned and waved to Jenny and Aaron, who were fast approaching. "It's okay," he said.

His wife grabbed Hillary from him and swung her up, "My big baby."

Things were great between them, right? Really great, only notice how she takes the kids from me when she can, like she's afraid some kind of weakness of character is going to rub off from my hands? Or maybe, another one will die because of some karmic debt I've built up. And hell, she may be right.

"She scared the deer off," Aaron sulked.

"There'll be other deer," Joe said.

Hillary put her small fists up to her eyes to wipe them of the leftover tears, and said, "Hungee, Mommy, I hungee."

Jenny glanced at Joe. "We're all a little hungee, right?"

Joe said, "There'll be a place in town. We can eat before we see Gramma."

"You mean 'the witch'?" Aaron asked.

Joe glared at Jenny who glared at Aaron who said, "What I do?"

Jenny said, "You know what you did."

Aaron shoved his hands deeper into the pockets of his jeans and watched the ground as if he could focus his shame in the dirt.

"God," Joe sighed, and then shouted, "I HATE THIS PLACE!"

His voice echoed along the river. The Paramount River flowed, eventually, to the New River, or maybe it was the Kanawha, Joe couldn't remember. His voice would echo down its stony corridors. But he had lied in his pronouncement: it had been his home he hated, a particular house, on River Road, not haunted or ugly or dull. But a house of nightmare, nonetheless.

"You're going to scare her, shouting like that, Joe, Jesus," Jenny said, clutching Hillary ever tighter. "Come on, it's not so bad. We'll only stay a week. You at least owe her that."

Aaron looked up at his father. "I kind of like it here, Daddy," he said, "I want to have another gramma, too. Even if she is a you-know-what."

And she is, Joe thought. *A witch. A nightmare in a housecoat. The woman who gives a bad name to bitches. Mommy Fearest. What would she be now that she was sick? A shriveled, tired, whining creature with claw hands and iron-gray head? Am I going to have to love her and care for her now? What had she said about his first novel in her letter? "It's like being invited to a great restaurant, with wonderful linens and silver and waiters and fine wine, and sitting down at the table, and having the waiter bring over a huge covered silver tray, setting it down in front of me, and as he lifts up the cover, I see that all that's there is a pile of dung. You'll never support yourself except maybe as a pornographer. Why don't you just go back into the car business?"*

And that had actually been one of her finer moments. She had shined at distant relatives' funerals, when she could go up to the family and tell the recent widow what a terrible wife she'd been to the deceased; or with his father, how she'd driven him into the ground practically inch by inch over the years of Joe's youth. Her affairs over the years, her cheapness, her open condemnations of others.

Am I going to have to love her now?

And then, one other thought before he got back behind the driver's seat of the car.

I don't want to feel sorry for her. I want to remember all the bad things she did.

It had taken him nearly seventeen years to make it back to this hellhole, and now he wished he'd done what he intended back when he was eighteen:

burn the fucker down.

But still, he drove on up to Colony.

2.

The town itself, beyond the lovely countryside, was not a feast for the eyes; but whether or not it deserved to be burned to the ground was a question best left unanswered. The rows of shops and houses up and down Main Street and Queen Anne Street and its vectors had been built during the Federal period, and then there was the P.O. and town hall, miniature Greek Revival buildings, gone to gray seed from neglect and lack of funds. Overseeing the business district, you would have an impression of green glass in windows and old hearthstone brick and black shutters. The streets were empty at noon, busy by three or four, and dead again as darkness seeped in. The shops had no defined hours of business; whenever proprietors felt like being there tended to be the hours of operation. Where the flat-topped roofs of the business district ended, the sharp corners of the neighborhoods began. Private houses grew like feeble crops from the center of town outward: people had a degree of wealth, once, along the Paramount River's banks, for every fourth house was enormous and sprawling, now owned by poor relations who would board up broken windows rather than fix them, and wrap tarp over a leaky roof. Now and then, there had been a fire, through lightning or arson, and the blackened foundation and chimney of a hundred-year-old house would stand amidst a peaceful neighborhood; so in its history, whether through an act of God or man, Joe Gardner had not been the first to wish the town would go up in flames.

Dale Chambers, a third-generation Colonial, didn't have anything on his mind as spectacular as burning the town down. He was thinking more along the lines of murder.

Murdering someone, particularly someone you care about, is never a simple matter of planning and then executing. Things go wrong, fate steps in, life tosses in a screw or two. Dale Chambers was finding this out on this fairly chilly day in November when he felt, at the age of forty-eight, that life was still good and that his prime had not passed. These feelings were mainly because of his thing with Lannie.

As affairs went, Lannie Barnes's with Dale Chambers was going pretty well—she had companionship at least three nights out of the week, and he got some nooky that his wife Nelda had been denying him for the past twenty years. It couldn't be said that the affair was a secret, but it also could be maintained that Nelda didn't give a flyer who her husband put it to as long as he didn't come wagging it at her. Dale had always lusted after Lannie, ever since the days he worked at the factory before he'd turned seventeen, long before he switched careers. All those times he had seen her on his drive home, at sixteen, on summer evenings, necking with farm boys out at the river.

That had been years ago, of course, when Lannie was still the tease of the county, and was known for not wearing any underwear underneath her crinolines; later, she earned the title of town tramp; as time went on she was known as liberated but deadly. She looked a bad forty, and had spun a hundred and eighty degrees in the other direction from her bare-assed youth —she ordered silky underwear from the Victoria's Secret catalog just to entice the men. She had reached the stage where she felt to be attractive she had to hide more than she revealed.

They were, at the moment Joe Gardner and his wife Jenny and their two children were heading towards the town, in a desperate embrace, tangled in the moth-eaten sheets of the Miner's Lodge. They had a private room upstairs, and had greedily devoured a plate of oysters and cheeses, and had downed a jug of Chianti. Lannie's blue eyeshadow had rubbed off on Dale's navel. Dale wore Cherries In The Snow lipstick imprints on some places on his body that even *he* had never seen. What made this an important coupling for both of them was that Lannie announced her impending pregnancy right at the moment Dale was about to enter her—his spirit wilted as quickly as did his flesh.

"I think I heard you wrong," he said, pulling away from her, the suction of skin slurping as he did so. And then, thoughtlessly, he added, "And you're too old, for God's sakes."

She drew back against the pillows and covered her breasts with the sheet. "As it would turn out, Dale, hon, I'm not. I saw Dr. Cobb on Tuesday and it seems there's a little Dale just gettin' his fingers."

This was about the point when Dale decided to kill her. It wasn't the most logical process. He didn't want his wife Nelda to know, of course, that he had gotten the town tramp knocked up; neither did he want to be a father. He had one bastard in town already, and didn't think there was room for more. To top this all off, he was furious with Lannie for letting this happen. She was supposed to be on birth control pills, which Dale felt was the woman's duty, and so she must've wanted to get pregnant—Christ, at her age—as a trap for him.

Well, it wasn't going to work.

Dale had killed someone once before, years ago, and no one had found out. It had been an accident, really. He had only been eight or nine, and it was another little boy who had tried to touch his weenie. That was a no-no as far as the Gump was concerned. So he had taken the kid to one of the old mine shafts, that had since been covered over because of just such incidents, and shoved him down it. His intention then was not to really kill the kid, but just to put him someplace where Dale would never have to see him again. Nobody ever looked down the shaft; the boy was gone for good; and Dale's conscience barely gave him a tweak over the incident. Dale Chambers was not quite as smart as he thought, though, because as he got older he would occasionally get the odd letter typed on a cheesy old Royal typewriter (he figured this out later, when he started using the ancient typewriter his wife used to write her pathetic poetry on). The letters said:

I saw you. Youre naughty.

Or,

I know you inside and out.

He had been scared of the letters at first. But the letters stopped just a couple of years before, and nothing had happened.

So, the idea of murdering Lannie because of her pregnancy was not that farfetched. He knew it could be done—he had studied murder cases in his off-hours, and a few on the job, as well. He knew that sometimes people got away with it; and the ones who didn't were stupid or scared or just plain wanted to get caught. Killing Lannie wasn't the problem, not for Dale, it was all the baggage that went along with it: the time, the place, the alibi, the proper technique. He was a particular fan of true crime books, mainly dealing with serial killers, his idols being Ted Bundy and the Zodiac Killer, in particular, although he certainly was an avid reader of anything having to do with Jack the Ripper, too. Jack was amazing—he got away with it, apparently. That Black Dahlia Killer, from the forties, he got away with it, too.

It could be done.

He leaned against Lannie, pressing himself closer, and kissed her cheek. She couldn't read his mind, could she?

"You want me to get rid of it, don't you?" she asked, sounding like a whiny kitten. "Well, I'm a good Baptist girl and I ain't gonna do it."

He kissed her sweetly. Like she was already a mother. She had always had baby hunger, hadn't she? She had been spreading her legs since she was twelve, and it wasn't for pleasure or money or acceptance, it was for the basic reason, the most essential reason for having sex. It occurred to him that Lannie Barnes might be the most old-fashioned girl in all of Colony, because she probably had only ever viewed lust's main function as procreation! And after nearly three and a half decades of trying, she had finally gotten the bun in the oven.

"We'll have the baby," Dale Chambers whispered, "but let's keep it secret for a while. You didn't tell Virgil who the father is, did you?"

She shook her head. Tears in her eyes; smile on her face. "Dr. Cobb ain't the type to spread stories, if that's what you mean. But I wanted to tell you first, before I told anybody else. I didn't want it to get back to your wife. Not yet. Not something this special. You love me, don't you, Dale? And you'll love the baby, too, won't you?"

He answered her with kisses.

After a bout of lovemaking where he pummeled her good, Dale Chambers showered, dressed, left the Lodge, and stood out in the early evening shadows, with the street lamps humming to yellow life. He wondered just how he was going to put Lannie Barnes out of her misery.

He got in his car and leaned out the window to wave to Virgil Cobb, possibly the oldest practicing country doctor in the county, let alone the whole state, who was carrying three sacks of groceries to his old beat-up car. "Well, hey, Doc, how goes the trade?"

Virgil was nearly seventy, but in pretty good shape, "spry" as the young called the old when the latter group could barely bend at the waist to pick up a penny, or manage a smile on a hot day. He was wearing his traditional Scots plaid bow tie, heavily starched white shirt, and tweed jacket; always in khakis, always with the argyle socks, always in penny loafers—Virgil was a walking add for 1958, which happened to be the year that Virgil's wife had left him and gone off to New York for a bigger life. Virgil set the groceries on the sidewalk and practically trotted over to Dale. The old man leaned into the car window and said, "Hey, Sheriff."

Dale Chambers smiled, and thought: *You don't know the real me, old man, I have a secret and nobody in this town knows the inside me, the thing I am inside, the one who gets the letter telling me how naughty I am, the one who's gonna make sure Lannie Barnes never sees too many more sunrises. The Gump is gonna do it, 'cause he's my inside man, my innard self, ho-ho.*

3.

After he spoke with Sheriff Chambers, Virgil Cobb picked his groceries back up and took them to his car. He was beginning to notice the change—not just in the temperature, although with this first nightfall of November, it was dropping fast—*it might get as low as forty tonight, maybe some snow down here in the lowlands in the next couple of weeks.*

But something else, too.

Like a reminder of his youth, he felt it: the town was changing in some way, maybe because half the young people left as soon as they could drive, and the other half took off when they turned legal age. It was a place people didn't want to stay in anymore. He'd only had a handful of patients in the past two years, mainly the ones close to his age who had always been coming to him. These days most of his patients drove over to Stone Valley to the spanking new HMOs and medical centers—they didn't trust an old man with their ailments. In the winters, which could get harsh come January, the Malabar Hills cut the town off whenever there was a good storm coming through; the summers had become unbearable with the mosquito population and the excessive humidity; and jobs. There were no jobs. People like Virgil couldn't even afford to retire— he knew it was just a matter of time before he got forced out because of his age, but how were young people to ever keep the lifeblood going in a town where the jobs were so limited, and so coveted? When he had been a boy, he had seen how Vidal Junction, at the pass in the hills, had dried up and become a ghost town, and there were other places, too, small corners of the state that had died when the mining towns had closed or had dried up and blown away because there was nothing solid to keep them in place. Towns had lives just like people did, Virgil knew. You had to feed them, you had to nurture them, you had to keep their lifebloods pumping.

Something his little brother Eugene (rest his soul) had told him once, when Virgil had first studied biology in high school. *Hemogoblins.* Virgil pricked Eugene's finger to get some blood to test and see what blood type he was, and he tried to explain about blood, about white corpuscles and hemoglobin, but all Eugene had repeated back was, *corporals and hemogoblins.*

Whenever he thought of poor Eugene, he remembered those silly childhood things.

For a moment, he saw a face through a darkened

shop window, and it startled him until he realized it was his own face. Looked like a ghost, he thought, for just a second, thought it was a ghost.

But it was the Virgil Cobb that had grown creaky and cobwebbed and stooped from what had been a rather handsome youth who had once turned down the advances of a few ladies because of his pursuit of the life of the mind: books and medicine. Loved books too much, maybe. Lived in them most of the time.

Escaped into them, you could say.

Half his bed at home was taken up with books and papers; he slept on the other half, occasionally feeling the spine of a hardcover as if tucking his wife in.

Tried to die, though, but can't. You can't die when you never really lived, can you? It would be redundant.

Virgil drew the collar of his herringbone tweed jacket up around his neck. Getting cold. He knew his thoughts were too depressing; maybe it was just his age. *Maybe you live life long enough and you expect the world to die before you do. Maybe you expect all of them to disappear, the candle to extinguish, before yours gets snuffed.* Virgil had been over the hill recently to see another doctor—well, not a doctor, who was he fooling?—a psychiatrist, which is a doctor, but not the kind that you could talk about openly in Colony—and the doctor had asked him to describe his symptoms. "Tired, forgetful, worn out. And sometimes I wake up thinking: it's a good day to get in the car and die."

The psychiatrist had asked, "Die?"

Virgil had chuckled, "Did I say that? No. I mean, it's a good day to get in the car and drive. Just drive, anywhere."

"Dr. Cobb," the psychiatrist had said, "you said, 'die.'"

And he had.

He knew he had.

Virgil Cobb didn't think he wanted to die, but the concept just crept in there, under the fence.

He put his groceries in the car and locked the doors. Used to be, you didn't have to lock anything in Colony, least of all your car; things had changed. He was going to go for a walk out to the cemetery, see his brother. Hadn't seen him in a long time. It'd be cold, but old Eugene had been out there with no one to check on him since maybe August. Virgil figured he ought to talk with him awhile, get some advice.

Virgil was beginning to wonder if most of his friends and family weren't out there, at Watch Hill, the ten acre boneyard just bordering the Paramount River, within the town limits. He could name at least nineteen people he knew who were currently (and indefinitely) underground, and might only be able to name another ten to twelve who were above.

There should be a prize for survival, he thought. Old Man Feely, he's almost ninety, he'd get the gold medal. Miss Risa DeLaMare would get the silver, at eighty-four. And Dean Lowell, weighing in at eighty-one, he'd get the bronze.

Darn, he thought (since he had never been given to swearing, even when polite society embraced verbal obscenity), *I wouldn't even make it to the Olympics of survival.*

Virgil Cobb went to the Watch Hill, now, just a few times a year. His brother, Eugene, hadn't died, at least not officially. There was a stone marker for him, because they figured, given where he'd taken off to, he wouldn't survive too long. But nobody knew for sure, except, perhaps, Virgil himself. Oh, he'd seen something happen to his brother, Virgil had, but what seemed real in an instant at the age of twelve, now, from the distance of an ocean of years, seemed like the paper-thin fragment of a dream. But Virgil had stuck to the official story: his brother Eugene had just disappeared, at fifteen, a runaway, perhaps, and there was no doubt in anyone's mind that Eugene had died somewhere in the intervening years.

4.

Byron Cheever was nineteen and home on a presumed break from college. He was a smart boy, they all said it, but he knew different, he knew how he had gotten the high score on his SATS in high school, and why he had graduated second in his class—a little blackmail went a long way in a town like Colony. He had landed at Washington and Lee University over in Lexington, a college which was hallowed in the South, but particularly sacred to Byron's family because he was the seventh Cheever since his great-great-grandfather to attend that university. The problem was, for By (as his friends called him), that he had just been expelled for cheating on his midterms. He was home for a few days, supposedly a fall break, but in reality, he knew he wasn't ever going to be going back to Lexington, Virginia, and he had to somehow tell his mother and father without being expelled by them, too, for reaping dishonor and shame and all those things that they spoke of so highly. It was worse for him, because he might never see his Lambda Chi Alpha brothers again, and for By, social life had been the be-all and end-all.

So he was doing what he always did when he got nervous—trolling the streets of Colony for a girl to ball

or a buddy to get plastered with. Driving his daddy's
Cadillac convertible, the top down even in the cold; By
didn't mind, he thought it was more studly that way.
And what to his wandering eye should appear, but a
girl of sixteen dressed in something that looked like it
was baby doll and slut combined, standing on the corner of Princess Caroline Street, with a girlfriend about
as ugly as any woofer on the planet.

He pulled over, almost jumping the curb, and the
dog friend stepped back into darkness.

The Beauty, as he came to think of her, stood still.
Smiled.

She looked the fuckingest he'd ever seen a girl look,
and he thought: *screw college, all I need is a nice tight
pussy and a Cadillac and this boy's in hog heaven.*

"Hey, Beauty," he said, "how's about a ride with the
Beast?"

"Oh," she said, stepping forward.

Then, looking back into the shadows, "Mind if I
bring my friend, too?"

By glanced at the other girl, shrugged: *hell, who
knows? Maybe have me a bite of a little sandwich tonight, hot damn.*

"Depends," he told Beauty.

"On what?"

"On whether you're gonna worship at my love tem-
ple tonight?"

"Oh," she said, not taken aback at all, "I'll do more
than that, Beast."

Byron Cheever grinned and got an instant boner.
She was one fine piece of flesh, Beauty was. He'd just
put a bag over her girlfriend's face, and give them both
the thrill of a lifetime. *Damn, it's good to be young and
hung and studly.* He'd have some good stories to tell
his buddies, that was for sure.

5.

You could hear the sound of the Cadillac's tires screeching, and the roar of its decrepit, sorry-ass engine as it careened up the street, turning left on Main, running the stop sign. In towns like this, the sound of a car burning rubber was like a cry in the night. Those who were at their windows, closing them against the cold, or locking up shop, listened to it as if it were a banshee's howl.

Main Street seemed to grow at night, with the yellow street lamps, and the feeble lights from storefronts. Everything was shadows and brick between the narrow streets. There were only nine streets in the town proper—Queen Anne Street, Princess Caroline, Main, North and South Angel, and then streets First through Fourth crossing each of these. The buildings were the old Federal style townhouses of the old towns built before the Civil War. Above every store was an apartment, many of them empty, going for the cheap rate of a hundred and fifty a month. A smart person could haggle the desperate landlord down to a hundred on a good day. Some of the college students from Stone Valley got places there—it was a forty-minute commute over the hills, but the savings were enormous on rent and utilities.

Minnie Harper, who was seventy-eight, had always lived above Logan's Market—she was a self-described spinster, and spent the early evenings at her window, dressed like a princess in a beaded gown and her hair all done up above her head, four strands of pearls around her neck, just watching the streets as if she owned them from above the market.

Winston Alden was still sitting at his desk behind the glass storefront window of his office. The lettering on the glass read: *W.H. Alden, Consultant.* Beneath this: *Opinions Expressed.* He would sit there for another two hours; he had little business these days, but he had fallen into something of a second childhood after having been a preacher when he was younger, then a lawyer, and finally a walking shambles in a three-dollar suit—he spent most of the better part of the day reading old copies of *Tales from the Crypt* comics. He cherished his back issues of *Weird Tales.* His old friend, Dr. Cobb usually showed up by nine for a glass of sherry and a cigar. They would exchange stories about the old days, when they had adventures, and remember the women they loved and the loves they'd lost and sometimes they talked about the not-so-great memories, too.

Across the block from him, Jack LaPree closed his bookshop by six. George and Cally's ValCo Gas stayed open 'til eleven, but you could only get gas after dark because Cally once had a gun stuck in her face by some out-of-town boy and she swore she'd never open her store's door after dark again. The First Stone Valley Savings and Loan had closed by five, although the automatic teller kept going until midnight. Logan's Market was open until nine. The Fauvier Art Gallery was closed, but Miles Fauvier was still inside finishing up on his accounts. Through the windows, you could see the large canvases with their pastoral landscapes of Virginia and West Virginia, a painting of the New River, and a portrait of a mining family from the old days. Three bars in town didn't start up until about six or seven, and it was in one of these that Becky O'Keefe, formerly Becky Petersen, went to do her shift as waitress-bartender-consoler of lost souls.

The place was called the Angel Wing Pub. Downstairs, it had several small round tables, and upstairs, the bar. Becky didn't love her work, but it was one of the few jobs in town that allowed her to work four nights a week and still bring in enough money to spend time with her son, Tad, during his waking hours.

And as she set up a boilermaker for Jack LaPree, who had his eye on a woman named Alice who, like Jack, came in every night until closing, Becky heard a voice. She looked up, and thought she saw a ghost.

"I know you, don't I?" she asked. "Joe? Joe Gardner?" She wasn't exactly smiling, because you never do when you see what you think is a ghost, you only gasp and hope you're imagining things.

(Joe wasn't about to admit this to himself, and maybe nobody was going to say it aloud, but it wasn't like anybody wanted him back in town, in this town called Colony with its long memory of a girl who was voted most likely to succeed and most creative at Colony High, only to die one day while crossing a bridge.

It wasn't so much the girl's death. Nobody blamed Joe; hell, he wasn't even driving that day.

It was what came after. The voices.

When Joe thought he was going nuts after her death.

What he heard, all through town, the sounds of human voices, the secrets, the whispers.)

So Becky was briefly praying it was only some creep who looked like Joe Gardner, like in the game she and Hopfrog used to play called facsimiles, where they'd pick out people in a crowd who look like other people, maybe famous people. She hoped this was a facsimile of Joe, not the genuine article.

Because sometimes she thought she'd like to kill him for the way he had mentally tortured her ex-husband, "Hopfrog" Petersen, and set him on a path of obsession which had pretty much ruined their marriage.

6.

Certain routines and rituals were being followed in Colony, that night, also.

Romeo Dancer, so named because he had proclaimed himself the greatest tap and toe dancer in three counties and the greatest lover in the world, was sitting on the stoop of his trailer out towards Happy Valley, jawing at his wife, Wilma, and she was jawing right back at him. He wore his black suit and his dancing boots. He was getting ready to go to the Creeker's Roadhouse out on the Post Road, but he wasn't about to take Wilma because, as he told her, "you get jealous too easy and I'm only dancin', darlin'." Wilma owned a pit bull and they lived in separate trailers, side by side, and sometimes, when she was angry, she and the pit bull looked like kin to him.

"You go there tonight," she said, "and you ain't never comin' back, I'm gonna set this house on fire, you old fart, and then we're gonna see who does the dancin' round here!"

Their voices carried on the wind. They had become legends to teenagers making out down at the Paramount River in their father's four-by-fours or in the backseats of old Chevys, who heard the caterwauling as it echoed loud and clear across the water and far banks.

Uptown, near the Lyric movie theater, Miss Athena Cobb, Virgil's niece, who was all of forty-eight and genteel as the day was long (and they were getting short with winter coming on), was out walking her doberman, Chelsea, and waiting for Melanie Dahlgren. Melanie was from Sweden and she made her living from her beefy arms—she was a masseuse, the legitimate kind, much to the disappointment of the local lechers. She had recently moved to Colony to paint and get away from cities. Melanie was older than Athena, nearly sixty, and wiser in the ways of the world. She had begun to show Athena a whole new side of life. Miss Dahlgren, as Athena addressed her, even after various intimacies, was usually walking her dachshund at the same hour. Athena didn't want to miss running into her, and if anyone had told her that it was puppy love, Miss Athena Cobb would've probably agreed.

The Lyric theater, itself, once a vaudeville stage, and now the most run-down green velvet curtained movie house that side of the Malabar Hills, was packed to capacity with what appeared to be every high schooler with five bucks in her or his pocket, popcorn buttergrease on chins. It was Horror Week, as the Lyric's banner proudly proclaimed, in honor of Halloween, a twenty-four–hour marathon of *The Haunting, Dr. Sardonicus, CandyMan, Carrie, The Fury, The Curse of the Cat People, Misery, Hellraiser Three: Hell on Earth, Halloween, Let's Scare Jessica to Death, C.H.U.D.*, and the current feature, *Scarecrows*. On the screen, the face of a scarecrow in a field. Tenley McWhorter turned to her date, Noah Cristman and whispered, "I hate movies like this. I like movies about real people and real life. This wouldn't ever happen. I don't believe it at all. Wanna go for a drive or something?"

Only the diehards would still be there by midnight, and by dawn, you could fairly predict that the place would still have a couple of pimply-faced kids having a blast.

Winston Alden, sitting in his storefront office, with the lights off, lit up a Cuban cigar. He set out two brandy snifters. He filled one and took a sip. Then he reached beneath his desk and withdrew a dog-eared copy of *Twenty Thousand Leagues Under the Sea*. He flicked on the desk lamp. He began reading, smoking, and sneaking a sip of Napoleon brandy while he waited for his guest to arrive.

Nelda Chambers, Dale's wife, had come across an old typewriter that she hadn't seen in years and decided to resume an old habit. She put a fresh piece of erasable bond in the machine and began typing a letter to her husband:

I know what you did. You naughty, naughty man.

There, she thought, *keep the mystery alive, you whore-chaser, see if you have any conscience left in you.*

When she had finished typing, she put the typewriter back in the closet, took the letter, sealed it in one of Dale's own envelopes, and set it under the front door. She went back to the kitchen, made some Celestial Seasonings Sleepy Time Tea, and went upstairs to her bedroom to watch television until she could fall asleep.

John Feely, also known as Old Man Feely to just about anybody who had lived in Colony more than a few years, was unlocking the door to a very private room in his farmhouse. He had a candle in his hand, and he leaned forward as best he could to light the other candles in the room. When this task was complete, he knelt down and clasped his hands together, looking up at a marble statue stolen long ago from an untended grave. The statue had no face.

Beneath the floorboard, he heard the child kicking at the wall, trying to get out, and John Feely prayed harder and louder and longer to block out the noise.

7.

And even while all this was going on, Cathy Zane, who handled 911 in town, got a frantic call from Wendy Hoskins who said that her son, Billy, had run away from home, "and we thought he'd'a come back before tonight, maybe go to one of his little friends, he's done it before, but, good Lord, nobody's seen him, and I think something's wrong, I think—" but then Wendy had begun sobbing, and her husband, Mike, had taken the phone, "get that goddamned sheriff over here right now, you hear me, my boy's disappeared, and you people better damn well find him."

8.

As in any town in America at the end of the twentieth century, there was evil being perpetrated; in this case, in the form of what children often do to each other in their haphazard rites of passage. Although it was nightfall, and the light of the world was extinguishing at the farthest rim of the western hills, two boys were bullying another out at Watch Hill, the cemetery. They had come across the field, pursuing the boy—and he had only come to sit on the ground next to where his grandfather was buried before going home to dinner.

His name was Tad Petersen, and his father had once been known as Hopfrog, his mother had once been known as Becky Petersen, but was now Becky O'Keefe. Since his parents' divorce, he had withdrawn into books and videos and the drawings he sometimes made of a fantasy world—but he knew he was sensible and sane, and that the other kids in town were primarily idiots.

This attitude may have accounted for their treatment of him.

The boys who followed him, Hank and Elvis, were big for their age (twelve), and far too hairy. Their clothes were small, and they were from the Bonchance clan who lived by the river.

And they had it in for Tad, always. No particular reason relating to Tad, other than, given the chance, he was an easy enough target: he kept to himself, he drew weird pictures, he read a lot, and he got too many good grades.

As Tad stood up, next to his grandfather O'Keefe's grave, he saw that Elvis Bonchance had a big old cat-o'-nine-tails in his hand. Tad knew that this was probably Mr. Bonchance's, because Elvis's father tended to be of the old school, and was fairly well thought of as a sadist in Colony.

Hank snickered, "Hey, Peterbutt, what you doing out here? Boneyard's for stiffs. You a stiff?"

Tad, very solemnly, said, "No, but I play one on TV."

Hank glanced at Elvis, who chortled, "Trying to make a joke, is you? Well, you woosy-ass, we think you been bad."

"Yeah," his brother said, "Real bad."

"Bad Tad," Elvis laughed, cracking the cat out to the side.

Tad said, "Shut up."

"Your mama's a whore and your daddy's a gimp."
Hank took another step closer to him.

"Bite me," Tad said. He started to walk away. There
was only one light on at night at Watch Hill, and he
was walking towards it when he felt something sting
his shoulders. He spun around. Elvis had just brought
the whip back. "Look, Elvis, why don't you just admit
that your dad beats the hell out of you and you can't
take it so you have to pick on kids my size just to feel
like you're better than everyone else."

Tad expected that the two brothers would actually
redouble their efforts, so he cringed a little, ready for
the next blow—knowing he would hightail it out of
there if Elvis raised that whip another inch.

Instead, Elvis screeched, *"What the hell you talkin'?
My daddy don't beat me! I ain't no pussy!"* He began
shaking; the cat-o'-nine-tails dropped from his hand.

Hank grinned. "You stupid fuckface. We're gonna
put you where the sun don't shine for that one."

Tad started to run, but he felt like his feet were
stuck in molasses. He moved his feet, but, somehow,
Hank and Elvis had managed to catch him fast. They
bound him with some twine and carried him over to
one of the vaults.

"We'll just see how you like spending the night with
the bones, cracker," Hank slobbered.

Tad could not resist. "If anyone's a cracker, you are."

For that, he got a whack across the face.

When he awoke, he was down at the bottom of a
freshly dug grave.

"Guys?" he asked, choking back the fear as best he
could. All he could smell was mud. "Hank? Elvis?
Guys? I take it back! I am a woosy-ass! You're right
about my folks! Guys?"

He could feel his heartbeat.

Above him, it was completely dark, save for the stars.

Tad began crying, knowing it was babyish of him, but he couldn't stop. He knew that he would be stuck all night, that he'd probably die, that he would freeze, or worse . . . he might be buried alive.

"*Hey!*" he shouted until he was hoarse. "*Hey!*"

Not long after, some college girls who claimed they were on a scavenger hunt lifted him out of the grave and untied him, giggling over him and brushing their fingers in his hair like he was a baby; as far as Tad was concerned they were angels.

He brushed as much mud off of himself as he could, and then went directly back to his father's house.

But he didn't tell anyone what he'd heard there, lying in that grave. The voices beneath the ground.

Children's voices, as if they were calling to him to come join them.

He recognized one of the voices, a kid named Billy Hoskins—

It can't be. It was just my imagination. I know it. It was just me being scared and scaring myself.

Billy Hoskins, beneath the grave, had said, "Tad, hey, Tad, hey, Tad, we're coming to get you. All of us. Coming to get you."

6

A BRIEF INTERLUDE: JOE AND MELISSA AND HOPFROG AND PATTY GLASS ARE KIDS AND THE FEELY BARN IS DARK

1.

In those days, more than twenty years before the disappearance of Billy Hoskins, the rain tasted clean and good. (Joe stuck his tongue out to catch a few drops. He closed his eyes.)

"Come on." Hopfrog's crackly voice was insistent.

Joe opened his eyes. He was standing beside Melissa Welles, whose light brown hair was plastered to the sides and top of her scalp from the downpour. She looked frightened, so he took her hand in his.

"It's Patty," Hopfrog said, and pointed towards Old Man Feely's barn.

Melissa squeezed Joe's hand. "Joey," she whispered, and he could barely hear her so he leaned into her, close to her face. "Joey, I'm scared. What if she got caught? What if he's gonna do something bad to her."

Joe grinned, shaking his head. "Aw, nothing bad's gonna happen. It can't. We're just kids."

"He had a gun," Melissa said, "even if he's not supposed to use it. Maybe he shot her."

"Old Man Feely, he went inside," Joe reassured her.

Hopfrog waited at the edge of the gray barn. Three cracked and broken boards created a small opening into the barn. Hopfrog slid another board to the side, and glanced within.

Joe was shivering. He told himself it was the cold. But it wasn't the cold, and it wasn't just because Patty Glass had cried out.

It was because he was getting a feeling like he had maybe once before in his life *(when a strange man looked at him funny at the Esso gas station when he was about six years old)*. It was a feeling that someone was talking to him, only he didn't quite know who it was or where the voice was coming from. He didn't like to think about this voice too much because he was afraid it meant he was nuts; and the voice had only spoken once before. Worse, the voice didn't seem to say anything that Joe could understand. It just whispered.

Suddenly Joe shouted, "Hopfrog, don't go in there!"

Hopfrog looked at him funny, and then went between the space in the old boards, into the barn.

"Melissa," Joe said, "something bad's in there. Something we're not supposed to play with."

"Give me a break," she said, and let go of his hand,

following Hopfrog's lead. "I'm not five. Patty may be hurt."

As Melissa Welles ducked beneath the rotting wood, she said, "I wish you weren't so chicken sometimes, Joey."

That was it. Weird feeling or not, Joe ducked in and around the boards. When he stepped inside the barn the first thing he did was gasp. The second thing he did was wet his pants, but they were already soaked from the rain so nobody was going to notice.

2.

"Holy," Joe was about to say, "shit," but it was a forbidden word, and even though he heard it enough from other kids, he wasn't the kind to say it; but he could think it.

The barn was dark, except for a ring of light which came from its center.

Hopfrog was standing in the shadows, outside the light.

Melissa hung back, waiting for Joe. She said, "What is it?"

"It's a well," Hopfrog said. He picked up the cross that straddled the rim of the cylindrical opening. He looked at the cross as if he'd never seen one before, and then set it back down in its place.

"That's not a well," Joe took a few steps forward. When he reached Melissa he was shivering so badly he didn't want to touch her lest he convey his fear (and he very quickly needed to prove to her that he was no chicken).

Hopfrog stepped into the ring of light. The emanation from it seemed to turn Hopfrog's rain-shiny skin to gold. Hopfrog held his hands in front of him. They shone. "Maybe its radiation," he said.

"You're being nuked!" Joe shouted. His voice echoed in the barn.

Melissa shushed him. She whispered, "Look." She pointed up to the rafters.

Joe looked up and saw crucifixes and Egyptian symbols drawn in some kind of fluorescent chalk all over the barn.

"It says something." Hopfrog knelt down, and put his fingers on the side of the gold cylinder. "I can't read it, but it says something."

"Maybe we shouldn't touch it," Joe said. He was getting that feeling again, and not just from fear; he felt a weight in the barn, a presence.

"I wish you were a little more like Hopfrog," Melissa said, and went towards the golden light. Joe, striking out in the bravery department, hurried over to them.

He looked down the cylinder; it was dark inside.

"It's some kind of a well," he said, "listen."

The sound of gently splashing water, as if an eel were moving through its waters.

Joe called out, *"Patty!"*

With his shout, the ground beneath his feet seemed to rumble, but it was only his voice echoing down the well.

And then, Patty Glass, from somewhere down there said something. Joe couldn't tell what she'd said, but it was as if she'd heard him and tried to say something back only she was too far away.

Melissa and Hopfrog were staring strangely at Joe.

"She's fell down there," Joe said.

Melissa put her hand up to her mouth; Hopfrog's mouth opened, but he said nothing.

"It's Patty," Joe said.

And then he knew that there was something behind him, something just outside the golden circle of light, something . . .

He turned and saw what appeared to be a boy taller than he was, made up entirely of blood.

It reached out and wiped its hand across Joe's face.

3.

But this happened so long ago that sometimes Joe felt he had dreamed it, or had not seen it right, whenever he remembered it. He had only a vague remembrance, anyway, of seeing something strange and frightening when he'd been a boy, something that made him not like Colony at all.

Joe and Melissa and Hopfrog made a pact after that, a pact that they would never tell anyone what they had seen in the barn, because if they did, they knew it would open something up that should stay in the barn until the end of time.

They kept their vow of silence, but every now and then through the years, at thirteen, and then fifteen, and finally at eighteen, they looked at each other and briefly remembered. But then packed the memory back into the murky area of the brain where all of childhood might be lost.

By the time Joe Gardner returned to Colony, in his thirties, the memory was a bad dream that was confused with a hundred or more other nightmares about his hometown.

4.

From the journals of Joe Gardner/when he was twelve:

This is a story about a boy who is a hero.

He went into a barn and saw a big well. He was going to save a damsel in distress.

When the blood dragon attacked him, he took out his sword of fire and drew a line across the grass. "You can not pass this line," the boy said, "or you will blow up."

The blood dragon wiped its dark claw across the boy's face and in a voice of lava said, "One day, boy, I will come and get you, but not today. Today you are strong. But one day when I am stronger, and you have forgotten, I will skin you alive and drink your blood from a golden cup."

The boy laughed at the dragon. He married the damsel and when the dragon returned, the boy cut the dragon with his sword of fire and the dragon blew up real good. The damsel, now called Princess Melissa, told the boy that he was the bravest in the kingdom. He was known as King Joe Dragonheart and he and the princess lived happily ever after.   The end.

5.

From the journals of Joe Gardner/when he was eighteen:

This is not the end of it, but I have to leave. I have to get the hell out of this place before I go crazy.

I have to stop the voices in my head.

6.

From the journals of Joe Gardner/before dinner, his first night back in his hometown:

I'm back.

Shit.

COLONY

TAD

1.

Tad Petersen was always being shuttled between his mother's and father's. As his mother would've said, "divorce is a bitch," even though he knew that he wasn't allowed to use the kind of language he heard fly between his folks whenever they ran into each other. It was always, "you do this," or "you never do that," between them, so whenever he could, Tad ducked and covered and tried to be invisible. His mother lived three streets away from his father, and still Tad had to stay three nights with his mother, three with his father, and every other Sunday with one or the other. It was enough to drive him nuts, and being eleven was driving him nuts all by itself.

So whenever he could (or maybe, just maybe it was whenever he *dared*) he'd hang out in his dad's woodshed, out behind what he'd come to think of as his second home, mainly to stay away from his parents when his mom had just dropped him off and needed to chide his dad about child support or about something from the past that had only just occurred to her; or like now when his dad was ragging on his mom for being an hour late with Tad, or because he had noticed that Tad's grades had slipped a little and *whose fault was that?*

Tad was sure that if you put his folks in a locked room with a jar of peanut butter, they'd figure out a way to argue about it.

His father's woodshed was really just a converted garage, separate from the house. Tad wasn't really supposed to go into it by himself, because his dad always told him that the machines were dangerous. But Tad was approaching an age in which he felt he was smart enough not to turn on the wrong thing. He knew enough not to fiddle with the jigsaw or lathe. Sometimes, however, he went and got a hammer and some nails and just started pounding them into a scrap of wood to make a design.

He went searching for the jars of nails; there were tons to choose from, but he liked the larger kind. Hammering seemed to eat up a lot of his frustration, and being a particularly frustrated kid, he wanted to do a lot of it.

He got a small jar with several fat spikelike nails, and grabbed a triangular piece of wood from the scrap pile next to the jigsaw.

And then, he thought he heard something.

The light in the woodshed was dim, and outside, the trees of the backyard obscured what little light of day remained.

It was as if someone had coughed and then disappeared.

Remembering what he'd imagined at the cemetery, Tad pulled his windbreaker closer around his collar.

"Dad? Mom?" he asked.

Then, he thought he saw a shape just beyond the woodshed door.

He shivered.

He was sure that someone or something was waiting there, just outside the woodshed.

He dropped the piece of wood he'd just picked up.

He could practically hear his own heartbeat.

"Who's there?" he asked.

He walked close to the shelves, away from the door. He opened the jar of nails and drew one out. He held it up in his fist, point turned towards the door.

"Who's there?" he asked again.

His dad came through the doorway. "Tad? I thought you weren't coming in here again without permission."

Tad caught his breath, and lowered the spike. "Dad, you scared the bejesus outta me. Is Mom still around?"

His father shook his head. "She left half an hour ago. I was wondering where you ran off to. And so, I find you in the one place where you shouldn't be."

"Oh." Tad grinned, knowing he would now have to charm his father out of his sour mood. "There's lotsa places where I shouldn't be. This is the one place where I should be. Maybe I'm just like you, Dad, and will be a world-class carpenter when I grow up. When are you ever gonna show me how to use the jigsaw?"

"In a year or two. Don't change the subject. This is not a place where you should be playing."

Tad cast his glance to his shoes. "I know, I know. It's just that when you and Mom start in, I want to be as far away as possible."

His father sighed. "Well, as long as you watch out for stuff. And we don't mean to start in."

"I know," Tad said, "it just happens."

"Sometimes," his father said, a sheepish look on his face. "Sorry about that, Taddo. Hey, you've got mud on your windbreaker."

And right then Tad wished that his parents had never gotten divorced, that they'd learn to get along for a while just so he wouldn't have to feel as if he were the Dad sometimes and that his mother and father were the kids.

He wished he could go back in time so that they were all living together again in the house again, because even with the arguments and stony cold moods, he felt safer and warmer when both of his parents were there all the time—

And if he got his wish, and went back in time, he would force them to love each other the way a mom and dad were supposed to. He would make sure it was a happy family where everyone got along and no one fought, and if that happened . . . if that happened . . .

Tad Petersen would probably go even more nuts, because he knew it wouldn't be his parents with him, but some robots or body-snatcher people. The thing he knew best about his mother and father was that they loved to disagree. "Dad?"

"Yep?"

"If you love Mom, and she says she loves you, why can't you both work things out?"

"It's not that simple," his father said, and pretended to be distracted with some out-of-sequence tools; he arranged some screwdrivers and hammers on one of the mid-level shelves. "Sometimes it takes more than loving someone to be able to have a marriage."

"It sounds simple to me. It's like being in school with kids I don't know or like much. I just decide that I'm going to get along with them, and then, if I try hard, it works out."

"Marriage isn't like that."

"Yeah," Tad huffed, "marriage should be easier, 'cause at one time you liked each other."

"We still like each other. It's more complicated than you can imagine."

Tad shut up. He knew when to shut up, because talking to his dad about these things was like talking to a wall. He watched his father fumble, trying to reach for the upper shelves where the drills hung. "Here, Dad," he said, "I can get it." He went over and stood with one foot balanced on the second shelf up. He reached for the smallest of three Black & Decker drills, and grasped it. He passed it to his father, who suddenly, to Tad, looked small and weak and completely helpless.

2.

When it was closer to suppertime, Tad went inside to wash up. His dad's version of supper tended towards the pizza delivery route, or the Quickie Burgers over on Main Street. Tad preferred those to his mother's almost exclusively vegetarian household; as he soaped his hands, in preparation for the soon-to-be-delivered pizza, he practically drooled thinking of all that pepperoni and sausage slathered across the thick cheese.

And then, he felt the hairs on the back of his neck stand up.

The feeling seemed to freeze him: someone was watching him from the window.

It was a stupid fear, and he knew it; he already had too many fears. Besides the Bonchance brothers, there was his fear of the dark, and his fear of getting bad grades, and his fear that he would never grow up and get married and be happy. Sometimes Tad thought he could pick a fear for any moment of the day.

Even though he knew better, he told himself not to look out the bathroom window. *Whatever's there will go away. Or maybe nothing's there. Maybe it's some leftover goblin from Halloween.*

Finally, he couldn't resist. He glanced at the bathroom window.

Just the bare trees outside, and the house behind them.

Tad, wiping his hands on a towel, walked over to the window. He looked out at the shadows.

He thought he saw something over at the Feely farm, just four houses behind where he was.

The field and orchard were dark, but there was an eerie light on at the house, and for just a second, Tad thought he saw a face in the light—

But how can I? It's so far away.

When he was younger, he had believed that he'd seen a witch fly across the moon at Halloween. But he'd been a baby then, maybe four or five.

The face was like a jack-o'-lantern, its feral eyes and grin outlined in the light of what seemed an enormous red flame behind the glass of the window.

How could it be? It was so far away, why did it seem so close?

"I'm not a baby anymore," he said aloud, and moved away from the window, refusing to believe that there could be anything to see beyond the shadows and the trees and the normal lights of houses.

3.

Downstairs, in front of the television (watching the video of *Jurassic Park*, which they'd both seen at least six times), in between pizza chomps, he asked his father, "Do you believe in ghosts and goblins, Dad?"

"That's a weird question. How's the 'za?"

"The 'za is excellent. You didn't answer my question."

"Oh. The goblin question. Well, I don't believe in them."

Tad thought about this a minute and then said, "Just because you don't believe in something, does that mean it isn't there?"

His father looked across the sofa at him, but said nothing.

On the TV screen, a *Tyrannosaurus rex* was chasing a man down.

Tad said, "There're things I don't believe in, but I have a weird feeling that they believe in me, and that's the scary part."

The action in the movie didn't seem half as terrifying to Tad as the memory of that strange face in the window of the old Feely farmhouse.

Tad wanted to ask his father if he knew about Billy Hoskins. There was a kids' network, an informal grapevine, no less powerful than television news, through which dirty jokes from ages past were filtered (about men named Bowels No Move and girls named Sue Pee), and songs about Comet which had never been on television in Tad's lifetime were sung, and the ancient ritual dance of bullies and wimps was observed. Local news, too, made it from grades one to seven, the mythology about the white trash family out in the shanty which drank their own spit from a Maxwell House coffee can, about the rich old widow who drank the blood of children, and now, about what the other kids were already saying about Billy, only a few hours after he'd disappeared:

about how something leftover from Halloween got Billy and ate him up just like candy corn.

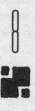

NO PLACE LIKE HOME

1.

"I thought you looked familiar in some high-school-flashback way," Becky O'Keefe said.

She brushed her hair back from her eyes, and gave him a warm smile and a frozen glance. She smelled good. Joe could smell her perfume across the bar. It was Yardley's English Lavender. He knew because when he'd been a kid she'd worn it. She still wore it, and she still smelled good. Her face, while not set in stone, was sketched with an expression of modified anger. He knew she had hated him for what had happened when they were teenagers, but he did not antic-ipate that she would feel the same so many years later. She looked great, kept her figure, seemed more attrac-tive than she had in high school—they had a mutual lack-of-admiration society between them, and it had come as a surprise when his best old friend Hopfrog announced at nineteen that he and Becky were going to marry since Becky had never been part of their in-ner circle of friends. That was just about the moment that Joe had taken off like a bat out of hell and had not looked back until now.

"Good to see you, Becky," he said, but it was a lie. It was terrible to see her. It was like running into the last person in the universe that he would ever want to see, although Becky was only a close second to dear old mom.

"It's you, Joe, then. Can't believe it. You been okay?"

"Sure."

"You see Hopfrog yet?"

Joe shook his head.

Becky said nothing. One of the customers called her down to the end of the bar. She went and got the order. He watched her. She hadn't changed much since high school; her hips had widened slightly, and she seemed taller and more confident. She was smok-ing now, which she had not been doing when he had known her. Back then, she'd been a drinker. After serving the customer, he watched as she lit a cigarette, took a long, slow drag, and then set it down in an ashtray. "I traded one addiction for another," she said, noticing how carefully he watched her blow the smoke out through her nostrils. "We all take our drugs in life, Joe."

"I get the feeling I'm an unwanted visitor."

She ignored this comment. "Your wife here?"

"She and the kids are downstairs. We just had dinner. Lou told me you were up here."

"You got what, two, three kids by now?"

"Two. A boy and a girl."

"I thought you had two boys. Somebody told me . . ."

He cut her off. "We had a son who died."

She took the cigarette up again. Another smoke. "Sorry to hear that, Joe."

"Well," he said, and then realized that he had nothing really to say to her.

"Well, good to see you again, Joe," she said, and walked back to ring up a tab.

He got off the bar stool and looked at the floor, as if thinking of something further to say. He caught her attention again, and leaned against the bar. "How's Hopfrog doing?"

She looked right past him. "Maybe you should ask him that. We got divorced a while back. Look him up, Joe, I'm sure he'd be glad to see you."

"But you're not."

"Right as usual," she said, and turned away.

2.

When he returned downstairs to the restaurant, Jenny was sipping decaf while Aaron stared, transfixed, at the long aquarium with the multi-colored tropical fish that was built into the wall. The plates had been cleared; Lou Harper, the manager who had been senior class most likely to succeed, was busing tables because one of his employees had quit earlier in the evening. Hillary was nodding off in her high chair, a jewel of drool at the edge of her lips.

Joe wanted a smoke very badly, but knew that he couldn't keep sneaking them like a teenager. He decided to fidget instead; he sat down in the chair beside Jenny and drummed his fingers on the red tablecloth.

"I don't get it," Aaron said, "how do they feed the fish, Dad? Look"—he rapped on the wall surrounding the aquarium—"how can they do it?"

Joe grinned. "Those fish don't look like they're exactly starving. In fact, they look like fat fish."

"I still don't get it," Aaron said, looking all around the edges of the tank. "Everything eats something. Do they just eat each other?"

Joe reached over and touched his wife's shoulder. Sometimes it was good just to make sure she was there. Sometimes he was afraid she wouldn't be. Jenny didn't smell like perfume, she smelled like Ivory Soap and Pantene shampoo. She smelled very Jenny. He leaned over and kissed her on the cheek.

"What's that for?" she asked.

"For not hating me the way everyone else on the planet seems to."

"Oh, don't assume anything. So, did you see her?"

Joe nodded. "She wasn't exactly thrilled to see me."

"Joe, is this the part where I find out that I married a psycho-killer or something?"

He lost his grin. It was getting harder to pretend that he could handle being home again. He looked at his nervous hands as they fiddled with the buttons of his jacket. "Aw, Jenny, maybe this is the worst idea, coming here. Maybe I should've just waited."

"Meanwhile, your mother dies, and I'm left with your guilt and anger about not seeing her. I watched my parents play that one out, no thank you, Joe. So what's the big secret? Why is it that you don't want to be here, and even your old friends don't want you here?"

"I don't know."

"You lie like a rug. Tell me."

"Remember what I told you before?"

Jenny nodded. He realized right then that she was too good for him, that he didn't deserve such a compassionate wife. She had supported him emotionally through the ups and downs of his life, and he had sometimes dragged her through the mud without intending to. And here she was, still Jenny.

He began, "Well, it wasn't just about that, about the accident. Something happened afterwards. Maybe a week later, after I got out of the hospital in Stone Valley. I heard her."

"Who?"

"Melissa Welles. And then, not just her."

"Joe, I don't understand."

"Not just her," he continued, "but everyone who had ever died in this town."

Joe Gardner didn't want to, but he felt them coming, the tears; not in his eyes, but somewhere at the back of his head, like a doorway that was greasing open, like the geometry of his brain was expanding and letting something out, this emotion, this thing he'd kept locked away. This memory. This town of the mind, where he had thought he was once somebody, but had found out that an entire town could turn against him. Somewhere between the first tear, as it reached his lower eyelid, and the kiss he felt from Jenny, it stopped, and he was able to put the teenage part of himself back into the compartment from which it had been loosed. He scruffed his son's hair up. He swung his now-waking daughter through the air as they left the Angel Wing, and went out into the yellow lamp-lit streets with the cars, with the shouts of teenagers, with the laughter of young love in bloom and the cries of cats down windy alleys, and above all these, he could hear the rush of water from the Paramount River as if it were all around him.

As they walked back to the car, Joe finished telling his wife the story of the voices.

3.

From the Journals of Joe Gardner/when he was nineteen:

I was at the old soda fountain having a root beer when I thought I heard her for the first time. Just like she was sitting next to me. Only I couldn't see her. All she said was something like "Joe." Not much else. I just knew it was her. So I didn't mention it to anyone. And then, I woke up on Tuesday and I hear her say, "You've got to go tell John Feely to let me out." I figure it's a dream, so I go to work and I'm in the middle of The Crying of Lot 49 *when I hear her say it again, only this time it's like a command, "Tell John Feely to let me out."*

Very weird. So last night I go see Hopfrog, and he's staring out his window. His mom says he doesn't seem to care about anything anymore. So, I sit down across from him, he doesn't look at me, and I ask him if he believes in an afterlife. He pretends I'm not there. I kind of hedge some more, and finally come out and tell him about hearing Melissa.

He waits a minute, and then turns and stares at me, kind of angry. He tells me I need to see a doctor, the mental kind. I pretty much agree.

And then I kind of get it, not about Melissa's voice—I figure I'm kind of losing it to hear voices—but about Hopfrog, why he's not talking to me, why he's so down. And I come right out and say it.

"You loved her, too," I say. And for once in all the six months since it happened, he started bawling his eyes out. And I go over, and he hugs me, and I tell him that it's okay that we both loved her. That I'm glad that he loved her, too. That it makes me feel less alone.

And then he says, "You know, Joey, I sometimes think I can feel my legs moving, or that maybe I can get up and walk again. But it doesn't mean that I can. They still won't move. I just believe I can. It doesn't make it true."

"What's your point?" I want to know.

He says, "She's dead. She's dead. You were there, too. She's gone. Joey. It's not her talking, it's you."

But then she tells me something, and I look at him. And I repeat what she says, word for word.

"I didn't drown," I say, "I didn't drown. You buried me alive. I'm not dead, why won't somebody help me?"

He looks at me funny.

And then I hear this guy tell me to tell Homer to listen up and listen good.

"Christ," Hopfrog says when I deliver that message, "it's Gramps. Christ, Joe, you crack your head open and got something inside it? They put a metal plate in or something?"

It scares me now, because Hopfrog is looking at me with wide eyes and goose bumps all along his arms, and he starts screaming for his mother because I can't help it, I can't help the fact that his grandfather starts talking through me and I'm beginning to think that maybe they did put something in my head when they sewed it up after the accident, that it wasn't a metal plate but some kind of receiver, some kind of copper wire and crystal, because I'm beginning to feel like the radio of the dead.

And then, just like last night, I hear them today. All day long.

All of them, talking at once, kids and old folks, most I don't even know, but I know they're out in the grave-yard on Watch Hill, out there at what we used to call the Flesh Farm, and I don't know if I'm crazy or if I'm sane, all I know is I can't stop them from talking through my lips, and Melissa keeps telling me that we buried her alive . . . and I can't sleep now, I can't sleep, I have to know, I have to know . . .

4.

"You were under a lot of stress then," Jenny said. She was just buckling Hillary into her seat. Joe leaned against the Buick, and dreamed of smoking. "You had just lost someone very close to you, you were young, you had all the problems at home, and you had seven-teen stitches in your head. Anyone would hear voices if that happened."

"Yeah, I know. Sounds logical now, doesn't it? Back then I thought I was either a prophet or looney."

Aaron, who had been pretending not to listen, as he so often did, chimed in, "Wow, Dad, did you go dig her up?"

"Aaron Gardner," his mother snapped.

Joe didn't answer. He got behind the wheel of the car, and when his family was safe inside it, he turned the key in the ignition. "It's almost eight," he said, "I guess we should go to Gramma's."

Jenny said, "I can see this is going to be a tense few days."

"You've only just come to that conclusion?"

"Might as well make the best of it. Tell you what, the kids and I'll check into a motel, and you go stay with your mom—" As she said this, his jaw seemed to go noticeably slack. "Joe, it's a joke, lighten up a little will you? You're thirty-five, you're a successful writer, she's a little old lady with asthma."

"My mother," Joe whispered so Aaron wouldn't hear him, "is a bloodsucker."

5.

Anna Gardner continued to live in the decaying colonial that had been her parents' home. It had seen her through her marriage to Joe's father with all its labyrinthine intrigues and infidelities. Now it would be her final resting place. The house was a large three bedroom with a wide wraparound porch and a screened-in gazebo in the backyard. Its brick was clay red, and its windows were small and perfectly square. It was originally the only lot on River Road, in 1911, when Anna's father had bought up most of the property along the river and had decided to settle there. The old house rested on two acres that overlooked the river from one of its steepest banks. Other houses had risen up during the sixty-seven years of her existence, and so the Northside, as it was called, consisted of a long thin row of homes, a few nearly as old as Anna's house, most newer and smaller, all with a view of the river. Although Joe's father had made a decent, even fat, income by Colony standards, the house had fallen into beloved disrepair when Joe was still in school—both drinkers, Anna and her husband preferred to maintain their pleasant levels of inebriation rather than maintain the house.

The approach on River Road was unspectacular. Colony was dying now and the houses seemed to have lost their shine. Yards were overgrown. Old cars sat up on blocks. For sale signs were posted in front of five houses. Only occasionally was there a perfectly manicured lawn, but even these were marred by the fake jockeys standing at the edge of the garden path or the flamingos and stone elves squatting alongside an azalea hedge.

"We used to have a tree down the bank," Joe said, as he parked alongside the river. "Me and Hopfrog, we tied a tire to it and used to swing out on the river all the time. That was before the big chemical companies upriver started dumping all toxic junk into it. Back then," he said to his son, "you could swim in rivers."

Aaron shook his head and grinned. "Jeez, you can still do that."

"At your own risk." His father shrugged.

He looked at the house.

His mother had left no light on.

"Maybe she's asleep," he said. "Maybe we should just get a room in town and come by tomorrow."

Jenny nudged him. "She's half blind. She probably doesn't even know the lights are off. Come on, let's go, onward, onward." She mock-shoved him forward.

"Oh, God, I don't want to."

"You sound like a baby."

I don't want to I don't want to, he thought, but his feet disobeyed him, and he walked up to the front porch, carrying Hillary. When he got to the screen door he rapped on it three times and realized that his mother, Anna Gardner, was already there, sitting on one of the Moroccan wicker chairs in a corner of the porch. She was lit by the orange light from a citronella candle, and he saw smoke from her cigarette drift upwards in the flickering shadows. He smelled the mint julep of her breath and heard her raspy cough. A radio was on, reporting the news of the region, and his mother reached across the small glass table before her and switched it off.

"Joseph," she said, "it's about time. Goddamn mosquitoes been eating me alive out here." She laughed. "It's November and the buggers're still breeding in the river." She rose on uncertain feet. She tossed the cigarette over the edge of the post and extended her arms to Jenny. "You must be Jenny, I am so, so happy to finally meet you."

Joe looked at his mother, and then at Jenny. Jenny stepped forward and hugged Anna. Then, Aaron went to hug her.

Finally, she approached Joe.

All he could think to say was, "You don't seem all that sick, Mom."

She smiled. "Well, I have my good days. But, hell, Joseph, I knew you'd never come see me again unless I was at death's door. And I was right, wasn't I? Now, give your old nasty mother a hug and a kiss, and, oh, this is Hillary, my God, she looks like me." But Joe knew that his mother couldn't tell who Hillary resembled in the feeble light from the orange candle.

Anna Gardner went and flicked on the porch light. "Let's get inside and have some cookies," she told Aaron.

She tricked me. Jesus, I should've known she would do that. Joe glanced at Jenny and realized that she was completely and utterly charmed by his mother. *You're not taken in by this are you, Jen? By the bourbon-*

soaked Southern accent, by the vulgar language heavily weighed down with syrup, by her seeming niceness? Jesus, this woman destroyed my father. This woman came close to destroying me.

He felt like a doomed man.

He watched as Aaron slipped his arm around his grandmother's, and how Aaron's face lit up as he went past his father. He wanted to tug his son free from the old woman's grasp, but it hit him that his mother was grasping no one. It was Aaron who was clinging to her. Jenny was opening the door for her to pass through.

She won. She finally won. She's going to take everything I have away from me.

But there was the tiniest shred of a voice in his head which told him:

Maybe she's not the monster you've made her out to be all these years, bud.

Maybe she's only human.

6.

Sheriff Dale Chambers picked up the phone. "Hello?"

"I need to see you." It was Lannie Barnes.

Christ, what if Nelda picked the phone up? Lannie was just fucking things up for everybody.

"Dale?"

He hung the phone up.

The phone rang again, but he quickly lifted the receiver and hung up. Then he turned the ringer off. He walked through the upstairs rooms, turning all the phones off.

Nelda was already in bed doing her crossword puzzles. Because she didn't like to be disturbed in the evening, she did not keep a phone in her room. When he passed the bedroom, she didn't ask about the phone call. She didn't even look up at him.

Dale walked slowly downstairs, just like he was going to take one of his usual evening strolls down by the river, or into town for a beer.

He knew where Lannie would be. She'd be at the Lodge having a drink, sitting by the pay phone, expecting him to call back. To come to her. To tell her how much he loved her and how much he loved the baby they were going to have, and how, if they ran away together right now, tonight, it would fix everything, that life would begin for both of them.

Dale decided against calling her back.

He noticed an envelope there by the front door. He squatted down and touched it. He almost thought he felt a barely perceptible shock, and then a chill run through him as he touched it. He got an instant erection, and didn't know why the touch of an envelope would arouse him. He picked it up and stood. He knew what would be inside. He was almost glad that it had arrived tonight. Whoever the mysterious voyeur was, the man who wrote the letters to him, now seemed an extension of himself.

He opened it.

I know what you did. You naughty, naughty man.

He didn't even realize that his free hand was down at his crotch, just touching his penis through the rough cloth of his chinos. He felt, for a moment, young again. All those letters over the years, and it was as if this mystery writer knew him, really knew what he was planning for Lannie.

It was like a letter from God.

He folded the letter neatly and slipped it back into

the envelope. He placed it in the inner pocket of his jacket.

He decided, as he walked out into the chilly evening, that he was going to wait until Lannie left the Lodge. She would go out into the parking lot to her car. She would be loaded—maybe four martinis if he was lucky. He would be there, in her car, in the backseat, waiting for her.

He would surprise her this time.

The letter was like an omen: this was the night, this was the moment to be seized.

7.

Byron Cheever lay with his head pressed against the milky smooth bosoms of the girl he called Beauty, while her friend sat over at the base of a large stone marker and smoked a cigarette. They had specifically requested the old graveyard. He figured they were kinky, and although he'd only gotten to second base so far, the way Beauty was grinding against him, he figured it wouldn't be long before he'd be slapping his prick against her snatch.

Beauty moaned, "Oh, God, By, do it, do it, just do it."

Well, it was all a boy like Byron Cheever needed, so he whipped it out with one hand, and spread her legs further with the other.

And as he pressed his fingers up to her crotch, he felt something lumpy.

For just a second, he thought it might be a purse or something that she kept down in her panties. *Maybe a Kleenex, or shit, a Tampax* . . .

But the thing grew in his fingers, and before the

knowledge reached his brain, his body already knew to draw back, and as he did:

Lightning blinded him.

Lightning?

He couldn't see.

Then, another flash.

"What the fuck—" he gasped.

Someone was taking pictures—it was her dog-girl-friend, or shit, not *her* girlfriend, *his* girlfriend, it was a guy's dick he'd been holding underneath Beauty's dress.

And as he stood, his dick out, his pants down, tripping over himself, he saw an entire sorority from Danville Women's College standing there in the graveyard at Watch Hill, with flashlights held beneath their faces, beginning to sing "The Man I Love."

Beauty stood up, brushed himself off, and pulled the wig off his head. He said to By, "Look, it was repulsive for me, too. I usually like a guy who treats me right." He withdrew the falsies from the bosom of the dress and tossed them to By, who dropped them immediately.

Beauty's girlfriend kept taking pictures, and the flash kept blinking.

She shouted, "This is what you get for what you did to Marti."

"Marti?" He didn't know any Marti. Did he? Maybe there had been that girl at the party one time who had squealed after they'd made it—was she Marti?

She had wanted it. Her name was Martha Wiley. She had wanted it. She had only squealed because she'd been taught not to want it. But he had worked her over good.

Suddenly, he became enraged. "You goddamn

bitches!" He lunged at the guy who was Beauty, but missed him and landed face first against a stone angel.

When he awoke, he was alone.

For a second he forgot what had happened.

Someone had pinned a note to him, and left him with a flashlight.

He tore the note off his shirt and scanned it with the flashlight's beam.

Dear Mr. Cheever,
Even if the law won't protect us, we'll do what we can. Marti will be happy to see these. And also Dave Hotchkiss, the guy you beat up for being queer last year. How the tables do turn. We have some photographs of you making out and fondling our friend Todd, and we even managed the shot where you have it in your hands. Nice photos. I'm sure your frat brothers will appreciate the, er, head-shots. Maybe even your folks. Maybe even your girlfriend over at Sweet Briar.
Warmly,
The Sisters of Vengeance,
Danville Women's College.

Byron Cheever dropped the note and the flashlight and sat back against a grave. He looked up at the stars and knew in his heart of hearts that his life was over.

He had a conscience after all, and it was bothering him, but not for his hump-and-dump incident with Marti Wiley.

His conscience bothered him because he had felt a thrilling warmth go through him when he had touched the growing lump in Beauty's panties.

For a young man his age who had always hated queers, had beat them up whenever he saw one, this was a revelation which only led to one place, and it was a desolate thought which sawed into his head.

He would have to kill himself.

8.

Joe's mother's house had not changed significantly since he'd left seventeen years earlier. Although it was neat, she didn't keep it very clean. The dust was thick on the banister of the stairs leading up to the bedrooms. The ragged hall curtains were shut. The books and newspapers, of which there were many, were stacked along the wall. The wood floors were scraped and stained. She had bought nothing new, and not one overstuffed chair or sofa had been reupholstered in over thirty years. Still, there was something comfortable about the place. It looked as if it had been well lived in.

"So," Anna Gardner said to Jenny, "you must be exhausted."

"Very."

"Well, I've had Joe's old room fixed up for the children. You and Joe can have my old bedroom upstairs. I sleep most nights down here in the den—the stairs are a bit too steep for me these days. I'm afraid that I, too, must retire shortly. Now that I'm an old bat, I can't seem to stay awake much past nine."

Joe hesitated, but then kissed his mother good night on her forehead.

"Joseph," she began.

"Mom, we're really tired," he interrupted.

"I know. But I want you to know I've changed."

"Oh." He drew back from her. Aaron stood next to him; he ruffled Aaron's hair.

"Well, I love you, son. I hope you sleep well." She turned and walked towards the den. Perhaps she had a tear in her eye, Joe couldn't tell. Perhaps she was faking it.

She's faked things before. She's faked love and caring and affection. She ran around with that doctor and caused the biggest scandal of the county. She destroyed Dad and faked innocence.

He put his arm around Jenny, and hefted Hillary up. "Well, Hilly, it's finally time for beddy-bye."

9.

When they were alone in the bedroom, Joe said, "I can't believe she lied about being so sick. I can't believe it."

"Joe," Jenny said, her voice low, "it's obvious."

"What is?"

"She wanted to meet us. Your family. Finally. She wanted to see her son again. Look at her. She's a lonely woman who's lost everything but her house."

"And what a housekeeper she is," Joe added, feeling nasty. He began undressing, tossing his shirt over the bedpost. He dropped his slacks and left them where they fell until he saw the look on Jenny's face. Then he picked them up and folded them and laid them across the trunk at the foot of his mother's bed.

"The nut doesn't fall far from the tree," Jenny said. "You could use some pointers in the housekeeping department yourself."

"I'm telling you, Jen, something's fishy. She's not like that."

"Oh, really? You've spent half your life telling me she's a witch and an ogre and a vampire, and all I see is a woman who lost her son because she was foolish and because he was unforgiving." Jenny went to the suitcase on the dresser and opened it. She lifted up a few items of clothing: a sweater, a couple of blouses. She hung these up in the closet. Then, she unzipped and stepped out of her dress, hanging it neatly, too. She wore a slip to bed, but didn't say anything further until Joe spoke again.

"Maybe I was wrong," he whispered as he lay down beside her. He could see the river from the bedroom window. It was black and placid, not turbulent, the way he remembered it. The orb of moonlight traveled across its surface. "Maybe she was only awful back then. Maybe things are different now."

"Well," Jenny curled into his arms, resting her head on his chest, "what we think is happening when we're children is different than what we know is happening as adults." He smelled her hair. It was arousing and comforting at the same time.

"Maybe," Joe said. "So much was going on back then. It wasn't just that Mom was the town scandal, it was all the other crap, too. The accident, Melissa's death, the way Hopfrog turned on me. All of it. The voices. Maybe I was nuts. Maybe Mom was just coping the best way she knew how. I always blamed her for destroying Dad, but he wasn't just some wounded bird. He was a tough man. I don't think he'd just stand by and let her destroy him. It's so confusing."

"Family," Jenny said, "is always confusing."

"Mine more so than others, I guess."

"But look, she produced you. Somehow in all that mess, she produced a writer and a good husband and a great father."

"Am I a good husband?"

Jenny sighed. "After all we've been through, Joe,

and I'm still here. Do you think I'd've stayed if I thought you weren't a good husband?"

Joe said nothing. He kissed his wife on the forehead and held her close. He rested the tip of his chin on her scalp and smelled her essence. He watched the Paramount River, with the moon and stars reflected across it.

After a while, Jenny said, "Besides, back to the subject of you being nuts, all writers are nuts, didn't you know that?"

He kissed her again. She leaned forward and up so that their lips met. She opened her mouth for him. He kissed her deeply. They made love as quietly as they could, trying to forget that the kids and his mother were in the same house.

10.

Dale Chambers checked the parking lot for Lannie's white Lincoln Town Car. It was parked in darkness, at the far edge of the lot. *Good.* If he had to kill her, he might need to leave her in the car, leave it parked here. He might have to, in his capacity as sheriff, accidentally put his fingerprints on the car. He pictured it in his head: *Take Jud along as a witness, pretend that maybe the woman in the car has passed out, open the door, touch the glove compartment, touch her throat, maybe even touch her arm and dress and blouse and sweater. Pretend that she's not dead, and then be shocked as hell when you pretend you only just discovered she doesn't have a pulse. Hot damn,* he thought, *you are so fucking smart.*

It was good to be sheriff.

Dale's weight sometimes got in the way of things.

Even though it had only been four blocks down to the Miner's Lodge, he was huffing and panting, and in spite of the night's chill, he was sweating. He was slightly afraid that the sweating might give him away. *Somebody just like him would see the Gump in him, the one who was going to kill Lannie Barnes—whoever wrote those letters—whoever knows I'm a naughty man. He'll know what I'm up to.* He stood still in the darkness. His adrenaline was rushing like the river in springtime.

He waited for over an hour for Lannie to come out of the back door of the Lodge.

Then he thought, *what if I just go in the back way, by the phones? Nobody'll see me. I'll hang back. She might be back there. I might be able to pull her out here, into the dark. I'll pretend we're going to fuck, and then I'll get her in the car and strangle her to death. Nobody will see me.*

He skulked around in the shadows, and finally made it to the back door.

He tried the door, but it wouldn't open. A sign on the door, which he'd never paid attention to before, read: *After Midnight, This Entrance Closed.*

Someone was coming out.

He heard two men talking on the other side of the door.

Dale stepped back behind the dumpster. He crouched down. George Fletcher and Gary Welles stepped out beneath the light outside the door.

"Well, all's I can say is, good luck with it, that's all I can say," George said, sounding his usual drunk-off-his-ass self.

Gary lit a cigarette. "Your kind of luck, George, I can do without," he said.

Gary had become a drunk since his daughter Melissa's death, so many years before. He had lost his wife and his house, and now slept in the back of his car most nights. "Son of a bitch, you're supposed to be my friend," Gary muttered. "George, you're supposed to be my friend. Don't nothing mean nothing no more? What's a man supposed to do when everything he loves gets taken away from him?"

"Sleep it off, boy," George said, walking off in an opposite and slightly loopy direction.

Gary Welles stood alone. With a cigarette in one hand and his dick in the other, he pissed a bright luminescent yellow snake down the parking lot. When he was done, he didn't bother zipping up. He shivered drunkenly and went to lie down in the shadows.

Dale Chambers inhaled the four-day old Lodge trash until both men were out of sight.

He knew he'd have to risk it.

You're sheriff, you can do it. You can do anything.

Dale Chambers decided to use the front entrance.

He couldn't wait for Lannie forever.

The Miner's Lodge was a venerable institution—it had been built in the twenties, first of wood, and then, when it burned down, of stone. It was the closest that the town had to a country club, although its rules of entry were less than stringent: as long as you could crawl across the threshold, you were welcome.

This was Dale and Lannie's bar, and although Lannie should've been there, on one of the bar stools, leaning over with a cashmere sweater on (a forty dollar cream-colored cashmere sweater he'd bought her last year, already with cigarette burns on it), with her big clinky brass jewelry clacking on the bar while she ordered another margarita or martini (she only ordered drinks that began with "mar" because Margaret was her middle name). He knew so much about her, so many stupid facts, the perfume she wore (Anais Anais), her shoe size (eight), the big purple birthmark on the left cheek of her butt—he knew her inside and out.

Dale looked from face to face at the bar. He checked the women's room, asking one of the other regulars to peek into the two stalls for Lannie. But she was not there.

"Could be she left," Harold Earle said, winking at him. Harold was fifty and had been the bartender there forever, keeping secret the sleazy affairs and misbegotten intimacies of Colony the whole time. But he did have his code words to special people; Dale knew that he, himself, was the most special person.

And what that wink had meant was:

Lannie Barnes is already upstairs in a room with another man, Gump.

11.

Dale Chambers managed to break into Lannie's car. He was deft with a coat hanger, and she might not notice the damage to the window, at least not in this lifetime.

He crouched in the backseat and waited.

As he waited, the night wore on and his anger lessened, replaced in his mind and heart by another emotion, a feeling which he didn't think he was entirely capable of.

12.

In the bed upstairs at his mother's house, Joe was dreaming.

It was the old dream.

Melissa, Hopfrog, and he, the Volkswagen beetle, the Paramount Bridge, the eight-wheeler.

Hopfrog, finally starting the car at the last second, but too late . . .

falling, all of them, hitting his head on the roof of the car, hearing Hopfrog's scream as something metal tears into his legs.

And waking up, beneath the water, in the car, believing he is dead. Hopfrog is no longer in the front seat. Joe doesn't know this, because it is too dark in the water. Later, he will find out that Hopfrog was thrown from the car just as it went over the bridge.

Later, Joe will learn a lot about this accident.

In the dark water, he feels her hand; they held hands as they went over.

Melissa, unconscious in the backseat with him.

Floating; water coming in through the broken windshield.

And then, as he tugs at her hand, something in that dark water,

tugging back, but not her, not Melissa,

something on the other side of her, tugging, and he thinks it is someone rescuing his beloved, so he lets her go.

Later, he will learn where they found her, downriver, two days later, her body bloated from excessive water intake and the skin sagging with it.

Later, he will learn how she had lost so much blood in the water that she was very nearly to her last pint when they found her body, that gallons of river water had burst from the places on her body that had been cut on rocks.

Wake Up! Joe yells at himself in the dream. *Wake up! Get the hell out of there, get the hell out of there!*

But the dream continues, and takes him to that place, that place on Watch Hill, early on a Sunday morning, with Hopfrog in his wheelchair; with a shovel, and a mound of dirt at his feet.

And there is something to find in the month-old grave, the resting place of Melissa Welles.

13.

Across town, in a white Lincoln Town Car, Dale Chambers was dreaming, too, dreaming that he and Lannie were holding a baby. When he looked at the baby's face it bore an uncomfortable resemblance to his wife, Nelda.

He awoke.

He snarfled, coughing up a snore and swallowing a gasp, and then realized that someone was unlocking the driver's side of the car door.

It was Lannie. And she was not alone.

"Oh, God, my car stinks, it just stinks," she said, her southern accent sour and sticky. He could hear her six bracelets clash together. He sank farther down on the floor in the back.

A man said, "Smells like you, Lannie, smells just like you, all lavender and honeysuckle."

That voice, Dale thought feverishly, *that voice!*

Unmistakable.

Jud Carey, his own deputy.

Mother of Pearl fuck!

Dale felt beads of sweat resume their onslaught

from his receding hairline right down to his quickly receding balls.

My own deputy, practically a son to me, wait 'til I get him alone, I'm gonna—

And then, he heard the worst thing.

The slap and spit of a kiss, a deep tongue kiss.

Oh God no, he cringed as he heard the sound of sweater and jacket unzipping and pulled over head, the light rustle of hair being finger-combed, another zip, that *zip* that meant Jud's thing was being drawn from his trousers.

"Lannie, honey, I only got an hour for break, and we already done it twice. You can't raise the dead," Jud said and gasped.

"I don't believe in predictions of failure," Lannie said, sounding sloshed and Southern and damned sexy. She said something more, too, only Dale couldn't understand her 'cause it sounded like her mouth was full.

Dale could no longer take it.

He covered his ears with his hands.

He wanted to die.

He didn't want to believe that Lannie was capable of this, the most heinous of betrayals.

And then that emotion surged within him, a tickling up his spine.

Love.

He loved her.

He truly and deeply loved her in his heart and with his soul.

He closed his eyes and waited for the act to finish.

Finally, he heard the triumphant and dreadful groan, the rezipping of clothes, the combing of hair, the clinking of bracelets being put back on.

Dale Chambers rode home to Lannie's, undetected, lying uncomfortably in the back, weeping to himself.

14.

Two old men sat at a storefront window in the semi-darkness.

"Is belief the problem?"

"I guess I don't believe in anything."

"Not even God? Virgil, really."

"Especially not Him. Not anymore."

"Everyone believes in something."

"Enough of the psychoanalysis, where the hell is that cigar you promised?"

The room was dark, save for a single lamp, set on a table, which cast only faint shadows of the two men who sat on either side of it.

"Here, Virg, try it."

The sound of a man sniffing.

"Cuban. Hand rolled?"

"Very good. You must've been a hound dog in your last life."

"Winston Alden, how in the name of Pete did you get hold of hand-rolled Cubans?"

"I've had it in storage since 1955. Hasn't lost its smell any, has it?"

"I haven't had one of these since . . ."

"Since before time, eh?"

"Thereabouts."

Smoke moved in slow circles around the lamp's glow.

The sound of liquid, pouring.

"Medoc. 1947."

"Must be a special occasion, Win."

A long pause. The man named Winston heaved a sigh that seemed to hang in the air with the smoke. He said, "It's coming, you know."

"Winston?"

"They're coming, Virg. I can smell them. They're coming."

"No more of that stuff, please. It's bad enough, the nightmares you gave me last time."

"I gave you? Who was it who found out about it? Look out there. The streets. How many towns are like this, do you think?"

"Like what?"

"Of no real consequence anymore. Why, Colony could just be gone tomorrow, and who would come around to check its pulse? Stone Valley would continue the same as always, and nobody else really cares or even comes through here. The furniture company just laid off fifty more employees. It'll be gone soon. We could go like that"—fingers snapped—"and it would be a day or two before anyone came around to investigate. If a snow comes, could be longer. Maybe two weeks."

They sat in silence for a while, with the shadow of smoke curling around the lamp. The silence was broken with the clinking of glasses as more Medoc was poured.

"I saw the writer, Virgil."

"You're talking in too many circles for me. What writer?"

"For a doctor you're not too bright, Virgil. The one who used to live out on River Road. Oh, the one with the voices. You remember."

"Anna Gardner's boy? He's back? You're sure?"

"Haven't lost all my marbles just yet. He stopped across the street for a paper hours ago. A woman and children in the car, too. Looks taller but he's still got that paunch. He's how I know. It's coming back again, soon. Got to make sure none of them come round my place, not like they did that last time. And don't you ridicule me, you hypocrite—you sit there drinking my wine and smoking my Cubans, and scared out of your mind because you know it's true."

From the dark on the other side of the table, the other man sighed. "I figured as much."

"'Bout time you admitted it. But there's only one problem, Virg. We're just too old to do anything about it. I don't have the same kind of strength I had back then. And I know you don't have the belief you once did. I know I don't."

Five minutes of silence.

"When you're right, you're right. So, what do we do?"

The other man said, "What, you think I've got a solution to every problem? I'll do what every other fool in this town does in a crisis and sit on my fat ass until doomsday."

"I suppose we could talk to John and see if he's got it under control."

"Tried that. He hasn't been answering his door. Got me worried on that count, too. He's too *much* of a believer, you ask me. When he goes . . . well."

"Oh, dear," the other man in the dark room said. "Me a doctor and you an ex-preacher, Winston, and between us we can't make it go away."

"Nobody can. Look at that town. Look at the streets. I can feel it out there. It's caught, but it wasn't meant to be kept down forever."

9

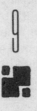

THE LAST NIGHT OF
BYRON CHEEVER

1.

Watch Hill was a lonely place on weeknights. On the weekend, teenagers often went to the cool stones and flat markers, and, with a crowbar pried back the doors to mausoleums—to make out, or camp out, or just to lie back and watch the stars.

But because Byron Cheever was out on a Thursday night, the graveyard was barren of life.

Out to the north he could see the orchards leading to Old Man Feely's place, and the river beyond it. To the east, he could see the town, with its flickering yellow lights. All the rest was wilderness. The beacons of Stone Valley shone from the ridge the other side of the Malabars. He had been born in Stone Valley, but his first memories had been of Colony, of the Paramount River, of the Old Town, with its stone houses and Federal-style buildings, the Civil War cannons over in front of the Post Office, the taste of ham and eggs at Wanda Mirkle's Pig in a Poke coffee shop, the smell of the river in spring when the fish were running and the girls were for the taking along its banks.

He became overly sentimental as he sat there on the flat raised marker of some lost soul from decades back. He was going to have to die, that's all there was to it. He had learned something about himself, something about his inner nature, and it terrified him. He didn't want to be anything other than what he presented of himself: a guy who liked pussy. It was the only Byron Cheever he had ever known. This other one, this man inside his skin who had been turned on by that other man, had to die. The only way By knew how was to kill both men, the one on the inside, and the one on the outside.

He thought he could hear the hum of the universe as he sat there. The airwaves of God, maybe, that kept the whole lunatic world somehow on track. And only he, *he* was tuned into it. His parents wouldn't hear it— they were so far removed from the workings of the cosmos, they were only into money and appearance. Byron, the inside man, was something of a poetic soul; he knew what suffering was, what true pain was. He knew how when he had pushed sissy boys down on the playgrounds of childhood, he *knew* that *he* was the one who had suffered the most—how those kids had *made* him push them down. How it was out of his control, how those kids had been laughing at him, on the *in-*

side, how they had forced him to push them and beat them and kick them until they were bloody and bruised. It was always them. And when he had beat off over his little brother, Hugh, when Hugh was nine and he was thirteen, even though Hugh wept and asked to be let go, he *knew* that it was Hugh making him do it, and he was right, wasn't he? Hugh was now a teenager and already a queer—it was Hugh who had made Byron Cheever do it to him. And how he had suffered for what Hugh had made him do! How different his life might be if Hugh had not made him hold him down and spit all over him and beat off against his thigh! He might not have this inner self now, telling him how much he liked to hurt boys and how it made him all excited.

God, if only all those other boys had never existed. It was like they were demons put on earth to torment him and other guys like him, *normal* guys, guys who liked pussy, who were smart and got ahead and were going to one day show all of them, all the rest of those people who had ever hurt or tormented him (he could name them: Hugh, Mark, Bart, Gus, Clay, Jimmy, Joe Bob) . . . he was going to show them just how much they had *damaged* him.

Byron had considered suicide several times before, but never intended to carry it out. He was too valuable to the scheme of things, he had reasoned. He was going to go on and make something of himself and destroy those who had made him suffer.

But with those photos, *those bitches* . . . Byron Cheever knew it was over for him. He was already dead. His frat brothers—particularly Beau, *oh, man, how am I gonna look Beau in the eyes again? He's my best friend, he'll never understand, he's so handsome and butch, he'll think I'm such a fag, he'll never want to*

be my friend again. Kicked out for cheating, and now,
this. Aw, what the hell's the matter with the world!
Why does it always happen to me? Who the hell fucked
up?

Already dead.

Already dead.

It was like a song going through his head.

Might as well die

Say bye-bye to By

'Cause I'm already dead.

What was the point? Why live? What reason did he
have for getting up the next morning, for facing the
cruelest of possible worlds?

Who cared about Byron Cheever and his suffering?

2.

He searched the trunk of his daddy's Cadillac. He
found some old *Penthouse* magazines, and a large flashlight, a toolbox (he didn't want to kill himself with a
screwdriver, although it might be possible), and beneath the spare tire, a thick extension cord. Good
length. That would be good for death. A good strong
cord around his neck—he'd beat off before, strangling
himself with one of his mother's silk scarves wrapped
around his neck. He liked the sensation. It was a
smooth feeling with the scarf. It would not be so
smooth with the extension cord, but life was a bitch
without tits, so what did it matter if there was more
pain at the end? It was all pain, all suffering, all torture. *What's another fuck? as one whore said to the*
other.

When he slammed the trunk closed, he thought he
heard something move nearby.

He looked towards the Connor crypt; turned the flashlight on it. The small building was intact, door closed. Sometimes kids were around. Maybe they were giggling at him. Maybe they'd been there all along, and they were going to go home and tell their mommies and daddies what they saw and heard, how Byron Sumner Cheever was a pervert, not just a homo, but the kind that got off only when he could hit somebody and make them cry.

They'd tell their folks that he was *not normal*.

Oh, God, hurry up and kill yourself.

He spun the flashlight's beam around the graveyard, all of its two low, sloping hills. Nothing but the wrought-iron gates, nothing but the luminescent stones, nothing but the flat November grass, and the silvery dew, like an early frost. Nothing but the dead and soon-to-be-dead.

He didn't ask, "Who's there?" because he was afraid someone would respond.

He imagined his family, here in a week, looking down at the coffin as they lowered it. Thought of the minister saying his Good Bookisms, thought of his mother, weeping tears of loss, his father, tears of remorse. They would hug and shiver. They would miss their son. They loved their son. (They hated Hugh because Hugh was showing signs of major queerdom, he couldn't play sports and he couldn't do boy things very well, he was walking funny—*Jesus, they'd only have Hugh, it was like having half a son. Good, let them suffer for once.*)

He turned the flashlight off. He tested the cord for strength by pulling on it, snapping it. He swatted the air with it, then slapped the cord down on one of the markers. He walked around among the raised stones and swatted them. When he came upon one of the stone angels, he whapped it hard over and over again until some chips flaked off from the angel's face.

He would like it to have been that fucking Marti Wiley for making him fuck her and then for telling her bitch friends that he had raped her. *Jesus, she had practically raped him, she had wanted it so bad.* The world was so unjust. He would like that stone angel's face to be her as he whapped it and slapped it and sliced it open with the extension cord. It almost made him want to live.

But, still, he climbed up the side of Watch Hill, to the top.

He wrapped one end of the cord around the lantern that thrust out of the Feely mausoleum. It was welded to the stone and was made of iron. This was the oldest building on Watch Hill, built by the Feelys when cholera had taken several of their children. It had faces of cherubic children carved into its stone walls. Engraved above the lantern were the words, "Cast Our Light Unto the Darkest Places." Byron Cheever, like all of the youth of Colony, had seen those words since his earliest days. He had broken into the mausoleum with friends and spray painted the inner walls. He had gotten laid for the first time up against the doorway on a hot night during the summer he turned fourteen.

There had been two other suicides here in the past sixteen years that he was aware of. It was an historical place. A twelve-year-old girl had drunk poison and left a note about beatings and worse, back in the eighties. Just a couple of years back, Angus Zane, one of the village idiots who had been in school with By, had slit his wrists, although no one knew why.

It was a lonesome and wonderful spot.

He secured the extension cord on the lantern and

held onto it. He lifted himself off the ground, did a pull-up.

It would hold.

It would do the trick.

He let go of the cord and went over to the mausoleum. There were plenty of loose bricks around the doorway after the countless crowbars that had been used to pry the door open. He picked up one of the large bricks and set it down beneath the cord. Then he went and propped the flashlight up so it would shine directly, he hoped, on his swinging body. It would be dramatic that way, if they found him at night. If they found him in the daylight, it wouldn't matter. He began to hope they would find him at night.

He inhaled the chilly air, deep and strong.

Coughed.

I look out at you, Colony, Paramount River, farm and town and hills, and I say, Fuck this.

Byron Cheever balanced himself on the brick. He wrapped the cord around his neck.

3.

It was a hard balancing act, because the brick was on its end, and By was not petite. He was a husky, strong young man, who had never had to balance himself before. He was hoping that he could finish his malediction to the world before the brick went, but it was not to be.

The brick toppled.

He swung.

He did not die.

He hung there, strangling, barely able to breathe.

He remembered reading or hearing something

about how, if your neck didn't break you would just hang there and strangle. And death would take its sweet ass time.

In the grip of a new panic, a panic that the suffering in his life had begun all over again, he saw something, a dark shape standing just outside the flashlight beam.

Someone was watching him, and he thought he heard the sound of a child giggling.

And then another sound, a booming, rending of bones and earth and wood and stone, as if every grave in Watch Hill were erupting with the rising dead of Judgment Day while the majority of Colony slept.

He realized this was a private vision, meant only for him.

At the crossroads of life and death, as he swung there, the shape, a child stepped into the light and told him what he must do.

What needed to be done this night.

And then, the child became something other than what might be called flesh.

4.

Enough people in town *were* asleep, but Sheriff Dale Chambers never seemed to get the chance. Since escaping unnoticed from Lannie's car an hour before, and having to hoof it all the way to the office, he was exhausted and wired at the same time. He was mentally kicking himself for being so weak as to fall in love with Lannie Barnes, to let his weenie lead him astray like that. He sat in his office, and read the report about the missing Hoskins boy; his deputy was out patrolling the streets, checking out leads, seeing if the boy was sleeping over at a friend's house. They'd find the Hoskins kid. He wasn't worried.

Truth was, Dale was a fairly incompetent sheriff, and he'd be the first to acknowledge it if anyone had ever had the balls to confront him with the truth. He despised most of the town, thought they were idiots and functional clowns. They were like a bad dream, or a sewer stink made flesh. He had always wanted out of the place, but there were chains holding him back, the invisible chains of marriage and obligation. And fear, too, that worst of all chains, the fear that there was no other world out there beyond Colony, no world that would support him or look up to him or kowtow to him.

He was sheriff, after all.

Folks looked up to him.

(Except that one person, that all-seeing person who wrote the notes.

Naughty, naughty man.)

It was almost two A.M. He knew he would be up all night, wondering what to do with Lannie and Nelda, each of them, the rock and the hard place. Lannie, the slut he loved, and Nelda, the icebox he married. It was always the same choice, he knew, all of womankind was either one or the other.

He started typing up a couple of reports for the morning, mainly his comments on the performance of his office.

And then, about the Hoskins boy, he wrote:

Possible runaway. Possible kidnapping. Possible murder.

He looked at those possibilities. Rubbed his eyes.

"Goddamn it," he said, slamming his fist on his desk. From the outer office, Cathy Zane, who worked the night shift dispatch, came in with a cup of coffee. "Who you gettin' pissed off at now, Gump?"

"You ever call me that again," he said, "your ass is gonna be grass."

"My ass already got mowed this week," she said, smiling. She set the coffee down. "White, like you like it. So, what's all the cussing for?"

"Oh,"—Dale waved his hand in a vague gesture—"that Hoskins kid."

"Billy? I'm sure he's fine. Boys always run off at that age and they always come home. Heck, he may just've snuck out to meet some girl." She sat on the edge of his desk and thumbed the dozen pieces of paper in his to-be-filed box. Idly, she said, "Two accidents out on Twenty-eight. Big rig and a trailer. Looks messy. Stone Valley's got it, though. The other one was some fool drove his car into the river. Don't know who it is yet."

"Ten dollars on Pearl Watson."

"I don't waste my money on a sure thing. We got Jud on it. Quiet night, 'cept for those two."

Dale couldn't keep another cuss in. The thought of Lannie taking Jud's thing in her mouth, well, it got his blood boiling but good. "Goddamn it," he said.

"Cross yourself when you do that."

"I ain't Catholic."

"Well, do it anyway. What is worth using the Lord's name in vain?"

"Well, I was thinking about Billy Hoskins. I mean, Cathy, if he's run off, we can find him or he'll come home. Right?"

"Right."

"But if he's dead—"

"Billy Hoskins? He ain't dead. He ain't. Don't say that. He just run off."

"But *if* he's dead, the state boys'll be down on us so

fast we won't know what hit us. I hate the state boys. They're always going through my papers, always trying to piss me off."

Cathy clucked her tongue. "My, but you are a worrywart. Listen, that kid might be lying in his own bed right now for all we know. You know how kids are these days. Lying, cheating, stealing, running, hiding, sneaking. No morals, no cares. He'll be back before dawn in his own bed, and if his folks're right in the head, they'll give him a whupping he won't forget." She slid off his desk and walked out.

Dale heard the static and distant voices as dispatch came on, informing Cathy of yet some other disturbance in the long night.

He leaned back in his chair and looked up at the ceiling.

Damn kids, he thought, *damn women and the fruits of their womb.*

5.

Byron Cheever reached his arms above his head. With his hands, he tugged at the extension cord as it hung from the lantern fixture. It did not give; it held too tight. The thing that had spoken to him, the thing that had looked like a child, it had given him some kind of *push*, some brief shot of energy, so that he was able to grasp the cord. Now it was up to him. Only he could save himself from the despair and madness that this town had doomed him to. Only he could be hero to his soul.

His finger tugged at the cord. It was so damn thick. He'd never get it to break. He'd never get out of it.

What had everyone done to him? They had made him want to die, want to *strangle* himself, for God's sake.

And then, it gave. He was stronger; it was as if his fingernails were sharp knives, cutting through the insulation around the cord, right down to the tiny wires inside. He split a finger open doing it, but he would be free in a moment.

Free to live and breathe and get back at them, all of them, everyone who had ever hurt him.

A reason to live. A point. A purpose.

Release.

Byron Cheever dropped to the ground, hunkering down like an animal. He inhaled clean, sweet air. Oh, he had thought he would never taste its like again.

The child thing was gone.

It had been, he knew, a vision, as had the others he saw in that brief time while he'd been hanging.

Others, rising from graves, not like zombies or ghosts, but like people, real people who had been buried all wrong, who had been buried alive by Colony and its minions.

He knew it because he had almost crossed over to them, almost given dominion to the assholes of town who would murder the sensitive and loving and intelligent in favor of lowlifes and scum.

He half stood, but crouched down again as his back hurt badly now.

His senses seemed heightened.

I've been touched. Touched by some great being. A gift from the most Holy of Holies. He sniffed the air, and smelled. *Oh God the air, the wet trees the bugs the dead possum rotting at the roadside the heat-stink of animals nesting nearby my own flesh oh dear God how sweet the smell that saved a wretch like me.*

And then, a stronger smell above all the others.

Coming from just beyond Watch Hill.

Rotting apples on the ground, sweet grass, dust of stone and wood, a house, a great house-stink and sweet sweet flesh.

He loped in the direction of that strongest, most vital of odors.

Byron Cheever felt a wave of greatness sweep over him, and he knew now that he was capable of the most wonderful and terrible things.

6.

The geography of Colony is simple: there is a town and a river surrounding it. It is not an island, however, by geological definition, for the river runs so narrow at certain points, particularly to the southwest, as to be a thin sliver of water going through rock; at its southeast corner, the river is completely underground, dripping through the man-made caverns which widened since the days of the old mines.

The night birds that rake their wings across the cloak of the dark are not silent; neither are the trucks out on Route 28. If your ears are attuned, you can hear beyond these noises, too, to the sounds of lusts and passions and snores and coughs.

If you are of the mind, the most hidden and precious gems of the mind, you can hear beyond, you can hear thoughts and wishes and prayers.

7.

Old Man Feely was on the toilet, having been woken up by the kicking noises. He rarely had a full night's sleep anymore; it seemed the older he got, the less time he wished to waste in bed. He was not a true insomniac, for he caught catnaps during the day, after lunch, before supper. Night was his time. He could read his Bible or clean his various collections—the guns and the stuffed carcasses of his favorite hobby, taxidermy. He could walk room to room of the great house that his great-grandfather had built with his own two hands, the farmhouse with rooms upon rooms and halls upon halls. Each room covered with a layer of dust and spiderwebs, each with gaslight in the window, each with mementos of family or of the past. God demanded so much from him. God did not forgive moral laxity. He tried to keep the farmhouse up, but his savings had been eaten away. He only had money for the most necessary items: simple food, enough nourishment for survival, and enough clothing for his thick frame. If cleanliness were truly next to godliness, then he was surely last in line.

He was on the toilet, reading from the Book of Abaddon, the Angel of Shadows. It was a part of the bible that his father's father heard in a dream, and had written down in the morning. It was the story of how the fallen of God's beloved, the Light Bearer, had been cast from heaven:

And so, the Light Bearer spake unto the Lord God Jehovah, "It is not for man that I love thee, but for thee alone, Creator of Light."

But God was not pleased, for created he man and woman, like unto Him. "My most cherished above all," the Lord God spaketh unto him, "ye must cleave unto man and woman lest ye betray Him whom you claim to love."

The terror of the Light Bearer was of the magnitude of oceans, likewise, his fear was of the depth of the abyss. He shrank from God's light, and hid among the blessed of the firmament, until Jehovah cried out to him, "Be ye known to me, beloved, shun not the light of the Lord Your God."

Revealed to the Heavenly Host, the Light Bearer uttered these words, "I will not love that which is beneath thee. I will not love that which is undeserved. I will not love the sinner called man nor the wanton called woman, just as I do not worship the eel or slug nor kiss the foot of the goat."

Lo, the most High Lord Jehovah cast the Light Bearer and his lovers down to the very clay they had despised. "May you and your generation live beneath the rocks of the earth, imprisoned within the waters of Creation. May the eel and the slug be thy sustenance, and may the goat tread upon thy dark kingdom. I bequeath to thee a hundred acres which shall be thy lot and thine own heaven. Man shall not be thy servant, but thou shalt serve his most base desires, thou shalt be the Lord of Murderers and the Drinker of Blood, thou shalt suck the breath from babes and milk blood from the teats of the wet nurse, be honored Lord of Maggots and Pestilence, and crowned King of Plagues and Throat of the Underworld, whereby its water shall cover thee and its mountains hide thee from my sight. Thou art no longer our beloved."

And so, as God spake, it was to the land of Calyx, west of Eden by ten hundred million leagues, to which the Light Bearer was driven, in the caves of man, and there he resides in Colony, so named for the hundred acres which Jehovah decreed when he cast him from the heavens.

And Jehovah said, "Let no man feed the hand of

the Light Bearer who now is named Abaddon, the Angel of the Pit, for thou hast foolishly snuffed thy Light and dwell in the Shadows of Sin and Damnation. For if man or woman so much as give themselves to his desolation, so shall they become as he and be damned from my sight."

Old Man Feely had pretty much memorized this passage from among the thirty pages of the Book of Abaddon. It was his favorite part, in fact, because it reminded him of his sacred obligation. Even being such a slow reader, he still read the entire book every night, particularly when the kicking became too loud, or when he heard the creatures below the house trying to scramble up from the pit.

He set his bible down. It was enormous, handsewn and bound by his great-grandmother, and printed in his grandfather's hand. He'd been told as a child that the binding had been made from the dried skin of one of the escaped devils.

He was finished with the toilet, and reached over for some Charmin (one of his few modern luxuries, for he could not abide uncleanliness down there.)

The roll was empty, the last roll. There were no rags or newspapers lying nearby.

"Father forgive me," he prayed, and tore one of the sheets from the Book of Abaddon out, putting it to a new, and less than dignified use.

8.

After leaving the bathroom, he went and checked the crosses.

There were thirteen of them, representing the Angel

of the Pit's place at the table, the Uninvited Guest at the Last Supper in the disguise of Judas. Some were old wooden crosses of his grandparents' generation. Others were newer, stolen from certain churches, all consecrated by priests and preachers. Although he had never seen the angel with his own two eyes, his father had told about how his uncle, an unbeliever, had once removed the last cross and had let out the angel until his father was able to put it back in its place of torment.

The gas lamps, too, were lit. The garlands of flowers and the profane blood of the innocent lamb dressed the marble slab altar across the threshold. The dried goat's foot hung suspended above the altar, and the water in the bowl rocked gently, for the creature in one of its guises was kicking at the floor.

He did not hear the sound of glass breaking at the window in the front room.

9.

Byron Cheever sliced his arm raw, but crept in through the window, all the while listening for the old man. He wiped his arm on his shirt and plucked two small shards of glass from his wrist. He did not bother to stop up the wound; it would bleed profusely, but he had more important work here, the work of the greatest of beings to attend to.

The house was feebly lit, but his eyes no longer needed brightness. He saw the spider as it lurked in the shadows, and even the shade was light.

He followed the scent of the old man until he came to the room at the bottom of the stairs.

He opened the door and saw the old man, one hand clutching a bible, the other a shotgun.

"Sinner," Old Man Feely said, "you ain't here on the Lord's business, I know that just by looking at you."

"Oh." Byron shivered with the overpowering stink of the old man, the smell of sweat from dilated pores, the perfume of blood and flesh. He felt something like an orgasm but without his dick, just that feeling that started at the base of his spine and shot up to the base of his skull, full with pleasure. "Oh, I am here for *you.*"

Old Man Feely hefted the shotgun up, eye level. "I can take that pretty look off your face right now. You been listenin' to the wrong side of the cow's tit, boy. Just back out real slow from here right now, right up those stairs. Or I'm gonna have to send you on to your Maker."

"Can't you hear them?" Byron asked. "Can't you hear them? Their sweet songs. All the children, all there"—he pointed to the baseboards—"buried too soon, too soon. But you can't hear them, can you? You have defiled yourself, Old Man." Byron Cheever grinned. "How much you want to bet, Old Man, that I can get you before you get me? You're ancient, you have no muscle tone. Perhaps ten years ago, you might've had the strength to resist. But now? Now, when your bones ache and your heart is sore tired. Who will win this battle, Old Man? You?"

Old Man Feely shook his head. "Meet your Maker, boy."

Then, he let Byron Cheever have it with both barrels.

10.

But Byron was faster. He had such power in him now, drawn so quickly back from the crossroads. It was as if some of the strength of the dead had infused his bloodstream. He dropped to the floor and crawled forward, as the shot whizzed over his head.

11.

Old Man Feely, known as John to some, Johannes to his mother, thought for a second that he'd hit the boy. Then he thought the boy was the devil himself, transformed into a snake at his feet, for he saw a blurry slithering form move faster than he had known a human being to move.

And then, the boy with the blood on his arm was upon him.

12.

Byron felt like a jaguar. He tore into the old man til there was no more struggle in him. He dropped the body, then turned towards the small closet door. He knocked the crucifixes off of it and wiped at the ones drawn crudely in chalk on the walls. He kicked the candles over. He barely noticed the heavy red drapes catching fire. He barely noticed anything save the sensation of pleasure that washed over him.

He flung the door open and let the dark light which was within the stone cave beneath the house draw across his hand. He followed the light downward, through the tunnel; the rest of it drifted smokily upwards.

The dark light covered the burgeoning fire, and soon the fire had stopped.

He felt the others down there as he clung to the damp walls, knocking down the crosses put there, snuffing the candles with his fingers.

Finally, he reached the round and wet bottom of the man-made cave.

The others moved, brushing by him, reading his flesh with their fingers, understanding him with dry tongues wiped across his neck and ear.

Byron, they whispered.

Their touch felt delicious to him. He felt an electric current run smoothly down his spine, through his testicles, up his chest, along his lips.

And then, he saw the angel.

At first, he thought he saw something that looked like a large insect, with a mosquito proboscislike tube beneath its multiple eyes. Then, it was more like a lizard with white skin and empty eye sockets. Then, it was a child. *Vision is a faulty sense, Byron,* the voice in his head said, *it leads us to believe that what cannot be seen by mortal eyes does not exist. You can only see what your mind can handle without being pushed too far. What you see is the most beautiful creature in all of creation.*

He saw the creature more clearly: a child with razor eyes that flashed with radiance. He was lashed with chains and crosses to two great stones. The dark light hovered across his face.

The child was Byron himself, the year he molested his brother.

The dark light painted a dim brilliance on the face. The razor eyes gleamed.

Byron dropped to his knees. "Oh, most beloved, I worship you."

The child reached out his hand, its shackles pulling at the stone. As it's skin met Byron's, he felt as if something within him was fighting to be born, fighting to burst through his skin, trying to burst his bones and flesh and blood outward in a spray of red.

He heard the sound of wet splitting, and where the child touched him, a bone broke through the surface of his flesh.

The child's mouth went eagerly to the bone and Byron, shivering and feeling cold, watched while he sucked at the bone of his forearm as if it were sugar cane.

But it didn't hurt, not then, oh, no, it felt different, but it did not hurt.

He shivered.

And shivered.

The shivering became exquisite.

The others, in the dark light, pressed their faces against his skin.

13.

The sheriff's office had been typically quiet, until Cathy Zane made a bat-squeak noise, which woke Dale up—he hadn't planned on sleeping, but had just naturally drifted off just before three and had been asleep for only a few minutes.

"Cathy?" he asked. He stood up, pushing his chair back. He went around the desk to his office door. He looked through the venetian blinds that afforded him some privacy at work. Cathy looked pretty much as she always did: bored.

She was sitting at the dispatch radio desk just staring at the machine.

He opened the door. "Everything running smooth?"

She didn't look up at him at first, but when she did, he thought there was a tear in her eye.

"They found a girl."

"You mean the Hoskins boy?"

"A little girl."

"Cathy? What's going on?"

"Dale, 'member back when we were in school, how those kids were playing out at the Feely place, and that girl fell down the old well?"

"Something 'bout it. It was Ginger Glass's little sister, wasn't it?"

Cathy said, her voice cracking, "Jud, he found her. Same as if she just fell down that well yesterday. Only . . ."

"What the hell—that's the most cockamamie—"

Cathy Zane said, "Jud found her, all bruised, all sliced up as if a wild animal had scraped the skin off her back. Bleeding all over, he said."

"This I don't believe. It's got to be some other girl."

"She was on her parents' front porch. Scraping at the door to come in."

Dale shook his head. He wasn't buying it. Maybe he was still dreaming, asleep at his desk. He went over and put his hand gently on Cathy's shoulder.

Her face had gone completely white. "They took her to Dr. Cobb's. I guess she's going over the hills to Stone Valley Medical next. She'll probably die." Then, she looked at him directly. "How could that be? How could a little girl from over twenty years ago still be a little girl? It ain't right, Dale, it ain't natural."

10

JOE SLEEPWALKS
& PATTY GLASS BLEEDS

1.

Joe was in the laundry room when he awoke.

He was disoriented, standing over the washing machine, looking down into its depths. The light was on. His mother's laundry was slumped on shelves and lay across the floor like debris from an explosion. She was an unrepentant slob, though he sort of admired her for that.

Joe didn't know why he was in the laundry room. He thought for a second that he'd been doing a wash or something, had suffered a spontaneous narcoleptic blackout. Then, he realized that not only was he in his mother's house, but that it was probably three in the morning, and moreover, he had been sleep-walking.

A voice behind him made him jump.

He turned around, leaning on the washing machine. "Aaron? What are you doing up so late, you scamp?"

Aaron stood there in his Jockey briefs, his legs and torso all skinny and birdlike, his dark hair all mussed, the sand of sleep at the corners of his eyes. "Daddy? I heard a noise."

"What kind of noise?"

"A noise like you bumping into things. I came out and saw you going by the stairs. I got scared. I called you, but you didn't hear me. It scared me. You kept talking and shaking your hand. You walked real fast down the stairs. You were mad. You were talking real bad things."

"How bad?"

Aaron rolled his eyes, "Real bad, Dad, trust me. You okay?"

Joe shrugged; nodded. "I guess. It's nothing to be scared of. People sleepwalk sometimes."

"You did it before?"

"I don't know. Maybe I have. Maybe this is the first time I've ever been caught. Hey," he said dropping his voice to a whisper, "let's go see what Gramma has in her freezer, okay? I bet she's got ice cream."

"Something I don't understand," Aaron said.

"What's that?"

"I thought you said Gramma rhymes with rich."

"Well, maybe, just maybe I was wrong. That happens sometimes," Joe said, and put his arm around his son's shoulder as they went out of the laundry room and walked across the hall to the kitchen.

They each had a scoop of Tin Roof Sundae ice

cream, and as they went upstairs to bed, Aaron whispered to him, "Promise me not to act like that again, Dad. I don't think my ticker can take it."

2.

After he put his son to bed again and checked in on Hillary, sound asleep in the old crib—Joe's old crib, in fact, something which he hadn't even realized his mother had saved—Joe returned downstairs to the kitchen.

He opened the freezer door. There was the faithful bottle of vodka, a family tradition with the Gardners since at least 1966. He had never enjoyed his mother's excessive bouts with the bottle, but at that moment, he was happy that she always kept something on hand for life's little emergencies. He took the bottle to the counter and brought down a highball glass. He filled it three quarters full. Added some ice. Hunted down some Martini & Rossi vermouth and dripped a bit into his glass. He stood there, looking out at the darkness, and took a healthy sip.

Don't need an olive.

He sighed as the liquor crept down his throat. *"Went down smooth," as my daddy would've said. "Smooth as cherry."* He hadn't had a vodka martini in years. It seemed to take away the conflicting pains that shot around in his head. Something about his mother's house always made him want to drink; it made *her* want to drink, too. He finished the drink, feeling more than slightly buzzed. He had to walk carefully back up the stairs and was happy that he didn't have to drive anywhere anytime soon. He was equally happy that neither of the kids (nor Jenny) could see how Daddy took care of the throbbing in his head.

He crept around to his side of the bed and as he looked at his sleeping wife, she looked like something else. The moonlight through the window was doing something to her face. It frightened him for a second, and reminded him of childhood fears of the dark. How the moonlight transformed ordinary things and loved ones.

But it was just the light and shadows, after all.

He slipped beneath the comforter and pressed his head into the pillow.

Joe fell asleep again. He dreamed some more about Melissa Welles, his first and truest love, and what she said to him, what she whispered in his ear as she bent down over him, with the smell of the grave on her white and shining body, was obscene beyond words.

3.

Across town at the small medical office, Patty Glass lay on the examining table, mute, while Dr. Virgil Cobb, who had just gotten into bed after driving back from Winston's storefront office when he'd been awakened with the emergency, checked her pulse. Patty's father and mother, George and Aileen Glass were sitting in chairs in the corner, both looking as if they might be going into shock. The sheriff's deputy was standing near them, a man who clearly did not believe that this was, indeed, Patty Glass at all, but some poor damaged girl who looked so much like the missing girl of years back that her parents wanted to believe in her.

Virgil was used to being awakened with emergencies, the births, deaths, and everything in between of a small community, but he had not expected to see Patty Glass as a twelve-year-old girl still breathing.

He was trying to stop the flow of blood from the little girl's cuts, but was having trouble. He knew that Patty Glass seemed to have more blood in her body than a girl her age and size would have.

He was afraid he knew why.

He did not want to believe the evidence of his senses, that the girl on the table had at least eight extra pints in her.

As if her flesh were some kind of storage tank for blood.

UNDERWORLD

Byron Cheever lay face down on the cold wet stones.

He could feel them crawling across his back, their thousand sand-dry tongues lapping at his skin. They'd torn the clothes from his back. He now knew ecstasy.

He had been the one.

Opened the door for them, for the Radiant One, the Light Bearer, the angel.

He tasted salt in the back of his throat and coughed.

They had drawn off the skin of his back with their tongues. They were lapping like kittens, millions of small and tiny kittens, at the blood and meat that he exposed to them willingly.

It was beyond pleasure.

The pain did not begin until their tongues stopped and his nerves began reacting, his muscles going into spasms, in response to their ministrations.

It was only then that Byron regretted his actions.

It was only then that Byron Cheever would wish he had hanged himself when he'd had the chance.

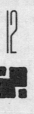

THE RETURN OF HOPFROG

1.

Homer Petersen didn't know what time it was, but it was late. He was up reading, taking the occasional swig from the Jack Daniel's bottle by his side, and scribbling in his notebooks. He wasn't exactly a polished writer; his notebook was barely decipherable even to him. In fact, he wasn't a writer at all and didn't pretend to be one. After an aborted attempt at college, he had been trained in carpentry by his father who had grown weary of his son's promises to strike out on his own. He had begun scribbling in his books with the optimistic thought that one day all the reading and thinking he'd done on the past would add up to something, some key for him, some way of understanding this small corner of the universe.

He sat at the desk in his downstairs study. Leaning back in the wheelchair, he caught his reflection in the front window. Round glasses, his yellow-blond hair scruffy and badly in need of a cut, his lips thin and tight, his jaw set tensely. He needed another drink. After he'd put his son to bed, he decided that one drink wouldn't be bad. Becky still persecuted him about his drinking, now that she had gone AA whole hog. Tad mentioned it, too, sometimes, but Homer could not relieve tension any other way. He'd already consumed half a bottle.

He looked at the glass filled with the brown liquid. *"A man works up a mighty thirst,"* his father used to say. *"Women, they don't understand what we go through, boy, about the pain and struggle of being a man."* Homer saw his father in the reflection, too, and realized that this was how he remembered his father: in his thirties, drinking hard liquor and bemoaning his fate.

He pushed the glass away. "I'm drunk enough," he said, feeling incredibly coherent for someone who had put away that much whiskey.

He rubbed his eyes and glanced down at the book. *Aliens in Our Midst,* by P. Courtney Seagrove. The book sucked, as did most books on this subject, and Homer flipped through the rest of the pages which he had not already highlighted, but found nothing of interest.

And then he heard creaking on the floorboards behind him, near the door.

He saw, in the window, the reflection of himself as a

little boy, standing in the doorway to the study. After a second, he realized it was Tad.

He wheeled his chair around. "Tad, what are you doing up?"

"I had a bad dream," he said. He rubbed his eyes and padded across the floor. He stepped around his father, glancing across his desk. "You read too much, Dad."

"I suppose."

"You drink too much, too."

Homer laughed. He was trying to hide his drunkenness. "You're right," he said. This was something his own father would never have said. (Something within him almost wanted to lie to Tad and tell him that it was okay to drink because it relieved the pain of being a man, but Homer knew his son was a little too smart to let that one get by him.)

"Why do people drink bad stuff?" Tad asked. He was too damned innocent. Homer wished he could keep Tad at this point, bonsai him to never grow up, to never have to experience bad things—even though the divorce had been a doozy, even though Tad sometimes tried to manipulate things between Homer and Becky just to get his way.

"I guess it may be that everyone is weak sometimes."

"Are you weak, too?"

"Sometimes."

Tad seemed to accept this without question. "I'm weak sometimes, too," he said.

"Like when?"

"Well . . ." Tad hung his head, as if with shame. "You're not gonna like it."

"What happened?"

"It happened when I guess I was having a nightmare."

"And?"

Tad looked his father in the eyes; there were tears along his small pebble eyes. "I had an accident."

"Oh"—Homer slapped the air in front of him—"we all have accidents."

"It was when she looked at me," Tad said, "the girl in my nightmare."

2.

Homer had adapted over the years to what he referred to as The Chair. It was not mechanized. He not only could not afford the kind of insurance that would've covered that, but he did not want it, for he preferred to think of himself as self-reliant. He had built up his upper body over the years so that when he climbed down from the chair in his son's room, he could sit in the regular chair by the bed and pull the sheet off, wad it up and toss it into the hamper, help Tad blot up the stain on the mattress pad before removing it, too.

"Someday," Homer said, "you'll stop wetting the bed, Tad. I used to wet the bed when I was your age, and Grandpa did, too, and his father before him. You come from a long line of bed wetters."

"That's good to know," Tad said, an almost perfect imitation of the way his mother would speak. "I just wish it would stop now."

"How often does it happen?"

Tad shrugged, "About every other week. I try not to drink any water or anything before bedtime, but it's like I store it up and don't know it. Can that happen?"

Homer grinned. "Anything can happen."

"When I get scared in a dream, it happens."

"But it's only a dream."

"Yeah, I know. But they seem real sometimes. Like when I opened my eyes, I saw the lady."

"There's a funny word for that, it's called hypnogogia. Don't even try to say it. It took me years. But it's when you're half awake and half asleep and sometimes your dream carries over." Hopfrog tossed the fresh sheet to his son, who began tucking it in. "So, when you saw this lady in your dream, a picture of her stayed in your head even when you were just waking up. Sort of like when a flashbulb goes off in your face. You see it later on, only it's not there."

Tad huffed. "You're treating me like a little kid. Of course, I know all about that kind of stuff. You're not the only one in the family who reads." He tucked the bottom sheet in haphazardly, then threw the quilt across it. "Hey Dad."

"Hey what?"

"If the lady was only in my dream, then how the heck did that happen?" Tad pointed to the window.

The orange-yellow glow of his lamp illuminated fingerprints across the glass. Not a small child's either. Homer maneuvered back into The Chair and moved over to look at the windowpane. He wiped at it with a Kleenex, but the fingerprints remained. "Is this some kind of trick you're playing on your old man?"

"Uh uh. I didn't do it."

And then, Homer noticed the bits of dirt, and perhaps even the dark berry stain of blood in the prints.

Someone had written with their filthy fingers on the glass:

HOPFROG

And beneath this:

Why

Homer looked at the scrawl. It was familiar, but his brain was taking a roundabout route towards comprehension. It finally dawned on him, and it seemed less unnatural than he had imagined.

Tad said, "So, did I dream that?"

His father said, "Not unless I did, too. You sure you're not just playing some trick on your dad?"

Tad sighed.

"I know you wouldn't do that. I wonder how this got here?"

"Well," Tad said, "if the lady from my dreams did it, she wasn't scary or nothing. She seemed really nice. It was all the other stuff that was scary in my dreams. The stuff about you."

Homer turned to his son, feeling a cold chill, and the small hairs on the back of his neck seemed to tickle. He felt his face go warm even while the rest of him remained cold. "What stuff?"

"Well, it's what really really scared me," Tad said. "But you're gonna get angry if I tell you."

As if hearing someone else speaking through his mouth while he was removed to a small portion of his own body, Homer Petersen said, "I promise I won't."

"Okay," Tad said, but couldn't look his father in the

eye. He glanced down at the quilt instead. "It was you and some other guy coming after me and there wasn't anywhere to run to. And you say to the other guy, 'he's one of them, he's one of them,' and I kept calling you so you'd know it was me, because you were acting all strange. You had something in your hand, a knife maybe, and you held it like this"—Tad held his arm in front of him as if he were about to cut an invisible person's throat—"and just when I thought you were gonna do it, she showed up. The lady. She's maybe in high school, and real pretty. And that's when I woke up, and I saw her for a second at the window. Whoever wrote that there was looking for you. You used to be called Hopfrog, Dad."

His father wheeled his chair over to Tad. When he was beside him, he placed his hands on his son's shoulders. "Tad, I'm not angry. I know you wrote this word on the window."

Tad drew back. "I did not. I told you, it was the lady from my dream." Tad seemed fairly calm. "She didn't scare me or anything. She may be my guardian angel for all I know."

Homer was shivering. He couldn't hide his fear from his son. *I'm drunk,* he figured, *I'm drunk and my son is telling me something that might sober another man up very quickly, but not old Hopfrog. Not me. I am jumping in my skin.* He continued to shiver even after he'd gotten Tad to settle down to sleep again (and how could that boy sleep after seeing that blood and dirt-stained finger painting on the window? How could a boy who had not even hit puberty have more nerves of steel than a man of thirty-six?); only another sip of whiskey slowed the shivering, and he just about polished off the rest of that bottle of Jack Daniel's down in his study. Homer rifled through his notebook. *Where were they? Where were those damned pictures?* He found them, tucked into an envelope in one of the more tattered notebooks, bound up with two rubber bands. His hands shook as he opened the envelope.

The pictures of her.

Melissa Welles.

A girl as bright and lovely as any which had existed. Shoulder-length hair, a sunny complexion, eyes that sparkled with some wicked delight. He could practically hear her: "No, Hopfrog," as he tried to kiss her that time, behind the bleachers at the football game, and then, when he hadn't taken "no" for an answer, she said it again, and pushed away from him. She had said to him, all fire, "You're supposed to be his best friend. I love him, Hop, that's not going to change for me."

And he, at eighteen, all hormones and confidence and looks and killer cool *(and legs—remember those? How they moved beneath you, how they carried you where you needed to go?)*, had responded, "I have always loved you, Melissa. Ever since the second grade."

It had come out like that, quick, a gentle breeze of unrequited love, and then it had dissipated in the frosty winter air.

She said, almost cruelly, "Don't even. I love Joe and that's all there is to it. Hopfrog, I am going to tell you something about yourself that you don't even seem to be aware of. You think that because you're handsome and wild and hip, that you can have anything you want. Well, let me tell you, there's one thing you're lacking, the one thing that you're going to have to spend the rest of your life trying to get and that's emotional depth."

At the time (*what did I know? I was eighteen and hot*) he laughed at this.

She said, "Laugh if you want. But it's something Joe has, and when your looks dry up and your ego crawls under a rock, Joe will still have it, and more. The only reason that I'm your friend at this point in life is because you are best friends with the man I am engaged to marry. You have been trying to use me to put a notch on your bedpost for at least three years. It will never happen, Hop. Never. Maybe if you'd stop betraying friends, you'd have a few left. Let's at least pretend we get along for Joe's sake."

She had seemed all venom then. Looking back, now, he knew it had been himself who had been the snake, trying to hit on his best friend's girl, trying to get her in the sack. The worst thing was that he did love her, damn it. He loved her above everything and everyone else; he just didn't know what that meant. He thought you could simply tell a girl you loved her, and then you got her, because you were Hopfrog Petersen. Joe Gardner, now he would've had a hard time getting girls. He was no prince, just an ordinary joe, still Baconhead to Hopfrog, a guy who would always take a backseat to other guys. (He remembered his thinking back then, that life was completely Darwinian, that the survival of the fittest meant that guys like Hopfrog got everything, and guys like Joe got whatever was left over. He wished he could go back and kick that old Hopfrog before the inevitable tragedy would occur, but *what could you do with the past? Unless you had a time machine, you were stuck in the here and now gazing with futility upon the roads less taken, the narrowminded path of least resistance, the way of all stupid teenagers who think they know everything.*)

As usual, just looking at her picture pressed tears

from his eyes. His head felt like it was melting down. He covered his face with his hands. He took a deep breath. It was the whiskey, that was all. He wiped his eyes dry. He set the pictures down one by one. He had used his uncle's old Polaroid Swinger camera to take them. Melissa at fifteen on the cheerleading squad, Melissa riding a horse over on the House Mountain trail, Melissa giving him a dirty look while she sneaked a cigarette behind the cafeteria. And then, that day, Melissa and Joe standing beside the Volkswagen, looking more in love than he had ever seen any two people be. A golden moment, plucked out of time.

"Forgive me," he said to the picture.

3.

He knew what the "why" meant on the window. At least he thought he knew.

The why was a question from the dead.

The why really should've been: "Why did you do it?"

Or, more specifically:

"Why did you kill me?"

4.

The books on his desk: *The History of Paramount County, The Sightings, Aliens in Our Midst, Vampires Among Us, The Paranormal, Popular Delusions of the Twentieth Century, Depression and Its Effect on Family, Folklore of the South.*

These, and other similarly titled books, had been his extracurricular reading for the past decade or so. On the walls of his study: photographs from childhood, his and Tad's and his father's, too, as if childhood were the only thing worth remembering.

In the book, *Folklore of the South*, he had marked page 173.

On that page, it was written:

Another story from the Night of Falling Stars, usually occurring on or about August twelfth, comes from the mountains of West Virginia. In the mid-seventeen hundreds, when a few dozen Mennonites settled on what was then part of the wilderness of the Virginia Colony, it was reported that God, in his wrath, tore the heavens apart and "cast the torches of the firmament down upon the earth," for there was popularly believed to be a war in heaven at the moment. One William Eaton wrote that a ragged band of angels was seen atop the mountains afterwards, and that the Godless Scots-Irish of the area took to hunting the last of the angels the way one might hunt deer. "The mother who suckled her babe was given to much lamentation at this, for if the Scots trapped God's own angels, what was to become of mankind?"

On page 42 of the book titled *Depression and Its Effect on Family*:

It is not uncommon for the person who intends to commit suicide to take with them those they are either most angry at, or feel the most love for, since love and hate, far from being contrary emotions, are, essentially, the same emotion. There are many cases of men who murder their wives and children, sometimes even the pet dog, before turning their weapons upon themselves; perhaps this is a way to stave off loneliness in whatever afterlife they imagine for themselves. More likely, given a depressed and irrational state of mind, it is because these men believe that whatever they look upon is owned by them, and so, by eliminating these others, they are ensuring that no one else will have them.

On page 133 of the book called *Aliens in Our Midst:*

A man named Fredericks who claims to have been abducted in 1982, has this to say about his captors. "They did not at first come to me in their real forms, but as familiar faces so as not to frighten me, I assume, although this certainly backfired, since the fact that I saw my long dead father was more terrifying than an alien could ever be. They showed me many things, most of which I have forgotten through some sort of induced-amnesia, but one thing stuck out in my mind, and that was that these beings did not think of our planet as any threat to their survival, but as a wastebasket of the cosmos, a place which had been used as both penal colony and trash heap since before the dawn of the human era."

Hopfrog fell asleep that night, again downstairs, in his study, the photos of his youth in his lap, his much-highlighted books as pillow.

In his hand, which rested upon the desk, a small rock, a chip from some ancient lava, shiny and rough.

5.

Usually the booze obliterated the dream, but sometimes it heightened it. It wasn't really a dream, anyway, not in the strictest sense, for it never changed. It came to him, first, like a long-forgotten odor, an odor of youth, sweat, champagne, the choking dust of an old car engine as it coughed to life.

He was driving the Volkswagen across the Paramount Bridge. He could watch himself from above, as if he were God. He could see right through the top of the VW, all of them, Hopfrog, Melissa, and Joe, squeezed into that tiny car; the rain coming down across the windshield; the truck, an enormous Kenmore that took up the entire bridge, bearing down upon them.

And the light in the sky, as if an explosion had already happened even before the truck hit them.

And Hopfrog's hand, tight in a fist on the stick shift, a ball of power on the shift.

Knowing that he could put the VW in reverse.

Knowing that he could get them off the bridge and to the side of the road, to safety, in a split second.

And in his head, like a worm in a rotten apple, the thought (heard aloud in the dream, for in the dream Hopfrog was God):

"I want to die. I want them to go, too. With me. Life is shit. Life is meaningless. Nothing will ever be the same. If I can't have her, well, neither can Joe. Why should they be so happy when life is so shitty?"

He didn't remember the words coming so quickly and lucidly, but he knew that those had been his thoughts.

The accident had taken forever, but if you were God, looking down upon the truck as it smashed into the Volkswagen, you would not cry at this scene, but laugh at the shortsightedness of children who think that death is the answer to the problems of existence. You would watch, detached, as the smaller car went through the rail of the bridge, over the edge, dangling for a moment before plunging into the water.

And being God, and a vengeful one, you decide that the teenager who made this decision would suffer until the end of his days for this foolish act. He will lose his legs, you decide, and the girl he loves, and then maybe you'll figure out a way for him to lose his best friend, too.

But that won't be the worst thing in God's plan . . . *But hell, Hop, you don't believe in God anymore, do you? Except as maybe some cosmic court jester, ringing his bells and giggling maniacally over creation. You believe in the idiot universe, don't you? You believe that we're all in the dark and nothing means anything—and there's only one thing that disturbs that deeply held belief in nonbelief—*

And it's what happened after.

The worst thing.

The thing that keeps you drinking at night and pathetic by daylight. The thing that keeps you reading quack books about devils and angels and aliens and vampires and werewolves, the thing that keeps you shivering when you see your old nickname scrawled across your son's window in dirty fingerprints.

The memory of another moment.

When you saw Melissa Welles alive, her face raw, her shredded lips pressed against the neck of the Fulchers' six-week-old baby, drinking as if it were the sweetest juice, making the piglike noises that only the very thirsty can make—*you work up a mighty powerful thirst after a car wreck, heh-heh*—on a moonlit night, three months after her funeral.

The baby's sour breath in the air, and the brown stench, as Melissa grins, her teeth, berry-stained and shiny.

13

A DAY LIKE NO OTHER

1.

Morning comes up slow in Colony in the autumn; slow and dark and then not dark at all—an easy birth. The sun was very much like the sun in other parts of the country, save for the fact that House Mountain and the Malabar Hills tended to keep the shade going to the west of town until nearly eight o'clock. On River Road there are a few joggers, fewer this year than in years previous, and several strollers, too, inhaling the deep aromatic chill of the Paramount River before going home to shower and change into their work clothes. The Colony Furniture Company, with half its employees since the layoffs in '91, has been operating since six-fifteen in the November dark. The woods echo a gunshot, for a hunter is after his family's supper. Machinery turns. Objects come alive: the grind and groan of wood and steel and stone and flesh that is town, all its disparate parts, somehow begin working together again after a long night off. The garbage trucks go first, lumbering down the narrow streets, and then the school buses, yellow and dreaded, with black exhaust coughing behind them as they travel neck and neck with the egg man's long, rugged van and the pale milk truck. The early commuters drive their old beat-up VWs and Chevys over to Stone Valley, or cross the state line into Virginia to work in Westfield. They will spend their hours in labor and thought, and when they return, it will be dark again.

Fourteen people did not show up for work at the Colony Furniture Company. Their spouses did not call in sick on their behalf. But then, absenteeism at the factory was at an all-time high since the layoffs; too many employees were taking sick days to head over the hills to find more secure work. Andrew Cross, the foreman at the factory, put the absent workers' names on a list and determined that he would make an example of them to the other workers so as not to allow morale to slip further.

But things had happened in the dark, before the sun had vanquished the shadows.

The landscape had subtly changed.

Romeo Dancer did not return to the trailer which he shared with his wife. She knew he had been out with that Wilmot woman from Westfield, drinking and carousing. Still, this was the first time that Romeo had not returned from such a night. His wife was actually worried that her man had met a bad end.

Tenley McWhorter, who had snuck into her bedroom window at two A.M. the night before, after being out with her boyfriend, Noah Cristman, slept late. When she eventually woke up, she was surprised that her parents, who were strict fundamentalists, had not gotten her up for school or yelled at her. She wandered around their small house, calling for them, but they were not home. She followed a strange and rotten smell into the fruit cellar, but when she got to the bottom step, she thought she heard someone there, in the dark.

She was afraid to take a step forward or back.

Tenley McWhorter, who had only recently turned sixteen, stood there for almost twenty minutes, terrified, as if she were only six. When she'd worked up her courage, she turned and ran up the cellar steps. After shutting the door behind her, she locked it. She had not seen anything, but the stench had become overpowering, and she was afraid, after having watched the *Scarecrows* movie the night before, that something like those evil scarecrows were in that cellar.

Athena Cobb awoke with a slight headache and turned over in bed, rubbing her friend, Melanie Dahlgren on the shoulders. Melanie's skin was aged-wrinkled, but felt right to the touch. "I need to go open shop," Athena said.

Melanie smiled, and said, "Not while we have an extra fifteen minutes," and then leaned forward to kiss Athena.

* * *

Gary Welles never slept, so waking was never an issue with him. He dried out overnight. He'd lain down in the azaleas that bordered the Miner's Lodge parking lot. He'd spent the night staring at the stars and sometimes watching people go by. He knew that it was only a matter of time until it happened again, how his daughter had been mutilated by that boy, and sure enough if he hadn't seen that boy back on Main Street again. Other people didn't recognize that Gardner bastard, but Gary knew him by his weasel eyes. Gary Welles knew that he was coming back to do bad things again and he had to be stopped. *Had to be.*

Gary had pretty much replaced the last town drunk, Ernie Craven, when Ernie had gone straight and married an ox of a woman over in Bluefield. Gary begged most of the time, and then his old friends who remembered him when kept him in sandwiches and beer; but he knew it was the Almighty carrying him through. He had a reason to carry on: vengeance on what that boy had done to his daughter.

It was not enough that Joe Gardner ran off and killed his daughter (no matter how many people called it an accident).

It was what Joe did to her after she was dead.

Gary had a gun, though, and he was going to use it. Use it on Joe Gardner, and now he was back.

Gary brushed the dirt from his heavy coat as he got up from the bushes. He crowed at the freezing morning air, his breath hanging in a mist as if a breath of fire.

Gary kept very little to himself these days, and so when Don Hoover asked him, in passing, what he was up to that day, Gary replied, "Gonna get me the boy who ruined my little girl."

* * *

Virgil Cobb awoke in his bed. After being up most of the night trying to tend to Patty Glass, he wanted to sleep extremely late, but his habit of rising before nine could not easily be broken. He sat up suddenly, feeling a clutching pain in his chest. It was not his heart; he knew that. It was anxiety from the nightmare he'd been having. He'd been dreaming about his brother Eugene, eternally twelve, standing over him, watching him while he slept.

He went to wash, then hurried over to his office, which took up one half of his house. When he found her, still there, still restrained as he had left her (telling her parents that she needed to remain with him overnight to make sure she would not go into shock), he took one of his scalpels and thrust it into the little girl's heart. There was very little blood left in her; he had spent the hour of four A.M. draining most of the blood in her into gallon jugs. Only a very small amount of blood spat out from the slivered wound.

It was then that she began to howl.

Dr. Cobb worked quickly and severed her jugular. Then, using other, more effective tools with spinning and jagged edges, he separated the girl's head from her body.

What he would tell the girl's parents he had no idea.

He spent the rest of the morning cleaning up his examination room.

Then he went to wake up Winston Alden, who had slept in his guest room that night, too terrified to go alone to his own house. Winston, who was lean despite all those years of drinking and smoking and stuffing his face to the point of gluttony, slept in his clothes and was yet unrumpled. He was very much the opposite of Virgil: terrified of his own shadow at times, addicted to horror magazines, and very much a child in an old man's body. Winston, barely awake, said, "I should check on John today." He noticed the blood on Virgil's work shirt. "You've taken care of it, then."

Virgil nodded. "As much as possible."

"Sometimes," Winston said, his voice almost boyish, "sometimes I've wished it never happened. That we never knew about it. What happened to Eugene. John Feely. All of it. Sometimes I wish I could just die in my sleep—that's how I've always wanted to go, Virg. Peaceful, in my sleep. Scatter my ashes to the four winds. All of that. But we won't, will we? Neither one of us. Since that day, we've just been marking time, like chickens in a coop, until the big guy with the ax comes by looking for Sunday dinner."

Virgil patted him on the shoulder. "I'll go with you to John's place."

"No, it's daylight. Nothing's going to happen with the sun up. You know that. You know how It plays by the rules," Winston said, and then did something uncharacteristic. He rose up from a sitting position and gave Virgil a great big hug. "You're my best friend, you know that Virgil." He stepped back and shook his head. "You're shaken up by it, aren't you?"

Virgil attempted a smile. "It hasn't really hit me yet."

"Tonight it will," Winston also smiled, sadly. "Tonight and the next night, and then—who knows? Maybe we'll stop it again. Hah! Two old farts with one foot in the grave, that's a good one."

Virgil had to catch his breath; he saw Winston, for the first time, as an old man. Not just an old man, but a man who had some trouble moving around, whose slacks sagged, whose head sagged a bit, too, as if tired of being held up for so long.

Winston left soon after having a cup of coffee. He

didn't ask about what was in the examination room. He did say to his friend, as he walked out into the crisp day, "I almost wish it had gotten us back then, Virg. I almost wish it had been us so we wouldn't have to live with this all these years. I think Eugene was the lucky one."

Virgil Cobb locked the door after his friend left.

A lone figure sat on Watch Hill, like a sentinel. His face was chalk white, his hair, white, also; he wore torn khakis and topsiders, but had no shirt on, even with the biting cold.

His eyes could be seen from a distance. Circled with darkness, in stark contrast to the chalk of the rest of his skin, they had a pinkish cast to them as if every blood vessel in them had burst.

The skin of his back was not pale like his front. It had a layer of red tattoos, designs of dragons and lightning, carved in excruciating detail along his shoulder blades and down his spine.

He crouched down and watched the town from a distance. When the sun was completely in the sky, he loped towards a mausoleum and rested in its icy stone shadows.

As he closed his eyes, faint with hunger and dizzy with lack of blood, Byron Cheever whispered to no one, "He chose me. He chose me. He chose me."

He began digging with his bare hands at a bulky stone cross that was thrust into the ground at the center of Watch Hill.

Yet, in spite of these developments, people like Nelda Chambers awoke in the morning still believing that the hottest news on the grapevine was that Joe Gardner was back in town. She called Cally Harper after she'd had her day's allotment of leaded coffee and said, "You remember his mother, don't you, Cally? Well, yes, yes, she still lives out on the river, never going out into town anymore, no thank you, but staying inside, as well she should. Leading a good man like Dr. Cobb astray and then breaking his heart. Well, that son of hers, you remember, what happened with him and the Welles girl. You remember him going around town and telling everybody everybody's business, and finally what he did. Yes, that's right. What he did to the girl's body. Oh, lord, wouldn't you know he'd be back? The chickens will come home to roost, won't they?"

After she hung up the phone, Nelda typed a letter on the old Royal typewriter:

You will lose everything you love if you keep this up, you naughty man.

She folded this, and slipped it into an envelope.

She addressed it, sealed the envelope, and set it out in the mailbox for her husband, Dale, to find when he finally came home from wherever the hell he'd been sleeping.

Others awoke, and the town's geometry seemed to expand with the movement of the living.

2.

Homer "Hopfrog" Petersen was up by seven. He'd slept badly, perhaps only three or four hours at the most. He could not remember the nightmares too clearly and was hungover, but this never hindered his performance in other areas. He even managed to get in a workout with his weights before eight A.M. His upper body strength was important to him, for it helped him to be less dependent on the outside world. His son, Tad, was staying over the week in compensation for Thanksgiving weekend, coming up in a few weeks, when Becky would take Tad to her mother's house in Richmond; there had been no custody battle, because Homer pretty much let Becky handle Tad's schedule, and because he still trusted Becky to be fair in just about everything.

While he still had his morning privacy, Homer tried to do his leg exercises. He stared at his knees and concentrated. Closed his eyes.

Give me strength, he thought. *Give me my legs back. I demand that my legs shall move.*

He thought this for several minutes; his head finally ached from the effort.

"It's never going to happen," he whispered, mostly to himself.

He went and got ready for his teaching job. He had never finished college, but because of his carpentry work, he had finagled a gig teaching woodshop at the junior high six years before when the carpentry work had dwindled. It was something to do. It paid the bills (barely) and got him out of the house on hungover November days like this one.

He went around to the back, along the paved drive, to his car.

On the way, he saw the footprints in the dirt.

He saw something, caught on the bare branch of one of the azaleas, as if someone had brushed up against it, in a hurry, and had torn part of her dress.

3.

Hopfrog's son Tad was on the bus to Colony Elementary before eight. He had a lunch box in one hand and two books in the other. He was fairly independent for his age and was used to rising early, making his lunch of peanut butter sandwich, banana, and Twinkies by himself. By eight o'clock, he was in his classroom and his teacher, Mrs. Wilkes, was taking roll. By nine o'clock, he had already given his book report on an old book from his father's library that he loved called *Neverland.* "It's not about Peter Pan or anything like that. It's about this bad kid named Sumter who has this shack he plays in with his cousin. And then he starts making really bad things happen, until the whole island he's on becomes this scary place. And it's really neat, because his teddy bear ends up tearing up his father."

Mrs. Wilkes said, "My goodness, Tad, what kind of book is that for you to be reading?"

"The kind I like," Tad said matter-of-factly, and then went and sat back down at his desk.

Mrs. Wilkes looked at him, and he knew that she was probably going to call his mother to check to see that he was reading the right kinds of books. It was something Mrs. Wilkes seemed to do a lot of. When the class had to write a short story and read it aloud for Halloween just two days before, he had written one where blood ran in the streets and dragons attacked from the river.

He had gotten a note home for that one.

He waited out the school day, as if it were a prison sentence. Elvis and Hank Bonchance sent a note to him which read:

gunna get u weenie.

He couldn't wait to get back home and do stuff with his father.

4.

Tad's mother, Becky O'Keefe was still sound asleep. She had gotten off her shift at two and had fallen asleep at home before three, but something at four in the morning had woken her up.

She looked out her bedroom window, but could only see the maple trees outside, their bare branches bending in a wind. Just as she was about to fall asleep again, she thought she heard something in the room itself. She switched her bedside lamp on. The room was bathed in a warm golden glow from the light. The pictures on the wall of Tad, from infancy onward, seemed to have been rattled, as if there'd been an earthquake (and surprisingly, several years back, there had been a mild earthquake in West Virginia, so she thought this might again be the case). She called to her spaniel, Whitney, which slept in Tad's room, even if Tad was off on one of his overnights. The dog didn't come running up, as was usual.

Disturbed, a little frightened, she reached for the pistol from the drawer of the bedside table. Taking it in hand, she grabbed her robe from the end of the bed, threw it on, and walked out into the hallway.

For just a second, she thought she saw a ghost, standing at the bottom of the stairs.

But the stairs were dark, so how could she have seen it?

She flicked on the light.

When she saw the spaniel's body, what had been done to it, she screamed and ran down the stairs.

It was freezing. The door to her house was open, and there were small muddy footprints leading from the dog to the doorway.

The bare footprints of a child.

5.

Joe Gardner didn't rise until almost eleven. The phone was ringing, and he covered his ears at first and tried to go back to sleep. But it was not to be. The telephone had an old-fashioned ringer, and its bell sounded eight times before someone picked it up. He opened his eyes. A trace of cold had slipped beneath the windowsill and made him want to snuggle with the comforter awhile longer.

But a full bladder got him up, standing, wiping sleep from his eyes.

His head was throbbing, a condition he didn't understand until he remembered the enormous vodka martini of three A.M. or so. He clutched his head and pressed his thumb into his forehead. The sun, so flat and brilliant as only encroaching winter sun could be, flashed across the window. Jenny was already up; he heard her downstairs talking with his mother (a horrifying thought), and there was the clatter of dishes.

He went to the bathroom to do the three s's: the first two being shower and shave. Afterwards, he pulled on jeans and a blue cambray work shirt; topped it with a gray wool sweater; jogged down the stairs, feeling better since the shower. Only traces of an ache in his head.

Jenny said, first thing, "You smelled like vodka."

He acknowledged this with a kiss on her lips. "All gone now, though. Found the Scope in your overnight bag." Jenny smelled fresh; baby powder and his mother's spice hand soap. Her hair, blond and recently chopped, smelled something like his mother, too. He wasn't sure if he liked it, but it didn't seem as terrible a thing as he'd feared.

His wife wrinkled her nose up. "I still detect liquor." She never liked him to have a drink. He knew it, her fear about writers and alcohol; it was a fine and destructive tradition, often taking with it the most wonderful as well as the most mediocre of literary talents.

"It was purely medicinal," he said, making a feeble joke.

Changing the subject, she said, "That was Homer calling a little while ago."

"Homer?" Joe had to think about that name; it sounded familiar, but he couldn't place it. Suddenly, a face dredged up through his memory: a handsome boy with strawberry blond hair and an absurdly winning smile. "Oh, Hopfrog!" And then, another memory: the last time he and Hopfrog had broken bread together.

What Hopfrog had said to him.

6.

"You've been more a brother than any brother," Hopfrog, nineteen, had said. "But this is driving me nuts. I can't sleep. I barely touch my food. I want to be happy in this life, Joe, and if I start thinking about this, all this . . . this . . . well, craziness you're talking . . ."

"But," Joe interrupted, "you saw it. You were with me. Remember? You saw it, for god sakes."

Hopfrog had closed his eyes then. "Joe. I don't know

that I saw anything. Maybe I did and maybe I didn't. You never heard of mass hysteria?"

"Yeah," Joe said sullenly, *"it's when you laugh in church. You saw what I saw Hopfrog. You helped me do that to her. Jesus, Hop. And for some reason, something got into me from it. Like a disease. But you know it, too, don't lie to me. You know it."*

Hopfrog opened his eyes, and looked at Joe as if Joe were an escaped mental patient, then. "I think you need help, Joe. That's all I can say. If you believe in all that crap, you need a good doctor and a good long rest. I think maybe you've cracked."

7.

"Hopfrog," Joe said to Jenny, "Jesus, they all come out of the woodwork."

"What?" she whispered affectionately so Anna, in the kitchen, couldn't hear, "you managed to alienate everybody in your hometown in only nineteen years of life?" She pinched his behind playfully.

"Apparently," he shook his head, laughing, "what the hell? It's old home week. Can't fight city hall." He was going to try to take a lighter view of things, he decided. The town was not that dreadful, nor was it peopled by monsters.

Jenny reached up and combed his hair neatly with her finger; what they called between them, "basic gorilla grooming." She took him by the hand, and they walked towards the kitchen. "He said he heard you were in town from the way everybody was looking like a bomb had hit. He was very funny on the phone. He told me they used to call you Baconhead."

"Oh, no," Joe had to laugh, "not that one. Just because in eighth grade, when my hormones struck, my hair got really greasy. I had to wash it three times a day. Well, better Baconhead than Hopfrog."

"Well, we're all going to catch up tonight at supper. At the Angel Wing at six-fifteen." She led the way into the kitchen. The sunlight through the large window was stronger against his eyes than any emotion he might have had, walking into his mother's kitchen, the same one where he used to find her bent over drunk, vomiting in the sink on some mornings.

Joe's mother was at the kitchen table talking rather seriously with Hillary about dolls and their personal habits. He watched her peripherally as he went to get a cup of coffee. His mother had never been good with kids before; yet, somehow, overnight she had transformed into Grandma Barney.

"Why don't you and Jenny take the day and go out, I'll watch Aaron and Hillary," Anna Gardner said, her voice far too sweet and grandmotherly.

Joe looked at Jenny. These women were in cahoots. He gave his wife the: *I can't believe you trust her with our children* look, but he was fairly sure she would ignore it.

"I already said it was okay," Jenny said, rather too authoritatively. "I want you to give me the whirlwind tour of Colony."

Joe looked from one woman to the other. One thing he had learned in his marriage, the one thing that set him back five hundred years, back to when troglodytes ruled the earth, was that no matter what, the woman was always right. It was the only thing that ever seemed to keep peace in the household. Jenny's eyes seemed so affectionate: she hadn't done it out of malice or naïveté, she had made this decision from her heart.

"Good," Joe said, "that'll be great. Then we'll come back and go out to dinner. Say around six? You remember Hopfrog, Mom. He'll be meeting us, too."

Anna Gardner's face brightened. "Thank you, Joseph. Thank you." She came over and planted a kiss on his cheek. "You're making an old witch very happy."

"Just don't take the kids down to the river. If something were to happen—"

"I know, I know. A feeble oldster like me couldn't do much. We'll stay in the yard," then, turning to Aaron, "and you know what I have in the yard to show you?"

Aaron shook his head.

"Your father's truck," Anna said, "from back when he was a boy."

Joe glanced at his mother. Sipped his coffee. "You still have that old rattrap?"

"I wasn't about to get rid of it," his mother said. She sounded slightly hurt by his suggestion. "I know how much that truck meant to you." She put her hand over Aaron's. "It was a gift from your grandfather. Oh! Aaron, you look so much like your grandfather, and he was the handsomest man in the state. He was smarter than I'll ever be, and he worked hard, and loved his family. But he was disciplined and ran a tight ship."

"That's funny," Aaron said, "Dad told me he ran a garage."

8.

Joe and Jenny took River Road, the long way to town. The river was noon bright, the water brown and yellow with sunlight. It was warming up a bit, so they kept the car windows down. Even though most of the

trees had lost their leaves, there were still enough
around with yellow and red bursts of color; the stone
houses, all in a row on the river, with the boat landings
behind them; joggers in sweats taking a lunchtime run;
the sight of the eastern bridge, its girders etched in
Joe's memory—he pointed out where he and Hopfrog
would hang off the end of the bridge and then jump
into the river below. "It didn't seem dangerous back
then," Joe said, "but we could've died doing it. Look
how far a drop that is. Whew."

He drove her by the old high school, Dabney Court-
land High. "Named for the county's only hero of the
War Between the States. Dabney deserted from the
Confederacy right about the time that West Virginia
separated from Virginia. Then he led the attack on Fort
Harris. Died at the Alamo. I know all about him. We
had to study him at least one day a year from first
grade on. And there"—he pointed out a large satellite
dish, smack dab at the edge of the schoolyard, bordering a brick house; the dish seemed taller than the
building—"we have the West Virginia state flower."
Joe grinned. The high school was closed down. It was
a functional and dull late fifties building, red brick, like
a large oven. Three of its windows had been broken. "I
guess the high school kids all go over to Stone Valley
for school now."

Jenny got out of the car. "Let's walk some."

The shopping district of town was just a few blocks
away and amounted to both sides of a very narrow
street. He parked the car, got out and stretched. Jenny
put a quarter in for the local paper (four sheets primarily of classified ads, with tidbits of local wisdom and
what they both imagined to be a rotating restaurant
review, as there were only four restaurants in town). As
they walked, Jenny browsed the classifieds.

Joe said, "What, are you looking for a house to buy?"

She seemed lost in an ad for a second, then looked up at him. "What? Oh, this. It's just that you can tell a lot about a place by its advertising. Look at this, house rentals, four bedrooms go for four hundred a month. Four hundred a month."

"Yeah," he said, "but it's a long way to Baltimore from here."

"I don't want to move here, Joe, I'm just amazed that there are places in this country that are still so inexpensive." A middle-aged blond woman was walking her dog. Jenny folded the newspaper up and passed it to her husband. She petted the dog, a rottweiler. She looked at Joe and they continued walking, as if they were going somewhere. They passed up two antique shops and a bakery. "Let's go in one of these," she said, and then her face tightened with concern. "You're almost pale, Joe. Is it that bad? Aren't you happy we came down here?"

"I guess I am. I didn't expect it to be like this."

"Neither did I. But I knew it wouldn't be as awful as you expected. You know something, Joe?"

He looked at her.

She clasped his hand. "I wasn't sure if we were going to make it. I wasn't sure I could . . . only now, I think I'm falling in love with you all over again."

It felt like a magic word to him: love. He began seeing Colony differently. The bricks which met haphazardly on the buildings, so ancient and so fresh, as if, when the town was built up again after the Civil War, time had stopped and there was no decay, neither was there poverty or squalor in this place. The streets were no hotbeds of commerce during the daylight hours, but those people he saw, the locals who worked at the bank or the real estate office, or who were taking their lunch breaks from their shops, all seemed to hold untold secrets of the good life. Rosy cheeks, sphinx smiles, bright eyes, expressions of subdued joy upon them—he had forgotten this in the years he'd been gone.

He entertained, for a moment, the idea of moving home, getting a nice old town house, and teaching his children about the quiet life of quiet towns nestled among quiet hills. Jenny kept turning to him with a look of mild surprise each time someone waved hello as if they'd known each other for years; she was born and raised in Washington, D.C., and had never known a town like this.

Joe noticed the birds: the blue jay and cardinals, the mockingbirds jabbering from the tops of the gingko trees that were planted along the row of shops on Main Street. He remembered being seven years old and how interested he was in birds, how he and his mother raised a mockingbird which had been abandoned by its mother. How his mother had taught him how to feed it with an eyedropper, how to teach it to fly by letting the bird grasp the end of his finger and then moving his finger slowly up and down. Joe had a good memory of his mother after all; then a flood of memories washed through him. He remembered his mother taking him to horror movies as a boy, because he loved them so much. He remembered when he hadn't studied for a test and faked illness, how his mother had taken him to the cliffs over the hills to look for fossils. He remembered how his mother had showed him how to plant flowers the correct way, so they'd grow and bloom.

And then, the most powerful memory:

He remembered how he had been sad when his pet mockingbird was eaten by a neighbor's cat.

And how his mother had given him a small typewriter when he was in fourth grade.

And she had said, "I want you to tell me a story about your mockingbird."

How he had typed and typed, learning how to use the machine, hunting and pecking, until he had written a page.

How his mother had read the story and cried.

He had said, "I'm sorry, Mommy, I didn't mean to make you cry."

And she said, "This is the most beautiful story I have ever read. You are going to be a writer. You have made me a very proud woman."

Joe stopped in the middle of the street.

"Joe?" Jenny tugged at his arm. "Joe?"

"It wasn't always bad," Joe said. "My mother wasn't always bad. She gave me my writing."

They walked to the opposite sidewalk, and Joe shared the story with Jenny. They sat at a table in a small tea shop and drank herb tea.

He said, "Something happened with her later. I don't know what. Maybe it was the alcohol. Who knows? Maybe it was Dad. Maybe she just had something in her that made her do the things she did."

"But you love her, Joe. Don't you see? You love her."

He sipped from the pottery mug and nodded, but didn't talk for a while.

Later, on the sidewalk, a policeman waved to him, "Joe? Joe Gardner? Baby Joe?" He came jogging across the street to them. He wore the tan uniform of a local sheriff, had a gut like a two six-pack-a-day Pabst

Blue Ribbon man, and the yellow teeth of a chain-smoker. His eyes were bright, and there was something that seemed familiar in the Elvis-like curl to his upper lip and the last wisps of hair on his shiny pate. The sheriff started yabbering a mile a minute about hearing that Joe was around, that he was back with his family, that he looked like the same old Joe. "Same old Baby Joe," the sheriff said.

Joe didn't recognize the man at first, but within a few seconds, listening to the chawed-up cadences of his speech, he realized it was Dale Chambers, the Gump. "You're sheriff now, eh?" Joe asked after they shook hands.

"For six years, cuz," Dale said, then, to Jenny, "we're only second cousins once removed, if you were to get technical, but that makes you and me pretty near kissing cousins." He hugged her and pressed his lips against Jenny's before she could protest. "Hey, Baby Joe, you married a live one, didn't you." He leered at Jenny. "Long and leggy, that's how I like 'em. Mmm." Nudging Joe, he whispered seriously, "You're not back here to stir up more trouble again, are you, Baby Joe? Don't tell me your wild days aren't behind you?"

After they got away from Dale, Jenny smirked. "That's your cousin? No wonder you haven't introduced me around. I could practically smell corn squeezins on his breath."

"Yeah, that's the Gump. It's a sad statement about this place if he's sheriff. When I was thirteen, he taught me how to spit tobacco at six paces. He's pure class." Joe found himself laughing. He grabbed Jenny's hand and together they walked down the sidewalk like kids in love.

"What was all that about 'your wild days'? He actually sounded concerned." Jenny shook her head, stopping to glance in a shop window.

"Oh, it's all that stuff that happened. I was hearing voices, I was seeing things. And without the help of drugs. Hell, maybe they were all on the mark when they said I was nuts. I did something I'm not proud of."

"Oh?" Jenny didn't sound interested. He knew she wasn't pursuing the subject because she wanted him to enjoy this trip, and not dwell on all the bad things again.

He loved her for it.

They went door-to-door to all the antique and knick-knack shops. Bought the ugliest garden sculpture possible, a fat little stone faun to sit among the ivy in their small backyard in Baltimore. It was too heavy to lug around, so Joe told the shop owner, Athena Cobb, that he'd be by sometime before closing to pick the sculpture up.

"It was too expensive," Jenny said, shaking her head as they left the shop. "We should've talked her down."

Joe shrugged. "I'm feeling pretty good. As Bambi's mother said, why not blow a few extra bucks when the mood strikes?"

He bought souvenirs for the kids: a sweatshirt for Aaron, and a dried-apple-headed cornhusk doll for Hillary. They had lunch at the Angel Wing Pub, and, to Joe, it felt as if he were on a second honeymoon with his wife after thirteen years. Someone at the next table was annoying him, going on and on about some lost little girl who had just shown up in town. Joe and Jenny were having such a lovely time that Joe wanted to turn around and tell this loudmouth to shut up because this was, maybe, one of the best days of his life, and could he keep his gossip to himself, please? But even with the loudmouth, Joe was rediscovering a love for humanity and life and small towns that he didn't know he had ever possessed.

9.

Winston Alden carefully got out of his ancient Corvair, bought in Stone Valley at auction for one hundred dollars in 1979 and still running like an asthmatic junkheap. He had parked at the edge of the road. It wasn't going to be dark for a couple of hours. He still had time. He had been postponing coming to the house the entire day. There had been ham biscuits to enjoy over coffee at breakfast, and then a stroll to the library to read newspapers; between noon and four, a nice siesta on the hammock he kept in the back room of his office.

And now.

The hour of doom, he thought.

He looked the Feely place over: it was completely dark inside. It had always seemed that way to him for as long as he could remember. The Feelys were hard, cold people who kept to themselves; they kept their secrets hidden.

Don't go in there, a voice in his head warned.

Don't be a fool and risk your life over something that you know is going to destroy you.

He touched the hood of his car. It was warm. He'd been feeling a chill beyond the afternoon frost. "You don't need to go in there," he said aloud as if coaching himself. "If John Feely's alive, you'll see him. If he's dead, well, then, what in God's name are you going to do old man?"

The stink of rotten fruit wafted down from the apple trees near the barn.

Winston felt in his pocket for his old Smith & Wesson revolver, model 10. He'd had it for fifteen years; before that, he'd had a shotgun under his bed.

The bullets were silver, because after decades of tossing around the thought of what had happened to Eugene Cobb back in the thirties, Winston Alden decided that it was high time to believe in something that might be supernatural. Something like vampires and werewolves and ghosts and ghouls. He kept his belief in a corner of his mind, what he referred to as his insane twin, the one who still believed that a man could see angels and dogs could go to heaven.

The belief came out only now and then in his life: when his wife died, when his sister lost her baby, when it happened to Eugene.

He had a vision of Eugene:

Flesh burnt where the crucifix had touched him.

The necrotic and scarred flesh sloughing off, molding new skin over Eugene's face.

Winston shook this memory off.

He walked up the path to the front door. Went up the porch steps.

Knocked at the door.

He didn't wait. It would be weak to wait, to admit his terror. He needed to be strong. He opened the door.

He called out for John. His voice echoed in the musty hall.

He went inside.

The walls of John Feely's house were papered with pages from the bible.

Some of these had been torn away; beneath them, holes and cracks in a yellowed wall. There had been some kind of fire, too, for many of the pages were burnt.

Winston walked down the narrow corridor which he knew led to John's bedroom. The master bedroom led to the other room. The room he'd seen as a teenager, the room he had tried to forget about his whole life.

He opened the door.

The room was in the same condition in which it had been when Winston had been a boy and had been ushered into the room by John.

John Feely said, "It has lived since before God created man. It was thrown from heaven by God and has dwelt in the rock since Adam first was expelled from Eden. It is called Abaddon. It is the Angel of the Pit."

Winston, at sixteen, stood beside an equally young Virgil Cobb and whispered, "And if there ever was a Pit, this is it."

The window had been long ago boarded up, but there was light from a single candle, which seemed an encouraging sign. Nervous, Winston drew the revolver out and held it up as if willing to shoot anything that moved. The dressing table and mirror were clear, as if no one lived within this room. The drapes were drawn shut on the ornate canopied bed; John Feely had once bragged that his great-grandfather had brought it over from Bavaria piece by piece and then had spent four years reassembling it. Its dark wooden posts had grown dull; the drapes, enormous red and gold, were caked with dust.

His hands trembled with the gun's weight.

Winston was about to turn away and go into the other room, that inner sanctum, when someone called to him from within the drapes.

"Boy," the man said, "Boy, you've finally come." It was none other than John Feely's own bray.

Winston sighed, "Oh, John, It's out, isn't It?"

"Oh, yes," John Feely said. A hand pulled the drapery aside, and from the darkness of the bed, Eugene Cobb, still a boy, leaned into the dim light of the bedside lamp.

When he grinned, his teeth were pasted with red. "Lights out," he said, covering the candle flame with his thumb and forefinger.

The candle let out a feeble hiss before the room went dark.

The door shut behind Winston. He did not want to turn around to face whatever was behind him now.

Winston began shivering uncontrollably. "It's not even night yet," he whispered. "I thought you only lived at night." He pointed the revolver towards the dark spot where the bed was.

It answered him, now with Eugene's voice, "Where I am, it is always night."

When something touched his neck, he panicked and shot the gun off six times, spending every round. After the first shot, he thought he'd gone deaf from the sound of the blast.

He felt lips on his wrist; the featherlike slice of a cold razor there, at his pulse point.

He dropped the gun.

He knew his life was over. He knew he was powerless.

Winston Alden stood in the darkness, waiting for it to happen.

And it took forever.

10.

When he got off the school bus, Tad Petersen figured he had a good fifty seconds to race down the street, make a right and then a zigzag left until he was just about to his dad's place. It was quicker to his mom's, but he wasn't staying at her place this week.

If he didn't make good use of those fifty seconds, he was dead meat at the hands of Elvis and Hank, who were like yappy dogs on his tail. He ran as fast as he could (he wore his old sneakers to school for just such occasions), but Elvis tackled him on the Withrows' lawn, throwing him into a pile of leaves.

When Elvis, already a good one hundred sixty pounds at the age of eleven, was sure that Tad was squashed, he began stuffing wet leaves in his mouth. Tad tried to shut his mouth, but Hank was on him, too, holding his jaw down.

"Eat it, woosy," Elvis crooned.

Tad was sure he was going to choke to death right there. Sure that his life was over, he only saw one alternative, but it was the kind of choice that a kid could not return from.

He reached up and started tickling Elvis just under the ribs. The boy quivered like jelly, and his face turned red as if he were about to explode.

And then, he started laughing.

Elvis Bonchance for the first time in his life started laughing from something other than sadism. It was truly a red letter day.

Elvis rolled off Tad, still giggling. He laughed so much, he farted, and this started him laughing all over again.

Hank looked confused. Tad spat the leaves out and

went on the offensive, attacking Hank, too, tickling him until he cried out for mercy.

When Hank was exhausted, Tad stopped and said, "In the Ming dynasty, the emperor would designate a special man as chief tickler. This man would torture criminals by tickling them to death."

"No shittin'?" Elvis was wide-eyed.

Even though he was making it up, Tad nodded. "It's true. I read about it in *National Geographic*. He would tickle murderers and blasphemers with peacock feathers and sometimes with a razor."

Hank recoiled. "Jesus, a razor?"

Tad nodded. "They would laugh themselves into a coma."

Mrs. Withrow came out onto her porch and called out, "What are you boys up to in my leaves?"

Tad shouted back, "Just being boys, Miz Withrow!"

Hank leaned back, gasping for air. "We was gonna beat the crap outta you, boy. We was." He erupted into a laughing fit again, as if he had never truly laughed before in his miserable existence. And knowing the Bonchance family, with its beatings and incest and tattoos, this was quite possible.

Elvis grinned, slapping his meaty thigh. "You sure are a funny guy."

Tad smiled, proud of narrowly surviving a Bonchance incident. "Practically a weirdo," he said.

After that, he went home feeling pretty damn good. He could not get the smile off his face for hours.

11.

When Joe picked his mother and the kids up for dinner, Aaron said, "I saw your truck, Dad. Gramma said I can have it when I turn sixteen. She's so cool. And this." Aaron held up a small blue spiral notebook.

Joe felt his face go red as he recognized the notebook. "You've kept that thing?"

Anna Gardner beamed. "Of course. Do you think I'd throw out one piece of writing by Joseph R. Gardner?"

Aaron opened the notebook and read slowly and haltingly from the yellowed typewritten page that had been glued to the notebook paper. " 'I lost a friend today. He was a bird. His name was Fred. He was a mockingbird. My mother and I found him on the ground outside. He was too little to take care of himself. And he was buck naked. He had not earned his feathers yet, and so we took him into our house. His mother, a big mockingbird who eats our crab apples, attacked us when we took him. She was a very mean bird, because she kicked him out of the nest too soon. But I learned later on that she didn't know better, because she wanted to protect her baby, but she wasn't able to do it because she could only do what a bird could do . . .' " Aaron paused, glanced up at his father and sighed, "Jeez, Dad, you were a terrible writer back then. You were worse at writing than I am at reading."

"Let's go to dinner," Jenny said, taking the notebook from him. She set it on the table by the front door and whispered to Joe, "When we get home tonight, I am going to sit up all night long and make you read that to me."

"I cherish those early writings of his," Anna said.

Joe shook his head in wonder. "Mom, I thought you didn't like my writing."

"Oh, you mean what you write now. I don't. Maybe if it was *about* something I might enjoy it, and maybe if it didn't have all the kinky stuff . . . You write like you're building bridges and dams, Joseph, I want to read books about people, about life in a way that I never thought of it before. Maybe I'm just a tough reader." Then, she patted his shoulder. "You can't expect to write a novel to please your mother, son."

Joe followed the rest of them out to the driveway, feeling as if he didn't know what the hell was going on anymore. Jenny stood beside the car door. The look on her face was unmistakable: love, lust, affection, warmth, all of it there in her eyes, in her smile, in the glow across the surface of her skin.

Life is good.

Aaron practically wouldn't let go of his grandmother's hand. In the Buick, he was scrunched in between Hillary and Anna Gardner, but he definitely looked happy. Hillary, too, would start talking excitedly every few seconds to her grandmother in a nonsensical chatter. Anna Gardner fielded all the questions, no matter how unintelligible, and reached over her grandson to comb her fingers through Hillary's wild blond hair.

They drove through town, Joe and Jenny talking nonstop about their afternoon. Aaron told about how Gramma showed him pictures of his dad from when he was Aaron's age. The streets were slick with rain; two collies ran circles around a tree, chasing a squirrel; Joe noticed how incredibly gorgeous the houses were, some of them built in the early 1800s, like mini-antebellum mansions. He was feeling pretty damn good, and was surprised.

What is it you want most, Joe? A voice from the past seemed to cut across Joe's brain.

What is it you pray for?

Just as they neared the Angel Wing, Anna Gardner gasped, "Joseph. Joe."

Aaron said, "Daddy, something's wrong with Gramma."

Joe looked in the rearview mirror. He saw such a pained look cross his mother's face that he almost went off the road.

Aaron threw his arms around his grandmother's shoulders and whispered, "Grandma, I love you."

14

TOWN AND COUNTRY

1.

Dale Chambers laughed and slapped Lannie Barnes square on the butt. "I do love you, chicken, you're the best thing that ever happened to me."

They'd just gotten into room 9 of the Miner's Lodge, and Lannie had barely enough time to notice that there were flowers everywhere.

"Dale, what's all this?"

He grinned, shaking his head like a boy. "I love you, girl, that's what this all is. I know you been seeing Jud, and I know you just want me to shit or get off the pot, so I wanted tonight to be special. I left her."

"You left her?"

"That's right."

Lannie went over and sat on the edge of the bed. She looked at her pumps. "You mean you left your wife?"

"You got it."

"After twenty-five years of marriage and three children, you left your wife."

Again, he nodded.

She looked up at him and said, "You incompetent noodle. Your wife was the best thing that ever happened to you."

It took a minute or two for this comment to settle into the back of Dale Chambers's brain. The creature called the Gump who resided there started knocking at some unopened door inside him. The Gump whispered, *See? They're all betrayers. They all are cold heartless monsters and they only seem warm for a while. They take take take. They're not even real. They're not even human.*

"What did you just say?" he asked.

"Now, honey," Lannie said, crossing her legs and reaching for a cigarette from her purse. "It ain't that I'm not hot for you and that I don't love you, I do. I love you more than squat. And if it wasn't for the baby—"

He interrupted, his voice a low growl now as the Gump emerged into his thoughts, "How do I even know it's my baby?"

Lannie lit her cigarette and took a puff. She wasn't even looking at him. She glanced around the room as if he weren't even worth her attention. "Oh, it's your baby, Dale, I only slept with Jud after I was pregnant."

"How do I know you haven't been sleeping with half the county? Hell, you may have done all of Stone Valley for all I know."

Lannie sighed, shaking her head. "Take it to a talk show if you want to, Dale, but trust me, I didn't sleep with anyone else at the time I conceived. Okay?" She waved the cigarette for emphasis.

She was cruel. She was so cruel. He could deal with her infidelity with Jud. He knew she loved sex like a mink. He could even deal with her coldness to him. But the baby. It was their baby! What kind of mother was she going to make? What kind of monster was she going to bring into this world.

But something inside him softened. He whispered, "We're going to have a baby, Lannie. We need to set things right between us."

She smiled, almost warmly. "That's right, Dale, a baby." She chuckled, then laughed out loud.

"What's so funny?" he asked, meekly.

"I'm going to the clinic in the valley tomorrow. I have an appointment."

"This is a night for surprises," he said, feeling colder and Gumpier by the second. "You mean . . . ?"

"Yeah, I am going to get rid of it. I could tell the other night you didn't want it, and frankly, I'm not so sure I do, either."

"You're a good Baptist girl, honey. You always wanted children."

"Well," she took a long drag on the cigarette so that when she spoke she looked like a fire-breathing dragon. "You can't always get what you want, like the song says."

"You're not gonna kill our baby." Dale crossed his hands over his chest and stood like stone. "You are not going to kill our baby."

"Yes," she said, "I am." Then she looked a little frightened, as if she thought he might hit her. He had never hit a woman before, at least as far as he could recollect, so this didn't sit well with him. She scootched back farther onto the bed, carefully keeping her legs together, bent at the knees. "Now, Dale, honey," she began, but she seemed like a sheep bleating—from her tight cap of overpermed hair to her dumbass eyes, the Gump saw that she was just a sheep.

Bleating as if it knew it was headed for slaughter.

(He would have to kill her, there was no way around it. He could not let her live if she was going to do something so immoral as to murder his unborn son. What other choice did he have?)

"Hey, now, bay-ay-by," the sheep stammered. She must've seen the look in his eyes.

He wasn't angry.

Oh, no.

The Gump didn't get angry over the little things in life.

He was calm.

That's what the sheep saw: his calm.

His eyes were placid pools of muddy water, his lips curled gently.

"Not our baby," he said, feeling as if he didn't have to walk towards her; all he had to do was shimmer in her general direction, like sunlight moving across a newly opened curtain.

(*Slaughter the lamb,* Gump told him.)

"Well, I was only thinking about getting rid of it," she said, "I went over to my mama's grave up at Watch Hill and talked to her for a while. She says you don't really want the baby. She told me you aren't a good man at all."

He sat down on the bed, twisting around towards Lannie. "Your mama's been dead a long time. You making things up?"

"You know how I still talk to Mama? How the spirit world's just in another room and we can talk to any of them if we believe? Well, she said I was too old for a baby and that you only love yourself. She told me something else about you, too." Lannie leaned back against the silky pillows, bringing her knees farther up. He could practically see up her skirt.

He caught her smell there, from between her legs. She slowly brought her knees apart.

No longer sheep, all he saw when he looked at her was sex. Both the inner Gump and the outer Dale liked that quite a bit. Idly, he asked, "What else mama tell you 'bout me?"

"About a little boy you put down in the mines a long time ago. Little bitty thing. How you killed him and left him and didn't give a whit." As she said this, something small and pink thrust from between her legs and his thoughts became jumbled—

baby's bein' born, good God, the baby's bein' born right now

givin' birth

what the hell is goin' on

While Lannie leaned forward and grabbed Dale's head, bringing their lips together—

the bloody thing emerged from between her legs—

He pulled back from Lannie, whose lips were bright red and moist—

The thing from between her legs was not an unformed baby at all, but the blood-drenched body of a little nine-year-old boy named Davy Hammond, a boy that the Gump had put down in the bottom of a mine shaft when he, himself, had only been nine. As Davy pushed out of Lannie's flesh, the flesh seemed to slough off, and Davy's eyes were fierce, and before Dale could say anything or move or even laugh like crazy because he had just lost his mind,

Davy got him.

2.

Just downstairs at the Miner's Lodge, Gary Welles sat at the bar and when he heard the high-pitched shriek from one of the rooms, he shook his head. "Too much of that going on these days. Folks aren't decent no more," he said. "Nobody, not even God. If God was a decent sort, why'd he let that weirdo kill my little girl? Nothin's decent no more."

The bartender brought him his fifth beer. "This is it for tonight, Gary. Closing up early."

The bar was empty and had been all afternoon and into the evening. This made Gary very happy, because sometimes he couldn't even sit at the bar but had to skulk off to a corner to drink himself into a coma.

"Life closes up early." Gary wagged his head around, and pointed at the bartender. "You, you think that life's great, but wait'll some sumbitch kills your little girl and starts talking crazy about how she's still around!" Tears soaked his cheeks as he spoke, feeling the old passion coming back to him. "Think about your little girl in her grave, and some kid digs her up and drives a spike in her heart and cuts off her head. Think about how that would make you feel, huh? And then, Jesus, he talks about her, on and on, about she's saying this and she's saying that, about how she's not dead even though you know this kid killed her!"

Then, quietly, "I'd like another Bud."

The bartender held up his hand in a "halt" gesture. "No can do. Five's your limit tonight."

"Please," Gary whimpered. He felt an always-present sweat increase at the back of his neck; his tongue was dry, his lips, parched. He knew that if he didn't have another beer in a few minutes that he would start shivering. It always went like that. He couldn't even remember anymore when it began. Maybe when his daughter died, way back, or maybe when his wife left him, his son, too, taking off in the night like thieves because they couldn't stand the sight of him. (*It was that Joe Gardner's fault, too.*) Maybe it was before all that, but Gary didn't think so. He could fairly specify the time and day right down to that car wreck in the Paramount River. The call. Dale on the phone, saying, "Gary, I have some news about your girl." The rest of what Dale had said might've been any kind of gobble-dygook, because that was all Gary heard. And then, at the funeral that boy having the gall to show up and go to Gary's wife and hug her and cry like he cared.

He wasn't crying later on, when he dug her up.

He wasn't crying when he took that spike and put it into her heart.

Even the dead got to be protected from some people.

Gary wiped his hand through his greasy hair. "He shouldn't'a never come back."

The bartender said nothing.

"You ain't gonna give me that beer, huh?" Gary pushed himself back from the bar, almost toppled, but managed to right himself and catch the stool before it fell. He didn't like being denied beer; it would mean maybe hitting Frankie or Wilson up for a freebie, and that could be humiliating. He spat at the bartender, "Maybe you'd have more business if you was nicer. I notice this place's half empty."

The bartender chuckled, "Aw, gee, Gary, I like to think of it as half full. What you gonna do tonight, big guy?"

"Gonna put a fella outa his misery." Gary shambled away, wanting another beer and hoping there was one somewhere out in the night; a beer and a gun and a man who should've died in a river when he'd had the chance.

3.

Athena Cobb had just turned the *Open* sign around to read *Closed*, when a man approached the door to her antique shop. He was soaked with rain, and must've been freezing because he wore no coat. She pointed to the sign.

The man said something which she couldn't quite hear.

She quickly unlocked the door.

As he stepped inside, she was about to tell him that her shop was closed, when she noticed the bloodstain which ran down his shirt—the blood continued to seep across the rain-soaked cotton. The man's knees buckled, and he fell down.

She caught him.

"Oh, my God," she gasped. He was heavy in her arms.

He whispered against her cheek, "Children."

She couldn't hold him any longer and let him slide to the floor. She crouched down over him and looked up when she heard a noise.

In the rain-dark street, there stood a little girl dressed in a muddy skirt and blouse. In between her lips was something that might've been a drinking straw.

A crazy thought flashed through Athena's mind:

the little girl had just sucked the man's blood through the straw.

This was her last coherent thought, because Athena Cobb knew that her fight for survival had just begun, a fight that would end with a straw that felt like steel being thrust into her trachea as several children leaned over her to suck her life.

4.

Noah Cristman was seventeen and love was driving him mad. He had tried calling Tenley McWhorter's house, but no one was answering, which was odd.

Noah was accustomed to Tenley's mother getting on the line to preach God and morality to him—he almost missed her whiny sermons. But Tenley hadn't shown up at school, so he drove around her house half a dozen times before swinging by Burger Palace (only to find out it was closed). Then he zoomed over to his buddy's house around six, only nobody seemed to be answering at that house, either.

It was weirding him out.

Noah had to see Tenley. Had to see her. Wasn't going to make it another hour without her. Main problem was, he wasn't supposed to go up and ring the McWhorter's doorbell. Mr. McWhorter swore he would chase boys off his property with a shotgun. In Colony, you didn't take such threats idly.

Finally, extremely frustrated, Noah parked on a side street and jogged across the slick dead leaves and asphalt back to her house. He snuck around through the neighbor's yard and jumped the chain-link fence into the McWhorter's side yard.

He was about to toss a rock up at Tenley's window, when he thought better of it.

He got another idea. There was something about Noah that even he didn't like to admit to himself: he was far too good at breaking into houses. He had a technique involving getting into the house through the basement and then tiptoeing up the stairs.

The McWhorters only had one tiny window in their basement. As Noah crouched next to it, he wasn't sure if he was going to fit through it. He used a rock to smash the glass, then carefully pushed out the jagged shards with his hands.

He slipped his head through, then his shoulders, arms first.

"Shit," he whispered. He was not going to make it all the way through.

He was about to withdraw when someone grabbed his arms, tugging him forward.

"Tenley? That you?" he asked, trying to see in the dark basement.

He felt other hands, small, like little kids', and they were trying to pull him in. He was scared, and tried to get his head back, when something touched his face.

Like a feather.

He opened his mouth to scream, but something in the dark shot into the back of his throat and down his esophagus.

They pulled him into the basement.

5.

These were just a few of the events around Colony that night, typical of how the town had begun its descent into darkness.

For some, it was just another cold, rainy November night.

Nelda Chambers was trying to cry herself to sleep, which was impossible. She had drunk six cups of coffee (trying to kill herself with caffeine), after Dale had packed his bags and walked out of the house.

Several families around town were watching the *Cosby Show* reruns, while more than a few were flipping between Connie Chung and Peter Jennings on the news; Melanie Dahlgren was doing yoga on the small oriental rug in front of her glowing fireplace, anticipating a visit from her new best friend; suppers were being cooked; dogs walked; the Angel Wing Pub was getting a few stragglers in from the inhospitable weather; on the surface, many things seemed the same as they had the evening before, like every rainy evening the town had ever known.

Becky O'Keefe, for example, was feeling like hell, as she did on any given night in the fall.

15

BECKY FEELS LIKE HELL

1.

Becky O'Keefe had been raised in Richmond, Virginia, and her parents had only moved to Colony, West Virginia, when she'd turned ten. After high school, her parents moved to California because her father felt there were more jobs out West. She had remained behind because she could not stand the idea of California, nor could she justify, at eighteen, still moving with two parents who could barely support each other, let alone an adult daughter. She had gone to work back then at the soda counter at the Five N Dime. Two years later, married to Homer Petersen, she went to work as a bookkeeper and receptionist for Dr. Cobb. Then, after Tad was born, she took two years at home. The bartender shift at the Angel Wing Pub hadn't come until six years back, when Dr. Cobb had severely cut back on his practice and his expenses. He was no longer able to maintain a full-time assistant because most of the medical business went to the medical center over the hills.

With the exception of her divorce, she had lived fairly peacefully until that particular day when her dog lay dead at the bottom of the stairs.

She awoke from a comalike sleep at four in the afternoon and stared at the ceiling for a full fifteen minutes before she could find the strength to get out of bed. She had cried herself to sleep over the death of her son's beloved pet, and when she awoke, she raged at the impotence she felt at the hands of whoever had committed the atrocity. Becky O'Keefe believed that she could not depend on anyone else in this life (her marriage had proven that), so she had not been surprised when Jud Carey, the only available representative of the local police, arrived at her door before she'd fallen asleep, took one look at her dog, then at the muddy footprints, and pronounced the verdict: "Your dog's dead."

For a good ten seconds, Becky stared at him. She had never truly assessed how dumb Jud Carey was until that moment.

She shouted at him until he left the house.

The dog was dead.

A spike had been driven through its skull.

When she awoke in the afternoon, Becky stared at the ceiling and thought about that. She knew the Bonchance boys, from the other side of the river, might kill dogs—they'd been known to burglarize the houses and stores on Main Street, and they'd been caught drowning old Risa DeLaMare's cats for some kind of perverse lark. Becky wished she could take those Bonchance boys out and shoot 'em. But she didn't believe that those twisted kids had killed the dog. The muddy footprints were those of a young child. *Maybe someone else killed the dog, and then some little kid found it and brought it inside. Now, that sounds suitably nuts.* She was thinking how evil the world was, how awful human beings were to do that kind of thing to some innocent animal.

And what was she going to tell Tad? *Some weirdo killed Whitney, Tad. Some lunatic who is so paranoid he thinks an eight-year-old mutt is going to tear him apart, so he takes a spike and jabs it against poor Whitney's skull, thinking it'll stop the voices in his head.*

Why did I think that? Voices in his head. Only person that could be would be Joe Gardner, the radio of the beyond.

That thought gave her yet another headache, which was all the impetus she needed to go to the bathroom to down a few Extra-Strength Excedrins. *Stupid police, stupid people. The world is nothing but stupid people. Stupid Homer Petersen, and his stupid obsession with those stupid stories that stupid Joe Gardner had fed him.*

"Lady," she said to the bathroom mirror. "You are a mess."

She had never wanted a beer so badly. She saw the small lines in her face, the way her lips seemed dry. She hadn't been to her AA meetings in Stone Valley in nearly three months—she thought she didn't need them. But the thirst was still there. It had been there after the divorce, like a lion waiting in tall grass, hidden from her daytime self. But at night, when she'd put Tad to sleep and sat up, watching TV, it was there. It was there when she was in the bar, serving drinks. Watching the others down beer and wine and Irish coffees. The thirst never went away. But she had control of it; she could keep it somewhere safe, deep down in the pit of her soul. The meetings had helped for seven years; she had kept away from the demon rum. (Only once had she broken her vows and gone off the wagon, and that was when she had the miscarriage. Only then did she drink a whole bottle of wine all by herself. Only then, back when she and Homer were still married. She had believed in God before that, before she lost her little four-month-in-the-womb child, and then, for a while, she had believed her punishment for drinking away her youth had been to lose the baby.)

But the AA meetings never quenched the thirst. She desperately wanted a glass of wine. *Just one glass. Just a few sips. Anything to take away this feeling.*

She waited at the bathroom mirror until the feeling passed.

After showering, she checked her messages. One from work, mentioning the all-night poker game that was to go on that night after closing. Two messages from Tad just calling to say hi and that everything was cool at his dad's. The last one, from Dr. Cobb.

All he said on the machine was, "Rebecca," he was always so formal with her, "I've done something terrible here at the office. Something truly . . . psychotic . . . I need some help. I need something. Please come see me. Don't call. I won't answer the phone, and when they find out what I've done they'll lynch me."

2.

"I'm on shift in an hour, Dr. Cobb," she said as she walked in the door to his office. It was brightly lit, not just the fluorescent bulbs, but every lamp in the place. When she saw the look in his face, as if his spirit had died, she wished that she hadn't sounded so harsh. "I'm sorry," she said.

Virgil Cobb sat in one of the waiting room chairs. "I told her parents that I had an ambulance take her over to Stone Valley. They were so exhausted from last night that they bought it. I made up some completely cockamamie story that if coma patients are disturbed in their first forty-eight hours that they might easily bleed to death. It was total fabrication, total, she's not in a coma, she wasn't even alive, not really."

Becky O'Keefe stared at him as he babbled on.

Finally she said, "What the hell is going on?"

Virgil Cobb looked at her sadly. "It's Patty Glass."

The name didn't register with Becky at first. Her mind sometimes worked like a computer, albeit an inefficient one. She could practically hear the *ticka-ticka-tick* of a machine as the two words, *Patty* and *Glass* rolled around until she hit the jackpot. She remembered a little girl in third grade with long hair and owl eyes. "She's dead," Becky said without further hesitation.

"I know," Virgil said. "Of course she is. Of course she's dead. Of course." His words melted into a loud booming laugh. As Becky stood there, her coat still on, she wondered if the pressures of a failing practice had taken its toll on her former employer's mind. *Maybe he should've retired before now.*

She immediately went to feel his forehead. It was

cool. He stopped laughing and, instead, looked at her with cool eyes, too. "You think I've lost it."

"Not totally. I just don't understand. Patty Glass died when I was ten. Unless you're talking about some other Patty Glass."

Without bothering to explain, Virgil Cobb stood up and wiped at his face as if it were dirty. He walked through the waiting room and into the examination area. She assumed he wanted her to follow. She had known Virgil as Dr. Cobb since she'd been able to speak, and had always had great respect for him. But everybody cracked every now and then.

Still, she gave him the benefit of the doubt.

She followed him into the room.

3.

The room was dark. The blinds drawn. She could tell from the shapes that the room had remained as it was when she had worked for him: charts on the wall, a stainless steel counter and cabinets taking up an entire wall.

Something lay on the examining table, but it was too dark to see it.

"What is it you believe in, Rebecca?" Virgil asked.

"Electricity, Dr. Cobb. Could we have some light in here?"

"Not yet. You're not ready."

"Okay. I believe in the basics."

"You mean, God, country, and all that jazz? What about the not so basics. What about the things under the bed, or the strange light at the window? What about the other side?"

"Dr. Cobb, I don't know—"

"The other side, Rebecca, from where we are. Maybe the dead. Maybe the not so dead. Maybe some species that exists between dimensions."

"Look," she said, "I've had a bad morning, what the—" and then she reached over to the wall, found the light switch, and turned it on.

Things happened simultaneously for her then:

Dr. Cobb was shaking his head as if she were a foolish child jumping ahead of the lesson plan;

she noticed that he had painted the examination room, green from off-white;

she noticed the blood on one of the off-white walls;

the blood in several large jars set on the stainless steel counter;

and, on the examining table, held down by leather straps, the decapitated and eviscerated body of a little girl.

Becky O'Keefe had never fainted before in her life— fallen down drunk or passed out, yes, but never a genuine faint.

But she saw pinpoint and swirling curls across her vision and thought:

am I seeing stars? I'm seeing stars for the first time in my life.

And then her legs gave out and at about that point she felt a sudden, precipitous drop in energy or perhaps even blood sugar.

She hoped she wouldn't hit the floor too hard.

4.

She awoke sitting up in a chair in the outer office. The plush, leather chair that she used to sink into in the late afternoons when she had been Dr. Cobb's office administrator.

Becky rubbed the back of her head; *no bumps here*.

Virgil Cobb knew enough about her not to offer her a brandy. Instead, he made some Celestial Seasonings peppermint tea. "Good for settling the stomach," he said, his voice cracked a bit, as if taken over by exhaustion.

"I'm glad I didn't split my head open," was all she could think to say.

"Me, too. I saw your skin go white. I knew you were going to faint. I managed to get over to you in time to catch you. I'm not as nimble as I used to be. Practically threw my back out."

A few moments of silence hung in the air. The tension was enormous. Her head was throbbing, but not from the faint. The room seemed suffocating.

"You did that in there? To that girl?" she asked, wanting to understand. She didn't believe Dr. Cobb was capable of murder, nor did she think he was capable of lying. Madness, however, was another issue.

"She was already dead, I promise you. I just had to do a little outpatient surgery."

He was trying to make a feeble and sick joke, which was unlike him. Her warning buzzer, the one that went off in her head whenever trust and some man entered her life in one fell swoop, seemed to remain dormant.

The weird thing was, she was briefly worried about work, as ridiculous as that seemed at a time like this. She knew that she should be calling into the pub to say she wouldn't be in. *"Oh, just because I saw a little girl slaughtered on a doctor's table and I think maybe the doctor's taken a touch too much of his own medicine on this particular night."*

She watched Virgil's face for some sign of insanity, but there was something so damned sane about the guy, it was as impossible to believe that he had murdered this girl as it was to believe that the body had really been Patty Glass's at all. The whole world outside of the office seemed to fade away. "How is this possible?" she managed, after a sip of scalding tea.

"Thank God," he said, "Thank God you came. I thought I was a madman."

She said nothing. She watched him and sipped. She was moderately surprised that she didn't fear for her own life. She couldn't get past a certain intuition she had that Dr. Cobb was not crazy at all, no matter how much her logical sense told her that he very well might be.

"She was one of them," he said. "She's the first one I've seen in years. I thought maybe we'd stopped it. Looks like I was wrong."

Neither of them spoke. She noticed that it was completely dark outside. She thought of Tad's dog and of Joe Gardner. Somehow her mind connected all of these things. She said, "You've been like a father to me, Dr. Cobb."

He drummed his fingers on the edge of the coffee table, covered as it was with magazines. "I'm going to stop you right there. You're already talking like I'm crazy. I'm going to tell you about Patty Glass. She disappeared at the Feely farm over twenty years ago. Both you and I know that. The children with her told the authorities that she might've fallen down an old cistern in the barn, but no body was found in it. Yesterday, she was discovered. She was at her parents' house. She was mute and didn't seem to be able to focus on anyone. But I recognized her, Rebecca, I knew what was making her run. I've seen it before. When I took her blood, she had several pints of blood more than the human body is meant to hold. Her heart had been eaten away at, as if by rats. She had not fed completely though, so she did this." Virgil Cobb stood and took his tweed jacket off, laying it neatly on the arm of his chair. Becky realized that he had begun shivering. Then he rolled up his shirtsleeve and extended his arm beneath a desk lamp for her to inspect.

She got up and went over to him. She took his arm in her hands and turned it gently.

A large black-and-blue diamond pattern just below the biceps. His forearm was swollen. She pressed lightly on it, and he winced. A small clear liquid leaked out from several marks on his forearm.

"I'd like to tell you that it's from a dog," Virgil said, "or from an enormous mosquito off the river. But it's not. It was Patty Glass. Not that she put her face against my arm and bit down. Nothing that easily vampiric. It was very fast, how she did it. It was in a fold of her skin, near her neck. You see, that must've been her own entry wound. When she fell down the well at John Feely's, whatever was down there waiting for her, it must've gotten to her neck first. But any major artery will do, I suppose."

Becky looked from his arm to his face. He was pale; sweat beaded the elderly man's forehead. She felt a chill run through her. "I don't understand," she said. Her brain seemed to be shutting its computer works down. She felt as if she had stepped off the neat plane of reality into the dimension of nonsense. The weird part was that it was beginning to make a kind of sense to her.

Virgil Cobb looked at her as if he were a child with his mother, telling the truth, and not being believed. He spoke slowly and deliberately. "I was bending over her at the table, checking her vision. Her eyes were dilated even with extreme light on them, and I wanted to see if I could detect any further abnormality there. I had already restrained her. To be honest, I already planned to . . . well, you saw for yourself in there. As I leaned closer to her face, her eyes seemed to retract back into her skull almost, like a snail going into its shell, threatened. My gut instinct was that something was wrong, so I drew back. But I was too late."

Becky watched the purple bruises on his arm. They were growing darker.

He gasped when he observed this. "I shouldn't be afraid of death. Not at my age. But I am."

"You're not going to die," Becky said, comfortingly.

"Not in the traditional sense, but Rebecca," he said, looking straight through her as if she had no physical body, as if he were not in a room with her, but alone in a dark universe with nothing to comfort him but the echo of his own voice, "I think I may already be dead. I think this entire town may be dead, too."

5.

Becky O'Keefe put her arms around Virgil Cobb and hugged him tightly. She closed her eyes. All she saw was the idiocy of darkness, yet it was oddly comforting to hold this man and to see nothing. His own arms were slack at his side, as if he didn't know how to hug another human being.

When she finally broke away from him, she said, "I don't know what any of this really means, Virgil," saying his first name for the first time in her life, "I know that there is a mutilated body in that other room. I know that you have always been kind to me. I consider you a very good friend. So I am willing to listen to anything you have to say. So please try and explain this to me in a way that I can get it. Because I'm not getting it right now. I can't even figure out what you're trying to tell me."

Virgil Cobb began another story, not about Patty Glass, but about something that happened years before Patty or Rebecca O'Keefe had even come into existence.

Back in the olden days of Colony, when summer seemed to last forever and was always green, when the river was not only swimmable but drinkable, when the world was smaller and Colony was bigger, back when an old man named Virgil Cobb was sixteen and dared his younger brother to run up to a certain porch of a certain house.

6.
Virgil's Story
My brother was always so active, always running and jumping, doing cartwheels. I thought he'd never stop. He was a terrific little brother, Eugene was, with his Irish mop of red hair, inherited from our mother, and his grin, like the devil himself on holiday. It was 1937, and in many ways the Great Depression had never hit us here in Colony, for we were all as poor then as we are now. My father was possibly the most well-to-do of all the locals, for he was also a doctor and ran his practice at an office in town, where my niece's shop is now. So we had material goods and food on the table at all times, that was true. And my friend Winston and I would get in trouble, usually with Eugene, the most adoring brother a boy could have. Once, I remember we three carried huge rocks from the quarry

all the way across town and piled them up in the middle of Queen Anne Street. It was late summer. We covered the rocks with corn, still in its husk, and then we went upstairs in Winston's house and waited to see if anyone would drive through the corn. Most folks had sense, and they drove around the pile of corn as soon as they came upon it. But the preacher, an idiot named Lee from over the hills, in his big shiny black Cadillac, drove right down the center of the road. He must've been thinking that he'd hit the corn and it would go flying; instead, he hit the rocks, and the engine dropped out of his car. Oh, we laughed about that one, and then hid because we knew somebody was going to come after us to tan our hides.

But Eugene told. Not on us, but just on himself. That preacher was angry as the dickens, and when Eugene volunteered himself as the culprit, my baby brother got whupped right there on the road. I felt guilty about that for months to come.

I just wanted you to know what Eugene was like. Even though he was my baby brother, he would take all the responsibility. He would let himself get punished instead of me.

And then, there was that dare. I don't know what month of summer it was, all I know is, it was hot as Hades. We both went around without our shirts, which my mother called uncouth and my father called unhealthy—the mosquitoes were positively rabid then, and I ended up with welts all over my back and shoulders. Winston got us to go over to the Feely place. Even then John Feely was called Old Man, and he probably wasn't much older than eighteen. But his father had died two years before, and his mother was something of an invalid, and there were three sisters of his to feed, too, so John became the head of the household. But the thing was, he used to run around with us, some, too. But as soon as he was running the farm pretty much by himself, he got reclusive, and shouted Bible phrases at us whenever we came out to see him. He called us sinners and such, and then when we got tired of it, Winston and I went and threw eggs at his house. And John Feely, damn him, didn't ever wash those blessed eggs off—they stayed there for weeks, drawing flies. People in town talked funny about John, how he would go out to Watch Hill and hammer crosses in the ground, even where there weren't any graves. They said he walked around at night, when no one else was in town. He was the town freak. So, Winston and I decided we'd break into his house one night while he was out. We didn't mean any real harm—you know, back then, folks left their doors unlocked all the time. Sometimes they didn't even close them.

So we drag Eugene with us, and he keeps telling us it's wrong, it's wrong, shaking his head, acting like a skunk. But we tell him about John Feely's stolen goods. Winston started that. He was always a better talker than me, and had read a lot of science fiction like Jules Verne and H. G. Wells. Winston convinced my brother that John Feely had stolen the old stone angel from Watch Hill, the one that used to be at the entrance. How that was sacrilegious and how it was only right that we go steal it back.

I didn't know that Winston was telling the truth.

Turns out, Winston had watched John Feely steal it one morning at five A.M. when Winston looked out his bedroom window and saw John walking down the street with it, plain as day.

So, it's maybe ten minutes to midnight, and we're all three staring at that old farmhouse. Our folks'll all skin us alive if they know we're out so late.

And then Winston looks at me and Eugene both and says something like, "I bet you're both too chicken to go in there."

To tell you the God's honest truth, I *was* too scared. I don't know what it was, but there was something about the Feely place at night that unnerved me. They say that there are some places where it can look perfectly beautiful and peaceful, but the eye detects something's wrong. Even though our minds can't notice what it is, our eye sees something without completely recognizing it. It's called the sublime. That's what I think it was, back then, that I felt. Call it a heightened awareness, but I was convinced when I looked at that dark old farmhouse that it was somehow alive, somehow it had some energy to it.

And it chilled my blood on one of the hottest nights of summer.

But Eugene was not attuned to that, I suppose. He accepted the dare from Winston. He barely waited a minute before he bounded up to the front porch and tried the door.

Unusual for us, the door was locked.

Eugene went around to the windows and looked through each one.

One window, a small one, was almost too bright with the lights on.

I was about to call to him to come back, to forget it.

But he saw something through that window. I don't know what.

When I saw him again, a few minutes later, and when we had gotten inside our house in the light, I gasped at the sight of him. He asked me what was wrong. All I could say was, "Your hair."

His hair, the bright red of fire, had turned completely white.

"It's because of what I saw," he said, and I felt it then. I felt that somehow my brother Eugene had become a ghost even though he hadn't died.

Now, I didn't believe him then. You won't believe me now when I tell you. He said that he saw something that looked very much like John Feely's old mother standing at the window on the inside, surrounded by candles. She was looking right at Eugene, although he was sure she couldn't see him because he was, after all, in the dark.

And then she reached up, placing her thumbs on either side of her eyes, and began to draw the flesh off her bones just as if it were our mother pulling skin from a chicken.

I didn't sleep that night, and I told him that we would never go back to the Feely place.

But apparently, you can't see them without wanting to go to them. It's part of the power they have. They're like some kind of Gorgon. You are turned to stone before them, powerless. You offer yourself up to them without even realizing it.

For the next morning, my brother Eugene had vanished.

He was gone for five weeks before I confronted John Feely. I was certain that Eugene had fallen prey to some strange glamour of what he'd seen in the window. I had to shout at John just to get a small response from him. When he acknowledged me, he nodded as if answering a question in his head.

John Feely looked at me sadly, and took pity on me.

He told me to meet him at his house before dawn, and I would see my brother.

My fear of John's house was overcome by my desire to see my brother as well as my insane curiosity. I awoke before the sun was up and rode my bicycle out to that accursed house. John greeted me soberly. He led me to the room where my brother had seen his terrifying vision.

There was a closet in the room, a closet that rose strangely from the floor, at an angle. This was surrounded with votive candles and every manner of religious symbol available, crosses of gold and brass and cornhusk, even a Star of David drawn on the wall in chalk; the Eastern yin-yang symbol, I think, also, and the Egyptian ankh. I was surprised a man of John Feely's limited education and interests would even know these, but he proved to be a self-educated man. His library was enormous and exotic. He told me a story about one of God's angels sent to this spot and chained by John's own great-great grandfather, a radical Mennonite preacher. The devil, John told me, still lived down in its tomb and had ravaged Colony more than once in the town's short history.

I was impatient. I wanted to know about my brother.

John Feely told me, "Something has happened to your brother, and I'm afraid it is my fault."

It seems his mother, out of curiosity, had removed the crosses and had stepped down into that cavern the very night that Eugene saw her through the window.

The devil had emerged in his mother's form and had seduced Eugene with what powers it had. Eugene had returned that night before John could make right the balance.

And you want to know something? I believed every word as we stood there. I bought it all. I could tell John Feely believed it, and I could hear, in his words, his own suffering and regret at the loss of his mother.

"How, if the creature is chained, could it escape?"

Before John Feely could answer, I heard my brother

on the other side of that locked closet door. I fought John to get to that door, remove the lock and throw off the crosses that hung from it, but something in me held me back. For as my brother shouted to me to open the door, I realized it could not be my brother Eugene at all.

That my brother would not use language such as this creature did, nor could he make the sound that I heard.

The sound was not human.

John Feely told me that if I listened too long to the devil that I would become his vessel.

Then he showed me what he had done to himself to keep from hearing the devil below.

He had punctured both of his eardrums.

I realized he had not heard anything I was saying.

I could stay there no longer. I ran out into the dawn, home to my safe bed, and never told anyone this story except for Winston Alden.

And now, you.

7.

Virgil Cobb looked into Becky's eyes for signs of belief.

She could not look at him. She sat on the floor, totally caught up in the world of that story.

"And what was beneath the Feely house, what took over my brother's body also took over Patty Glass," he said. "For some reason, it is able to get out now. That means only one thing."

"Old Man Feely's dead." Becky was totally drawn into the story he'd woven.

"That's right."

"But I don't see what it is. Is it a devil?"

"Of a sort. It is what they called in the olden days unspeakable."

"Nothing's unspeakable."

"You haven't seen it."

She caught her breath. "You did?"

8.
Virgil's Story

It was nearly a month later; the moon was full. I had watched my parents mourn the loss of their youngest, while I grew more guilty each day. Yet I had sworn to John Feely that I would not tell anyone. He told me that my brother was lost as soon as he gazed upon that creature and I believed him.

Then, one night, I heard a rapping at my bedroom window. My room was on the third floor of my folks' house. I figured Winston was down below throwing pebbles up.

But instead, I looked out and saw something that looked exactly like my brother, in the big old oak tree just beyond my window, dressed in the overalls I'd last seen him in.

He was sitting among its branches, I thought. But as I watched him in my frozen terror, I saw that he wasn't sitting at all. Eugene was standing on nothing. I thought that he was floating in air.

And then I saw them, in the moonlight that cast its beam between the shadows of leaves and branches: something coming out of his spine, holding him to the tree. They were like the thin, curved legs of horseshoe crabs, that was the closest I could come to determining what they were. Or feelers. Some kind of antennae sprouted from his spinal cord.

I bit the inside of my cheek to make sure I wasn't dreaming.

Eugene spoke to me through the open window. He said, "Why did you leave me there? Why didn't you protect me, Virg? Why did you let it get me?"

And then, it dropped out of sight into darkness.

Only later did I find out about two children of the neighborhood, a boy and a girl, taken from their home. They were found down near the river, their bodies torn, drained of blood.

I went to John Feely, and he took me up to Watch Hill and showed me how it could come up from some of the graves, how the ones without crosses on them could be used as doorways for it.

I had snuck the Bram Stoker book, *Dracula*, from my uncle's house. It had been banned from the local library for twenty years. I knew about creatures that drained blood. I wrote down in the dirt in front of him, "Vampires?"

And he crossed that word out.

John Feely had never heard this term before. He looked at me and said, "No. Angel of the Pit. Abaddon."

We went through Watch Hill that day, looking for where the creature may have come through.

When we found a newly dug, but empty grave, John Feely dropped several crosses down into it and covered them with a thin layer of dirt.

It wasn't until the winter, when another grave was dug up there, that I saw my brother again and pursued him at dawn across the snowy ground to try to catch him. Winston was with me, and he had gone ahead (believing it all, because he believed everything) and had drawn several crosses in the ground around the grave.

I chased my brother, swinging a crucifix I'd been keeping under my bed—borrowed from St. Andrews'—as we ran.

When my brother arrived at the grave, he saw the crosses and stopped dead in his tracks.

He seemed to freeze. He stared at the crosses as the sun slowly rose to the east. Only a purple light. Faint light.

Winston and I were able to walk up to him, then.

We had our equipment ready. We knew now that this was a vampire we were up against.

It was easy. He continued to stare at the crosses in the ground, like a bird hypnotized by a cobra. It was the strangest thing I've ever seen.

Eugene continued to watch the ground as I brought the stake I'd carved up to his chest.

And then, I couldn't do it. I began bawling like a baby. Suddenly, with the light coming up, I didn't believe that my brother would be a monster. I didn't believe.

I started erasing the crosses with my feet. Something compelled me to it, and I remembered how much I loved my brother, how I protected him, how I was never going to hurt him in any way.

And when I turned around, Winston was screaming.

Eugene held my friend with one hand, clutching him as if Winston were a chicken whose neck was about to be wrung.

Something was rippling beneath my brother's face, and remembering Eugene's own vision of Mrs. Feely tearing her face off, I watched something begin to emerge from Eugene's left eye.

I didn't wait to see what Eugene would transform into.

I took the stake and jumped him, jabbing him over

and over in the vicinity of his heart until I was sure that it had stopped.

I sat on top of his body in the bloody snow. Winston, rescued, helped me with the rest of the procedure.

When we were done, when we had finished what we knew had to be done to vampires, we took him to the frozen river and broke the ice. We dumped his body into it. We waited for weeks for someone to come across it; the river ran low the following summer, but his body was never recovered.

I never spoke to John Feely again, and I tell you it has been fifty-some years since that day, and it is as fresh in my memory as yesterday. You may wonder how I stayed sane after that.

I will tell you.

I kept watch for them. Winston and I both. We had a hunch they came back at least once, but somehow John Feely kept it contained.

But whenever a child goes missing, I get a chill, knowing that it might be that thing that has it. That thing that's living beneath the very ground we walk upon, trying to find a way out of its prison. I think it uses children mostly because it requires some belief. As we get older, we lose that, even, sometimes in God. But children believe in things, and it feeds on their beliefs as much as it does their bodies and souls.

9.

Virgil Cobb finished his story. He no longer seemed to be a doctor to Becky, but a very weary, very old man who had come a long way in his life to end up here, frightened of ghosts and goblins. She had begun to believe parts of Virgil's story, at least insofar as he himself believed it, but she knew that this was not sane. What he was talking had no basis in the world. Becky was not a major believer in anything, although she held to her Protestant upbringing a bit—the part of it that didn't directly involve God. She held to the morals and codes and attitudes engendered by the church of her childhood; the supernatural element she didn't buy into at all. She firmly believed that man made his own errors, and that perhaps there was a karmic debt built up, but it had a swift and effective collection agency: *you cheat on your husband, you end up divorced, you lie to a friend, you lose your friend.* She sat there, understanding that Virgil Cobb was, perhaps, talking in metaphor about the loss of his brother. She thought that he truly believed that his brother had been turned into some kind of vampire. A more disturbing thought struck her as she sat there: *if he isn't telling the truth, if he is experiencing delusions, then the little girl in the examination room isn't Patty Glass, of course you gullible idiot, she's some poor girl that Virgil dug up from some grave and mutilated. Or worse, she was alive when he performed his surgery.*

She wanted to believe him, because he had never broken trust with her. He had helped her as a teenager when her father had become too abusive in his drinking, and again when he was her employer. Finally, when the divorce came, he got her inexpensive counseling over in Stone Valley. She wanted to believe him. But she could not. Something within her rebelled.

The desolate thought that remained was that she was listening to, at best, a ghoul; at worst, a murderer and sociopath.

She still felt for him. She took his hand in hers. His hand was cold.

It was just beginning to rain outside. She heard a

wind come up, and then the clicking of the rain as it hit the shingles of the house.

"You must be tired," she said. "Let's get you into bed first thing. We can figure the rest of this out in the morning."

"I am very tired," Virgil replied. "More tired than you can imagine. Thank you for believing me."

She could not look him in the eye.

At least, not until they both heard the cry from the next room.

The examining room.

The cry of a young child, which, as the rain picked up, became a wail.

Virgil said, "Whatever you do, you mustn't go back into that room. It is night now. It must hear its master, like its own heart, beating beneath the house, in the very ground upon which we live."

He rolled his shirtsleeve down to cover the bite on his forearm. "I suppose I'm what it needs to harvest, Rebecca."

As if it were the most important thing in the world (and knowing at the same time that it was totally ridiculous), she said, "Call me Becky, Virgil."

"Becky"—his voice softening as the child's wailing ceased for a moment—"I called you because you're the only person smart enough and trustworthy enough to help me. I'm afraid my friend Winston was already taken. I'm afraid others, too. I don't know who. I just know it is loose in this town. You can run away from it if you want. It's too late for me. I imagine that before the sun is up tomorrow I'll be dead and then it will take me over. I want you to run, actually. I want you to be safe."

"I still don't want to believe this," she said, her

words carefully measured. "Why would this be happening now? Why right now?"

Virgil shook his head. "I don't know. When I was young, it was as if it leaked out. It was as if just by looking at it, we gave it some kind of power. Maybe someone else has given it power, too, whatever it is."

"I just want things to be the way they were before you called me." She said these words as if she were already removed from the immediate problem which involved Virgil and the girl in the next room.

"I understand. You go get your son and anyone you love, and you run, Becky. I understand completely." He nodded.

"No"—she shook her head—"I can't, though. Someone killed my son's dog this morning. I don't know who. They pushed a spike right into the dog's skull. I thought then that it must've been some monstrous juvenile delinquent. But the footprints. Muddy footprints, so tiny, delicate. Like a little girl's. Do you think there are other children?"

"I don't know. If John Feely was somehow stopped last night, there could be any number of people who have been taken by this thing."

"Then I can't leave. I have to go get Tad, and then there's Homer—I won't leave him here. How can I leave any of them to this?" She brought her hands up to her face, covering her eyes. "I feel like we're already lost."

The rain came faster and harder.

Don't think of the body of that girl in the room. Don't think of what he had to do to her.

Minutes passed.

Becky felt rooted to the spot.

Then, the door to the examination room creaked open, behind her, and before Becky could turn around,

she saw it in Virgil Cobb's eyes as he watched what
came through the door—it was not so much terror, as
an expression of such absolute emptiness that for a second she thought Virgil was no longer in his body, but
had already died and left a shell which continued to
twitch.

Becky turned towards the open door.

16

PATTY'S BLOOD

1.

What emerged from the doorway of Virgil Cobb's examination room did not walk across the floor, but crawled from the top of the door frame across the ceiling. The light from the halogen floor lamp cast rays from the thing's main body, which rolled, at first, in a fluid motion as if it were some thick liquid spilled on the ceiling. But it was a body, a small body, moving, reaching as it moved across the acoustic tile of the ceiling.

Virgil Cobb would have trouble describing it later,

for although it seemed human, a child, perhaps, it had no skin. Neither did it seem to have a head. Instead, it had arteries and musculature and hanging yellow fat as if the child's body had somehow been turned inside out. It possessed other qualities, too, but somewhere between his eyes and his brain, Virgil could not make out the various forms that ruptured along its spine; his mind seemed to scramble, unable to determine what it was he was seeing. For a moment, he thought he saw the child again, Patty Glass, even her face; and then, it was some kind of animal, like a bloodied badger; and then, something so geometric that it seemed a crawling crystal formation.

Like a spider, it crawled, pausing above Becky's head for a moment.

Virgil was about to tell her to move, to tell Becky to run out of there, but he could not open his mouth fast enough.

She seemed mesmerized as she stared at the creature.

And then, it dropped:

A rain of blood showering down upon her.

2.

Becky was no longer in Dr. Cobb's waiting room, but in

a dark place, her arms across her chest. It was hard to breathe, and when she tried to move she felt as if she were bound with chains. She tensed and tried flexing her muscles, but nothing would budge—

and then she heard the voice of her grandfather, whispering in her ear, "Join with us, Becky, you've come round at last."

"*Grandpa, where am I?*" she asked.

"*You died, sweetie. Now you're with us, now you're one of us.*"

A spear of light grew from a corner of the box she was in and she realized that it wasn't just a box, it was a coffin, and the people pulling the lid off the coffin weren't just any townspeople—

there was Billy Hoskins at the foot of the coffin, cackling and dancing around like a monkey

Tommy Masello who had died when his dad had mistaken him for a deer on a hunting trip three years back—

Linda Marrow, who seemed more beautiful in death than she ever had in her short life of seven years, her wispy blond hair wreathed with withered roses—

Deke Hunt, who'd been run over by the eleven o'clock train that took a piece of him (they said) all the way down to New Orleans; reaching his gangly arms into her coffin, grabbing her by the ankles and tugging—

And above her, Grandpa and Grandma O'Keefe, their skin dried like leather against their bones and skull, Grandma with her scraggly white hair hanging down to her elbows—in her arms her toy poodle, Buffy, its eye sockets empty, its fur gone, but its tiny mouth opening and closing in a dusty yap. Grandma said, "*We're so pleased you came to us, dear, we've had all these children to look after.*"

The sky was red, and a wind picked up.

"*I'm dead,*" Becky said, remembering the bloody creature dropping onto her at Virgil Cobb's office. She knew it had killed her, and she was buried, and now, what was she?

"*I'm a vampire?*" she asked.

Grandma O'Keefe grinned, a pink worm spitting

from her crusty jaw. "*I wouldn't say that,*" she said, "*I'd say you were just about ripe for picking is what I'd say.*"

"Indeed, yes," Grandpa O'Keefe chortled.

Billy Hoskins leaned into the coffin, into her, right down her belly as if sniffing out her womb.

Then, he attached his lips at her navel and started sucking.

She could not move no matter how hard she tried.

Billy watched her face, but kept his lips to her navel. He made gurgling sounds in the back of his throat. She felt nausea in her stomach, and then, something else, something worse than pain—

a terrible, sweet feeling, as if she were about to enjoy what he was doing to her too much—

excess blood spilling from between his puckered lips—

and then, they all fell on her—

She heard Virgil Cobb say, "It's all right, Becky, it's gone."

She felt as if she were being vacuumed out of her skin, and she realized she was still in the waiting room. She tried to open her eyes, but it was dark. She heard Virgil near her, felt his hands on her shoulders, but she remembered the shower of blood that had come from the ceiling only seconds earlier, and she began thrashing wildly.

"What the hell, Jesus!" Becky gasped, pushing away what felt like insects crawling across her skin. She couldn't see; her eyelashes felt like they were glued together. She brushed frantically at her face. "Get it off me!"

Virgil Cobb was busy wiping a damp towel across her forehead, and around her neck. When he was done, she managed to open her eyes.

Becky looked at her hands. They were dry. There was no redness to her skin, no splotches of blood down her arms. She looked at Virgil. "It got on me. I saw it fall. I saw the blood come down." She glanced up at the ceiling, but it was as if it had been wiped clean.

She convulsed into sobbing, and Virgil Cobb took her in his arms and held her. "What is it?" she whimpered, her face pressed into his neck. "Oh, God, Virgil, what is it? Am I crazy? I was dead—the children—my grandparents—God, oh, God help me."

"No, no, dear," he whispered, patting her back. "You're sane. It's gone now. It's all gone."

For just a moment it was like being a little girl in her father's arms again. She felt safe and warm and dry.

3.

The phone rang. Becky and Virgil looked at it as if it were completely alien to their understanding. Then Virgil picked it up. "Hello?"

He glanced at Becky. "It's Winston." After a minute, he hung the phone up.

"Is he all right?"

Virgil looked as if he had been drained of vitality. "He says he's with Eugene."

A sharp pain cut into Becky's head.

"Tad," was all she said.

THE HOMECOMING

1.

About the same time that Virgil Cobb was finishing up his story for Becky O'Keefe, with the corpse of a little girl in the next room, Joe Gardner pulled his Buick Skylark over to the side of the road. His mother, in the backseat, was clutching the area near her heart with her right hand. Her left hand was rigid. The car grazed the curb. The rain started coming down in sheets, and the wind was blowing hard. Joe felt a panic such as he hadn't felt since the death of Melissa Welles, a choking sensation in his throat, palpitations of his heart. He managed to turn the ignition off before completely succumbing to the feeling of encroaching darkness in his brain, as if he were about to shut down.

Jenny was talking quickly: hospitals, doctors, heart attacks, strokes. He saw a look he remembered from the past across his wife's face, a look he'd seen on someone else's face once. It was a face with a shadow across it; his vision blurred.

Don't shut down, Joe, don't shut down, he told himself, *it's not that bad.* He knew he was a coward most of the time, and it was nothing special to overcome as a writer sitting in a room typing away; but with his mother dying in the backseat . . .

He did it. He broke through the ice of his inertia and unbuckled his seat belt. He quickly wiped at the tears forming in his eyes. He opened his door and got out of the car. He went to his mother's side of the car and opened the door. The rain was cold. He tasted it on his lips.

He was normal again. He was behaving normally, he knew. He slid beside his mother, who seemed small and frail, like a baby bird dropped too early from its nest.

"Mom," he said, putting his arm around her. She felt like a silk handbag, full of bones. He was afraid he might crush her.

Weakly, she said, "It's over, it's over, I'll be fine." She rested in his arms. Joe sighed. His heart continued to beat rapidly. He tried to bring his breathing under control. For a second there, he thought she might go, and then what was he to do after all these years of hating her, love her for one day and then, nothing? He glanced at Jenny, who had tears in her eyes. Aaron, beside them, was silent, his eyes wide.

His mother, a bird in his arms, a thin small bird with

no strength whatsoever in its frame. She smelled like
lilacs. He saw a thin spot on the top of her head. Her
skin was less wrinkled than it was like butterfly wings,
so thin as to be translucent to the workings of the pink
and blue veins beneath it.

"Mom, don't you die on me," he whispered to her,
kissing the top of her head.

"I won't," she sighed. She seemed to fold herself
into him, weary and in retreat.

"Your the only mother I've got."

"And you're my only son."

The rest of the world disappeared for a few moments: the car, the rain, even Aaron, Hillary, and
Jenny. He held his mother as if she were a baby, and
rocked her.

When she had recovered some strength, she told
him the truth.

2.

"I have had heart problems for sixteen years," she
said, "at first, nothing much. My heart has never
pumped all that well. I spend abut three weeks a year
at the hospital. I go to the pain clinic over the hills
once a week. If there's a minor problem, I just go to
Dr. Cobb and he takes care of me. Well, after all, to go
to Stone Valley, I have to take a cab, and it costs a
small fortune, and takes forever—there's only one
driver in this whole damn town. I know it's punishment for the first half of my life."

"Shh, Mom, that's not true." Joe cradled her.

"It is true. I was awful to you and your father. I was
an unfit mother. I don't know why. I don't know what

possessed me in those times. Perhaps it was some undiagnosed illness. Who can say now?"

Jenny said, "We should drive over to the hospital."

Anna Gardner shook her head. "It's fine, now, really. I'll go in tomorrow morning for my appointment, anyway. I have some pills at home. I should've remembered to take them, but I was so excited from today . . ."

"You're talking too much, you need to rest," Joe said. "Let's go back home. I'll call the restaurant and get a message to Hopfrog. We'll spend a nice night at home."

He looked at Jenny. There was something in her eyes, more than tears, a glimmer of something so corny he could only call it the innocence of love, for he knew that she was looking upon him again as she had when they were first married.

He hadn't expected that his wife would ever look upon him again with that innocence, not after what he'd done. He'd never thought they could recapture that.

Joe kept his arms around his mother.

Jenny slid over to the driver's side, and drove them home through the rain.

The whole way back, Joe felt something break inside, something that he had repaired years ago, through anger and strength and stubbornness. But it broke again, just like it was china knocked off the shelf. It wasn't anything like his heart; it was that part of him that believed in things, in happy endings, the part that wasn't so cynical about the world. As he sat with his mother in the car, he didn't think he would ever regain that part of himself again.

3.

Even back at his mother's house, he thought about that: what he believed in. What could possibly be believed in this world. Joe sat on the stairs, just as he had when he'd been a boy, sneaking down to watch late night TV (which his mother would sit up and watch while she drank in the parlor). He sat with his hand cupping his chin. Hillary was tucked up against him, her legs dangling slightly over his knees. She was almost asleep, her small nostrils flaring slightly as she breathed, her eyes closed. He kissed her on the scalp a few times.

Jenny came out of the bathroom. "She's taken her pills, Joe," she said. "Anna seems fine. She needs to rest. It'll be all right."

Jenny stood on the landing. Aaron was out on the front porch, watching the storm. Joe felt the invisible tentacles of family emanate out from him and touch each one of them, to make sure they were okay. "Sometimes it seems like my only job in life."

"Joe?"

"I was just thinking. About when I was a kid, and now. How I always wanted to make sure that nothing bad ever happened to anyone. I look at Hillary, and Aaron, and I think about all the bad stuff they're going to have to face. And other kids, too. All sweet and pure and bright, and how they're going to have to go through what happens to everyone, but shouldn't. I wish I could be there to stop whatever bad's going to happen."

"Like Holden Caulfield?"

"Right: catch them as they go over the rye field. But he wanted to because he thought adults were phonies. I don't think that. I think adults are just overgrown kids who maybe looked in the funhouse mirror and believed what they saw."

"I don't understand," she said. She took two steps up the stairs, and sat down just beneath him.

"I guess in my heart of hearts I've always felt it was me who drove my mother away. I've always felt it was me . . ." That was about as clearly as he could put it. He hugged Hillary tight and rocked her back and forth against him. She smelled like shampoo and rain. "I don't want my kids to ever feel that. To ever feel like they did anything wrong."

"Joe." Jenny placed her hand on his knee. Her voice was low and soft and steady. "Maybe we should go home. Maybe this is too much right now."

He shook his head slowly. "No. I want to be here now. This is my home."

He began stammering on these last words. Finally, he said, "I don't want her to die."

He barely heard the phone ringing.

4.

Hopfrog Petersen and his son had been sitting at the corner booth downstairs at the Angel Wing for half an hour, when Tad got the brilliant idea. "Why don't you call them? I'm starved."

So Hop had wheeled on over to Lou's phone—Lou sat it upright on the host podium for anyone to use— and dialed Joe's mother's house. In all those intervening years, he hadn't forgotten the number, which was less a tribute to friendship than it was to Hopfrog's unnerving memory for minute and less than important details. The phone picked up on the fifth ring.

A woman said, "Gardner residence. Hello?"

He hesitated. This didn't sound like a little old lady, and it definitely wasn't Joe Gardner. "You're Jenny," he said.

"Hello?"

"This is Homer—this is Hopfrog Petersen."

"Oh." Her voice had a strain of sadness running through it. "I'm so sorry we didn't call first. Joe's mother isn't feeling well, and we had to come back home. Let me put Joe on." Before he could get another word in, the voice changed.

It was Joe. "Hop?"

"Joey?"

"Hey, long time no see."

"Well, you woulda seen me had you kept your appointment with destiny." In a split second, the two of them had fallen back into the speech pattern and cadence of their adolescence. "So, how's it hangin'?"

"Oh, Jenny told you. That was Jenny, my wife. Wait'll you meet her." This was said in gusts of breath, and then, the sadness. "Mom's not doing too well tonight. We had to come back. She's doing a little better now."

Hopfrog said, "I have so much to talk about with you, Joe."

"Me, too. I want you to meet my kids and Jenny. I guess this just isn't the night for it."

"How 'bout if my boy and I swing by there?"

"Let me check," Joe said, and then the phone went silent. Hopfrog figured he must be punching the mute button. When Joe came back on he sounded like an excited sixteen-year-old who got the car for the night: "Hey, Hop, Jenny said she'll stay here with Mom and the kids. I feel sort of guilty leaving them . . ." From the background, Hopfrog heard Joe's wife say, "You're not going to sit around here and mope all night," and then Joe said, "I can meet you down there in about fifteen minutes."

5.

It took less than ten minutes, actually, and Joe was sopping wet from the rain when he walked into the pub. The place was full and smoky; Joe had a bit of a problem with asthma, so he started coughing right off, and that's what made Hopfrog look up to the door.

Joe stood there, his dark hair a little too long (although certainly very short by the standards of their boyhoods), his glasses round and schoolteacherish. In all that time, the guy had still not changed his style of dress: khakis, topsiders, white button-down shirt, and a blue windbreaker. It made Hopfrog laugh out loud to see him, and he practically did a wheelie as he cut a path to the door. The two men hugged, and Joe was the first to say, "I missed you, ratface."

Tad came up and stood beside his father, looked up at Joe and said, "It's about time. I'm starved."

6.

Lou moved their table to the back room, where there was less smoke than up front owing to the great open patio (Joe was still coughing, but it wasn't quite as bad as it had been in the front room). The rainstorm raged outside, but it was not so cold as to be uncomfortable, and the three of them were the only ones in the small room.

"So tell me about my dad when he was a kid," Tad said.

"I don't know if he wants me to do that." Joe winked. "Your father was a geek from the word go. He didn't have a neck and he walked pigeon-toed."

"Figures," Tad said.

"Don't do much walking anymore," Hopfrog said, and then when he noticed that Joe's face got all sad when he made this reference to his legs, he laughed. "It's a joke, Joe. I don't miss my legs all that much. Do I, Tad?"

The boy shook his head as he took a bite out of an enormous hamburger.

"How's the woodworking business?"

"Fair. We had a fire last year out on Connaught Road, and so I got a lot of work there redoing kitchen cabinets and some detail work on staircases. The factory hires me four months of the year to do detail work on the rockers, too. Then I teach shop at the junior high a couple of days a week. I get by. How's the book business?"

"Let me put it this way," Joe said. "If I had it to do over again, I'd've studied accounting. Or plumbing. But it's all I seem to be able to do."

"Your Mom?"

"She took some pills and fell asleep. She claimed that she'd be fine if she got some rest. I feel a little guilty running out the door, but Jenny was okay with it." Then, turning to Tad, "I wish I'd dragged Aaron down to meet you, Tad."

Tad, finishing his hamburger quickly, looked at his father and then at Joe, as if scrutinizing them. He said, "Mom says that whenever you two get together, it's all she can do to keep from jumping out a window."

All three of them laughed. "Well, it's true," Joe said. Tad shook his head. "I like it. Dad doesn't have any friends, not really. Only me, and I don't count 'cause I'm blood. I'm really happy he has a best friend."

Later, after a couple of beers and talk about family and work and places traveled, Hopfrog turned to Joe and said, "I have to ask this, even though I'm not sure I want to."

"Shoot."

"Did you come back because of what happened?"

Joe looked a little confused. "I came back because of my mother."

Hopfrog wasn't buying this. "No, you didn't. You came back because It wanted you to come back."

"Hop? What are you talking about? It?"

Now Hopfrog felt a little angry. He said, "Don't play games with me on this, Joe. Remember? That night? When you convinced me that we'd find it empty— remember?"

Joe said, "I don't know what you're . . ." and then stopped himself. Joe glanced at Tad, who was watching him. "I don't know if we should talk about this right now."

"It's okay, Joe. Tad saw her last night. I didn't really believe him, not 'til this morning when I found this." Hopfrog reached into his breast pocket and withdrew a shred of silk fabric. He passed it to Joe.

Joe took it in his hand and turned it over. "Any number of women might wear this . . ."

Hopfrog shook his head. "Don't even start. You know and I know. What, you move away and you forget everything?"

Joe didn't answer for a minute or more. He seemed to forget where he was. He finally looked up at Hopfrog. "It's not that I forgot. It's that I thought I was crazy for a little while back then. That's why I never came back 'til now. I thought I was crazy. I didn't want to get crazy again, not like that. I didn't want to be-lieve it had happened."

"Believe it," Hopfrog said. "She's out again."

Tad, who had been pretending to finish off his 7-Up, looked at each of the men: first his father, and then Joe Gardner, as if they were speaking a foreign language.

"Are you talking about that ghost I saw?" Tad asked, looking at his father, then to Joe.

And then, he told them. Not just about the girl he saw at his window, but about the newly dug grave at Watch Hill, when he thought he heard Billy Hoskins calling to him from underground. When he was through talking, Tad had worked up a sweat because it frightened him more just remembering than when it had happened.

Both of them were staring at him in a way that made Tad aware that he hadn't just imagined any of this. That it was as if Halloween had never ended.

Joe said, "Oh, my God. Oh, my God."

"What is it?" Hopfrog asked.

Joe said, "I can hear her again. She's talking to me."

"Who?"

Joe's face went completely white. "Melissa."

7.

What might have been the voice of Melissa Welles, long dead, or what might have been a thread of in-sanity in Joe's head whispered,

Welcome home, Joe, we've all been waiting for you for a long, long time.

18

FAMILY

1.

At Anna Gardner's house, Jenny had just finished getting Hillary fed and to bed. Aaron was up watching television. Jenny was emotionally wrung out from the trip, and was half wishing that Joe had accepted her offer to turn around and go home. *Not this place, but our real home, back in Baltimore.* She had been aware when they'd planned this trip that it might be stressful, but she had had no idea how exhausting it would be. Jenny was used to carrying the brunt of the labor, after having practically raised her five siblings, so working at the *Weekly*, raising the kids, and keeping house were the norm, but when she had to coddle Joe, too, sometimes it drove her a little nuts. She had been hoping for a brief vacation, these four days, but given both the internal and external weather, it was beginning to look like this patching up of family bonds would be a whole new career.

She went downstairs and plopped down on the sofa beside Aaron. A mindless comedy was on the tube about a family which had the kinds of problems you could solve in thirty minutes or less; it was relaxing. She fell asleep and then awoke again. The same show seemed to be on; she glanced at Aaron. He looked over, too, and smiled.

She felt warm.

"What time's it?" she asked.

He shrugged. "How should I know?"

"Where's your watch?"

"Upstairs."

"I think it's late."

"It can't be. This show's over by nine-thirty."

"Okay," she said, and fell asleep again without wanting to. Her whole body seemed to fall down on feathers. She heard the voices from the television as if in a newly born dream.

When she awoke again, the television was still on. The room was dark but for the blue and white flashes from the TV screen. Jenny rubbed her eyes. Aaron was no longer on the sofa with her. Where he'd been sitting, the crease from his body as if he'd only moments ago gotten up from the cushion. She yawned and stood up. Rain battered the windows; lightning sounded like bombs blasting over the river. She sleepily walked to the kitchen. Poured herself a glass of water, and drank it. She looked out at the lit porch, the rain, the flashes of lightning.

Something was moving outside, just beyond the porch light.

Something like several men hunched together, forming one large shadow in the rain.

It's the lightning.

She checked the kitchen clock. It was only quarter to ten. Not all that late for Joe to be out with his friend.

Again, she looked through the window.

The shadow of something passed, fluttering, across the incandescent light bulb on the porch.

The light went out.

My imagination, she thought. But Jenny was not given to wild imaginings or to seeing things that weren't there. She was sometimes too practical, too commonsense oriented, but not given to seeing specters where there weren't any.

"You need to replace the bulb on the front porch," she would tell Joe in the morning, "it burned out last night in the storm." She would tell that to him, and then it would seem silly that she had ever been scared about some kind of shadow on the porch that had covered the light bulb.

The lightning flashed. It reflected out on the river and illuminated the night.

And there, on the porch, stood a teenager, she thought, maybe a very young man, his hair white and snaking out from his scalp in a static wind, his naked torso tattooed with swirling designs. He was looking directly at her in the darkness of the kitchen, trying to shout over the crash of thunder.

Jenny Gardner suddenly felt cold, as if her body temperature had dropped several degrees in just a few seconds.

2.

Aaron couldn't sleep through the thunder, as much as he tried, pulling the pillow over his head. His usual solution to this was to go bother Hillary—in some respects he had never gotten over the idea that she was his own private toy to tease and annoy to his heart's content. He slipped out of bed and padded over to the guest bed.

He sat at the edge of the bed, staring at the shadowy form of his sister in the dark, the occasional flashes of lightning illuminating the room. "Hey, Pipsqueak."

Hillary woke up, annoyed, making her snarfling noises.

"I said hey Pipsqueak."

"What you want?" she asked in her authoritarian princess voice. "Leave me alone."

He giggled. For a baby, she was so haughty when it came to him. "I can't sleep. You want to play some games?"

She shook her head. "I tired."

"We can play hide and go seek," he said.

Then, a flash of lightning lit up the room, and Aaron thought he saw someone on the other side of the window, a boy just like him, with his eyes wide, his skin blue, his hair matted.

3.

Anna Gardner slept soundly, until the lightning was so bright that it jolted her awake. She sat up, feeling her heart racing a mile a minute, and reached for the pills at her bedside table.

As she reached, she felt a chill—someone had opened the window—rain was pouring in—

Her pills were not there, and as she groped around the table in the dark, someone grabbed her hand.

It was as if she'd stuck her hand into a hornet's nest.

19

BYRON

He owned the night. He owned this house, too, this woman who looked out at him, he owned everything in it. He was not just Byron Cheever, oh, no, he was the lord of the dark—he had already taken others, women, men, children, taken them to the Radiant One, watched while their blood was drunk, tasted the warm liquid and rolled it between his tongue and cheek, the warm, shooting blood. He felt that surge of power that only a god could feel, the energy flowing through him—

the electricity of life as it drained from the human body!

There were no words for it—all those years of his education had been shit, piles of meaningless shit. His mind had been opened and lit with the fires of his master, and when the children had drunk some of his own blood and eaten half his flesh, tattooing onto him their stories, their histories and legends, he had known all about them, all about the evil which had been perpetrated against his master, all the evil these blood holders had done in the name of their vanity. The crosses, the hieroglyphs, the incantations, to keep his master down in the prison.

But now. *Now!*

He shouted against the thunder, "I will tear your flesh open and drink your holy wine, bitch!"

The woman must've heard him, the woman at the kitchen window, for she wore an expression of terror.

He danced across the porch, and when the others came up to him, he knew that this would be the night of blood, and all creatures of darkness would rejoice.

20

HOPFROG'S RESEARCH

1.

Joe and Hopfrog drove in their separate cars back to Hop's house after supper. Tad went into the den to play video games while the two men settled into the study.

"I wasn't sure how much to say in front of your son," Joe said.

Hopfrog shrugged. "I don't think he needs to know the gory details, but he *is* the one who saw her. I tried to make him think it was a nightmare, but I know differently. I don't believe it was actually her, either, Joe.

I don't believe it was ever really her. I would call this an It, for lack of a better term."

"We called it vampire back then," Joe said. "You know what she said to me at the pub? She told me that she was faithful all these years. Waiting for us. Not just me, but you, too."

Hopfrog's mind seemed to be somewhere else for a moment. "Vampires. We were so influenced by horror movies. I have my own horror movies, made in the past ten years, Joe." Hopfrog wheeled over to the small television at the edge of his desk, and pushed a button on the VCR beneath it.

The screen came up blue. The word "play" appeared and then disappeared on the screen.

A static picture of what seemed darkness began to move as bright lights trembled.

Hopfrog's voice said, "All right, before I get put away by my wife, I decided to go down here a ways. Don't try this at home, kids, especially if your legs don't work."

The camera was moving and it was apparent that Hopfrog, filming this cave, was sliding down the shaft, clutching the camera and shoving some kind of brilliant light along beside him.

"I am going down into the mine. I've got my ropes on, and God willing, I'll make it. There," he said, and the camera and lights suddenly swung out to the wall of the cave.

When the picture came into clear focus, it was a close-up of the rock wall. There were scratches and dark stains all over it. Hopfrog's hand came into the picture and touched the wall.

"They were trying to get out. It's had others, too. Maybe It still manages to get others."

As the camera got closer, as it zoomed in on the rock

wall, and as the light brightened, something else was there, besides the scratches and the stain.

It was the formation of the wall, like a bas-relief, the images of children's faces as if pressing from the other side of the wall, trying to move outward.

Hopfrog pressed the freeze-frame button on the VCR. "It is something beyond what we thought, Joe. I don't think it's a vampire in the mythic way. I think it's some kind of other species living beneath this town. See those faces? Can you identify any of them?"

Joe looked closely at the television, but the children's faces were so out of focus it had taken a leap of faith to even believe that these represented real children.

"The one to the left." Hopfrog pointed to the screen. "Patty Glass. Remember? Look at the bridge of the nose."

"So, what are you saying, Hop? That Patty Glass was embedded in rock? That she's a fossil?" Joe actually had to laugh. "That something is down there which makes imprints in rocks out of children's faces?"

Hopfrog's face wrinkled in anger. "That the dead rise? That Melissa Welles came back and drank a baby dry and then came for me four and a half months after she was buried? That she and other dead people spoke through you when you were a teenager? Go to hell, Joe, if that's how you're going to deal with this."

"I'm sorry."

"You should be."

"Okay, so what does this mean?"

"I'm not sure. What if this is something that takes Its victims and re-creates them? So that these formations in the rock are just the impressions it needs to mold the body? I've been reading"—Hopfrog waved his hand towards his stuffed bookshelves—"about everything from angels to aliens, and none of it makes any more sense than what you and I went through back then. But at least one alleged survivor of an encounter with aliens (assuming you buy into it), claimed that a cast was made from his body because the alien had no form itself beyond a sort of gaseous light. This was in France, in Brittany, 1973. Several other reports have mentioned that the extraterrestrials appeared as a will-o'-the-wisp sort of light, too. Since this town has existed, in any form, there have been disappearances and there have been rumors of that damn angel that pointed this town out to the first settlers. All I know is what you and I went through when we saw Melissa leaving her grave. All I know is that a kid just went missing the day before yesterday, and I suspect he's been taken by whatever is down there."

"What, the boogie man lives beneath Colony?"

A look crossed Hopfrog's face, a look that wasn't anger or frustration, but disdain, as if he had been betrayed by Joe by that one question. "I believe that whatever is here in this town has been here for a thousand years, maybe more. I believe that it is from another world, either from up there"—he nodded towards the ceiling—"beyond our own solar system, or from some other consciousness, and that thing found a bridge between the world it inhabited and our world."

"Well," Joe said, "I guess it doesn't sound any screwier than my undead theory."

"Did you know that in 1865, the summer after the end of the Civil War, Watch Hill was set on fire? It was in the Stone Valley papers—some kid had lit the grass, and burned himself up with it. Nobody knew why, but there had been ghost stories about the dead soldiers haunting the area. And before that, during the war, twenty children were missing, mostly boys, but after the fire, their bodies turned up, stacked and bled dry in the Feely vault?" Hopfrog drew a looseleaf notebook from one of his desk drawers. He opened it to a page, and passed it to Joe.

It was a newspaper clipping from the Charleston paper, February 12, 1904. The article headline read: *Fifth Child Vanishes In "Colony Mystery."*

"That clipping's about a rash of unexplained disappearances, and then"—he reached across and flipped the page for Joe—"see? Two weeks later, look."

The clipping read: *Grave Robbing In Colony.*

"They caught a man a few weeks later, digging up some fresh grave. He was arrested for grave robbing, and then they found the bodies of four children, decapitated and eviscerated in his basement. He claimed that he had put them to rest, that they weren't children, but the walking tools of Satan. None of these children could be identified, Joe, because none of them were from that time period. But, look, here's a picture of one of them."

Hopfrog turned the page again and ripped out the clipping.

He held it close to Joe's face. Joe had to lean back in order to see the photograph clearly.

"Oh, my God," Joe gasped. "When was this taken?"

Hopfrog half grinned. "Thank God I'm not insane, Joe. Without someone to share these with, I was beginning to think I was insane, that I was ready for the state hospital. I didn't trust anyone else to talk with about what this might mean." He wore an expression of equal parts relief and hope. "I missed you so much, Joe, all these years. You're the only one who would understand."

Joe wiped his hands over his face. "When, Hop?"

"This photo comes from the 1904 newspaper out of

Stone Valley, what was then called the *Press-Enterprise*."

"It can't be," Joe said.

"It is. Remarkable."

"Patty Glass," Joe whispered, looking at the girl in the picture. It felt as if he were saying something too blasphemous for human ears.

"Patty Glass," Hopfrog confirmed. "Age twelve, not looking two minutes older than when she disappeared in Old Man Feely's barn. And this was one of the bodies that had not been hurt. She was still alive and according to the paper unable to speak. She vanished again. No one from that time period ever saw her."

"Patty." Joe's voice broke. He wasn't crying, but he could no longer speak.

"Need a drink?" Hopfrog asked, reaching for his trusty bottle of whiskey.

Joe nodded. After Hopfrog took a swig, he passed it to Joe. Joe looked at the bottle, then at his friend. He set the bottle down on the desk. After a minute he spoke, "I want to stay sober for this. So what does this mean, I mean if it's really Patty Glass in a photo taken decades before her birth?"

Hopfrog retrieved the bottle, drank again from it. "Well, you could look for the complex explanation. Maybe someone is playing an elaborate hoax on anyone who knew Patty and has managed to put a faked photo into the microfiche of the library. Or, the simpler one, in which somehow Patty Glass traveled backwards through time. And forward, too."

"Forward?"

"You haven't been in town long enough to hear the buzz, but this morning, I heard the kids at school talking about it. She showed up at her parents' door yesterday, good as new, and still about twelve years old."

"I don't believe it."

"And this." Hopfrog drew some papers out from a folder, passing them to Joe. "If you read through it, you'll see that in 1931, one of the mines imploded, killing sixteen miners, and trapping four. Of the four, only one survived, and he gave this account at State, where he ended up living for the rest of his days. He claimed there were ghosts haunting the shafts. He claimed that he saw what looked like a giant crab down there, too. He lived off the bodies of the dead for two months before they were able to locate him. When they did, he told the authorities about children with wings and that the entrance to hell was down in the mine. He may truly have been mad, but read this part." He pointed to the second page, resting in Joe's hand.

Joe read it aloud, "James Woodard said, 'The devil told me he was looking for one of his children, that one of his babies had gotten trapped down here and he was looking through all of time for him. He said he wouldn't drink my blood if I brought others to him. I got to get him some blood, y'see, I got to.' " Joe let the pages drop from his lap to the floor. "I don't believe it. I don't."

"Joe Gardner, you can sit here after what we've been through and say that . . . Jesus, Joe. You hearing voices, these disappearances, what we went through . . . The point isn't that this miner saw the devil, the point is that something's down there, only no one but maybe you, me, and maybe this James Woodard ever saw It and came back."

Joe interrupted, "We didn't go down there."

Hopfrog nodded. "Technically, no. But what we saw in that barn, It was this . . . devil, vampire, alien, whatever you want to call it. God, you don't know what a relief this is just to be able to sit and talk with you about it, Joe." He wiped his forehead and then his dry lips. "I've been holding this in for so long, slowly doing my research, slowly putting things together. Just take this for what it is: we know Patty vanished when we were kids. According to this photo, she appeared in 1904. According to current rumor, she appeared yesterday in town, and this is according to kids who weren't even around when she first vanished. Now, either Patty's some kind of god, or this thing, let's call it an angel, is living beneath this town, and it's somehow feeding off these children, let's say. Maybe the way we saw Melissa feed off the Fulchers' baby. Maybe it needs the blood to survive and empower it, just like an engine needs gasoline. Only this engine makes the machine go forward and backward in time. Maybe it's drawing blood from generations of residents of Colony. And why Colony? Why not somewhere else? I think I figured that out, too. Maybe the blood here is a little better because of something in the soil, something that gets in the water, hell, we have our own wells here. I'm not a geological genius, but I also am aware that certain cancers are higher in this region than even right over the hills, less than an hour away. I don't know what it is; maybe it's some mineral we haven't even classified yet. But this thing, this It, is down there, I know it is, milking us, milking our children, and for some unknown reason, it needs to travel backwards and forwards in time. It sounds insane, but after ten years of devoting my free hours to this, that's what I've come up with."

Joe took a long breath. "Okay. Okay. I don't quite follow you. But, as far as I see it, if this It needs blood, why doesn't It just attack all at once?"

Hopfrog half smiled, as if waiting for this question.

"Why buy the cow when you can get the milk for free? Why kill the golden goose? It's been living here for centuries, maybe. Why screw up a good thing?"

"Oh, jeez, Hop, you don't even see what you're doing. You're creating a pattern around all these incidents and making sure it all fits, when in reality each may be completely random and separate."

"I'm not going to say it again, Joe: fuck you. You saw what the corpse of Melissa Welles did, you helped dig up her grave and what we found . . ."

"I know, I know," Joe said, and covered his ears with his hands just like a four year old because he didn't want to hear this, it was screwing with his mind, it was making him go haywire inside, remembering . . .

the voices, as he opened the coffin,

and it was empty, but the bottom of it had been clawed at and opened, and something had gotten out of it, moved down through the earth, down through the root-encrusted ground, dug its way like a mole downward to some final destination.

The voices of the dead had said to him, "Joe, come on down, boy, make yourself at home, we want you and Missy to be together for always, throughout eternity, together, just you and the love of your life."

2.

After looking through Hopfrog's scrapbook, Joe looked up at him. "What does It want?"

"What?"

"Well, someone always wants something."

"Maybe just blood. Maybe this mineral in the blood."

Joe shook his head. "I just don't get it. You said something about an engine. About blood being like gasoline. If It needs blood, why? Is It going somewhere?"

"I don't know. Back in time?"

"Or maybe It's stuck and is looking for a way out?"

"I'm either drunk or you're making no sense whatsoever." Hopfrog laughed.

Joe looked at the window and saw his own reflection against the dark, rain-spattered night. "And why now? Why didn't this thing, whatever it is, do this last year? Four years ago?"

"Oh, I sort of figured that one out"—Hopfrog looked up at him and said, unhesitatingly—"it's because you've come back, Joe. I think—I believe It needs you."

Joe turned to face Hopfrog again. "What?" he whispered.

"I never wrote or called because I didn't want you here again," Hopfrog said, his voice barely a whisper. "You were like my brother, but I didn't want you here because when you were here, it happened. You heard the voices, Joe, you were It's receiver."

Joe closed his eyes, trying to wish the world away in a heartbeat. When he opened his eyes, the room and Hopfrog and the books were still there. He said, "I don't understand. Because of the accident?"

"I've been trying to piece it all together ever since then," Hopfrog said. "I'm not sure why. Maybe it's 'cause It almost had you back then. Maybe because of what you did . . . to yourself."

Joe went and took a drink. The whiskey went down his throat burning. He glanced down at his wrists. The scars were healed years before, but the whitest of lines, like creases in the fabric of his skin, were still there, jagged and long from his wrists up to his fore-arms. *Eighteen years old, crouching down in the mine shaft, the razor in his hand, waiting for death and for Melissa to come to him, to take him with her.*

"Maybe you came close to It then. I don't know, I don't know." Hopfrog pressed his hands up to his face and began weeping. It was the saddest sound Joe had ever heard. "I have been trying . . . so long . . . to understand why it happened . . . On one level, I might just be making it up, but on another, I know it's true: why Patty Glass is in a newspaper that was printed decades before her birth . . . and what we did the day she disappeared. What we did in that barn . . . as soon as I heard you . . . that you were here . . . I knew it was going to happen all over again."

"But Hop," Joe asked, *"why me?"*

"I'm not smart enough to know. It's something from beyond . . . I have read every alien-abduction book from the past twenty years, and why do you think some moron from the backwoods gets abducted and not Ein-stein?" Hopfrog had gone from crying to barking. "Why does anything happen to anyone? Christ, Joe, I don't fucking know. I'm just an idiot carpenter in the land of Bumfuck. How the hell am I supposed to know everything? All I know is It exists, It's here, It's going back and forth in time, It's used children, and Patty Glass appeared about the same time you did. You fig-ure it out."

Tad came and stood in the doorway. "Daddy, are you fighting?" He looked both sleepy and excited.

Hopfrog wheeled over to his son and plopped him onto his lap. "Just debating. It's bedtime for you, kiddo —we promise to keep it down from here on."

Tad looked at Joe. "My mom says you're a bad influ-ence."

Joe couldn't even smile. Mechanically, he said, "Does she? Well, she just may be right."

3.

Ten minutes later, Hopfrog closed Tad's door and wheeled along the hall to where Joe sat at the staircase. "Let's go back in the study," he said, "I've got to tell you something."

4.

"Remember at that well?" Hopfrog asked. "Over at the Feely barn."

Joe nodded. "When Patty disappeared."

"Yep. What you did, Joe, do you remember that?"

Joe thought a minute, trying to conjure up a picture: inside the Feely barn, the golden light at the well, the crucifixes and Egyptian symbols as if it were some ancient tomb. He couldn't remember exactly what had transpired. "I remember being there. Not much else."

"It was what you did." Hopfrog grinned. He looked a little mad. Beads of sweat sprouted along the lines of his forehead and he had a glimmer in his eyes. "You did something really important back then, only you didn't know it. I don't know how you did it, but it protected us, you, me and Melissa, at least then. It only got Melissa later." Looking down at his useless legs, he whispered, "It only got part of me."

"I just remember all that light. The golden light."

"What about the boy? All covered with blood? Only it didn't always just look like a boy—it looked like a bug, too."

Joe shut his eyes, trying to draw the picture-memory from his mind: *The warm light, he bathed in it, practically, and touching the markings on the well—although now, as a grown-up, remembering, it seemed less a well than a metal tube, some kind of thick, shiny metal . . . Hopfrog was there, on two legs, and Melissa, close by, too . . . and then he saw him, the boy, the blood boy—*

But Joe saw through the boy, too, and it wasn't a boy at all, but some kind of insect, or machine, something with multiple eyes, something with shriveled vestigial wings in a row along its carapace . . . the Thing's lampreylike mouth gasping as if for air . . . it was some kind of dragon, and it must've taken Patty Glass— but Joe knew it wanted all of them . . .

And then the memory became confused, as if Joe had superimposed another memory, one from his imagination—for he was no longer Joe in the memory, but *King Joe Dragonheart, and he withdrew his flaming sword of valor and struck the dragon a blow to its heart . . .*

Joe opened his eyes. "I don't remember it clearly. I'm not even sure it really happened. Maybe it was mass hysteria, Hop, maybe we were so scared we made up a story about it."

"I think maybe you killed something there in that barn. I don't know how." Hopfrog's grin slid into a tight-lipped line. "Or maybe you know how to protect yourself from It, Joe. Maybe the reason It's out now is because It wants you most of all because you're the only one who can stop It." Then Hopfrog drew something out from his pocket. "Look at this," he said. He passed what seemed to be a rock to Joe.

Joe turned it over in his hand. "A fossil? What is

this, maybe a trilobite or something?" The chip of volcanic rock was curved and shiny at the center, as if it were studded with bits of mica. The impression of an insect or some many ribbed animal, about the size of a fist, was at its center.

Hopfrog half smiled. "You'll never believe what it is."

"I'm beginning to believe a hell of a lot."

"What would you say if I told you that that rock is only about twenty years old?"

Joe shrugged. "That's nuts. I'm no rock collector, but it's obviously some kind of lava with a fossil of an insect or crustacean in it. If it's twenty years old, it came from Hawaii or something."

"It's not lava. It's from the mud in Old Man Feely's barn. After you killed that thing, Joe, I found it there. It's what attacked us. It's not what we saw, I know, but it's the thing behind what we saw. It's what you managed to kill. And it burned into the mud. I slipped it in my pocket afterwards and kept it. I kept it so I would never forget what happened then."

Joe held the rock up to the light, but shook his head. "This thing is what we saw there?"

"Not what we saw. We somehow created what we saw from this. This is the raw material of our nightmare, Joe."

"Joe Dragonheart," Joe said.

"Huh?"

"King Joe Dragonheart. That's who I believed I was when I slew it. I believed it was a dragon. I really believed so hard, Hop, so hard . . . it seemed true."

Several minutes passed before Joe noticed that someone was ringing the doorbell, and he dreaded finding out who or what might be on the other side of that door. It was as if the world had come to a stop just so he and his old friend could talk about something that seemed more forbidden than anything that had ever existed in the world before.

21

JENNY

Jenny tried the phone, thinking that she'd try to track down Joe at the Angel Wing Pub, but the line was down, and that weird kid was still standing on the front porch, staring at her.

If she had known that his name was Byron Cheever and what he was currently capable of, she might've gone for a knife, but instead, she went to the door, and opened it a crack to ask the young man what he wanted.

Before she could say anything, lightning struck a nearby tree, lighting up the sky so that she could see the children in the yard, all standing near the older boy. Seven or eight children, she thought, but the light was so brilliant as to be blinding, so there may have been more.

Then, the electricity went out.

The very darkness seemed to move towards her.

THE NIGHT COLONY

22

SIEGE

1.

Joe opened Hopfrog's front door.

"Becky," he said, wearily.

She was rain soaked and her face was shiny with exertion. "Where's Tad," she said, brushing past him, taking the stairs two at a time. "Is he in bed?"

Virgil Cobb stood out on the porch. "Hello, Joe," he said. "Hello, Homer."

Hopfrog wheeled over and extended his hand. "Dr. Cobb, good to see you."

Lightning burst across the sky, like fireworks lighting up the whole neighborhood. The rain was thinning out. For a while, it turned to sleet.

Virgil said, "It's back again. Tonight."

Hopfrog nodded. It was as if they'd all stepped off the smooth world of sanity and had fallen into this pit of belief in anything and everything. "Yes."

Incongruously, Virgil said to Joe, "How's your mother, Joe?"

Joe felt as if he had just swallowed his heart. "Oh, Jesus, my family, Hop, we've got to get them, too."

And that's when they all heard it: the scream, blood-curdling, chilling, the kind of scream that could bring a grown man to his knees.

It was Becky.

2.

It was only the beginning of the screaming and wail-ing that would continue through the night, as house-holds in the small town of Colony, the town which produced the world-reknowned rocking chairs, found that their children were gone.

Others found that their children had returned for them.

Romeo Dancer returned from a night of boozing to find his wife Wilma's body drained of blood, and his four, normally hungry children looking quite full and bloated; Tenley McWhorter and her boyfriend Noah Cristman had already begun bleeding his father, tied up to one of the famous Colony rockers, his veins torn and pulsing with the last of his life as he watched something that did not seem entirely human shoot from the back of Noah's mouth, something which re-minded him of a bug's antennae; Elvis Bonchance had his baby brothers, both under two years old, in his pudgy fingers, their eyes open and pink, their bodies pure white, a large smear of black red across the front of his overalls; and Davy, the little boy freshly back from the dead who had begun sucking on Dale Chambers's bones as if they were sugarcane, sat on his haunches on the motel bed as if waiting for a signal; house to house, there were less than twenty people still alive in town, and within minutes, this figure would be reduced to a handful.

Night had descended upon this corner of God's earth, and it was a darkness which would not give in to the light.

3.

Joe found Becky sobbing at the top of the stairs. He wrapped his arms around her. Peering into Tad's bedroom, he saw the window open, rain coming in to the room, the flash of lightning outside.

"Please," she said, "please let me go, I have to go find my baby!" She tugged away from him, but didn't move again. Instead she shivered and wept and did not even seem to be conscious of her surroundings.

Hopfrog had crawled up the stairs, using the special bars positioned beneath the banister. He knelt beside his wife, speaking soft words of comfort to her, flashing anger at Joe. "I have a gun in the top drawer of my desk. Get it for me now. I am going to go out and get my son."

And then, it struck Joe. He was suddenly caught up in a nightmare which was not just personal, not just years built up of fears and fairy tales and the hyper-imagination of a young creative man—this was a nightmare which he had stumbled across years ago, which had remained dormant, like a volcano waiting to blow.

He forgot about getting the gun for Hopfrog, forgot about the present tragedy of Hop's son Tad being missing, forgot anything and everything except for the picture of Jenny and Hillary and Aaron. It was as if a dam had burst within him, a dam that had been holding in fears and terrors and suspicions and beliefs—the muck of a childhood revisited in a moment. *MY FAMILY OH GOD DON'T LET ANYTHING HAPPEN TO MY FAMILY, PLEASE GOD, PLEASE.*

That other voice, too, not of anyone dead, but of Mister Fate, always there in the background whispered,

What do you want most, kid?

You want happiness? Love? Fortune? Family?

You want to see what happens when you return home? You want to see everything you've ever loved die again and again and again?

You want to know what happens to kids who defeat the dragon and then grow up? The dragon comes back, King Joe, It comes back and It's hungry for blood.

4.

Had he run to his Buick? Joe couldn't even remember, for the fever had taken him, the fever and the fear, too. It had been a blur, since holding Becky as she wept for Tad, abducted somehow from his room without anyone noticing, and seeing someone who looked like grizzled old Dr. Cobb, the man who had been perhaps too close a friend to his mother in the past, and down the driveway to the car; fumbling with his keys in the rain, dropping them, picking them up, dropping them again. Joe had just about put them in the car, when someone called his name.

He spun around, half expecting an assault, and there, in the rain, stood a spindly dried up old rummy of a man, barely a hair on his head, his plaid flannel shirt untucked and half buttoned, his coat ragged, his eyes burning with fire. "Joe? That you, you son of a bitch?" It was Gary Welles. Joe recognized the voice. "You killed my baby and now I'm gonna kill you."

In Gary Welles's shaking hand, a gun. Joe didn't know guns very well, but this one seemed real enough. "I knew I'd find you at your old buddy's house—I knew you'd come back and laugh at us little people the way you laughed at my little girl!"

Joe held his hands up. "Please, my family . . ."

Gary gnashed his teeth. "What about my family, you son of a whore? What about my little girl, Missy, my baby Missy, the most precious . . . oh, you sweet-talking pervert, you lured her and then you made sure she got killed, and then my wife left me, and my son, sure he was gimpy, sure he was a feeb, but he was my boy! Now, he don't even talk to me—he's too good for me, now, but he weren't back then—it's 'cause of what you done, you lowlife shit-eater! And then you had to dig my girl's body up and do that—disgusting, sickening—you're no better than that Jeffrey Dahmer feller was, but at least somebody put out his lights, just like I'm gonna do to you."

Joe was about to say something (although he wasn't sure what) when he saw a bright light, something that wasn't quite lightning, and then he felt blood rush like the sea in his head, and he realized he'd been shot. Rather than feel the numbness that he'd always heard was associated with getting shot, he felt a tremendous heat spread like a rash around his side. He fell to the muddy ground.

Gary Welles laughed triumphantly and knelt beside him. "When you're in hell, boy," he said, "send 'em my regards and tell 'em I'll be along in no time."

The man started laughing, waving the gun around in the rain.

Then Gary put the gun to Joe's head and pulled the trigger.

5.

The gun made a clicking noise. Then Joe heard nothing.

Then he heard the rain, spattering on his face.

Then he heard Gary Welles cuss and shout and click the gun a few more times.

"Shit," Gary said, tossing the gun onto the drive, "I paid good money for it, too."

By that time, Joe was able to sit up and, with every ounce of strength left in him, sock Gary Welles as hard as he could in the jaw.

Then Joe slid back down to the ground, to blissful unconsciousness with the one last thought before darkness took hold: *just when you think you know who the monsters are* . . .

6.

If you had wings, you could fly over the tops of the houses and look down at the woman who lay in the street, one leg propped up on the sidewalk, her body in the curb, her own daughter, not more than four years' old, giving what appeared to be mouth to mouth resuscitation, but which on closer examination might be something else, for the little girl had blood across her cheeks as if she were a messy eater; Jeptha Bonchance had just finished nailing boards across the bedroom which contained four of his children, but one of them, Hank, was still there, behind him, watching his father with what Jeptha might call a Wild Turkey grin, his hands torn and ragged from clawing his way through the walls. Minnie Harper, at seventy-eight years old, was sitting, as usual, in the window of her apartment above Logan's Market on Main Street. Outside, at the door, a child was wailing as if for his mother, so Minnie began to move slowly, practically hearing her bones creak as she went. Cally Harper was fixing some late night tea when they got her, a whole gang of them, and she thought at first that it was still Halloween, because they had drawn, almost shriveled faces, like raisins waiting to be plumped. If you had wings, you could fly and see all of this, and when you came to the dark house at River Road, the one with the mailbox with the word Gardner on it, you would know that something wicked was going on inside this house as well.

7.

In the upstairs bedroom, what had once been Joe Gardner's room, Byron Cheever took the body, and cutting just so, sprayed blood onto the walls in a pattern.

He dipped his fingers into this and wrote the words which his Great Master had commanded him to write.

8.

Joe awoke in the rain, with Virgil Cobb kneeling beside him. The old man said, "It's not too bad, just grazed your side, but there's some bleeding. How are you feeling?"

"Bad. Where's Gary?"

"He's inside. Passed out. Becky and Homer are inside, too."

"I need to get home," Joe said.

"Not right now." Virgil shook his head. "I'll need to get you down to my office so we can clean this properly."

Joe shook his head, tried to rise, but sank back down. "For a graze this sure hurts."

Virgil took a length of gauze and wrapped it around Joe's side. "With a little pressure the bleeding should stop."

"My family," Joe said. "I've got to get them."

"Yes, you do," Virgil said. "After I clean this out."

"No," Joe said, "now!"

9.

Joe felt his adrenaline pumping as Virgil drove the rain slicked streets.

"I've met this before," Virgil said. "This adversary."

"I have too."

"I know. Homer told me. There are ways of stopping it, at least temporarily." Virgil reached to the floor of his car. He brought a bag up and set it on the seat between them. "Tools of the trade. Screwdrivers, crucifixes, even some holy water I've stolen through the years from the church in Stone Valley."

"You think it's a vampire . . ."

"No, I don't. But it can be stopped the same way. John Feely put religious symbols everywhere in his house to keep it out. He would even go to Watch Hill and hammer in extra crosses. Did you know Watch Hill was once the main entrance to the mines? It's where the tracks had been put in to load coal and take it down to the river, where they'd load it onto barges."

"How many mines were there?"

"Twenty-eight in all, all interconnected. They ran for five square miles."

"Under the whole town?"

Virgil nodded.

"Christ," Joe sputtered. "The whole town."

"John Feely learned to put the crosses up from his grandfather, who must've had his own encounters with whatever is down there. And you, too."

"Huh?"

"You've had your encounters with it. I remember the voices, the stories you told people. I had the body of Patty Glass in my office. Before I put a scalpel through her heart, she told me something that involved you."

Virgil brought his car into the driveway of Anna Gardner's house. He said, "She told me that you were what she was looking for. It wasn't Patty's voice, but a synthesis of many voices, and one voice. It told me that It needed Joe Gardner's blood."

Joe looked at his mother's house: it was dark, and seemed to be empty.

10.

Joe searched the house from room to room. It seemed empty. Joe pointed his flashlight's beam into every closet, half expecting something to jump out at him. Virgil called to him from one of the upstairs bedrooms. Although his side ached and burned, he climbed the stairs, feeling as if he was moving in slow motion through viscous air. When he got to the open doorway to his old bedroom, Virgil had his flashlight on the wall.

"I am sorry to say that I found your mother's body," Virgil said.

Joe read the words that had been written messily in blood:

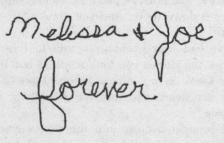

Then both men turned at a sound. The sound of someone sucking, as if siphoning the juices from ripe fruit.

Joe felt frozen, no longer in pain, but numb and perhaps dying somewhere inside his flesh, at least the part of him that had ever been happy or ever hoped or ever dreamed.

The beam of his flashlight struck the blood-soaked figure of Byron Cheever, naked, slick, as he lapped greedily at Anna Gardner's ankle.

Flinching at the light, covering his eyes, Byron turned towards them. "Joe," he said, his voice thick as if he were completely glutted. "Your mother has proved quite the treat. I'm sure when my Master has your children, he will find them equally delightful."

Virgil drew something from his bag, and held it into the beam of light.

It was a small cross, and it cast its shadow across Byron's face.

Byron drew back, but did not hide from it as Joe had expected. Instead, he seemed hypnotized, even stunned by it. He remained motionless.

Virgil said, "Notice how it reacts to the cross. Not afraid, just stunned."

And then, still holding the cross before him, Virgil walked cautiously over to him. He knelt beside Byron, pressing the cross into Byron's forehead. With his free hand, he took the screwdriver and jammed it swiftly and surely into Byron Cheever's heart. He said to Joe, "Now I need to operate on him, because the physical body needs to be completely incapacitated or there's a chance It can still use this body to harvest."

Joe stood there, holding the flashlight, but in his mind he had already gone to a dark silent place, a place with no family, no love, no warmth, no life. He was a statue now. All of this pain around him, all of this fear, all of this tragedy, was a dream world, where the real world was darkness and a frozen wasteland. He remembered having felt that way when he had attempted suicide after Melissa's death, as if he were in some arctic country, as if he could not even imagine that life existed anywhere else. He had placed himself here because of physical pain and the pain of knowing that everything he loved was dead.

Somewhere in that deep state of isolation, he

thought he heard his son cry out for him, and for a moment he hurtled through the rooms of his consciousness, trying to find the door that would lead him back to sanity.

He thought he saw, in his mind's eye, his son, Aaron, running towards him, only it was not his son, for the skin on his body ripped off as if caught in barbed wire, and instead, was an angel, not of death or of mercy, but The Angel of the Pit, its face smeared with red juice, winging its way to embrace him.

"Joe." Virgil's voice cut through his numbness. "Joe?"

Joe Gardner opened his eyes.

There were three children in the doorway, moving towards them like wolves.

Joe shined his flashlight across them. They flinched at the light, but kept moving. Their clothes were bloody rags, their hair twisted with mud and leaves.

One child, a girl who had only recently been known as Tenley McWhorter but was now simply one of the pack, stepped forward. "We have eaten your wife and your mama, Joe." She grinned, her hands clawing at the shreds of her own dress. "Your children are with us. Your mama's blood was like warm jelly, Joe. So delicious."

Virgil reached for the cross, which he'd left by Byron's body, but could not find it in the darkness.

"Your little girl will be the flower of hell." Tenley giggled. The boy who was with her hunkered down on all fours and leaped across the floor to stand before Joe.

He made a grab for the flashlight, but Joe slammed it against the boy's head. He fell. What seemed to be glowing white worms burst from the side of his skull. The boy grabbed Joe's ankle.

Joe heard Virgil cry out, but Joe had to turn his attention to the boy. He kicked the kid against the wall, and then, using one of the spikes in his belt, smashed it into the boy's chest, ripping through the cavity to find his heart. It happened in a matter of seconds, and when he brought the flashlight up, he saw that the girl and the other little boy had Virgil down on the ground.

Joe gripped the flashlight under his armpit and held it on the girl; then he made the sign of the cross with his fingers.

The shadow burned into the side of the girl's face, ripping skin from her nose and cheek.

She screeched and fell away from Virgil.

At the same time, Virgil found his cross and jammed its pointy base into the boy's throat. He wrestled the boy to the ground and then the two men performed the operations necessary to ensure permanent death for these creatures.

"Don't think of them as children," Virgil said. "Think of them as the Thing that murdered your family."

11.

When it was done, Joe's side ached where the bullet had grazed him and he slumped down against the wall. "I want to sleep forever," he said, "but my body won't. Its like something in me is fighting."

"Survival instinct," Virgil said matter-of-factly. "There'll be more of these after us. Let's get back to the others and try to fortify ourselves for one night. We can continue the fight in the morning."

The words in blood burned into Joe's mind: *Melissa + Joe forever.*

12.

"Oh, good lord," Virgil said as he brought the Buick to a stop two houses from Hopfrog's house. "It's like a last stand."

Joe, who was feeling hyperaware, was not even surprised by the sight that greeted them: twenty or thirty children surrounding the house, shadows and shapes in the bushes and trees, some crawling up the walls, some already on the roof.

"I hope Hop and Becky made it. I hope they're alive," Joe said.

"And how do we destroy all these?"

"Don't look at me. It's not like I have all the answers."

The front door opened, but it was too dark to see what was happening.

It was a man, standing, so Joe assumed it wasn't Hopfrog.

"It's Gary Welles," Joe said, "what the hell is he doing?"

13.

Gary was feeling a little better now. As far as he knew he'd gotten one good shot at Joe, and next time he saw him, he was going to finish him off for sure. He'd managed to kick down the fucking door to the room they'd locked him in, stumble through the dark house, avoiding anyone in it. He stepped out on the porch and laughed at fate. He shouted, "Fuck you all! Fuck you stupid Colony for being such a dumbass town, for killing my girl and poisoning my marriage! Fuck you all!"

By the moonlight, he could see the shapes of children all around him, and although he thought this was odd, he was still fairly drunk and wondered if these might not be pink elephant sightings.

Before he could think much else, the children were upon him, and Gary felt dozens of small mouths close around his pulse points, their teeth digging in, their rough little tongues lapping.

14.

Joe gasped, *"Jesus!"* He reached over to open his door but Virgil grabbed his wrist. *"We can't let him die like that!"*

Virgil said, "It's too late, Joe. They have him."

"No." Joe shook Virgil off and got out of the car. He held the cross up and ran into the circle of children, slicing them across their scalps and faces with the cross. He could smell it then, they had the stink of death, of worms and earth and sulphur. He took his spike and began ramming it indiscriminately into each child, as if he were working an assembly line, and although they grabbed at him and bit his arms, he kept stabbing, gutting, slashing—

By the time he was finished, he was laughing, laughing so hard he thought the world, the universe and God were all laughing with him.

He looked at the piles of bodies.

You have driven me insane. You have made me inhuman, he thought.

Joe Gardner fell to his knees, dropping cross and spike. He laughed until he couldn't remember ever not laughing.

Becky came out of the house. She wrapped him in a blanket, but he kept laughing, knowing that there was no saving them. There was no way to stop the children, no way to stop It, no way to slay this dragon.

Morning was a long time in coming. As the sun slowly lit the sky with its purple and blue dawn, the house was thick with the corpses of children and with crucifixes fashioned from bits of wood and anything that could be turned into a cross.

Hopfrog sat beside Joe's bed as he slept, and in the morning told the others that even in his dreams, Joe was laughing.

23

PREY

1.

Joe Gardner slept until late in the morning. He was not plagued by nightmares, neither was he disturbed by the chill, for he had left the bedroom window open as if hoping that his children would crawl over the frame after some adventure with Peter Pan. When he first awoke, he saw the sun and the frost on the windowsill. He watched his breath as it clouded the air. He heard the ticking of the hall clock. He closed his eyes again and fell into the blackness of sleep.

In the frozen sunless dreamscape, he felt nothing,

but heard the endless beating of its wings, of the Angel of the Pit, as it drew Its arms around him.

Joe was not a man who ever rested well, but the surface Joe, the one who loved his wife and kids and who had memory and pain and suffering, had gone underground. The Joe that was left was merely body: he breathed, he slept, and when hunger and thirst dried his lips and clutched at his stomach, this is the Joe which awoke at noon.

He sat up, pulling the blue-and-green quilt up around his shoulders. He shivered from cold. A crick in his neck from sleeping on the wrong side. The itch of stubble along his chin. The slight creaking of bones as he stretched his legs out in a body yawn. A sound, like a high-pitched whistle, as if there were a throbbing pain somewhere running through his being, only he had managed to block it out, as if the drug Virgil Cobb had given him had not only numbed his body, but his mind, as well. (What had happened? Had he crawled into bed? Had Becky and Hopfrog come by to see him as Virgil cleaned his wounds? Where had consciousness ended and sleep begun? He could only remember snippets of dreams, faces, someone in his room scrubbing the walls, scrubbing the words *Melissa + Joe forever.* Had Becky leaned over at some point in the morning and wiped his forehead with a damp cloth? These seemed to be memories from another life.)

For a second, he thought he was a boy again, in his old bedroom. On the wall, three posters: Peter Frampton, Jackson Browne, and Linda Ronstadt, fading and tattered at the edges, the Scotch tape yellowed and peeling the paint from the wall. *Don't look at where they scrubbed the walls, he told himself, don't look over there. You don't want to see what is over there. Don't look where you last saw your mother, either, where there's probably a stain. Don't see anything that's going to hurt too much.* On the dresser, apparently ancient bottles of British Sterling and Old Spice, exactly where he had left them when he was eighteen. His twenty-gallon aquarium on the bookshelf, empty now, thrust between his leather-bound copy of the *Thousand And One Nights*, and Herman Wouk's *Youngblood Hawke.*

It wasn't until he saw Aaron's black denim jacket on the chair that he started sobbing. He had just bought Aaron a sweatshirt, too, which Aaron wore to bed that night. Aaron's duffel bag leaned in a corner, full of wadded-up socks and underwear, jeans, and two extra pairs of sneakers. *Didn't Aaron know to put on his jacket? It would be cold out there.*

(All your children, a voice inside him whispered, *first Paul in the crib, and now Aaron and Hillary, and your wife, we took her, too. What is it you wish for Joe? Love? Happiness? Children? Family?)*

Joe leaned against the pillow. He could smell Aaron's hair there, as if Aaron had just gotten out of bed and was down the hall, in the bathroom. The smell of his hair was like Prell and grease and Aaron.

Joe had to press his face into the pillow to control his tears.

Then, he awoke from this dream-within-a-dream, to the bedroom at Hopfrog's house.

2.

After a while, he sat up and said, "No."

He was almost disappointed that he had not lost his mind.

3.

Becky was sitting on the front porch, a large down jacket wrapped around her shoulders. She sipped from a cup of coffee. Virgil Cobb sat across from her, smoking a cigar.

Addressing no one, she nodded towards the sky, "Looks like snow, doesn't it? It's cold enough."

"Last year it didn't snow 'til December first. Year before that, it was October," Virgil said.

Joe stood, hugging the quilt to him, staring at both of them. "It has my kids."

Becky glanced up. "Joe."

It was unspoken, what she seemed on the verge of saying: *you're alive. Didn't expect that from you at this point. Thought this might be too much for you, all the shock, the trauma, the nightmare. Good to see you up and running.*

Something else, too:

All our children are gone, Joe, all of our children. Your tragedy's no worse than anyone else's, so quit complaining. And we're all numb and dehumanized and traumatized and shocked shitless, so don't expect much sympathy from this quarter.

"Temperature dropped last night," Virgil said, blowing a smoke ring. "That'll help, maybe."

"You don't know," Joe said. "You don't know. Nobody knows, do they?"

"Joe?" Becky could not manage a smile, but seemed to be trying hard. "You get some rest?"

"Nobody knows anything. This whole town's a graveyard. We're all dead. We might as well just go to that thing, that angel or vampire or martian, or whatever it is. We might as well just let It have us, too."

Virgil said, "Not everyone in town is dead. Hopfrog's going out to see who's left."

"You happy about knowing it got your baby?" He pointed to the street. "You'll just sit here drinking coffee while your baby's . . ."

Becky set her cup down. Steam rose from it.

"What kind of mother are you?" Joe snorted. "You should've taken your baby and put him in the car and gotten the fuck out of here, if you were any kind of—" He began foaming at the mouth, and felt as he was having some kind of seizure. His thoughts rushed faster than his brain would allow them. His mouth couldn't move in sync with the rest of him. He tried to fight the overwhelming urge to run, to run away as fast as he could from this awful place.

Becky spat, "Look, you may decide it's better to be a lunatic, but I am trying to hold out hope that there's a way I can find my son and make sure he's unharmed. I don't know how to do that, but I know it is not by ranting and raving." Then, she calmed. "I did all my screaming and crying last night. We don't know that Tad is dead, just like we don't know that your family is dead, either. Why was it you found your mother's body, but not your wife's? Maybe they got away, Joe. Maybe they got out."

Joe went inside and got a pack of cigarettes, hidden in his black denim jacket's inside pocket. He lit one and went back out to where the others waited. He passed a cigarette to Becky and they began chainsmoking until the pack was gone. "Sorry about the outburst. I'm just nuts now."

Becky accepted the apology. "I promised Hopfrog I would help. We'll do what you two did the last time. We'll take them apart one by one. We'll stop it somehow. If there's a chance that Tad's alive, or your family . . ."

"No," he said, wiping at his eyes. "We won't. We'll die and become like them, some kind of storage tank for that thing that lives down in the mines."

"We can't leave anyway," she said, walking to the edge of the porch. "Not until we stop It. It has Tad. It has your children. How can you be sure they're dead? I don't believe they're dead."

Joe wanted to tell her what he thought, that they were dead, dead and now vampiric corpses, and maybe tonight they'd come for him and for her and for Virgil and for Hopfrog.

But he knew that he had to stay.

"The phones haven't come up yet," Virgil Cobb said. "One of us could drive over to Stone Valley, but what would we say? 'Everyone's dead in Colony, and all the children are taken. It wasn't the Pied Piper who did it, but some creature living beneath John Feely's property.' Well," he huffed, "that might take a while to convince them. Three hours up and back over icy roads, and then three days before they get their rear ends over here to check it out."

Joe shrugged. "Or they might throw whoever told them in jail."

"And meanwhile," Becky said, softly, "my little boy dies."

4.

Hopfrog was back by two and Becky helped him into his chair from the car.

"Anything?" she asked.

He shook his head. "I'd like to tell you that everyone's fine, but if someone besides us is alive in Colony, they're hiding really good. I tried the stores. I tried six different streets. There're some tire treads out by the Paramount Bridge which lead me to believe some foks got out. Maybe they'll spread the word. Maybe they're too crazed to do much of anything. I hope they got out." Hopfrog had become good at hiding tears. He closed his eyes. "My cousins, all of them, Becky: Kyle and Frankie and Janie, all of them. I found Frankie sleeping under his own bed, blood across his mouth. Eight years old. Now, one of them. I had to, God," he began, but was silenced by a gasp that seemed to come from within his soul. When he'd recovered, he continued. "I drove a spike through each of their bodies to ensure that they would not come back tonight."

Becky hugged him. She drew warmth from that ragged place inside herself and offered it to him with that embrace, pressing her face against his neck.

"I've got to go find Tad. Maybe if we get to him before dark, he'll be alive. Maybe there's a chance . . ." His voice died the way the wind died, all at once. Then, he told her to go look at the back of his car.

Becky stepped around, shielding her eyes, and looked through the dark glass. "Jesus, what the hell is all this?"

"An arsenal. I collected it from about six different houses. Miles Fauvier had the Uzi."

"The gallery owner? Jesus." She shook her head, started laughing. "It looks like Los Angeles or New York, not West Virginia."

She looked back at him with such a warm smile on her face. After all the sadness and frustration of the night, it was like sun, seeing her like this. He almost said it. *Almost. Becky, I can't make it without you. I love you. You are the only woman for me.* Then her face sharpened. "I thought weapons wouldn't work on It. I thought we knew that."

"Maybe not on It, but what It does to the kids, their corpses. We can at least stop them from getting us. Becky, they're like wild dogs. For all we know, they're hiding all over this town. Or down in the graves at Watch Hill. Just waiting for night." Hopfrog leaned back in his chair, drawing the collar of his leather jacket up around his neck and ears. He whispered, "I love you."

"What?" she asked, moving closer to him, kneeling beside him (which always made him feel like a baby, only now it felt good).

"Nothing," he said, feeling warm wherever she touched him.

She looked him in the eye. "We have to go find Tad. I won't let him die."

"I know. We'll go soon."

"You think he's already dead, don't you?"

"No."

"I can tell you do. But I don't. I'm his mother. I know he's still alive."

Hopfrog wheeled back towards the porch.

Virgil Cobb nodded to him. "Mr. Petersen, good morning."

"I got some guns and gasoline," Hopfrog said. "I think we can set fire to most of the houses. If they're in there, we can shoot them when they come out. I have these." He tossed an assortment of spikes and screwdrivers, hammers and mallets, onto the round patio table. "From my woodshop. If we're going to kill some vampires, we might as well do it in style. As I recall from stopping one of these vampires in my youth, a good Phillips head number six does the job, and isn't as hard to make as a genuine stake. Between these and the bullets, I figure we have a chance."

"Silver bullets," Virgil said. "They follow the rules of mythology. Silver bullets and stakes through the heart and crucifixes. I don't know why they do."

"Yeah." Hopfrog shook his head, wondering how far from sanity they all were at this point. He half expected witches and trolls beneath bridges and goblins and ghosties. "Joe's inside?"

"Went for a walk," Virgil said. "Just ten minutes ago. Said he wanted to think about things. I told him you'd be back soon, and then we could start."

"Isn't it weird," Hopfrog said. "Only us."

"Only us?"

"Only us. Nobody else. A town of nearly two thousand, small by any standards, but a hell of a lot of people anyway. It looks like Guyana out there, or Waco. I found bodies piled like stones, drained of blood. No children. It has all the children now. But of all those people, you, me, Joe, Becky—why?"

Virgil said, "Maybe because we saw It's face once. Maybe It's playing with us. Or maybe we have something that scares It that nobody else has. Maybe we have a power we don't even know about."

"Or maybe we're dessert," Hopfrog said.

5.

Joe was careful to avoid the slick edges of the road where the ice had not melted to slush. He put one foot in front of the other. *Got to keep moving. You stop moving, you die. You die, you can't help your kids. If your kids are still alive. If your kids are still alive, you've got to go down that well in that barn and face whatever it was you couldn't stop when you were a kid.* The sky was bright and still clouded over to the east. Storm clouds, gray on the underside, white on the edges. The air had that clean, strong smell that came just before snow. He was walking along the road, trying to think, but his mind was still not up to speed. He was a jumble of fears and images: *Melissa, Jenny, mother, house, river, bridge, truck, car, blood dragon, crucifix, ankh.* He stopped, pressing his fists against the side of his head.

Just two days ago. He didn't have to come back. He could've sent a plane ticket for his mother. He could've come home by himself, and then Jenny would still be alive, Aaron and Hillary would still be playing in the den at home.

If only . . . the two most miserable words in the English language. *If only.*

Clouds swept across the sun, and for one horrific moment, Joe thought night was descending soon, that the world had spun out of its orbit and had plunged into darkness. When he glanced at the muted sun, it briefly took him out of his sorrow. *Heaven.* He had never thought much about it before; he had never really believed in it. *If the world is so horrible a place, there must be one, or why even hope for it? It may not be paved with gold or have pearly gates, but there must be some peaceful happy place for those for whom life is misery.*

The sun broke through the clouds. He felt that it was a sign from the universe to continue, to fight the vampire, to not cower at Its enormity.

6.

When Joe returned to the others, he had a plan.

He told them. "We have a couple of hours until dark. We've wasted too much time. Hop, you and Virgil go round up some crosses. Becky, we'll go get some food, since we don't know what kind of night we're going to have, and we've got to stock up for the long haul."

"Okay, but, what—we go rip off all the churches?" Hopfrog asked.

"We won't have to"—Virgil drew his tweed overcoat around his shoulders—"John Feely must've had three hundred crucifixes all over the place at his house. Even if most of them are destroyed, we can probably find more there in his closets than in all three churches here in town."

Virgil and Hopfrog took off in Virgil's Honda Civic.

Becky said, "Who needs food? I don't care if I ever eat again. We're going to die, Joe. Our children are dead, and we are going to die."

Joe tossed his arm across her shoulder and said, "Now you're the pessimist. I guess that's healthy. But I had a sign from the heavens today. And you know what it said?"

She shook her head.

"It said, 'It ain't over 'til it's over.' We stock up on food today, and tonight"—he let go of her, and led the way outside—"I'm gonna whup some vampire butt."

Becky stared at him, shocked.

"I know," he said, "I'm crazy. I'm running on empty and I'm running scared. I'm probably teetering on the edge of sanity. But, you know what? I'm just going to go with it."

24

THE HUNT BEFORE DARK

1.

The weird part was, Colony looked normal outwardly, as if this were an afternoon right after lunch, before the workday was through, before children were released from school, when silence prevailed. Each street met neatly with another, each corner squared with its partner. There was no apparent damage, except for the occasional corpse in the street, but even these few seemed somehow to fit in with the sleepy winter atmosphere. "I don't even feel afraid anymore," Becky said. "It's as if the whole world just changed."

"I'm not quite to that point yet," Joe said, feeling in his pockets for anything that might remotely resemble a cigarette. "You got a smoke, Beck?"

"Left my purse at home," she responded, and then giggled. When she started giggling too much, he pulled over to the curb. They were on Princess Anne Street, right across from the movie theater.

Her giggles died out. He said, "You gonna make it?"

"I don't know. Let's break in to the market."

This is actually the fun part, Joe thought. They got out of the Buick Skylark; he didn't even bother parking particularly well.

Logan's Market was another block up, and he supposed he could've moved the car forward, *but what the hell? A little walk'll do us good.*

He was still a bit wary, too. He had armed himself with a small cross; Becky had a tiny one on a chain around her neck. "It was my mother's. Lucky for me she was a good Irish Catholic girl."

"Got your spike?" he asked.

She held it up. "I don't know if I'll be able to drive it into one of them, even if they are the undead, Joe, they still look like kids."

"After a couple," he said, "you get used to it."

Walking up a block, they saw curtains drawn at all the apartments above the shops. "I bet they're resting up for tonight." Joe rubbed his hands together for warmth. "You know what's sad?"

"Joe. After all this."

"No, I mean sad in a goofy way."

"All right: what?"

"I was beginning to like this place. I was beginning to remember all the good stuff."

Neither of them spoke again for a while, even while Joe smashed a rock into the glass door of Logan's Market. He opened the door for her and quickly flicked on the fluorescent lights before she was halfway through.

Becky got a shopping cart. The two of them went down the aisles, tossing everything from toilet paper to apple juice into the cart. When they passed the checkout counter, Joe grabbed seven packs of Marlboro Light 100s and stuffed them into his coat pockets.

"Paper or plastic?" he asked as they began bagging their loot.

Becky's face was horribly altered, and he only just noticed it. She was old now, old the way people got old when life turned on them, old and curdled like milk. Joe knew that he was the same, too. That this wasn't just going to end and they'd bounce back from it.

This was it. Even if they survived and destroyed the monster, this was it. Life was never going to be fine or good again.

Don't think about Jenny or Hillary or Aaron or Mom. Think about survival.

"He was just a little boy," Becky said, her face crumpling, almost caving in. But no tears, not even a trace of wetness in her eyes—she could cry no more.

Joe stuffed the fruit and fresh vegetables into the paper bags.

2.

"Look at that," Hopfrog said, lowering himself from the car to the ground.

"You need some help? I can get your chair," Virgil said.

"Sure, thanks, yeah," Hopfrog said. He was dragging his legs, using his muscular arms to propel him forward towards John Feely's barn. "Yeah, sometimes the chair is good. But look at that. At least we know the kids haven't gotten in there."

Virgil, walking around his car to get the wheelchair from the back of the other side, looked up and saw three Pennsylvania-Dutch-type hexes painted above the barn door, and a cross hanging in between them.

Hopfrog glanced back at him. "Would ya hurry it up with that chair? The ground's freezing."

Virgil unfolded the chair and pushed it up the drive to the path that led to the barn. "John Feely was well prepared for this event."

"Not too well prepared. It must've gotten him, right?" Hopfrog had a system for slipping into the chair, which was like second nature for him; he grasped one arm of it, and then slid into it so quickly that at times it was startling. Virgil gasped as he watched him. "Didn't know I was so light on my hands, didya, Doc? I've been working out my technique for years. So, what do you think? In the barn? When I was a kid we saw a bunch of crosses in there. Tons. You think it's safe?"

"I don't know." Virgil felt something, not anything as wonderful or dreadful as a premonition, but a vague but persistent thumping—a pulsation in his body. He wondered if it was his heart, because it was beating rhythmically, but too fast.

Hopfrog, noticing the look that had crossed Virgil's face, said, "Dr. Cobb—you doing okay?"

"For someone my age, I'm doing better than expected," he said. "I should've had a heart attack by now, you know, bad living, fatty foods, wine, cigars, a sedentary existence. I'm amazed I'm *not* dead."

When Hopfrog leaned back in the chair, Virgil got behind it and began pushing it. "If they follow most of the vampire rules," Virgil said, "they won't attack us even if they are in the barn." They went to the barn door. Virgil set the chair to the side, and stepped up to open the door.

Once inside, they found sixty-two crosses, and then some.

"We're right above It's lair," Hopfrog said, circling around the well at the center of the dusty barn, "and It can't get us."

"It's lair is the entire network of mines. All It needed to do was find a break somewhere. I'm willing to bet that John Feely had the whole town well mined with crucifixes and hex signs. But someone must've overcome John before It could wreak Its havoc. It must've been a human being, someone who wanted to let It out. Maybe in exchange for power."

"Christ," Hopfrog said. "What a world. This is where we faced off with It, when we were kids. Me and Joe and Missy. It got Patty, but we did something to send It back to wherever It came from. I saw Joe do something that was like magic."

"What was that?"

"I don't know how he did it. But he somehow transformed himself. It was like a trick of the light—there was this brilliant glow where It stood, looking like a boy covered with blood. And then Joe took up this stick that was on the ground and started using it like it was a sword. It was like he was possessed, like he knew what he was doing. I had to practically pinch myself, because I didn't really believe it. For a second, I thought he was all dressed in armor and wasn't a boy, but a man with a crown on his head and a sword in his hand. And the Thing had become this big lizard, almost like a Godzilla thing, and Missy whispered to me, 'It's Joe. Joe can make believe anything he wants,' and even though I figured we were all hallucinating, that was the moment I knew she didn't love me. When we were kids I knew she loved him. She believed in him, and he believed in himself in a way that I never could in anyone." Hopfrog leaned forward and gathered up some of the crosses. "Jesus, it's belief, isn't it?"

"What do you mean?"

"Joe, his imagination—that's why he heard the voices from the dead people. That's what almost drove him nuts back then. He was in tune with it, like It fed off his mind. Like It knew he had that power and was feeding off of him. He didn't even know he had it." Hopfrog leaned back in his chair, his arms thrust out at his sides, looking for all the world as if he were experiencing some kind of religious conversion. "That means he can stop It. He has the power. If he can just do that again . . . What do you think?"

"I think that what is below ground here is a monster. I think It's fooled a good many men over the years into believing something that isn't true. I wouldn't want to chance your friend Joe to a theory."

"Yeah." Hopfrog shrugged off his own idea. "And a crazy theory at that. You want to check the house next?"

Virgil wanted to say "no," because he, in fact, dreaded the idea of ever setting foot in John Feely's house, but he knew that at this point, the dreadful and the inevitable must intersect. "Yes. As long as it's daylight."

3.

Joe and Becky loaded the groceries—enough for a week—into the trunk of the Buick. Joe ripped open a pack of cigarettes and jammed one between his lips.

He punched the lighter in the car. When it popped up, he brought it to the end of the cigarette. He took a puff. "Delicious," he said. "I wasn't even addicted before today."

"Give me one of those," Becky said, leaning beside him, against the car. They chain-smoked three cigarettes each before they were sated. "I feel like I'm playing hooky from school."

Joe coughed. "I never was a good smoker. To smoke well, you have to be unafraid of disease and death. I've always been kind of terrified of those two."

Becky flashed an almost flirtatious grin. "That's the joy of smoking—the fear of death combined with the pleasures of nicotine." Then, she said, more seriously, "Will you come with me to my place? I want to get a few personal things. They seem silly right now, but I want them."

Joe stubbed out the last of his smoke. In his best redneckese, he said, "Got me a crucifix and got me a stake, we gonna kill us a heap o' vampires."

4.

When they got to Becky's house, Becky looked at the front of the building and gasped, "Someone's in there. Look."

Joe leaned forward, and looked up to the second-story window, where he saw nothing.

"It's Tad," Becky said, "I know it is." She had an excitement to her voice like a little girl on Christmas. "Oh, my God, Joe, it's my baby, he must've gotten away from them. He came home!"

And before Joe could stop her, she had bolted from the car and run up the front steps to her house.

The door was already open as if someone were expecting her.

5.

At the Feely house, once Hopfrog had wheeled himself through the front door into the foyer, the stink hit him. It was worse than anything he had ever had the misfortune to step in. He imagined that the primary odor came from the rotting corpse of John Feely himself which swung before him, strung by his feet in the hall.

Hopfrog covered his mouth with a handkerchief and tried not to breathe through his nose.

John Feely had been gutted like a deer and the cavity of his chest and ribs was stuffed with maggots.

Carved in his forehead, the word: *angel.*

Behind Hopfrog, Virgil Cobb said, "Dear God."

"What's that room?" Hopfrog asked, wheeling closer to the hanging body.

"John's bedroom. There's a closet on the other side of it. It's the inner sanctum. John told me, when I was a boy, that he kept the Angel of the Pit there, as his grandfather had, as he would until judgment day."

"Today," Hopfrog said, "is judgment day. Think you can get that body down so we can get through?"

The truth was, Virgil didn't think he could cut John Feely's body down any more than he thought he could face the night. He was shivering, terrified, feeling his heart beat so fast he was sure he would keel over at any moment—he'd had at least one patient in all his years of practice who had died of fright, a woman in 1972, who had a series of nightmares which literally drove her to an early grave—and he felt that he was going to shortly fall victim to fear, as well. He no longer felt like an old man, but like the boy he had been when he had seen his brother Eugene coming for him, coming with blood on his face. The fear he had felt when he and Winston had plunged the stake into Eugene's heart, had operated on his brother's body, and then had watched as Eugene's own blood rose up in an almost human form before evaporating before their eyes.

Virgil went to John Feely's kitchen and got a large carving knife. He was shaking as he cut John down, hacking at the rope that kept him tied to the spike that had been driven into the wall above the door frame. When John dropped to the floor, black and green flies rose up from his innards.

"Lord of the flies," Hopfrog said. "Beelzebub." Hopfrog wheeled around the body, into the bedroom. "Would you look at this?"

Virgil went in the room, and whatever fear he had possessed seconds before solidified into a feeling of certain doom.

The room was sprayed with blood, as if someone had taken a hose and attached it to several human bodies.

Winston Alden's skin had been dried and tacked to the far wall.

"I can't go in there," Virgil said, not knowing if he was weeping or wailing or even speaking aloud. "I can't go in there."

"Holy shit," Hopfrog said, seeing that his wheels were now soaked with the blood from the floor. "This is fresh."

"Let's not go in there," Virgil said. "Maybe when the others get back . . ."

Hopfrog said, "Did you hear it?"

"What?"

Hopfrog's eyes were wild, his face sweaty. He turned and clutched at Virgil's coat. "My boy. Did you hear it? I heard him. He's down there."

"No, Homer, only that thing is down there. No one alive is down there with It."

"No," Hopfrog said. "Don't you hear him? Oh, Jesus, he needs me, he's hurt, I've got to go—"

Before Virgil could stop him, Hopfrog leapt from his chair, and using his hands and arms for leverage, dragged himself across the bloody floor towards the closet.

Virgil wanted to stop him, but he couldn't move. The terror that gripped him was immense. He stood at the threshold of the doorway and called out to Hopfrog, but Hopfrog kept calling out to his son, calling to find the place where his son had been taken, and when he stopped calling, there was nothing but silence.

Interrupting the silence, briefly, a cry, a human cry as if the man who was now in the lair of the Angel of the Pit had seen the most beautiful and horrifying vision, and could not express what he had seen in anything other than the unspeakable language of screams.

6.

Joe ran up to the house after Becky, his crucifix drawn, and followed her upstairs to the second floor of her house.

He heard Becky cry out, "Tad! Tad, oh my God, Tad, you're alive, you're—"

Joe took the stairs two at a time, his heartbeat so loud that he could hear it as if it were in his ears and brain rather than in his chest. He drew the screwdriver from his belt, and went through the doorway into Becky's bedroom.

There was Tad, or what had become of Tad, his arms around his mother, her arms around him, and all around, in the room, mirrors and chalk drawings of crosses and bowls of clear water.

"Look"—Tad showed his mother—"they bit me three times, but I got away, I got away."

"Oh, thank you, God, thank you, thank you." Becky wept until her weeping sounded like laughter.

After a few minutes, Joe asked, "How did you do it, Tad? How did you get away from them?"

Tad grinned, but his eyes were sunken, his face wan and dirty—the kid had been through hell. "I lied to them. This helped," he held up a thick Swiss Army knife. "You can hurt them if you try. And they're real dumb. I was in my bed, when something came out from under it and grabbed me. It was Elvis Bonchance, but I knew he was a vampire. He and his brother and some girl dragged me out on the window ledge, and I almost fell out the window, except they could practically fly. But I always have my knife with me, so I stabbed Elvis real good in the eye, and then I ran. I was two streets over, and I remembered that Granny gave Mom this cross, so I ran over there, figuring Mom would be there and I could get help. So I came up here, only there was a bunch of 'em. And then, I figured out something: if they're vampires, they're scared of lots of things." He pointed to the bowls of water. "I told 'em it was holy water. I pretended real hard, just like I do when I lie, and you know what? They believed me. They hung around for a while, but when I started throwing the water on them and making up fake church curses, you know, like 'Be Thou Returned to Thy Lord Of Darkness!'

stuff like that, they went running. I believed as hard as I could, and they're really, really dumb vampires, if you ask me." Then, settling into his mother's arms, he whispered, "I was too scared to go anywhere today. And I'm really hungry."

"Well," Joe said. "This is your lucky day 'cause we have a ton of food down in the car." As he stood there, he wished it were his son in this house, he wished that his son and daughter and wife and mother had been this lucky. He took some comfort in finding this one child still alive and healthy and strong.

"Let's go," Becky said, taking Tad's hand. "Your father's going to want to see you."

"You guys thinking of getting back together?" Tad asked, carrying a bowl of phony holy water with him ("just in case," he whispered mostly to himself). "I mean," he added, "I believe in that, too."

Becky didn't answer him, but seemed to have been revived into life again, as if the wavering flame inside her had almost extinguished and was now resparked.

7.

Twenty minutes later, Becky, Tad, and Joe were back at the house. Tad was exhausted. He went to sleep in his mother's arms, on the living room sofa. She would not let him go. She rocked him, and closed her eyes, and fell asleep, also. Joe sat up and had a Coke and bologna sandwich. He switched on the portable radio from the kitchen. The news of the day was coming on—broadcast from Stone Valley, and another one all the way from Washington, D.C. As he listened to it, he was amazed how normal the world seemed. He half expected that the Night Children would've already taken over the planet.

When Virgil finally returned it was four-thirty, and the sky was darkening.

"Hey," Joe said, getting up to glance out the front window for Hop.

The driveway was empty.

"I walked all the way back," Virgil Cobb said, and in both his slumped posture and the way his eyes glazed, Joe knew that the man had lost it. Just lost it.

No surprise there. We should all have lost it by now.

All Virgil could say was, "It got Homer. It got him."

Joe pressed his eyes closed. *Survivors. We are the only survivors. Countdown to the last living souls in Colony, West Virginia.* He envied to some extent those who were already dead; their terror and pain were behind them. He opened his eyes and said, "We found Tad. He's okay. A little scared and tired, but fine. Let's go tell Becky."

8.

After the weeping and sadness, before night had descended, Virgil said to the others, "I am going to find more crosses. We got some up around the Feely place —there were tons there. Egyptian symbols, too, and Stars of David, even a couple of pentagrams—apparently any religion keeps the vampire at bay. There's maybe another forty minutes of the sun."

Joe glanced at Becky, and she at him. They could telegraph their thoughts: *the old man's lost—crushed —doomed. Like it's his fault that Hopfrog died.*

"Stay with us," Becky said. "We can set up some

more crosses in the yard. We can make it one more night."

"You should leave. All of you." Virgil could not even bring himself to look at them. "You have your son. Get out while he's alive. While you're alive."

"We've talked about that," Joe said. "I am staying because I have to see this thing through. It killed my family. I can't walk away from this."

"You could leave, Becky," Virgil said.

"No," she said, shaking her head. "Not until it's over. We're safer together."

"When I come back with some crosses," Virgil said, "I think you should get in the car and drive over to Stone Valley. You're putting your son in too much danger."

Becky said, "I won't leave Joe alone to deal with this, and I can't send Tad by himself. Maybe in the morning. Maybe then." She seemed set in stone, and Tad, next to her, was curled against her side; since hearing about his father's death, he seemed to have crawled to a place inside himself from which he could not be extricated.

"Whatever," Virgil said. "I need to go. I need to find out if there's anything salvageable in this town. I need to."

Virgil left in Hopfrog's car to go gather up what weapons he could before the dark.

9.

"I am going to the Feely barn," Joe said. "I am going to go down those stairs. I am going to do what I can to destroy the Angel of the Pit. I want you to know that since I may not come out that you should not leave here until morning. Set the crosses up, get the spikes ready in case one of the Night Children slips in somehow. Keep your back to the wall." He opened the door to his Buick.

"I am going with you," Becky said.

"No. You have to wait for Virgil."

"Virgil isn't coming back, couldn't you tell? He isn't coming back." She was not hysterical, but calm, as if she had decided her own fate and would not waver from that decision. "You're the only one now who has ever fought this before, Joe. Don't leave Tad and me here. If we stay together we might be safer. I am not going to run away from the monster that killed my son's father."

10.

"It'll be dark in ten minutes," he said, driving the slick streets.

"We'll be there in less than that." Becky leaned back in her seat; every few minutes she reached over and touched Tad as if checking to make sure he was still breathing. "Hopfrog told me you fought It before, Joe. You were Tad's age. How did you do it?"

Joe said, "I'll tell you what I remember. I don't know if it's going to help us or not. What happened when we were little . . ." and he began the story about Patty Glass and Hopfrog and Melissa on a rainy spring day when King Joe Dragonheart thought he'd killed a dragon. The story lasted until he'd parked the Buick beside the barn and walked in and showed Becky and Tad the well that had once seemed to be a metal cylinder filled with golden light. It was capped with a crucifix and etched with ancient symbols. They sat near John Feely's old work bench.

Tad seemed to not be listening to the story at all, but huddled against his mother, staring at the well, as if expecting at any moment that something would emerge from it.

25

THE CHILD WITHIN

1.

After he'd told Becky the story, he said, "And then, you know the story about Melissa's death."

Becky nodded. "Hopfrog felt so much guilt about that."

Joe shook his head. "It was an accident."

"He never told you." Becky leaned back against the work bench.

"Never told me?"

"He had nightmares every night for years, and in all of them, Melissa was there, and sometimes, you, too. He told me it was right after the accident, and he was standing on the shore. Both you and Melissa came out of the river, moving towards him. He said she kept saying, 'Hopfrog—why? Why?' Eventually, he told me. He wanted to kill himself that day. He was in love with her, too. He knew she didn't love him. He wanted the car to crash. He wanted all of you to die." Becky reached over and placed her hand across Joe's. "I know he didn't mean it. He felt like he was going to hell his whole life because of it."

Joe closed his eyes, angry at the world. "I don't believe now it was Hopfrog. I don't believe it. I think the bloodsucker got Melissa. I think each one of us was picked out when we saw that It could be stopped. I think that no one is allowed to see It's true face and live. I think It's been scared of us all along, because we have something that can hurt It. If I could only figure out what that is."

"He tried to kill himself twice that I know of," Becky said. She reached back over to Tad, still mumbling to himself, his fever cooling as he slept. She felt his forehead, then his cheek. "Look," she said. "Let's put some of these crosses up in the yard around here before it gets too dark. They'll be coming out soon."

Joe and Becky gathered up as many as they could and went outside. The sky was almost completely dark, with an incipient light, the last light of day, over the western ridge of the Malabar Hills. Using a mallet and hammer each, they drove the crosses into the ground until the land around the barn looked like a graveyard.

Then, they secured the barn door with a cross and laid down in some ragged blankets next to Tad.

Tad shivered. "Will they come in tonight?"

"Nope. We have enough religious symbols out there to open a revival meeting and then some. If they follow the rules like they've been doing, we're safe tonight.

Tomorrow morning, I'm going to go down and get It while It's sleeping."

"Why not tonight?" Tad asked.

"It follows too many of those vampire rules, that's why. Now, you go to sleep. You need your strength."

Becky wrapped her arms around her son and fell asleep immediately. Joe sat up awhile, thinking he heard noises. Gradually, he, too, drifted off to sleep.

In the morning, he awoke suddenly. Becky was already up.

"Wish I had some coffee," she said.

"Me, too," Joe said.

"Wish my ex was still here," she said, sadly.

"Me, too."

"Tell me the rest," Becky said. "About what happened after Melissa died. Homer told me that you went down there before."

Joe nodded and resumed telling tales. "I tried to kill myself, too, back then. It would've been happy if that had happened." Joe began spinning the story of his eighteenth year. "It was after Hop and I saw Melissa again. After she was dead. We dug up her grave—there was a lot of rain, and the ground was easy to break, although it was backbreaking work. I needed to know if she really was a vampire, or if we both were just going insane. The coffin was gone, only a tunnel in the earth downward . . ."

2.

From the Journals of Joe Gardner/when he was eighteen:

I left Hopfrog above the grave and slid down through the shaft beneath it, holding onto the chain with my dad's gardening gloves. Hopfrog had tied the chain to his chair, so if I started to fall and grabbed on, the chair would block his falling down, too. I tied flashlights to my hips, and kept a large one tucked uncomfortably under my armpit. I lowered myself down until I came to a kind of burrow, as if somebody had just dug under the moist earth. It reminded me a little of the stories of tunnels that people made to get under the Berlin Wall. It reminded me of a gopher hole.

I didn't start shaking until I lay down in the burrow and let go of the chain. I had to dig through some of the dirt that had already fallen across the recently dug path.

After a while, controlling myself from screaming from that feeling of being buried alive, the tunnel opened onto a chamber.

After that, I can't remember. I really can't. I know something happened down there. It's more like my body knows it than my mind does.

I think maybe I saw something, but I don't remember what. I was blind for about an hour afterwards, and I was back in that tunnel, trying to grab the chain so Hopfrog could pull me out.

When I got out, Hopfrog said he didn't know what to do when he heard me screaming. I said, screaming? I was screaming?

Three times, he said, like nothing he'd ever heard before.

Bloodcurdling, he said. Three screams.

I don't remember any of it and I don't want to.

We waited at the grave until just before dawn. When Melissa came back, bloated and grinning, I threw her onto one of the slabs and drove the screwdriver into her heart until Hopfrog told me to stop because I had plunged it all the way through her back.

The voices stopped, then.
For a while.
I'm writing this because it's my confession.
Tonight I'm going to kill myself.
I can't live with what I did.
I don't want to live knowing what happened to Melissa.
I want to be with her more than anything.
I want . . .

3.

"I wanted to die," Joe said. "I didn't want to go on. The more I thought about it, the more the idea of death seemed appealing. But I couldn't do it. I just couldn't. It was like I was King Joe Dragonheart again, and he would never kill himself. Now, I know I'm going to die. But I have to stop that thing."

Becky glanced at her wristwatch. "It's ten A.M. If the sun ain't up, we're all screwed." She glanced at the barn door, with its boards across the inside, keeping the Night Children out. "Do you want to do the honors?"

Joe managed a smile, as if survival were enough. He felt this was all a grim duty, that life had lost what little savor it had ever possessed. "Crosses. God bless Old Man Feely for having them, for knowing how to keep them at bay."

He stood, and went to the door. He got a whiff of himself—he stank, from his jeans to his sweater to his black denim jacket to his sneakers.

He drew the latch and board from the door, pushing it open. The door creaked on its hinges. The morning air was biting cold.

The apple orchard and the Feely house seemed empty of all life.

He turned to Becky, "They're in their beds today. All the children of the world."

"Good. Now, we have to go kill their owner."

Joe leaned against the door. "No. I am going to kill It. You are going to stay here and make sure your son lives. I am not going to let another child die in this town so help me God. If you won't get out of town now, you certainly aren't going down in the mines with me to find the Vampire."

4.

Some of the Night Children were asleep in Old Man Feely's house, along the stairways, and four, in the bed, looking as innocent as if they were truly human children dreaming of Wynken, Blynken, and Nod, rather than the puppets of some alien creature. Joe put a spike to the first one, but Becky could still not bring herself to do it. Instead, she went and stood in the doorway, in the sunlight, with Tad, wrapped in a blanket, sitting on the porch. "I'm sorry, Joe, I just can't."

"They aren't children anymore," he said. "They're just cast from children. The real children have been consumed. Remember. These are just re-creations of the children." He felt robotic inside, as if he, too, were merely a re-creation of the Joe Gardner who had once been.

When the work was done, he took a flashlight from Becky and a cross. In his belt he'd stuck a mallet and screwdriver to take care of whatever he was about to find down below.

His only thoughts were for those whom he had loved who had been taken from him.

He didn't say anything to Becky or Tad. He wasn't sure if they would get out of this alive. He just turned, and went to the room.

The rotting body of John Feely lay in the corner. What had once been religious symbols and icons had either been defaced or destroyed and lay about in clumps beside the small doorway to the closet on which was scrawled:

He is risen.

Joe opened the doors to the closet and shined his flashlight into it.

The beam of his light hit a winding stone staircase.

He unhesitantly took a step down, then another, and another, until he felt as if he were descending into the farthest pit of hell.

5.

He heard a fluttering like wings, and then someone grabbed his hand, knocking the flashlight from it. He heard the flashlight clatter to the ground. Instinctively, he reached for the screwdriver, intending to use it as a stake, but the darkness spoke to him in soothing tones.

It was Melissa's voice, her hand, too, guiding him in the dark.

"I've been waiting for you, all these years," she said, "in my prison."

Don't give in to her. It's not Melissa. It's the vampire.

"My mind is free to wander, but I am not free of this existence."

Joe asked, "Why don't you kill me?"

"I want to do more than kill you, King Joe."

"King Joe?" The stairs ended abruptly, and as he continued walking, the walls of John Feely's cellar gave way to the walls of the mine, shining with a yellow phosphorescence as if rubbed with fireflies.

As the darkness receded, he glanced at Melissa, who, for a moment was clearly visible, wearing the same clothes she had on the day she had died, soaked to the skin, smelling of river water. "King Joe Dragonheart, the boy who managed to lock me in my cage again when I was almost out."

Then Melissa seemed to evaporate, right before his eyes. Joe blinked twice, looking around in the darkness. The room that had been built into the rock gradually gave way to earth. He saw the shape of the mines, the chambers that led off to other routes.

The light came up, blinding, as if he were in some celestial presence too brilliant for human eyes. The golden light was sensual. Joe felt as if his skin were being brushed with thousands of feelers. A humming sound accompanied the light, until it was deafening, millions of locusts swarming around him, locusts made up of light and dark, spinning atomic particles of fire yellow and night; his arms, his whole body, in the light, seemed transformed as if by Midas's touch, until he could not separate himself out from the light—he no longer sensed his own body.

And then, something like wind, but like a jackhammer, slammed into him; he felt as if something smashed through him, through flesh and blood and bone, and he was falling to the ground.

It's going to kill me, he thought, *I've just delivered myself to the monster who killed my family*—the spike he'd brought to stab some vampire in the heart had dropped to the ground, the intent he had to destroy this creature was lost to the sensations, the electrical currents, running through his body.

6.

Joe lifted his head up. He was forced to shut his eyes for a good minute or two because the light was like fire—and then it dimmed and he could see the yellow-gold fluorescence of the creature. Its multiple eyes were small and shiny, and the proboscis which jutted below them swung like an elephant's trunk out along the chalky walls of its prison. It had two pair of vestigial wings along its spine, and these fluttered slightly, but they were tattered as if from centuries of abuse from thwarted attempts to escape. It was half melted, its thorax ending at a scarred abdomen which ended at the halfway point; he was reminded of pictures of mosquitoes and ants trapped in amber.

He wondered why he was able to see It. *Why me? Why Joe Gardner from Colony? Why not any of the others?*

And then, a voice. A voice far more dreadful than any he could've imagined from this creature. Upon hearing it, he felt as if his heart would stop.

"Joseph," his mother said, and she was standing there before him in one of her housecoats as if she had only woken up a half hour before and was putting on coffee. There was nothing inhuman about her. It wasn't just his mother, it was the mother he had always wanted, for she seemed warmer. She wore the kindest expression he could imagine on her face. Her arms were outstretched to him. "Joseph, thank God you're here. Oh, my baby."

"No!" he shouted, clawing at the air as if he could make her disappear.

A flash of lightning across Joe's vision as he was thrust into the middle of a movie of his own past:

the Volkswagen going over the bridge

Joe reaching for Melissa to save her

the crash, water pouring into the car

reaching again for Melissa and touching something else,

something other than Melissa.

"You believed," Anna Gardner said. "You understood. You knew about losing what you love. You had great belief, even for a child."

His vision faded to the blue again, and he saw the creature. The tentaclelike arms rubbed together, and the voice resumed, *you knew what I felt.* Then, it was his mother. Her skin was pale and shiny, and reminded him of a larva. She was weeping. "Oh, Joe, Joseph, I'm so frightened. Why do you hate me so much?"

"You're not my mother."

"Joe," she sobbed, her hands going to her eyes. "What did I do to make you hate me so much?"

"Don't do this to me," he said, fighting back every instinct he had to go and embrace this woman. "Don't do this to me. You're a monster."

Anna Gardner grinned. Blood tears streamed down her cheeks. "Yes, I am a bit of a monster, aren't I?" She advanced on him. "A bit of a monster, fucking other men, hating your daddy, hating you for being born. You're the destroyer, Joe, did you know that? You're the Antichrist. Look: everything you touch turns to shit. How many people have died because you came back here? How many? All those children, Joe. It was you who killed them. Just by stepping back over that bridge, you sealed their doom. And Aaron, my grandson. Oh, my Lord, you should've heard the squeals when his skin got ripped off—like a little piggie at the slaughterhouse. Hillary? We boiled her. We made a big pot of baby soup. Her skin slid right off her back after ten minutes. It was like skinning a tomato. I sucked her myself, Joe. Her blood was so pure and fresh."

"Stop it," Joe whispered, shivering. He felt as if he'd been thrust into a freezer. His skull felt like it was scraping the inside of his head raw. "You're a fucking monster!"

"Let me tell you about Jenny," his mother cackled, throwing her head back. "Oh, Lordy, Joseph—she was the difficult one. You married a cunt. She fought, she scratched, she bit. She was the trophy, I'll tell you. Do you know what a woman sounds like when you have her own child open her up down there? It's not even a scream, Joe. It's like air escaping a balloon. It's very amusing. The wonderful part was she called your name out, Joe, in the end. You should be proud. She called your name out. 'Joe—Joe,' she gasped. Where were you, Joe? Why weren't you there to help her? 'Joe!' she cried." Anna Gardner erupted in a fit of giggles. "And all because of you, Joe. I wanted you here. We all did. You could have saved your family and friends, if only you'd just come down here in the first place. I learned all about you from your wife before she died. She told us the most shocking things. She said you fucked some other bitch behind her back. She said you weren't a very good father. And your poor old mother's such a witch, is she? Well, look at yourself for a change."

Trembling from the cold, Joe said, "I know you're not my mother." He tried to block the images this creature was conjuring in his mind, but he saw them: *Aaron bleeding to death while some horrible being*

crouched over him lapping at his wounds. Hillary
screaming as children pushed her into scalding water.
Jenny's face tensing and calling out to him in her last
moment.

"Why the hell are you doing this! What is it? Do you
need us for fuel? What the fuck is it?" Joe cried.

Anna Gardner shook her head, sadly. "I'll tell you
why, Joe. You want to know? Why the children, why
blood? Why vampires and demons and the whole mas-
querade? Because I like it. Because it's fun. Because
your kind is so disgusting to me that I can't think of
anything I'd rather do than fuck you over. I am your
god, you stupid fuck." His mother's eyes beamed.
"And you're my baby. You're my little Joey, writing his
little stories about things that can't come true. All the
bedtime stories are shit, Joey. Mamas never do get
their babies back."

Then, it came to Joe. An insight, as if pieces of a
puzzle had just come together. "You had children,
too."

"What?" she said, caught off guard.

"You had children, too. We killed one of them.
Maybe the last one. Maybe Old Man Feely killed
some, too. Maybe his father and grandfather and great-
grandfather killed one or two. Me and Hopfrog and
Melissa, we killed one, too. That day at the barn.
Somehow, we killed one of your children."

A piercing shriek came from the creature. Joe had to
cover his ears. Even then, his head pounded from the
noise.

"My own. My children!"

Through the image of his mother, as if this were her
skeleton, he saw the creature rear up, its shriveled
wings beating against the fetid air.

Joe said, "What, are you going to kill me now? Go

ahead, damn it, just do it! You've taken everything away from me, you hear me? Everything! My wife, my son, my daughter, my little girl, how—you could do that to a little girl!" He could no longer weep. All he could do was scream and slam his fist into the rock floor.

When he quieted down, his mother said, "They are all here, for they are in my blood, they live, Joe, all of them, and Melissa, too. I will give you a taste."

From between her lips, a proboscis shot out and fell across his neck. He felt a brief, sharp pain, and knew It had drilled into his artery. He wondered if this was what mainlining heroin was like, for suddenly he felt lighter, and happier,

and he was

sitting on a grassy knoll with Jenny, who held Hillary on her knee. Out by the river, Aaron was catching a frisbee that Joe himself had just tossed him.

Jenny looked up at Joe and said, "It's about time you relaxed and enjoyed your surroundings a little, Joe."

But it was no longer Jenny, but Melissa, settling Hillary down on the grass, turning, standing, reaching for Joe, pressing her lips against his ear and whispering, no one dies here, Joe. No one.

Joe bit down as hard as he could on his tongue. The pain jolted him back into the golden aura of the creature. "It's all a fake," Joe spat out. "It's a show so that I'll give you what you want. Did you do this to the kids? Did you take Patty Glass and get her to see her folks? Or my son—did you let him think he was going to join Mommy in heaven? Is that why you started out with children? Because they're easy. But adults, we're harder. We aren't so happy to give up our lives, are we? We're not so easily fooled."

His mother came closer to him, kneeling beside

him. "Children believe, Joe. Their belief gives them power. Their power gives me strength. You believe, too, Joe, no matter how you fight it. You believe in me, don't you?"

"No," Joe said, "I don't believe you have any real power, if that's what you mean. I believe you prey on the weak and the young. Like a jackal. You know about jackals? They go for carcasses, too, and children, and the sick, and the helpless. Maybe you're just a jackal, or worse. Maybe your own kind imprisoned you here so that they would never have to deal with you again."

His mother's breath was sweet, like apple blossoms. She stroked his scalp. "Oh, my baby. You were the only one I spoke through. I trusted you because I knew you believed. I could drink your blood now, Joe, if I so choose. I could take the life from you. My sweet baby boy."

"Then do it. *Do it!*" Joe shouted, wrenching his neck —the pain was white hot as a sucker tore at the flesh around his jaw. *"Do it right now and when my blood is inside you, you bastard, I will make you suffer through eternity for what you've done to everything I've ever loved!"*

He drew himself to the creature and when he was close enough, it was no longer a monster or his mother, but Melissa stroking his scalp as he lay, head in her lap, in the back of his truck. The sky was purple. Night was coming. Melissa had daisies pressed into her tangled hair. She smiled at him and he grinned because he had never been so in love in all his life as when he'd been a teenager, never had he felt such an incorruptible bond of love. Her smile broke apart and she said, "Just think, we're getting married soon and we'll get the hell out of here and you'll write novels and I'll do . . . whatever it is I'm going to do."

She brought her hand down to his chin. She rubbed her fingers against it. "You cut yourself shaving? You've got a scar."

"Oh, probably," he said, caught up in the vision, and then, feeling the soreness on his neck, "you're not Melissa, though, are you? You're a phantom, a delusion. You're just that thing in the mine, sucking my blood out."

She giggled. "You're right. But you don't mind do you? It's not so bad. If you needed human blood to escape from your prison and find your only child, wouldn't you make some sacrifices?"

"I guess so. But you want to know something?"

Melissa raised her eyebrows, as if she couldn't tell what was on his mind.

"I know something about you that you don't even know. I know about believing in things. If I believe in this vision of you, and being in the truck, I am at your mercy. The old guy was right—Virgil was right. But the reason why you've mainly gone after children before now is that you could use their belief. But see, I know something you don't. I have an imagination like a child, but I have the mastery of someone who can shape my imagination. I can believe what I want. And what I believe right now is that you may be drinking my blood, but I am drinking yours in return. And your blood is belief, that's why the crosses can keep you down, that's why you can be imprisoned. It's not because you are some Christian devil, it's because it's part of your makeup to believe in everything, isn't it? You can't not believe."

Melissa's flesh began running, bleeding skin against her nose, her eyes dribbling together like runny eggs.

It was his mother again. Anna Gardner brought her face close to his. Pressed her lips against his lips.

Opened his lips with her tongue.

He pushed her away, knowing it was the vampire and not his mother.

"You can't not believe. So here is my religion, here is my belief," Joe gasped, and felt it to be true in his innermost being. "I believe that my blood is poison to your kind. I believe that it is like drinking your own child's blood, I believe you are burning your throat with my blood, *fucker!*"

The vision raked itself away and he was again in the sputtering light of the cavern. Above him, the creature's body pumped and had sent shoots of Its own flesh into him, into his arms, legs, stomach, thighs, forehead, neck, and through the peristaltic pulsing of the fleshy shoots, Joe knew that the creature would quickly drain him of blood in minutes.

I'm going to die, die, die.

And then, something rose up in his memory, the little boy who lived within him, dormant all these years, the little boy who had somehow managed to terrify this creature before:

King Joe Dragonheart. He saw the boy, eleven, with a crown on his head, a knight's armor on, a flaming sword of valor and belief in his hands—

He was no longer face to face with the creature, It was now a dragon, breathing fire, Its long neck wriggling as It regained Its strength—

I need more belief, I need more belief—

King Joe Dragonheart felt her, suddenly, not a voice, not even a face, but her, Melissa, inside him, as if she had never died, and Hopfrog, too, there with him, not grown-up, but as they were kids brave and faithful, in the Feely barn, enveloped in the gold light—

What struck Joe like lightning next, what illuminated the mystery of his existence, was the simple fact:

we turned Its own belief back on It.

we reversed Its own power.

we brought It to Its knees then because we believed we could.

He felt weak, but he kept the thought in his mind, the belief that became *belief,* not just his own, but King Joe Dragonheart's, and Melissa's, and Hopfrog's, all of their power as children—the light within him created a world in which he was more powerful than the alien, *powerful light righteous strength—*

Joe imagined the children helping him, too, all the dead and lost children throughout the history of Colony, coming back with a united belief in the destruction of this fiend—

I am your betrayer, I am the one who has come to end your suffering.

And then, Joe realized he was about to pass out. He prayed that his blood sacrifice was the venom for which there would be no antidote.

(I am a snake, a cobra, a rattler, and you milk your own doom, you press my teeth against your skin and draw into your veins the last of me, which is the last of you, like karma, like justice, his mind railed as he slipped into darkness, and then he barely saw his son, Aaron, shouting at the creature, *I'm rubber and you're glue, whatever you do bounces off me and sticks to you,* until Aaron and the world and all of life apparently was snuffed out.)

And when the light came up for Joe Gardner, he was kind of hoping he'd be in Heaven, or at least somewhere warm. Instead, he was right back with that Thing, its thousand eyes watching him, Its limbs scrambling in the earth trying to move, Its wings beating against the stale air.

It was fading, as if It had lost any power It had ever possessed.

It cried out, "my children, my children . . ." and then Its words became some otherworldly language, a language of flickering lights and sparks and gasps.

Joe had no energy left.

He watched as the light around the creature faded, and when he was sure It was dead, when Its wings had stilled beside Its body, he opened his mouth to cry out for help, but his voice failed him.

And then, what had been the creature, the Beast, became as insubstantial as light itself. Joe watched as a flash of light burst small and feeble from the place where the creature had been trapped.

He too, waited to die, happy, at least, that he had saved Tad and Becky.

7.

When he awoke again, it was Becky, with a spike in her hand, leaning over him.

She said, "Joe? Joe?"

"Becky," he gasped. "I'm alive. I'm Joe. I'm not a vampire. Don't kill me, please."

8.

When he awoke a third time, he was above ground, and a light powdery snow was falling from a morning sky. Becky was looking down at him, as was Tad, who said, "I knew you'd do it. Dad always said you could do anything if you put your mind to it. He was right about you."

Joe whispered, his voice like a scrape of pain. "It's snowing. Look."

Becky, her eyes circled with dark, her hair greasy and stringy from having come through a nightmare, shushed him. "You're all scarred up, Joe. You've lost some blood. You crawled all that way up the stairs, bleeding the whole time. I thought you were a goner. You need to rest."

"Did It die?"

"I saw a light, a funnel of light, like a cyclone, and it swept from the house outside," she said, as if she had just undergone a religious conversion and now believed in something larger than life itself.

9.

Several hours later, late in the day, he sat up in some sort of rough bed—it seemed to be all straw sticking in his back. He glanced up—it was Old Man Feely's barn.

When he felt a bit stronger, he stood up on unsteady legs and went to find the survivors.

When he found Becky, sitting on the Feely front porch, rocking Tad in her arms, he hugged her and wept. She wept, too.

"Is it over?" she asked.

"I don't know. Its body is destroyed, but I don't know if It is."

"I'm so tired," she said. "I am so damn tired."

"You and Tad sleep for now. It'll be night in a couple of hours. There may be some of the children left. I'll burn these in the house, the ones I can't get to. If others come, I'll be ready for them," Joe said.

But he was exhausted, too, and not even feeling as if he were alive. Inside him, it felt as if something brilliant, some fire, had been sucked from his soul, and now he was just an animal living on instinct. He trusted no one. He walked the mother and child back to the barn, checking to make sure all the crosses were in place.

Tad, who had been feverish, lay down beside his mother in the barn. Joe wrapped them in a blanket and two coats from the trunk of the Buick. One of the coats had been Jenny's. He brought it to his face, pressing into it for brief comfort before laying it across Tad's sleeping body.

Becky whispered, "I almost just want to die. I just don't think I can go on. Not one more night."

Joe wanted to tell her that there was still hope, but he felt that there was none. It was as if the light of the universe had been doused.

He knew that he had to stand watch during this night, in case It was still there.

In case It was not through with them.

He knew that if he were smart, if he were sane anymore, he would get Becky and Tad and get the hell out of that place. But there was something inside him, something he could not name or describe, something which he could only think of as a vague hope, a wish, a prayer for a miracle.

He glanced up at John Feely's work bench, in the shadows. The tools John, and perhaps his father and grandfather had used for over a century to keep It's creations from multiplying: screwdrivers and mallets and spikes and hacksaws, alongside crucifixes and ankhs fashioned from horseshoes.

The power of belief. Not the creature's belief, but the belief of those who held the instruments. It was not the cross or the ancient symbols which held power, it was John Feely, believing completely in them, having a faith like a child's imagination. Joe remembered a biblical quote: *Whosoever shall not enter the kingdom of heaven as a child shall never enter therein."* That's what it took to stop the monster, a faith and belief so strong as to be incomprehensible to It.

That's why It took over children. They were fountains of belief, towers of faith. They believed in God and Santa Claus and the Easter Bunny and the Bogeyman and Vampires and even the World—they believed so strongly that the World was the right place to be.

It had been the foulest of creatures, to use children, not because of their blood or their flesh, but because of their souls—their souls had been the fuel It used to move through Time, to find Its own children, lost millennia ago, destroyed, no doubt by some early ancestor of man who had been given the gift of belief in order to protect himself from such intruders.

Exhausted, Joe sat down beside the sleepers and wept for all the children who had been lost to It, not the least of them, his own.

Without realizing it, he fell asleep again, and something warned him, a voice buzzing around in his head, that they were still out there, the children, the ones who were left, the ones who were still servants to the devil which he had destroyed.

He dreamed that his son came for him and was drinking the first blood from the tip of his finger.

26

IN THE BEGINNING

Joe awoke suddenly, brought to consciousness by a smell.

Another sense, too, something he'd acquired recently, nothing specific, more instinct than sense, something within him that told him his quarry was near. It was as if he had a radar for some of them— *maybe if you know them, you sense them, or maybe (heh-heh, my insane friend) they sense you and send out unseen feelers to find you.*

He reached for the mallet. It was still there, beneath the rags he'd used as a pillow. His whole body was soaked with sweat from whatever fever dream had been buzzing inside his head. He wiped the back of his neck with his left hand. His neck and legs were sore.

How long had he been asleep? Sleep was a problem. After all he'd been through, his body was wearing him down, forcing him to sleep too much. And he was supposed to be on watch. He had appointed himself the one who would not sleep and the last thing he remembered was he had been sitting up, listening for them, waiting for them. Somehow, he'd been tricked into falling asleep.

He trusted no one now. Joe was careful not to wake the others as he rose up from the straw. Only three of them left. Only three. *Me, Tad, Becky.* His side still ached from a recent wound. He managed to force the pain down deep into his flesh, to forever pretend that the pain was only a vestige of some past incarnation. Had to bite his lip, too, because when he finally stood, it felt as if his legs would buckle and he'd fall again. He held onto the edge of a wooden post that was draped with chains and hooks.

Blood had dried on one of the larger hooks; blood and some hair. Maybe some skin, too, matted with the hair and blood, or maybe he was so used to the grue by now that he imagined it everywhere.

He glanced at the others. He didn't want to alarm them with what he was about to do. He was still not positive that any of them were who they claimed to be. The sleeping forms, wrapped in blankets and straw. They didn't have the smell to them, but he mistrusted his own senses more than anyone or anything.

He moved silently through the workroom, grabbing the tool belt from its peg on the cork wall. He could've taken a gun. There were plenty to go around, a veritable arsenal, but a gun never seemed to do the job right. What he had learned in the past twenty-four hours was that it was not enough just to do it and walk away—it took some time, it took patience, this kind of job. You had to watch them suffer before you knew they were truly dead.

He hefted a mallet in his right hand, swung it back and forth as if it were an old friend, and walked out the barn door. His palm was sweating around the mallet— he wondered when the mallet would become a part of him, melded into his flesh, until he was, himself, no longer a man, but a function of something higher—a tool of flesh and blood and wood and steel. He had never had much religious sense, but sometimes the voices told him what to do, sometimes he believed what they said. Sometimes he thought he was meant to be here, this time, this place, this hour.

The light was hazy, not dark yet, and he knew that if he was going to kill them it was going to have to be dark, because he wanted to look into their eyes and see the thing that he was killing—not them, but what was behind them, what gave them their inspiration. He tried not to think of them as Them, with a big T, because it was making him nervous as hell to even think about what they were without adding the larger fear to it. *What if I'm crazy? What if I'm one of those psycho killers who imagines that everyone else is a them?*—a fleeting thought, through his brain; he ignored it.

It wouldn've been almost impossible to find them in daylight, anyway, but at night, hell, they'd come to him. They'd approach as if they were supplicants coming to the altar and he'd just take them out.

Well, it wouldn't be that simple.

He'd probably get some fight out of at least one of them, maybe all. Who wanted to get his head bashed in, anyway? He knew he was crazy, thinking these things, but what was a man to do? He couldn't just let it all go, all the hurt, and give in. *When you give in, they get you. When you give in, they take you over and do things to you you don't want done, they get you over to their side, and then everything looks different.*

The trees leaned, cowed by the strong wind, as if his arrival had made them bow down. *But you're not God, remember that,* a voice told him, *you're just you, and you're going to look them in the eyes, one at a time, and you're going to have to bash them and spear them and they're going to know you, what you're thinking, they're going to have already half crawled into your brain, punching buttons as if you're a computer until they find out what's on your mind, and then they're going to do whatever they can to stop you.*

He could smell one of them in the air—they stank, had that stink of humanity—the wind was icy, and the stink made him want to retch. He clutched the mallet more tightly. The worst of it was, they smelled like people, just like people who maybe haven't bathed in a while, the strong stink of human flesh.

In the grove, at the edge of the property, he thought he saw someone standing there.

He felt for the tool belt, for the screwdriver.

He'd gone hunting once, when he'd been young, and learned of a phenomenon where a hunter, looking for deer, sometimes took a shot at another human being because the hunter wanted to see a deer so badly that he actually mistook a man for a deer. Not just any man, either—it was often a friend.

It was the problem with them, they looked so much like anybody else. You couldn't really know for sure until you plunged the screwdriver into them. It wasn't simple, Life. It wasn't gray, either—things were definitely black and white, at least for him. *Good and Evil,*

*and you're either for us, or against us. The only way to
live, now. Well, the only way to survive.*

But what if he was wrong? He could look in their
eyes, but if he didn't see what he was looking for,
would he kill them anyway?

*Maybe I'm just a madman, maybe I had a breakdown
and the stress of the shit-hole world has dropped down
on my shoulders. Maybe I'm just another Ted Bundy or
John Wayne Gacy out to hammer everyone I'm paranoid about into the ground, bash their faces so I don't
have to see their eyes staring at me, twist the old Phillips head number two into that sweet little place between their ribs where a nice plump heart's just waiting
to get skewered.*

*Have to keep my mind on right here, right now, no
veering off. They'd want that—you go careening off the
edge of a cliff in your mind, and they got you. Once
they get you, they put you where they want, and who
knows what happens to you, how they hollow you out
like a canoe and turn you inside out and then you're not
who you think you are, oh, no, boys and girls, you're
something altogether different and you look in the mirror but you don't see yourself, no no no, you see something else and then you want to break the mirror because of what they did to you, no thank you, ma'am, I
ain't buying none of that.*

He watched the bent over trees. The sky was darkening—not much after four, but getting dark fast.
*Never find them in their hiding place—have to wait,
sometimes, 'til they come to you.*

"Hey!" he shouted. Friendly like, neighborly, putting the mallet behind his back a little so whoever was
standing there wouldn't completely suspect him. They
weren't too smart, these people, and when they were
fresh, before they ripened, they had a little bit too

much of what they used to have, so they weren't always the smartest things.

You are insane, the voice inside him said, *this is just a dream, it has all been a dream, you've been drunk and abusing your wife and family and you drank a couple of six-packs of Rolling Rock and you went over the Edge.*

(The voice in his head knew about the Edge.)

Someone came out from among the shadows of the grove. It wasn't an It or a Thing or a Them.

It was a boy. Dark hair, pale skin, wearing a hooded sweatshirt with the hood pulled down. On the front of the sweatshirt, which was blue, were the words: *If Virginia Is for Lovers, Then West Virginia's for Us Decent Folks.* He couldn't actually read the sweatshirt from that distance; he just knew what the words said because he'd bought the sweatshirt for the boy, himself, not two days before, thinking it was kind of funny.

He knew the boy.

He's one of them, though.

The boy smiled.

Joe stood motionless. His fingers felt numb.

The boy started running towards the man, shouting.

Joe pulled the mallet from behind his back.

When the boy reached him, Joe took him in his free arm, and brought the mallet to the side of the boy's head, ready to bash it.

You are insane, the voice inside said.

Am I? Well, go to hell, he told it.

He held the boy's head tight in his arm, and stared down into those eyes as darkness blossomed all around them. He was looking for the light there, to see if he could see the boys' inspiration, if he could see the thing that fueled the boy. If it still existed there.

Tears shone in the boy's eyes.

"Dad? Daddy?"

Joe would only have a few seconds to perform the operation.

But he had to be sure.

He had come too far, from such a far-off land—the territory of sanity and reality—to lose it all in a moment's hesitation.

But he had to be absolutely sure that the boy was one of them before he carved into the boy's heart.

They were tricky that way, because you might slip up and stab one of your own kind—it wasn't like in the movies or books, where all it took was a good jab in the right place—it was bloody and you had to stab them over and over, until there was nothing left pumping—it was just like killing your own kind, only they weren't, they were another species, practically, and if you didn't hunt them down, they'd hunt you.

You'd be the deer in the forest to them.

The voice inside him said, *you are tired of this, aren't you? You just want them to take you so you'll be one of them, so you won't have to fight anymore. You don't need to fight anymore. Everyone you love is gone, everything you've ever lived for, vanished. If you kill him, you kill yourself. Look at him, look at his face, his skin, his eyes, you were once like that, remember? When you were his age, in this very place, you set this in motion, you and your friends. What has brought you to this place? You have brought yourself. Who is this boy? He is you so many years ago, running through the groves, setting this in motion so that you will one day return only to pierce your son through the heart as a just sacrifice for what you and your kind have done.*

And Joe knew then that he was insane, because, although he was holding the boy and raising the mallet to strike, he saw what he thought was the light of day come up all around him, a color of light that he had never seen before, and the boy was not what he had seemed a second ago, but a creature of mutilation and putrefaction. The world became liquid all around them, until all light was like a river, and the man fumbled with the mallet and dropped it. He tried to reach for the screwdriver to press it into the boy's flesh before it was too late, but something grabbed his hand and pulled him through some kind of opening, as if the world were only a removable layer of skin.

And on the other side, she stood there as beautiful as he had ever remembered her. *Melissa.*

She opened her mouth to speak, dark water spilling from between her lips.

"I know you're not her," he said. "I know I'm standing outside a barn, holding my son in my arms. There's a town just down the road. And apple trees. It's cold. It's getting on night. I know you can't be her. I don't know what you are, but I know you're not her." Was he shouting? He couldn't tell—his breathing was difficult. He felt a pain in his chest as his heart beat wildly. Unbidden tears streamed down from his eyes as he tried to see her as she was, rather than the way she presented herself.

Her face froze in its expression. Then, for a moment, he knew clearly that the voices within him were the beacon of his insanity: she was, indeed, who she looked like, and she was trying to talk to him, but the voices in his head were getting louder, more raucous, shrieking across his nerve pathways. He knew the world was not the insane place that he had been living in, that it could not be, that the creatures he had been slaughtering could not be anything more than simple human beings. His own obsessions had brought him to this.

He felt the screwdriver in his hand and turned its blade towards himself.

You failed once before, the clearest voice in his head said, *so do it, do it right. Do it now.*

He pressed the blade against his chest and was about to give it a good shove, when he felt a searing numbness in his leg, and he fell to the ground—the sound of a gunshot—a burning around his right calf. He closed his eyes. Rock salt? When he opened them, it was night, and the boy stood over him, looking at him. He could see the barn and the darkening sky. From nearby a man shouted, "What the hell are you trying to do to that boy?"

Shot, I've been shot, damn it, you don't shoot your own kind.

But of course you do, you always kill your own, its the law of man.

And what you don't kill, the wild things get.

He looked up, and recognized the other man, it was Virgil holding the gun. He tried to cry out to him. Although he trusted no one at this point, he knew that Virgil thought that he was rescuing the boy from the clutches of a madman. Virgil would try to help the boy.

Joe knew it was too late, knew that they'd tricked him, almost made him kill himself, and now they would descend upon Virgil, too, and all would be lost.

The game was over.

Now he knew the boy was one of them. His son. Aaron.

The boy, who looked just like a boy, a perfect imitation, resembling so closely, in so many insignificant details his own son, looked at him.

Then the boy turned his head in the direction of the man with the gun and sniffed at the air just like a wild animal detecting its prey.

Joe lay there and for just a second, like another scent, came the smell of memory and all that had happened in just a few days. All that had turned him from a sane man into someone who believed that darkness had fallen across the universe.

He grabbed the boy in a full-nelson stranglehold. With his other hand, he brought the screwdriver to his chest, pressing on it. Tears blinded him, as he felt his son's pulse. His son began sobbing, trying to break away, but he held him there. He held Aaron close to him.

"Daddy," the boy gasped (*but he's not a boy, he's a monster, he's one of those monsters, he's just pretending to be a boy, he crawled into the little boy suit after that creature ripped the life from Aaron, your son. He's a puppet, he's a repository for blood, an alien harvester, not your son!* the voice in his head screamed).

"Please," the boy gasped as Joe carefully brought the mallet up—*you have to act fast with them, you have to stop their hearts before they can get you, you have to eviscerate them to make sure they can't function.*

Joe whisked the mallet through the air, but let it go, let it fly and land harmlessly on the ground.

Joe barely got to his knees, the pain in his leg too much.

"I can't," he said, letting go of the boy. He touched the frozen ground with his hands. He knew that it would get him. He knew that even though he had slain the dragon, that this boy It had created from his son's body would now destroy him.

But then, something lifted, a great stone, as if the universe had been darkened and was now redeemed by light. The sky seemed to tear apart for an instant, and then was whole again.

It's dead now. I didn't kill It down there. I killed It here, I didn't give in to It. All of this, because It wanted to kill my son. All of what I did down in the mine would be nothing if I had sacrificed my own child.

He felt the boy's arms around his neck and heard voices, outside himself, voices which he didn't think he'd ever hear again:

"Joe? Is that you? Oh, my God, Joe!" Jenny cried out. He heard Hillary, too, bawling as if from hunger.

When Joe opened his eyes, he saw the miracle which he had not dared to hope for.

He saw his family again. His wife, his son, and daughter, not Its, not Things, not Drinkers of Blood, but his family, innocent and whole, and alive.

Alive.

He had believed in so much, but not in miracles. He grabbed his son, looking into his eyes. "Aaron? Aaron?"

His son was sobbing. Over his shoulder, Joe saw Jenny, her face filthy, her clothes torn, with Hillary in her arms. Joe cried out, not a word, but a yawp, a human cry of joy which he had forgotten that he had ever possessed.

They fell on him, arms around his neck, weeping, happy, ragged.

EPILOGUE

THE RIVER RUNS

1.

From the Journals of Joe Gardner/when he was twelve:

It wasn't just me, it was all of us, I could feel it. I don't know what it was. It touched me and It seemed to read my mind and make what I was thinking come true almost. I don't get it. But Hopfrog was part of it, and Melissa, too.

I think we slew a dragon.

2.

Joe had some fight still in him. He had belief in the universe at his back, faith that the cosmos was good, that love survived even death. He found strength in these thoughts. *With my family back, my boy, my daughter, my beautiful, wonderful wife with me again* . . . They made a big funeral pyre with most of the bodies of the dead; they didn't want to take the risk that there was still a spark of the vampire in any of the corpses. Some of the other bodies were left where they were. There was time enough for the authorities to come down over the Malabar Hills and deal with what had happened.

Jenny was strong. Joe wasn't sure if he had expected that or not. Later, they would both deal with the horror and the grief. Virgil, in his hunt for the children, had found Jenny and the kids huddled together in the sacristy of the St. Andrew's Episcopal Church. There were others, hidden, too, in places where there were crosses and symbols and concrete expressions of man's beliefs. The Night Children attacked his mother's house, his mother fought bravely, Jenny said, but she was attacked before Jenny could help her. Jenny had gotten Aaron and Hillary out of the house and had made it the three blocks to the church. Jenny had no faith, no religion, but she instinctively knew to go someplace where others had beliefs and creeds. She told Joe she would've gone to a synagogue or a mosque, or even a tent revival, if any of them had been within the town limits, but St. Andrew's was the nearest incarnation of religion she could find. "I took them there because I didn't know where else to go," she said.

Joe didn't bury his mother, but left her remains in

her bed, covered with his grandmother's quilt, as if she were just taking a nap and might awaken at any moment. He thought: *She still lives in my dreams, so I have not lost her, only her body which had become ravaged with ill health and the markings of some alien being.* Virgil Cobb, who Joe recognized after all these years as a man who loved his mother deeply, stayed at the house with her. "I'll be fine," he said, "I just don't want to leave her alone, even now. You go get some help, send some people over here to clean this place up. I'll make some tea, and wait."

"I know that you loved her," Joe told him, feeling his anger dissolve about the affair his mother had with this man. In its place, he felt kinship, as if both held the flame of her memory.

As he and his family left Anna Gardner's house, he thought he heard his old buddy Hop wishing them all well. There was something in his benediction that was like a soft touch on the shoulder, a nudge from a friend to continue to go up that road, to care for and protect the living, because somehow the dead would get along just fine.

The rain mixed with snow kept coming 'til noon. They gassed up at Cally's ValCo Gas. It was less strange than Joe had thought it would be to steal fifteen bucks worth of premium unleaded. He looked at the town, at Colony, and saw nothing but the markers of time in the form of stone and wood and steel. It was like viewing a corpse, a loved one who has died, and knowing that she is not there, not in that shell, that the one you loved had already moved on in her journey to some distant land. So, too, Colony had vacated its shell, and the ghost town that remained seemed as slight as a pile of leaves waiting to turn into debris.

In the car, back on Main Street, Becky and Tad fell asleep in the backseat. Aaron snoozed a little, but seemed to start with fear every time the car hit a bump in the road. Hillary was fairly calm—Joe doubted that she was even aware of what she had experienced. Jenny said, "Maybe we should keep hunting them. Maybe we didn't stop all of them."

Joe shook his head. "There was only one. The rest were Its hands and eyes and teeth. I believe It's gone. It's done." He was not sure if this were true, but for that moment, he knew it was more important to get the hell out of Colony than to debate the finer points of the unknown.

They drove out of town, along River Road, and took the turn off to Lone Duck Road. Here, the rain turned to snow. Joe was worried that the Skylark might not make it if the road were to freeze over. But the tires, bald as they were, cleaved to the road. The storm seemed to calm. When they were almost to the Paramount Bridge, Becky gasped, waking.

She pointed ahead. "It's gone."

Through the wipers slicing across the windshield, Joe saw what she meant.

The Paramount Bridge was still there, at least skeletally, but edges of it had been struck by lightning and were blackened and smoldering.

Joe pulled over and parked in front of it. He stepped out of the car. Becky and Tad also got out. Jenny stayed back with her children. Joe looked at them and shook his head. "Something has always kept me from crossing that bridge to get out of town."

Tad said, "Maybe that's good. Maybe we've always needed you here. I know Dad did."

Joe looked at that boy and could not help but hug

him. They walked to the edge of the road, right where the blackened and smoking bridge began.

Snow on face, eyes, lips. Joe sat down and tossed a stone into the river. The water was running high and fast, just as if it were oncoming spring instead of oncoming winter.

He turned to Tad, who sat down beside him, and said, "Would you look at that."

Snow was in his hair. The rain had stopped. Nothing but the whiteness of snow slowly blanketing the dead-grass hills and frosting the ridge and banks of the far shore.

"Would you look at that river," Joe said. He could not laugh, or cry. "It's so clean, that water, right now. You can drink that water."

Tad said, "No, you can't. It's polluted."

"Not right now. Not anymore."

They sat there a long time. Becky went and got a jacket from the Buick, and wrapped it around Tad. Jenny and the kids came over and sat beside Joe. He clung to Hillary, kissing her forehead. It was so silent. As the day grew long and the snow began to stick, Jenny said, "Let's go. We can head south and take the road up the Malabars. I saw some others taking that road."

"It'll be slick. The Buick won't make it. We can go steal someone's four-wheel drive I guess."

Aaron piped up. "I know where a truck is."

Tad looked at Joe and whispered, "I know I shouldn't be scared, Joe, but I don't want to ever go back there."

"Oh," Joe said. "There's nothing back there anymore. Nothing like what happened. It's gone."

Tad said, "I don't know. I can hear my father, Joe. I can hear him."

Tad began shivering.

Joe hesitated before asking. "What's he saying?" He glanced at Becky. She had a concerned look on her face beyond the exhaustion.

Tad said, "My dad says we should wait here. He says we should watch the skies. He says It may come back."

"No," Joe said, "we need to go before the snow blocks the roads. Once we're out of the area, we can find somewhere to call someone—I don't know who yet, maybe the police—and try to tell our story." Joe took him by the hand. They walked back to the car. Tad didn't object; if anything, he was overly compliant. Joe was shivering just as much as the boy. They all got back into the Buick, and drove to town, parking in front of the Gardners' house. Jenny, Aaron, and Joe went to the back, to the garage.

Joe slid open the old garage door, and as the light of day skimmed the place, he saw another miracle.

His old Ford truck, yellow and still shining, as if kept just for this moment.

His mother, all those years, had kept it clean, had made sure it was in good shape. Just waiting for him to come home again. He found a particle of joy in the midst of the tragedy of that week: that love survives even the wrecks and mangles of life. He loved them all, *my mother, my wife, my two beautiful children (no, three, for my baby Paul had died a few years before). Melissa, Hopfrog, Patty Glass*—a tremendous and profound love was born in him at that moment. He realized then that he would lose everything he ever loved in life, and yet love would not die in him because of it: *I believe this.* He hugged his son against his chest as if he could absorb and keep him safe in his bones; then, he let go. His mother was with him; he could feel her presence. Not in a garage with a bright and well-oiled machine, but in his heart, in the place she had never left.

He checked the tires, started it up after a bit of fooling around under the hood, and then they squeezed in, packed like sardines, children on laps, Jenny squeezed so close to him it almost felt as if they were one person. They drove up the side of House Mountain and took the route over the Malabar Hills, until they came to Stone Valley.

Joe got two connecting rooms at the local motel, all of them falling asleep almost as soon as they touched the beds.

When Joe awoke, in predawn, he looked out at a white snow morning, a silent world, and laughed out loud when he saw a child on the icy street, rolling snow around to make a snowman, breaking the cut-crystal silence with a shout to his friend that there was no school today.

The light came up, and he went about the business of the living.